PIERCING

THE

DARKNESS

A CHARITY ANTHOLOGY FOR THE
CHILDREN'S LITERACY INITIATIVE

Edited By
CRAIG COOK

NECRO PUBLICATIONS

— 2014 —

FIRST EDITION TRADE PAPERBACK

PIERCING THE DARKNESS © 2014 by Necro Publications
Cover art © 2014 by Daniela Owergoor
Personal Gallery: http://dani-owergoor.deviantart.com/gallery/
Books & E-Books cover / Commissioned work:
http://pinterest.com/danielaowergoor/commissioned-book-and-e-book-covers/

This edition February 2014 © Necro Publications: necropublications.com

ISBN: 978-1-939065-56-8

Book design & typesetting:
David G. Barnett: fatcatgraphicdesign.com

"King of Shadows" © 2013 Joe R. Lansdale
"Quiet Bullets" © 2013 Christopher Golden
"Haven" © 2013 Kealan Patrick Burke
"Brave Girl" © 2013 Jack Ketchum
"Dealing With Mama Lila" © 2013 Sandy DeLuca
"Husband of Kellie" © 2013 T.T. Zuma
"Obedient Flies" © 2013 Greg F. Gifune
"Exit Strategy" © 2013 Tim Waggoner
"Abattoir Blues" © 2013 James A. Moore
"Cannonball Lycanthrope" © 2013 Janet Joyce Holden
"Throwing Monsters" © 2013 Jonathan Janz
"The Fierce Stabbing and Subsequent Post-Death Vengeance of Scooter Brown" © 2013 Jeff Strand
"The House in Cyrus Holler: A Will Castleton Adventure" © 2013 David Bain
"Cooked" © 2013 Jonathan Maberry
"Miz Ruthie Pays Her Respects" © 2013 Lucy Snyder
"Letting Go" © 2013 Mary SanGiovanni
"The Viking Plays Patty Cake" © 2013 Brian Keene
"Shadow Chaser" © 2013 Simon Wood
"The Folly" © 2013 Robert Dunbar
"Spider Goes to Market" © 2013 Gerard Houarner
"Pest Control" © 2013 C. Dennis Moore
"I'm So Sorry for Your Loss" © 2013 Ronald Malfi
"Timothy Meek" © 2013 by Gord Rollo
"Traps" © 2013 F. Paul Wilson
"Searching" © 2013 Monica O'Rourke
"Fire" © 2013 Elizabeth Massie
"Dance of the Blue Lady" © 2013 Gene O'Neill
"Dinosaur Day" © 2013 Gary A. Braunbeck

ABOUT CHILDREN'S LITERACY INITIATIVE

MISSION STATEMENT

Children's Literacy Initiative (CLI) is a non-profit that works with teachers to transform instruction so that children can become powerful readers, writers, and thinkers.

Our goal is to close the gap in literacy achievement between disadvantaged children and their more affluent peers. We know that early reading = lifelong success. We also know that there is no stronger lever for improving student outcomes than giving teachers high-impact instructional strategies.

We invest in schools by providing training and coaching to teachers and administrators and quality children's books to classrooms. We work school by school—pre-kindergarten through third grade to strengthen instruction and create a culture of literacy. We develop a Model Classroom in each grade level, supporting consecutive years of high-impact literacy instruction for students.

Over the past 10 years, teachers coached by CLI have taught more than one million children.

For more information about CLI, or to donate, go to:

www.cli.org

ACKNOWLEDGMENTS

Thanks to all the authors who graciously donated a story for this anthology. Your willingness to share your work exceeded even my wildest expectations.

Thanks to Daniela Owergoor for producing and donating the gorgeous cover art.

Thanks to my wife, Kellie, for patiently enduring my long hours stressing over this project; and to my children, Emma and Ethan, for always wanting Daddy to read them books.

Thanks to David G. Barnett for stepping up and offering to publish this anthology, and for guiding me every step of the way.

Thanks to Kealan Patrick Burke and C. Dennis Moore for their support and advice when I was trying to get this project off the ground.

Thanks to Tony Tremblay, Nanci Kalanta, Thad Linson, Christopher Jones and Janet Holden—it's been quite the journey, and I look forward to continuing it with you all.

Last, but not least, a very special thanks to professor Daniel Mahala, Liz Tascio, and all the kids at Story City, for teaching me to look beyond myself and make a difference in the lives of others.

TABLE OF CONTENTS

*—Never before published

INTRODUCTION

I n January of 2013, my final regular semester at the University of Missouri-Kansas City, I attended a course titled *Language, Literacy, and Power.* I had no idea what the class entailed, only that it was one of just a few options I had to complete my writing minor. As it turns out, the class contained a service-learning component, something I'd never heard of but would impact me greatly.

In addition to our normal class time, my classmates and I were broken up into smaller groups (roughly 4-5 people) and assigned to a particular service-learning project. The group I chose to be in met every Friday afternoon, after regular school hours, at a school for underprivileged children. We worked with a group of about forty children, split into two groups, from 1st through 7th grade. Our goal each week was to lead them into creating their own (very) short story.

During my time with them, I discovered an overwhelming need to do more for these kids. They had next to nothing. As we were discussing a character during our second week, and what that character wanted in the story, we asked what some of the kids wanted in their own life. "A mom," said one. "A book," said another. It was heartbreaking. And to see those kids light up when we worked on a story, how they literally climbed over one another trying to voice their ideas and opinions, it was amazing. Looking back on it, it was easily one of the best college classes I ever attended, and easily the most life-altering.

Throughout the summer, my mind worked overtime trying to figure out a way to help not only these kids, but the illiteracy problem with underprivileged children throughout the country. And I thought an anthology, with all the money going to charity, would be perfect. Book sales helping buy books for kids who don't have any. I loved the idea. After thoroughly researching various organizations, I decided on the Children's Literacy Initiative, a non-profit organization that works directly with schools to help young children become better readers and writers.

But the question remained—could I recruit enough authors to contribute a story? Could I get *any* authors to join me, knowing that I had no resources from which to pay them? Could I find a way to publish the book on my own? These questions haunted me while I tried to start planning, but then something amazing happened. An author agreed to contribute a story. Then another, and another, and it began snowballing from there. Then, thanks to author C. Dennis Moore, the anthology found a publisher.

Stories started rolling in, a mixture of brand new tales—written just for this anthology—with some obscure reprints, and I could tell many of the authors were not only donating a story, but they were *proud* and *excited* to be a part of the book. And now, a year later, you hold in your hands the final product. An anthology featuring an All-Star lineup, with all the proceeds from sales being donated directly to the Children's Literacy Initiative. Now sit back, relax, and delve into the darkness...

— Craig Cook

KING OF SHADOWS

JOE R. LANSDALE

L eroy was as shocked as if someone had handed him an electrically charged wire. He got the shock when he learned he was about to have a little brother, and that his surprise sibling would make his first appearance at the age of eleven. Being fourteen him self and knowing full well how babies were made and where they came from, it twisted up all kinds of images in his head, and he didn't like a one of them. Some of them he hated with a deep sincerity that only a Biblical literalist could grasp.

His mama told him about his new brother and told him the boy's name was Draighton, and that Draighton would share his room with him, because there wasn't any other way, the house being small and all.

"I have a little brother? And he's eleven? And he's named Draighton? That's a real name?"

Now that the image of an eleven year old springing from his mother's womb ready to start fifth grade had fallen out of his head, a new idea came to him. His father had had a child by someone other than his mother, and there had been a discovery, and now this new child, branded with the name Draighton, would soon be coming to live with them, in his room, sharing his bed, eating part of the food that before Draighton's arrival had been his except for sharing with his parents and the garbage disposal.

He thought his mother was taking this all rather well, this new-found son by another woman, till she said, "Now, he's not your brother by blood. He's a friend's boy, but he was good friends with your daddy, and this fella, Jimmy Turner, well, he was a nervous sort. And just the other day he took to drink and lost his head. He killed his wife, then himself. Cut her and his throat with a big old razor. He left a will that wanted Draighton to come live with Herman and me, and the court, after a bit of finagling here and there, decided to let him."

"Why didn't his daddy kill him too?" Leroy asked.

His mother thought this was nothing more than a simple question, but it was really a statement of disappointment.

"He was on a camping trip with the Boy Scouts when it happened. It was a two week trip. In some mountains or another out in New Mexico, or Arizona. Some desert place. Jimmy starting acting a little odd at work. Everyone said so. And he must have known things were slipping, and that's why he made out the will. Did it two, maybe three months before the tragic accident."

"It don't sound like an accident."

"Well, technically, I suppose you're right."

"Technically," Leroy said, "ain't it a murder and suicide?"

"Technically, yes."

Well now, this was all intense and surprising news, and Leroy took it the way he took most unpleasantness. Badly. He went to his room and jacked off twice, thinking he ought to get some of it out of his system now, since the operation was going to be more difficult in the days to come, and he was not the sort of boy that liked the idea of talking about such things with a friend, or even a new brother, and the idea of them sharing in such an endeavor was unappealing, though some of the boys at school liked it, and had even participated in what they called a circle jerk. The thought of this alone made Leroy's stomach churn. The mere vision of some other boy seeing his equipment, or heaven forbid, touching it, sent shock-waves through him. What surprised him was that the other boys thought the whole thing funny and could see no homosexual attachments to the project, yet, due to his glasses and not overly attractive appearance, were quick to call him queer or fag, or at the least, four-eyes.

Leroy had only in the last year gotten to the point where he viewed the whole notion of sex as more than a fire that drove him to such episodes as he had just completed, lying on his bed drying from a humiliating activity with sticky Kleenex in his lap. He had lately realized the connection between his apparatus and that of the female of the species, it having been explained to him in the manner of plug and outlet by a senior boy, and the thought of it disgusted him. But none of this was as confusing or disturbing as the notion of a new brother, full blown with a personality, and close enough in age the kid might want to fight, and might even be able to beat him up. This was a real concern, as he had already taken two sound whippings from a girl at school, who besides being cursed with a massive facial outbreak of impetigo, a curse that extended throughout most of the first through eighth grade to such an extent that when those divisions of the school were on the playground it looked like a goddamn leper colony. And if that wasn't bad enough, like all the impetigo-cursed, this girl's sores were covered in a purple iodine medication that gave her the look from a distance of being a spotted pup parading on hind paws. Besides the impetigo sores, she was sick-bird-scrawny, had one eye that wandered, and rode the short bus to school and had to have help to find it at departure time every afternoon.

And this beating she gave him, it wasn't a beating he thought he deserved, having merely tried to point out that if she was going to stand around with a ping-pong eye, she might want to wear sunshades or some such thing, a pirate patch maybe. This suggestion had resulted in a sudden explosion that led to a legendary ass-whipping, that, a year later, was still referred to in quiet whispers, least the Wandering Eye Girl, as she was known, get wind of it, and take to beating someone else's ass to the point of near terminal embarrassment.

It made no difference that six months after the fact it was discovered she wasn't retarded at all, just contrary, and that a doctor had fixed her eye and her impetigo had cleared up and her parents had moved her to another school, where rumor was she had gained weight, looked good, made excellent grades, and kept tabs on the old school and things that were said there by a horde of hidden informants.

Leroy thought this was all doubtful, but still, he was careful in what he said, least any reference to the former Wandering Eye Girl might in fact inform some hidden stool-pigeon and lead to her return for an even more brutal whipping and the final cap on his embarrassment, that even now resulted in his being called all kinds of names other than queer, fag and four-eyes, among them Retard Punching Bag and Ass-Whipped Fellow.

Therefore, the idea of a new brother who would attend the same school and might be willing to fight him was nervously unappealing. That's all he needed, was a new addition to the list of all those who could whip his ass, which already included just about everybody.

What he thought he might do was jump the little bastard and beat him down right up front, therefore dispelling any future notions Draighton might have of pugilistic superiority. Of course, there was always the possibility of the turn-about. That he, instead of Draighton might in fact be the one who came out on the short end of the stick, even if he did spring a surprise attack and get in the first few licks.

And there was another thought. Though he had yet to meet Draighton, the name itself implied to Leroy that the boy might be a biter. Those old style hillbilly names often designated just that, though the fact that Draighton was a Boy Scout might temper his savagery a bit. They were supposed to be good citizens, though the truth was a couple boys he knew in the Scouts were great fans of the circle jerk, and found their camp outs perfect for such shenanigans. Bottom line was, it was hard to fight a biter. He knew, because this brought back an equally disturbing memory, one right there side by side with him having taken a severe trouncing from a thought-to-be retarded, wandering eye girl, and that was when he was nine he had tried to bully his seven year old cousin Wiley, who, in spite of generally wearing a sheen of dirt encrusted snot, proved to have the mind and tenacity of a pit bull. He bit. Leroy still had the scars. At least that little bastard went to a different school.

So it was with major trepidation that Leroy awaited the arrival of his new brother, Draighton.

«««—»»»

Draighton came on a cloudy day when there was a threat and smell of rain and a severe push of wind. Leroy had been forced to take a bath and clean behind his ears and wear church clothes, and he thought this was ridiculous, dressing up for some kid with a goofy name and no parents. But he had to do it, least his mother break out the fly swatter, and when the moment came, he stood with her on the front porch, waiting. His mother was as nervous as if she were anticipating final judgment, moving from one foot to the other and talking as if words might be a shield against the weather, which, along with the rain and wind, was turning as cool as a well-digger's ass.

He watched as his dad's Chevy pulled up at the curb and his father got out, and a moment later the door on the far side opened and a boy knee high to a midget climbed out, proving that there was no truth to the rumor that the Boy Scouts had height requirements, a factoid laid on him by the local Scout Master when he sought to join up. He'd have to look into that, this height business. He was beginning to think, for some reason or another, the Scout Master had lied to him.

The boy wore leg braces over his pants, carried a little bag by a handle and walked as if he were in a Nazi military parade, kicking one leg out front to be followed by another kick, and another and another. Leroy half-expected Draighton to give a stiff-armed salute.

Draighton didn't have a whole lot else going for him either. He had what was called a bowl haircut and his hair was the color of a fresh turd and his head was big and he wore thicker glasses than Leroy and his face looked as if it beaconed to receive flies and custard pies.

In spite of this, Leroy's mother came down off the porch and practically darted out to Draighton, grabbed his head as if she might make a free throw, and gave him a kiss on the forehead, said, "Aren't you just the sweetest-looking thing."

Leroy was astonished at such a bald-faced lie, as he felt Draighton might be best used to scare crows in a corn patch, provided you could teach him to stand on a stool and a phone book.

"This here is Draighton," the father said, as if he suspected Leroy or his mother might be anticipating someone else. Leroy came down the steps and went over and stuck out his hand the way he had been taught to do, and the boy took it, his little hand lay like a damp mitten in the palm of Leroy's paw. Leroy had a sudden charge of excitement. He was bigger than this boy in both height and hands, and probably equipment. The idea of having someone around might not be so bad, especially if he was superior to in size. It seemed unlikely that with those leg braces Draighton would have any chance of beating him up, or even chasing him down. A series of ideas ran through Leroy's head, some of them involving trip-wires, all of them ending with him in some mode of triumph, Draighton lying on his back, struggling to flip over like a toppled cockroach.

«««—»»»

The first thing Leroy did was lay down the rules.

"Reckon you can put your stuff over there in that corner, long as you keep it organized and don't get it mixed with my goods or use any of my stuff, except maybe some of the crayons, if you ask."

"Thank you," Draighton said.

"All right, don't mention it. I was taught to be kind. But it's important you know whose turf is whose turf, lest we come to a mis-understanding."

"That's very nice of you."

"Just want you to know how things are. We'll share the bed, but I get the side I want, and if you fart, then you hit the floor with a pillow and a blanket. I get the bathroom first, if I want, and I get the towels first."

"Won't I have my own towel?"

"Doubt it. We don't do the towels that much. My mother says it saves on soap and water bills if you just dry with the same towel for awhile, and you'll be using whatever one I finish with, I reckon."

"All right then."

"Your legs hurt?"

"They do. I had some kind of problem with them, and with my spine. Doctor says I might outgrow it."

"Don't count on it. Doctors and mothers and such like to give you the good side, so you'll have hope and won't kill yourself or some such thing. I was you, I'd just plan on being a cripple. You could maybe get a wheel chair when you grow up. Get a job, licking stamps and envelopes and such. They got some chairs now that are pretty good. There's a kid I see now and then, a waterhead, and he's got one of them chairs. You could maybe do that. He sells pencils. It ain't heavy work and it ain't rich work, but it's work, and thing is, you don't have to have no education to get it."

"I like to think optimistically."

"See where that's gotten you. Your old man killed your mama with a razor then cut his own throat, and if you had been in town, instead of off with the Boy Sprouts, you would have been cut up too. He might have even taken them braces and sold them before he done

16

himself in. You never know what kind of plan a crazy might have. And I ought to tell you, don't get too comfortable, you might not be around here long. My guess is the welfare will come get you. You might have to live in one of those big rooms with a bunch of cots. Just preparing you on how things are."

Draighton broke into tears and clanged out of the room, down the hall to the bathroom.

Leroy grinned, took a deep breath and tossed out on the bed.

Life was good.

«⟨—⟩»

Thing amazed Leroy was that the cripple seemed to like him. Draighton followed him around, and Leroy could hear him banging about behind him, as if everywhere he went there was nearby a dreadful machinery break down. It gave Leroy the creeps. If he sped up, Draighton sped up, and if Leroy looked back Draighton might be in the distance, but he would be coming as if on a mission, his face determined, his legs swinging out wide, tossing him onward.

At school he saw him in the halls, and Draighton never failed to acknowledge him by calling Leroy's name and waving. He seemed truly excited that he was Leroy's brother, and told others this was the case, though Leroy always said he was a homeless kid they were helping out. Considering Leroy had no status to begin with, having a miniature cripple for a brother was not beneficial, and tossed him into a rank just below the retards and the booger eaters who lined up outside during lunch hour to dessert on the contents of their nose in plain sight, relishing their bottom rung position as if it were an award.

The Draighton Connection made it so he was the butt of jokes that he wished were intended for Draighton. But no, he, as if by osmosis, collected Draighton's insults. "Hey, Four-eyes, you and your Mom have to oil your brother much." Or, "Have you thought about selling him for scrap?" Or, worse yet, "When you suck his dick, do the braces cut you?"

It was less than stimulating, and Leroy felt that it was only fair that some of this meanness directed at him should blow back on the source material.

17

«‹‹—›››

About a month went by. Insults didn't seem to bother Draighton. He rode those out like a pilot in a hurricane plane. But there finally came a vulnerable day. It was the day they all went to the house where Draighton's father had killed the kid's mother and then himself.

The plan belonged to a therapist Draighton was seeing. The therapist felt enough time had passed that it would be a good idea for Draighton to confront where it had all happened. Leroy had heard his Mom and Dad talking at the bottom of the stairs one night, while Draighton was snoozing in bed. He had come out on the landing and hid up there to listen. They were discussing Draighton's condition, how fragile he was, and Leroy's father was against something or another, though Leroy was uncertain what.

"That fella hasn't ever been out of that goddamn office, except maybe to hang around the University or such," Leroy heard his father say. "What the hell does he know about the feelings of a little boy? Common sense should tell you that doing something like that ain't a good idea, even if it came with money and added six inches to that little kid's dick. Though I reckon in that case he'd have to have some lifts built into his shoes."

"Darling," Leroy's mother said, "you shouldn't talk like that."

"Maybe not, but I'm telling you, it ain't a good idea."

"He's the doctor."

"Yeah, well, I think we should actually talk to someone who's studied medicine, not a bunch of hooey."

"He has degrees. Certificates."

"Yeah, so does the tire man at Wal-Marts, and my goddamn tire came off. Remember that?"

Few days later, Leroy figured it out when Draighton was taken for a private discussion in the kitchen. Leroy leaned against the wall near the doorway and listened. They were going to take Draighton back to his old home, to look around, to make peace with its existence and what had happened there. That's what he heard his mother say. "Make peace with its existence." Leroy thought, well, it ain't the house cut the little kid's mother's throat, so what's the beef there?

It was all obvious now, Leroy's father didn't want Draighton going back to the house where his parents died, and it was the therapist's suggestions they were debating that night, but, in the end, Mother and the therapist prevailed. Leroy thought. Therapists and mothers, they can be so dumb.

«««—»»»

The day was wet and cold and the clouds were full of shadows. The therapist, a skinny man who wore glasses and had a complection problem, and gave Leroy some idea of how he might look when grown, sat with them in the car, in the backseat between Draighton and himself. Leroy's mother sat on the front passenger side, and his father, grumbling all the while about this and that, drove. Leroy was glad to be along. He was supposedly there for Draighton's support, which he thought was funny. He was sort of hoping Draighton would have some kind of episode, break down in tears, or maybe just flip out and have to be hauled off in a straight jacket, live out the rest of his time in a padded room.

The house wasn't what Leroy expected. It was just a house. Nothing creepy about it. No spider webs hanging from gables, and no weed-grown yard. Someone had kept it mowed and it was a brightly painted house, the only purple house on the block. The only thing bleak about it were that the flower beds were empty of blooms this time of year and the sky seemed to sit down on the roof of the house like massive wads of cotton that had been stained with sin.

The inside of the house was no less deflating. It too was as common as hand soap. There wasn't any blood and nothing was knocked over and there wasn't a chalk line on the floor. Not even a yellow ribbon with POLICE: DO NOT CROSS had greeted them at the door.

Nothing was unusual about the house in any way. The therapist said, "Now, you weren't here when it happened, Draighton—"

"And that's the point," Leroy's father said. "He wasn't here. He's not dealing with anything. This is just not necessary and there ain't no way it's good for him."

"It's okay," Draighton said. "I want to see."

The therapist pursed his lips, as if to say: Told you.

19

"Now, according to the police," the therapist said, "part of what happened took place in the back bedroom."

Draighton nodded, as if this was only logical.

They went past the couch and opened the door and went into the room, and finally something was strange enough to have made the trip worthwhile. The walls were painted black. The windows were marked up solid black, and the instruments that had turned them that way lay on the floor under the window sills. Dozens of black markers. The bed had been turned over and was thrown up against the wall, and the closet door was thrown open revealing clothes hanging on a rod. The carpet in the bedroom smelled, and in one spot it was heavily stained and the stain had made the carpet in that area stiff as a wire brush.

"Here," said the therapist, pointing a finger at the carpet, "is where your mother was found, Draighton."

"This is just goddamn cruel," said the father. "It's okay, Draighton. You can go if you want."

Draighton shook his head. "No, sir. I don't want to go."

"I don't know Jimmy would have wanted this," said the father.

"Obviously, the father was confused," said the therapist. "He wouldn't have known what he wanted. Or, rather, what he wanted wasn't all that good."

"You know what I mean," said the father, standing up tall, pushing out his chest.

The therapist stepped back.

Leroy's father sighed, crossed his arms and looked defeated. The mother looked about the room carefully, as if more murderers or victims might be propped up in the corners.

"I think we'll go outside," the father said, and he and his wife went. They were in such a huff, they forgot Leroy standing there, actually enjoying himself.

Wow, Leroy thought. A murder. Cut from ear to ear. Wow.

"The room wasn't black when I went to camp," Draighton said.

"He must have finished a day or so before the murders," the therapist said. "No one knows why he made the room black, why he blacked out the windows. It's even possible he did it after the murder. No one knows."

"Is this where daddy killed himself?" Draighton asked.

The therapist shook his head.

"No. When he finished here, he went out this way."

Leroy and Draighton followed the therapist into the living room, then down the short hall that led through the kitchen, and to the door that led to the enclosed garage. They went down the short steps into the garage. The therapist asked where the light was, and Draighton turned it on. The car was still in the garage, sitting there like a great bomb waiting to be loaded. The place smelled really bad.

"He died here," the therapist said, and he pointed to a little storage door inside the garage.

"He went inside there, sat down on a stool, and cut his throat."

Leroy thought, wow, this therapist is great. If Draighton isn't fucked up now, he's sure gonna be.

Draighton stiff-legged over and opened the door to the closet quickly, as if he might do it so fast he would travel back in time and rescue his father from his final moments. When the door was open, Leroy leaned over Draighton and looked in.

The stool was still there and the place smelled of blood. When Draighton flicked the little closet light on, roaches darted away in a clicking rush. For a moment, in one corner, where shadows seemed to remain in spite of the light, it seemed to Leroy, at least for an instant, that the roaches gathered together and rose up into a tall, broad shape, then fell apart and scuttled away into…Well, he didn't know where they went. It had all happened in the blink of an eye. The floor and walls seemed tight together, didn't seem to provide any means of retreat, even for a roach. But, nonetheless they were gone and the corner no longer seemed to be shadowy. Leroy felt cold, as if water from an iceberg had been suddenly flushed down his back, and his testicles sought high ground, tightening up like string-drawn bags of tobacco.

Leroy looked back at the therapist, who was standing back in the garage, having paused to light a cigarette. Leroy had a feeling the therapist loved all this, and maybe hoped Draighton would seize up or go the other extreme, into a hissy fit.

Neither happened.

Draighton just stood there in the shadows, and then he walked inside and moved around the room, from one corner to the next, very slow, and then he sat down on the stool, lifted his head and looked up.

Leroy looked up as well. All that was up there was a fly-specked bulb of about forty watts. Draighton, however, took an inordinate interest in it, before lowering his head and letting it nod this way and that.

"Did he die on this stool?" Draighton said loud enough for the smoking therapist to hear.

The therapist came to the doorway, said, "Yes. Well, they found him lying beside it. His hand was outstretched toward the wall."

"Where is the razor? Do the police have it?"

"Well, Draighton, that was part of a little mystery. They didn't find it. They think it was a razor because of the way the cut looked. It could have been a knife. But the weapon wasn't found."

"Then why would they think he did it?"

"Because he wrote a note."

"Oh."

"It said, 'I had to.' And that was it."

The therapist studied Draighton carefully, and Leroy thought it was because he was still waiting to see Draighton go off his nut. But, if this was indeed his plan, he was disappointed.

"But where would the razor go?" Draighton asked.

"I know. It sounds more like murder. No murder weapon. But, the police believe, that due to the note, and the blood on the wall, your father cut his throat, and, well, hid it."

"But where?"

"It is a mystery, isn't it? But, that doesn't mean it was anything other than what it appears to be. A murder, suicide."

"He cut his throat and then hid it?" Draighton asked. "Wouldn't that be hard?"

"It would, but they think that's what happened. There was a cat in the house—"

"—Snowball," Draighton said,

"Yes. Your cat. And they believe it may have taken the razor in its mouth and wandered off with it. You know, the blood would have attracted him."

"Snowball carried off an open razor in his teeth?"

Leroy thought Draighton was asking some pretty good questions. Damn. This was great.

"I don't know, Draighton," the therapist said, "I'm telling you what the police thought."

"They're dumb," Draighton said.

"Well, they are the police."

"They're dumb. Even I know the cat wouldn't do that, and I'm a little kid. Where's Snowball?"

"Well, they determined the cat was in the house, but the window was open over the kitchen sink, and they believe he went out that way…He…Well, Draighton. He got run over."

"Killed?"

"I'm afraid so."

Draighton, finally overwhelmed, sitting there on the stool, hung his head and began to cry.

Leroy thought: Priceless. Even the cat is dead.

«‹—›»

A few days went by and Leroy found himself growing somewhat pleasant toward the stiff-legged invader. Perhaps it was because he was impressed a bit with Draighton. He had liked the way he had talked to the therapist about the shortcomings of the police, and he felt, in spite of his temporary breakdown on his father's death stool, that he had recovered reasonably well. He even saw fit to sit with him at lunch at school.

But another thing had crept into the mix. He had helped William Townson with his homework one afternoon, or was forced to was more the truth of it, and William had taken a kind of liking to him. Oh, he called Leroy Four-Eyes and Numb Nuts, but from William they were more like terms of affection, like the sort of nicknames you might come up with for a beloved, if somewhat belabored relationship with an unattractive pet. A dog missing an eye, an ear, or a leg, possibly one with a cut off tail, or perhaps the whole list.

This relationship grew, and pretty soon Leroy found he was in the company of a number of the cooler and better respected boys, and that William ran interference for him. Saying stuff like, "Well, he may be a dumb shit, but he's my dumb shit. Don't hit him but once. And on the arm."

Leroy thought it was okay for William to say that stuff because it put him in the company of a number of the well-respected boys, and this began to rub off on him. This was a good thing. Girls came around.

23

Certainly, they weren't interested in him. But it was as close as he ever got, outside of sitting behind some nubile sweetie in class, or passing them in the hall, riding home on the bus with one of them sitting in a seat nearby. They never even knew he was there, but when they came around and talked to William, who was smooth with them and was willing to touch them, Leroy felt that through his connection to William he was able, via a kind of pet ownership, to sniff at the asses of the female population, have dreams of someday mounting their legs. It was as close as he thought a dog deserved to the prize.

It was a dream, and it wasn't much and it wasn't going to happen, but it was all he had.

And then there was Draighton.

Therein lay a problem.

Now, for a time he had felt Draighton's presence was acceptable, because at school, it gave him a kind of pet, someone he could look down on and humiliate, but somehow stay connected to, but when William embraced his company, his stiff-legged, pseudo-brother became not too unlike a wound that wouldn't heal.

One time, out in the parking lot, smoking cigarettes with William, not because he liked them, but because he knew they made William look cool and therefore thought they might make him look the same, William said, "Who's that little retard I see you with from time to time? The gimp?"

"He's staying with us."

"He don't look cool, Four-Eyes. You hang with me, you got to hang with the cool. And I don't need two bumps on my ass. I ain't sure why I got the one, you know what I'm saying?"

"Sure, William. Sure."

"You got my homework?"

"Yeah."

"Miss a few? You got to. I get too many they know I'm a cheating sonofabitch."

"Our papers are different," Leroy said, scrounging in his pack, pulling it out. "I think I even managed to do it like your handwriting."

William took the paper and looked at it. "You four-eyed little prick. You didn't give me a folder to go with it."

"Oh. I have it here."

Leroy produced it and William clamped the papers inside. He flipped it opened and studied it. "This here looks good," he said.

"Thanks," Leroy said. "I did my best."

"I know you did," William said.

«« — »»

After that moment, Leroy began to push himself even farther away from his unwanted companion. Refused to sit with Draighton at school lunches, and instead sat with William and his friends. He was insulted there and made fun of and poked and sometimes tripped, but they wouldn't let Draighton sit with him, so when he came around the long table toward Leroy, Leroy stuck out a leg and tripped Draighton, sent his tray and food and utensils flying.

Draighton fought to get himself back on his feet, without so much as a helping hand, did this amidst ridicule and laughter, gathered up his plate and utensils, put them on his tray and kicked back toward the center of the cafeteria.

William stuck out his fist and Leroy stuck out his, and they bumped knuckles.

He was in now.

«« — »»

That night, up in their room, Draighton sat in the corner, his back against the wall, his bound legs stretched out in front of him. Leroy came in from having showered and found him that way. He assumed he had fallen and couldn't get up, but he didn't offer to help.

Draighton looked up at him, said, "Why, Leroy? Why did you do that?"

"Do what?"

"You know what I mean."

"Yeah. I know. Because I could."

«« — »»

Over the next month Leroy noticed a change in Draighton. He no longer even tried to be friends. He was sullen in the room, and had taken to sleeping on a pallet near the far wall. This was all right with Leroy. It gave him all of the bed and he didn't have to put up with him at school. Seeing him now was like seeing a ghost. Nothing really there. Just a wraith kicking its way around the house and the halls at school.

When it all but seemed Draighton had turned to smoke and disappeared, Leroy began to notice peculiarities. Once, he awoke and saw that Draighton was gone. It was no big thing, as he assumed he had gone to the bathroom, but the next night it was the same, and from his window, which was cracked to let in some of the winter wind, he heard a clanking sound. He arose and looked out. The moonlight was dim, but he could see going along the sidewalk, moving quite briskly in spite of his leg braces, the figure of Draighton. He watched until Draighton had kicked his way into darkness.

Maybe he'll get run over, thought Leroy. Or kidnapped. Maybe someone out there has a thing for cripples. If they did, it would be handy, because they could chase Draighton down quick and kill him. Maybe commit sexual abuse. Leroy had a hard time trying to imagine that, why anyone would want to have any kind of sex with Draighton. A robot, maybe. Someone made of steel. There might be some kind of appeal there. Outside of that, there was the killing part. Someone might do that. Someone who didn't like cripples.

Wouldn't that be a thing?

It was something to hope for.

Leroy went back to bed.

«««—»»»

One night late in the bedroom, Draighton was over in the corner sitting on a stool, Draighton's daddy's stool, a lamp light on, his little bag between his outstretched metal-strapped legs. Draighton had the bag open and was plundering its contents. Leroy was in bed with pillows propping him up. He watched Draigthon go about his business with a kind of amazement. It seemed it was only yesterday when the room was his and it was large, and now it was his to share and it was small.

"What are you doing?" Leroy asked.

"Looking for something," Draighton said, without glancing up.

"That bag ain't that big. You ought to be able to find anything pretty quick."

"I already found it."

Leroy watched as Draighton took out a long wooden box.

"What's that?"

"It belonged to my daddy."

"Well, what is it?"

"A razor."

"Like the one he cut your Mama with, then himself?"

"It is that one."

"It can't be."

"It can, and it is," Draighton said, balancing the box on his knee.

"It can't be, Wire Legs. It was never found."

"I found it."

"You been back to the house?" Leroy knew that he had, of course, or where would he have gotten the stool. Still, it was somehow a stupefying thought.

"Yes," Draighton said. "I've been back to the house."

"That's where you go at night?"

Draighton nodded, opened the box and reached in and took out the razor, and even from there Leroy could see that it was crusted with dried blood.

"Good God," Leroy said.

"He cut his own throat, put it back in the box, and hid it behind the wall in the garage storage closet."

"We looked there. The police looked there. There wasn't any place for it to be. He wouldn't have had the strength to do it."

"He cut his throat and he took it over to the wall board and pulled it loose and there was a little place for it back there. He put it in the box and put it away and sat back down on the stool and died."

"You can't know that."

"I know it."

"He cut his throat, he wasn't going anywhere. You know that."

"He did though. Did you know that there are eleven dimensions?"

"What are you talking about?"

"There are eleven and they bump against one another, and sometimes they collide. They can collide with great force, and perhaps in the past that was the source of the Big Bang, the colliding of dimensional matter. The dimensions exist alongside ours and we can't see them or touch them, except now and then when something slips through."

"Are you taking some kind of drug? They got like a drug they give cripples? I know you go to the doctor now and then. Mom and Dad take you. Is the doctor having you take something?"

"There is a lord of all things sharp, and he lives in one of those dimensions, and he can be called. He can be invited. He can slip through. His is the world of the razor, and he is the lord of the razor. The King of Shadows."

"You don't sound right. Where you getting this hogwash?"

"It's true. You cut yourself with the right tool, it can open your mind and it can open the worlds. The dimensions. Eleven become one. Sometimes, when they bump just right, they multiply, on down to the singularity of existence, and beyond. There is time beyond the singularity. Can you imagine that."

"No. I don't know what a singularity is."

"I've seen the distance. The great distance. It is forever and can make you mad. It's amazing. It's so much more than this. I tell you, you can open your mind."

"Only if your head is split," Leroy said.

Draighton shook his head. "No. You can open your mind with a simple cut from the right tool." Draighton held up his left hand. From there Leroy could see there was a big red mark on his thumb. A cut.

Leroy was beginning to feel nervous, because Draighton, sitting there draped in shadow, the razor in his hand, the box for it on his knee, didn't sound like Draighton. He wasn't talking like Draighton. He wasn't talking like anyone he knew and he wasn't talking about anything anyone knew.

"Way it works," Draighton said, "is the razor is made from a specific metal that was created when the dimensions collided so hard so long ago and banged everything into existence. When the great boom happened and all manner of matter knocked against itself, some of it was matter from planes we do not perceive, with physics we do not understand. My father, he bought the razor in an antique store. He thought it was strange. He accidently cut himself right before I went to Boy Scout camp. I remember. He cut himself and he said what I'm saying, and I thought it was strange. Mom thought it was strange. I understand it now. I don't think it's so strange at all. You know, there are cuts in all manner of tools if they are blessed with the words of opening, and these tools, like the razor, they can open your mind, and you can fall, fall, fall, down deep into forever."

"You're making me nervous," Leroy said.

"Am I?"

"Yeah."

"You made me very nervous at school. What you did, it embarrassed me. It made me feel even smaller than I am. It made me feel insignificant. But now, I feel less that way. The cut, it can open your mind."

With a flick of the wrist, Draighton sprang the razor open.

"Well," Leroy said, shifting in bed. "I didn't mean to. Make you feel small, I mean."

"I think you did mean to."

"Maybe. I was out of line. I admit it."

"You do?"

"I certainly do."

Leroy watched as the shadows that had been made by clouds and had come through the window to nest with Draighton moved away from him, and now he was just a little four-eyed dude with metal clamps on his legs, a big, open, shiny razor in one hand.

"You might want to clean that razor," Leroy said. "Clean it and put it away."

"Think so?"

"Sure."

"You seem nervous, Leroy."

"I'm fine. I just don't want you to cut yourself. That thing is huge. I don't see how anyone could shave with that thing."

"I don't think it's meant for shaving," Draighton said, and then Leroy watched as a kind of film moved away from Draighton's eyes, and they were just Draighton's eyes now, small and piggy, desperate behind his glasses.

Draighton studied Leroy for a moment, looked down to see the razor in his hand, closed it carefully, placed it in the box and put the box in his bag. He continued to sit on the stool, just watching.

"You look like some kind of owl over there," Leroy said. "You ought to go to bed."

"Guess I ought to."

"I don't think you ought to sleep up here in my bed. Go on and lay down on your pallet."

"Okay."

Leroy reached over and turned out the lamp light, which didn't seem to be giving the room much of a glow anyway, and pulled the covers up to his chin and turned his head on his pillow so he faced Draighton. He closed his eyes, but parted them slightly to watch. Draighton hadn't moved to go to bed. He hadn't moved at all. He just sat there on his daddy's stool with the razor box on his knee staring into empty space as if it were not empty at all.

Leroy didn't like it, and he thought he'd watch to make sure things were okay, but it didn't work out. He went to sleep anyway. But once, during the night, feeling cool, he semi-awoke to pull up the covers, and there in the dark he saw something that disturbed him. A wad of shadows in the corner on the stool were illuminated by a strand of moonlight wagging through the window. Very clearly he saw a figure on the stool. Draighton. Had to be. But he looked bigger and he was wearing a tall top hat. Then the moon was lost to cloud cover again, and there was only the squat shadowy shape of Draighton on the stool.

Leroy tried to awaken, but couldn't. He fell back down into darkness, knowing what he had seen to be a bad and strange dream, something he could wish away. And he did. And in spite of the strangeness, or perhaps because of it, he fell asleep.

Once more, near morning, he awoke, and there on the stool, a notebook in hand, writing furiously, was Draighton. He was sure that Draighton had been up all night. He thought about that a moment, then realized it was Saturday, no school, so he closed his eyes and drifted off for a while.

«««—»»»

That Saturday when Leroy went down for breakfast, Draighton was nowhere to be seen.

"Where's Draighton?" Leroy asked.

His mother, who was busy serving him breakfast, said, "He came down early. He wasn't hungry. He said he was going to the park."

"The park?"

"That's what he said."

Leroy sat in his chair with his plate in front of him and watched it fill with eggs and bacon. He thought about what he thought he had seen last night, about the bad dream, and now, in the clear light of day he was uncertain what he had seen, if it was a dream, if it was real.

No. Couldn't be real. That didn't work. Did not compute.

"Your father and I are going to go visit your dad's aunt," his mother said when he had finished his breakfast and was polishing off a glass of milk. "She's been quite ill. We won't be back until late. Maybe very late. You can watch Draighton, can't you? Lock the house up before it's dark. Don't go out after it's late. I'll give you money for you and Draighton to buy hamburgers and go to the movies before dark. But after dark, I want you home."

"Sure," Leroy said.

"We hope to leave within an hour. That's where your dad's been. Down at the station getting gassed up. When he gets back, we're going to go. Sure you'll be all right? We could find Draighton and we all could go. As a family. But I'm not sure you two boys would want to sit around a hospital all day."

"We'll be all right here," Leroy said. "I'll go find Draighton in a bit. Make sure he's back here around dark."

«‹‹—››»

When his dad and mom left, Leroy went back upstairs and looked around. He looked carefully at the stool. Yep. It was the stool he had seen in Draighton's house, out in the garage storage room. He picked it up to see if he could see blood on it, and thought in fact he could. When he did that, something fell out of the stool.

A composition notebook. It had been in a kind of slot under the stool. A magazine slide or some such thing. You couldn't tell it was there just by looking, but you picked up the stool, you could see it.

He put the stool down and picked up the notebook and flipped it open. It was full of gobbledy-gook and drawings and bits of writing and some of the pages had dark splatters on them. Blood?

As Leroy thumbed through, he was startled to see a crude drawing that made him suck in his breath. It was a crudely drawn figure shaded jet black, wearing a top hat. He had very narrow ankles

31

and his feet were fit into the open mouths of decapitated heads, wearing them like house shoes. The blackness of the man was not the blackness of a negro but the pure empty blackness that lay between the stars. This had been achieved by constant pencil shading, but there was something almost otherworldly about it. The teeth in the open mouth of the man, if man was the word, looked like needles and they had been colored with a kind of silver color with some kind of marker. It was crude but there was something about it that made Leroy uncomfortable. The main thing that made him feel that way was what the figure was holding. A razor. A large open straight razor.

Leroy turned the pages and saw there were drawings of old style razor blades, double-edged, and pictures of knives and a picture of what seemed to be a Roman soldier sticking a spear into the side of an almost stick-figure Jesus, positioned on a cross. Leroy had to turn the notebook upside down to see this, as it had been drawn in such a way that Jesus's head and that of the Roman were at the bottom of the page. Had it been drawn upside down purposely, or had he merely turned the page wrong when he began this drawing? Or had Draighton drawn it at all. Maybe it was Jimmy, Draighton's father. That made sense.

He examined more pages and found that the writing was often English, but more often than not it appeared to be nothing more than symbols. As he tried to read, his head began to spin and the symbols appeared to move on the page.

Leroy tossed the book into the corner of the room, and as the pages fluttered shut, they gave out shadow and the shadow cut like the edge of a razor across the room and across Leroy.

Leroy felt cold, and for a moment he felt as if he were falling. Sideways. But when he put out his hand, he discovered he was not moving sideways at all, but was standing upright.

He stumbled toward his bed, and then he noticed something he should have noticed before, but his preoccupation with first the stool, and then the composition book, had distracted him. Lying only partially covered by a blanket from Draighton's pallet were Draighton's leg braces. And Draighton wasn't in them.

«««——»»»

Leroy began at the park, but he didn't find Draighton. He went down town, and with the money his mother had given him for Draighton and himself, he went into the drugstore/cafeteria and over to the counter where food was served. He bought himself a hamburger and fries and a large cherry Coke made at the fountain, then he went next door to the movies and watched a horror film and went home.

Draighton was still not there.

Leroy read a couple of comics. The room darkened. Leroy got up and looked out. Night was not far away. His parents would probably not be back until late. What to do. Television was a thought, but he didn't feel any great drive toward that, and he didn't like sitting downstairs in the big living room alone.

Instead, he picked up the notebook again and thumbed through it, and had the uncomfortable feeling that the figure of the dark man with the razor had moved from one side of the page to the other, and that he was moving from the center of the book toward the front of it, because the page he was on now only held part of him, and one of his head-encased feet was in the gully of the notebook and extended onto the opposite page.

The light went out of the window and the darkness came in, and Leroy felt surrounded by it. He folded up the book, then jerked his hand to his mouth. A paper cut. He hated those damn things. He tossed the book aside. The room fluttered like bat wings with shadows, and Leroy decided he didn't want to be there anymore.

He got his coat and went outside and started walking. He went to town again, had another hamburger, then started walking, thinking he ought to go back to the house. But the notebook was there, and he didn't like the idea of it, and he determined that when he did indeed return home, he was going to burn the damn thing.

He sucked at his paper cut as he walked, and without really thinking about it, he found himself standing outside of Draighton's old house.

It looked different at night. More forbidding than it had looked in the daytime. Leroy went up the walk and came to the door, but he didn't try the knob. Locked most likely. And even if it wasn't, he felt uncomfortable going inside. He went around to the side of the house, to where the black painted bedroom was, pressed up against the window with his face cupped in his hands, and looked through a spot where the black markings were not quite complete.

Being as it was dark and the room was dark, there was little to see, and Leroy was about to withdraw from the window, when something moved.

Draighton.

Leroy had only caught a glimpse, but it was him, and he was moving swiftly, not in his usual way. This baffled Leroy. How was he getting about without his braces? Had he been suddenly healed? And what was he doing back here?

"Draighton," Leroy said, but his voice was soft and he said it in a way that didn't sound like he really meant it.

He thought again of going home, but decided against it. He didn't like Draighton, but he wasn't crazy about being alone anymore. He thought about William, and how maybe he could go hang with him, but then the realness of it all occurred to him. He didn't know where William lived, and William didn't know where he lived, and probably didn't give a damn. William just liked him around so he could slug him on the arm from time to time, have someone to punish for any empty moment that might occur. There was no real relationship there.

Leroy took a deep breath. Damn. Thing was, he didn't want to do that anymore. He wanted to take William's place, make Draighton his bitch. That's what he wanted. He didn't want to be William's plaything anymore, he wanted one of his own, and so far, that hadn't worked out the way he expected. Shit had not flowed downhill enough. Some, but not enough. He was, after a great moment in the cafeteria, tripping the little turd to the floor, losing his ground, and he was letting Draighton control things, and there was no reason for that. Now he felt he should take command, set things right. And finding out Draighton didn't need his leg braces might give him an edge. Draighton was maybe messing with everyone, for sympathy. And it seemed to Leroy that he had heard that as long as Draighton was in those braces, he got some kind of government check. He wasn't sure about that part, but he believed that was right. This could give him something to hold over the little bastard's head, like an anvil on a very weak string.

Leroy went back to the front door, feeling courageous now. After all, what could a little turd like Draighton do to him? He felt angry that he had allowed himself to be overtaken by irrational fears, allowed a notebook to scare him. Yes sir, for certain he was going to burn that damn thing when he got back home.

But for now, he was going to take over, and quit letting Draighton pull all this mysterious stuff, all this boogie man shit. He was going to lay down the law and get that little gimp bastard back to the house. He had to still be a gimp. He didn't just get up one day from being stick-legged, to suddenly having juice in his limbs. He must have on another pair of braces. And he must have been wearing them when he saw Draighton through the window. He had moved quickly, all right, but that didn't mean he still wasn't on braces. Of course, where had he concealed the extra pair? They wouldn't fit in his bag, and there really was nowhere else. He couldn't just pull them out of his ass. And there was still the other possibility that he didn't need them at all.

Leroy stalked around to the front door and took hold of it. It was in fact unlocked and he pushed it open and stuck his head in and called out Draighton's name. But his voice hadn't been as strong as he intended. The name seemed to cautiously enter the house and not go too far into the shadows, like a mouse that feared the presence of a cat.

He tried again. A little louder. Draighton didn't answer.

"You need to come on now. Mom and Dad have gone for the day, but they'll be back later, and we need to be home. I've got some money for you a hamburger."

Draighton didn't answer.

Leroy slipped inside and gently closed the door. With it shut it was very dark. The house felt odd, as if he were in the belly of a beast, swallowed whole, awaiting digestion. He wished now that he had brought a flashlight. He thought of opening the door to let in more light, but the idea of leaving it open might reveal that he was in fact trespassing, and there was something thrilling, as well as frightening, about being here, and it wasn't all a bad feeling. For the moment, anyway.

Leroy moved through the living room toward the garage. He had a feeling that's where Draighton would be, out there looking over his father's death scene. When he came to the garage door, just off the kitchen, due to moonlight through the kitchen window, he saw that a large rat had been crucified with thumb tacks to the door and that it had been cut open and blood from it was smeared on the door in those strange symbols Leroy had seen in the composition notebook.

This was almost too much, but then Leroy remembered being alone at home and no one to have as his slap monkey, so he turned the garage door knob, horrified to discover that the knob was coated in blood. He wiped the blood on his pants without thinking, then felt the worse for it. That would be something he would have to explain. He was going to make sure Draighton got a good beating for this. Oh yeah, he was going to beat him down and kick him around like a soccer ball.

Leroy took the steps down into the garage cautiously. The garage was completely empty now, someone having removed the car and some of the junk that had been there, and there was nothing to see, but Leroy felt the hair on the back of his neck prick up, and this was almost enough to send him running. Then he thought, Draighton. He's in here. I can take a cripple.

The door to the garage storage was open, and Leroy went over there and looked cautiously around the end of the open door, into the storage room.

It too was empty.

<<<—>>>

The garage made Leroy feel as if a heavy weight was lying on top of him. No. It was more as if the shadows were like a thick wool overcoat, and that they were trying to hold him. He went up the steps and back into the kitchen. As he did, he heard the front door slam.

Leroy rushed over there, but the door was jammed shut. He pushed at it, but it wouldn't budge enough to open. Finally, he went into the bedroom where Draighton's mother had been murdered, and pushed up a window there. As he was climbing out, he had the distinct feeling that someone, or something had entered the room. He practically fell out the window, and when he looked back at it, there was nothing there to see, except the frame of the open window and the empty darkness of the room.

Leroy went around to the front door and looked. A stick had been shoved under it. It couldn't be pushed forward. Damn that Draighton, Leroy thought. I'm going to get him.

Leroy hustled on home, the air full of the smell of rain, the clouds thick and the darkness dripping. At one point, he saw a car that looked like his parent's car. It was parked near the curb and the door on the front passenger's side was open. It looked so much like his parent's car, he started to go over and look at it more closely, but then he saw, up the block, walking fast, what he felt for certain was Draighton. He was rounding the corner of a house, walking as briskly as if the bones and muscles in his legs were brand new, but there was something about his feet. Something strange that Leroy couldn't quite identify from that distance.

Hurrying onward, Leroy tried to catch up, but when he came running to the corner of the house and looked around, all he saw was an alleyway. He took it and crossed over to another street and walked up and came to his house, looked in the drive to see if his parent's car was there. It wasn't. He went up the steps and put the key in, but when he did, the door came open before he could turn it.

Draighton. He had a key too.

Inside it was dark, and when Leroy switched on a light, nothing happened. He tried other lights with the same results. He looked around downstairs but didn't find Draighton. He thought the house smelled funny, and was too cool. With the electricity off, Leroy assumed the heat had gone out of the house. As for the smell. Well, he wasn't certain. Surely the power couldn't have been off long enough for anything in the refrigerator to spoil.

Leroy started up the stairs, and as he climbed, he felt something sticky on his shoes. He paused, leaned on the railing and lifted one foot. He couldn't tell there in the dark, but he put out a finger and touched the bottom of his shoe. It was something wet.

All right. That was it. His parents got home, he was going to catch shit, not Draighton, not the cripple. And he was going to catch it because this loser had tracked in something from the street. He went on up more quickly, angry, and when he came to his bedroom at the top of the hall, he found the door open.

He went inside.

《《《—》》》

The room was full of moonlight and it framed around the shape of Draighton at the window. He was sitting, leaning back against the sill, and for just a blink of a moment, it had not looked like Draighton at all, but then the moonlight went behind a cloud and it was Draighton, and then the light was freed and it wasn't Draighton.

It was a tall dark man wearing a top hat with silver winks of razor blade in the hat band. He had silver stick pin teeth, and he smiled them at Leroy. Leroy tried to pull his feet out of the floor, but they seemed nailed there. At the end of the long thin legs were two large balls of something. Leroy squinted.

They were heads. Like in the drawing. And this man...this thing's feet went down and into them, and now Leroy realized that the car alongside the road had in fact been his parent's car, and they were back early, had pulled over to give Draighton a ride...and....

He couldn't figure it. Not really. He didn't know what to do. He wanted to run. He wanted to scream. But all he could do was look at those heads. Those shoes. The heads of his mother and father.

"Slicing through dimensions is like slicing through flesh, except the dimensions have to be in the position to be sliced, and it is not so easy to achieve that, as it is to find and slice flesh."

Leroy was really frozen now. The thing had spoken and the voice was like cracked glass and tumbling razor blades. And the thing, it was smiling big, and Leroy knew as sure as he knew the Pope crapped in the Vatican, that he should run. But he couldn't. He felt warm all of a sudden, and urine ran down his legs and onto his shoes and the floor.

When the acrid odor of his mistake filled the room, the thing in the window stood up and sniffed the air. "Nectar," said the voice, and it dropped its hand to its side, and Leroy could see dangling from it the huge razor.

"Draig...Draighton?" Leroy said.

"He's here," said the thing, tapping his chest, "trapped by the shadows, held by the moon, one foot in, one foot out."

Leroy had no idea what this meant. A shadow rolled across the moon again, a cloud sacking it up, and when it did, there stood Draighton. He wasn't wearing his glasses. He stood there squinting, holding the razor. The heads were on his feet, his legs jammed down into the cracked-wide mouths of Mom and Dad.

"My daddy," Draighton said, "bought the razor in an antique shop. It's very old."

Leroy swallowed, found his voice. "Draighton. You're not well. Mom. Dad. How could you?"

"They help open the worlds. Enough blood. Enough death. All manner of things can slide through."

Draighton stepped forward. There was no mincing movement in his step. It was sure and firm and without braces and the heads on his feet plopped nastily against the floor.

"He demands sacrifices," Draighton said.

That was it. Leroy's feet finally came unfastened from the floor, and Leroy bolted, and he could hear the movement of Draighton behind him, pursuing him. He looked over his shoulder as he came out into the hall and up against the railing, and when he turned, there was Draighton, his mouth wide open, clopping forward with his feet in the heads, and Leroy thinking in spite of himself (How do they fit?), and then he was running, almost making the stairs.

Draighton had him. Draighton grabbed his shoulder and spun him. When he did, Leroy saw the razor coming down. Instinctively he shot out both hands and grabbed Draighton's wrist, and the force of stopping the blow slammed him against the railing, and he heard the railing crack, then give way.

Leroy and Draighton fell through space.

The couch below broke their fall and they tumbled onto the floor. Draighton somehow rolled out from beneath Leroy and stood on those horrible shoes he had made and staggered back into the shadows, which seemed to consume him, and then Leroy saw a hand come out of the shadows, Draighton's hand, and it took hold of the living room curtain and jerked it loose.

Moonlight jumped into the room and Draighton was not Draighton now, but the strange thing. What had Draighton called him. Lord of the Razor.

"Cat and mouse," said the Lord of the Razor in his strange voice of broken glass and tumbling razor blades, two pounds of gravel and the screech of a dying cat.

Leroy was up and running. He went through the living room and into the kitchen and he could hear the plopping of those feet behind him, and he began to scream. Still screaming, he hit the side door and it came open and he leaped out into the night air, onto the yard, and when he did, the moonlight was bagged again by shadows, and Leroy realized now that the moonlight wasn't all there was to it, but it was part of it. He turned and saw Draighton coming. He kicked out hard and hit Draighton in the groin and Draighton doubled a little, but kept coming. Leroy, with nothing more than an instinctive move, stepped aside and slapped out with both hands and caught Draighton across the back, sending him stumbling in his horrid shoes, stumbling across the yard and up against the house next door. He hit his head with a sound like an anvil being dropped on a pumpkin, and Draighton fell and rolled over, his face facing the heavens.

Leroy looked up at the sky. The clouds were rolling across the heavens and some of them were very dark and he could smell even stronger the aroma of rain in the air. He saw too that soon all the strands of clouds would pass, and the moonlight would be full. He rushed to the storage shed against the house, jerked open the door and got hold of the shovel.

He rushed over to Draighton, and as he did Draighton's eyes opened and the moonlight shone and Draighton's face began to change. Leroy lifted the shovel with both hands, brought it down with all his might on Draighton's throat.

There was a sound like someone cutting a garden hose in two, then there was a spray of blood, and Draighton's hand that held the razor fluttered a couple of times, opened. The razor lay in the flat of Draighton's dead hand.

Just to make sure, Leroy gave Draighton's throat another slam with the shovel, this time freeing the head from the body completely. Leroy stumbled back and sat down in the yard. The yard was full of moonlight now and it lay over it like a thin coating of butter.

Leroy didn't know exactly what to do. He wondered if anyone would come out of the house next door. They didn't, and lights didn't go on. No one had heard or seen anything. He looked across the street. The houses over there were dark as well.

How was he going to explain this? What about Mom and Dad?

He wasn't sure he was doing the right thing, but he began to dig, and finally he had a big trench in the yard. He rolled Draighton and the heads of his parents into the trench and kicked Draighton's head in there with them. He covered it up.

As he finished, he saw that the razor was lying in the grass. He picked it up.

He carried it in his hand, walked back down the street to his parents' car. Their headless bodies were there. Blood-covered symbols had been drawn on the inside of the windshield.

Numb, Leroy walked back to his house and went upstairs and sat on the stool that had belonged to Draighton's father. He sat there for an hour, then got up and got the composition notebook. He opened it and looked at the drawings, the symbols. They moved on the page.

He sucked at his papercut.

He looked out the window.

It was rainy.

Soon the rain would pass. It was that kind of rain. Pushing hard and passing quick. It would still be nightfall. The moon, which was full, would come out. Maybe the sky would clear of clouds.

He sucked the paper cut on his finger and looked at it.

His finger was the size of a frankfurter and it pulsed. The cut on his finger spread open as he looked. There seemed to be something there. He got up and found a match he used to air out farts, struck it on the window sill and held the match close to his finger. The heat from the match felt good. The cut on his finger spread open and he looked at it carefully. There in the wound made by the composition book with all its symbols, he could see more than eyes should be able to see. It was as if he had telescopic vision.

He saw his mother and father's heads hanging on hooks. Draighton's head hanging on a hook. And beneath them, sitting on a stool made of leg bones and rags of flesh, the Lord of the Razor, looking up and out the wound, smiling those stick-pin teeth. Closer he looked. There were all manner of bodies as well as living human beings, flayed alive, screaming, coming to the fore of the wound to look up with pitiful wounds for faces. All manner of strange bat-like things flapped up against the wound but did not come out.

The Lord of the Razor waved a hand that was like a flash of shadows and the bat things fled and the flayed things fled, and there was just the Lord's face, looking up and partially out of the wound. Smiling those silver stick-pin teeth.

Leroy dropped his hand. He went back and sat on the stool. He looked down at his feet. He needed to do something about the way they looked. He thumbed through the composition notebook, used the razor to cut the paper cut on his finger open wider. The blood came freely. He wiped it on his pants at first, then he used his finger and the blood to draw in the notebook. He understood the symbols. They did things to the world. A small part of it. They helped crack open dimensions. They made things as the Lord, the King of Shadows, wanted them to be.

When he finished writing, he sat very still on the stool, the open razor in his hand. Waiting for the rain to come. Waiting for it to pass. Waiting for the moonlight. Waiting for the change.

QUIET BULLETS

CHRISTOPHER GOLDEN

I
f Teddy had seen the cowboy's ghost at night, he probably would
have wet his pants. When he thought about it later, he had to
admit to himself that if he had been in his bedroom, or reading a
book in the sliding room, and looked up to see the gray specter of a
gunfighter looming in the doorway or some dark corner—maybe
even blocking his ma's view of the TV, as much as a guy you can see
through could block anything—it would have scared him right out of
his socks. As it happened, though, the worst he got was a serious case
of the chills, and an even bigger dose of curiosity, mostly because, at
first, he didn't even know he was looking at a ghost.

On that early October day, Teddy walked home from school the
usual way. He knew from reading and from movies that October
could be nice and cool in some parts of America, but in Tucson,
Arizona, most days were still warm, like the heat from the long
summer had been stored in the ground and didn't want to leave even
when the days turned gray.

He walked with Mike Sedesky and Rachel Beddoes most days,
except when Sedesky got in trouble and had to stay after school,
which seemed to happen more and more often. The boy just didn't
know how to keep quiet. One time Sedesky had told Teddy that his
daddy drank some, and took the belt to him if a note came home from
the teacher. Sedesky had taken to writing his own notes back and
forging his father's signature. One of these days, Teddy figured his

friend was in for a hiding like none he'd had before, but he did not say that to Sedesky. He could see that Mikey—which was what Rachel called Sedesky—knew exactly where all of it would lead.

Teddy and Sedesky were both ten years old and in the Fifth Grade at Iron Horse Elementary School. Rachel, a year older, had moved on to the upper school right next door, but never seemed to mind walking home with the boys despite the difference in status. Privately, though, the boys had debated whether or not the pleasure of walking home with Rachel—something that did make them stand a little straighter and lift their chins with pride—was worth the beatings it sometimes earned them from Artie Hanson and the goons with whom he palled around.

The older boys didn't like Rachel spending time with Teddy and Sedesky, and any time they crossed paths after school, Artie and the others would block their way, or worse. Sedesky made noises about giving those guys "the business," but Teddy had never been able to figure out what "the business" was, unless it included getting their books dumped in the shrubs, their noses bloodied, and their arms twisted behind their backs so hard they'd ache for days afterward.

There were Indian burns and wet willies and cries of "uncle," and those were the good days. On the worst day, Artie had tried to force Sedesky to promise never to speak to Rachel again, and when Mikey wouldn't promise, the goon had broken the pinky on his left hand.

Rachel had avoided them for a week after that. For their own good, she said.

After, when she started walking home with them again, none of them brought it up. Teddy assumed that Sedesky had persuaded her that he wasn't afraid, but he wished that the two of them had consulted with him before any decision had been made. He liked his pinky fingers just the way they were, thank you very much.

On the day he first saw the cowboy's ghost, they had walked home without encountering any sign of Artie Hanson. Teddy and Sedesky had said goodbye to Rachel at her gate, and then a block later Sedesky had taken off between houses, cutting through backyards on his way home.

Teddy and his mom lived in a small house on a quiet street, but it was neat and tidy and Mr. Graham and Mr. Hess—who lived on either side of them—had pitched in to paint the house just this past spring. They'd said it was the least they could do to help out, what with Teddy's daddy dying in Korea and his mom ailing. Teddy, who'd still been nine, had been their helper that day. He still remembered it with a smile.

But on the afternoon when he spotted the cowboy in front of his house, his thoughts weren't on painting or on his daddy. Instead, he mostly thought about Sedesky and Rachel, and how come Rachel seemed not even to see Teddy when Mikey was around. It made him feel bad—kind of small, really—and he didn't quite know why. Girls were a mystery, and not one he felt in much of a hurry to solve. They just didn't understand most of the things that were important to him, like cowboy stories and rockets.

With these thoughts in his head, he turned the corner onto Derby Street and noticed the cowboy walking up to his front gate. A smile blossomed on Teddy's face instantly. The cowboy looked like the real deal, from the hat to the long coat to the tips of his boots. If Sedesky had been there, Teddy would have bet him a quarter that the cowboy carried a Colt revolver. Maybe two of them. He picked up his pace, wanting to talk to the man, wondering why he seemed to be headed to Teddy's own house.

Two things happened at once. First, Teddy noticed that the sunlight passed through the cowboy—that he could see the fence right through him. Second, the man walked to the front door without opening the gate, just stepped right on up as though the gate did not exist.

Teddy stopped short and stared. The cowboy cast no shadow. The longer Teddy looked, the more transparent the man seemed. It scared him a little, knowing a ghost stood on his front stoop, but with the afternoon sun shining down, and the fact that there could be no denying this was an honest to goodness western gunfighter—maybe someone who'd been shot right here in Tucson—after a couple of minutes he felt a lot more *Wow* than spooked.

The cowboy turned, tipped him a wink, and gave a nod toward the door, as if he wanted Teddy to follow him inside. Then the gunfighter passed through the door and vanished within.

Teddy followed. What else could he do? It was his house.

«‹‹—››»

The weirdest thing about opening the door and stepping into his house was how ordinary it seemed. Dust motes swirled in the shafts of light that came in through the windows and eddied along the floor on a breeze from the open door. Teddy stood on the threshold a few seconds, but nothing seemed amiss. The stairs leading up to the second floor were dark with shadow, the hallway vacant, and from the living room came the sound of the radio playing low.

With a frown, he peeked into the room. His mother lay on the sofa, hands resting on her chest, tuckered out after a long morning. She woke up early every day to fix his lunch and send him off to school and then sat down at her sewing machine. Teddy's ma did great work as a seamstress—everybody said so—and so her mornings and early afternoons were spent hard at work to earn enough money to buy them food. What little money the government gave her every month—she had explained that they paid the money because Teddy's daddy had died in the war—covered rent, but not food or clothes.

In the afternoons, she turned on the radio and took a nap, sleeping so deeply Teddy had to shake her awake at half past four so his ma could make dinner. The radio stayed on, then, until dinner was ready. His ma said she liked the voices. They kept her company. Most days, Teddy did his homework at the kitchen table while Ma made dinner, and sometimes she laughed softly at things he either hadn't heard or didn't understand. Radio things. Even when he had no idea what had made her laugh, he would smile. Ma had a beautiful laugh.

She looked pretty when she slept, but kind of sad, too, and he always wondered if she were dreaming of his daddy. They didn't talk much about him. Teddy wanted to, but he had the idea that maybe that would hurt too much for his ma.

So that afternoon after he followed the cowboy's ghost into the house, it surprised him to find nothing at all out of the ordinary. The radio voices talked and his ma slept on, the sound of her deep breathing filling the living room. A song started to play, one with lots of horns. Teddy always liked music with horns—trumpets, saxophones, anything. Confused, he looked back toward the hallway, but still saw no trace of the ghost. He might have thought he imagined the whole thing if not for the creak of a door opening.

Now Teddy's heart skipped a beat. He felt his face flush and his breath quickened. The sight of the ghost outside on the street had seemed weird and wonderful, but that creak of hinges made the hair on the back of his neck stand up.

With a glance back at the sofa to make sure his ma hadn't been disturbed, Teddy went to the doorway and peeked out into the hall. He had left the front door open and a light breeze swirled along the floor, gently swaying the door to the closet under the stairs so that the hinges creaked just a little.

Teddy frowned—he didn't recall ever seeing that door open before. Most of the time he forgot it was even there, but now he walked over and gave it a closer look. The top of the door had a diagonal slant that followed the angle of the stairs. At some point the door had been painted over, so that the iron handle and the deadbolt were thick with the same dark green as covered the wood. Even looking at it now, the deadbolt seemed stuck in place, like it would be hard to move. He doubted he could slide it to the right to lock it again, and wondered how it had come unlocked.

Well, he didn't wonder much. In fact, a smile spread across his face as he glanced around. It had to have been the cowboy's ghost. The only other person in the house was his ma, and he could hear her softly snoring in the next room.

"Excellent," Teddy said, nodding as he stared into the closet. "Totally, totally excellent."

A single bulb dangled from the ceiling in the closet. He pulled the chain, but the light didn't come on. Nobody had changed that bulb in forever. Still, enough light came down the hall that he could see inside well enough. There were old pantry shelves, mostly full of dingy coffee cans full of buttons and nails, shoe boxes, and faded old table cloths. Teddy could not remember his ma ever using a tablecloth.

Somebody's moth-eaten sweater hung from a hook on the back of the door. There were other hooks in the closet, to either side of the shelves, and to the right hung the thing that he had focused on since first glancing inside. The gun belt looked worn by age and coated with the same dust that lay over everything else in the closet. The empty holster disappointed him, but he took the belt out anyway, putting it around his waist. His daddy had been a big man and even at ten years old, Teddy had some of his size, so when he cinched the belt as tight as it would go and cocked it at an angle, he just managed to keep it from sliding down over his hips.

Now he felt like a gunfighter. He opened his stance a little and imagined himself preparing for a shootout at high noon. His hand dropped to the holster and he made a little face when it closed on nothing. *Right. No gun.*

Where had the belt come from? It must have been his daddy's, maybe the one he had worn in Korea. The thought sent a shiver through him, but the good kind. Curious, now, he investigated the closet shelves more closely and immediately noticed the triangular wooden box with its glass top. Teddy stopped breathing. He took it down from the shelf and looked through the glass at the American flag that had been draped over his daddy's casket.

Teddy's eyes felt hot. He didn't remember much about that day, but now that he saw the flag a memory surfaced of soldiers folding it up and one of them handing it to ma and then saluting her. The soldier had saluted Ma. Boy, he had loved her that day. Through all the tears he had felt proud.

He slid the wooden triangle box back onto its shelf, sorry to have disturbed it. As he pushed it back into the shadows it knocked against something else. A frown creased his forehead and he moved the flag box aside, stood on his tiptoes, and reached into the back of the closet. His fingers closed on something round and metal and he drew it out, smiling when he discovered it was a Christmas cookie tin. Through the dust he saw the face of old Saint Nick, an antique-y sort of Santa Claus, and he remembered that Christmas was only a couple of months away. Maybe if he took the tin out and cleaned it up, his ma would make some cookies to put in it.

Only the tin felt pretty heavy already, and he wondered what was in it. He crouched and set it down on the floor of the hall with a clunk, and even as he pried off the lid, somehow Teddy knew what he would find inside.

The gunmetal had a bluish-gray color, which surprised him. He had expected it to be black. Teddy's heart beat loudly in his ears as he lifted the gun out of the cookie tin, glancing over his shoulder to make sure his ma hadn't gotten up from the sofa. He held the gun in both hands, barrel aimed at the floor, fingers away from the trigger. If there were bullets inside, he didn't want to fire the gun in the house.

As tired as his ma always seemed to be, and even though she hardly ever got mad at him, he had a feeling he'd get whooped worse than Mikey Sedesky if that happened.

He whistled through his teeth, the only way he knew how. The cookie tin had a coating of dust, but the gun looked clean and almost new. Handling it like the snake charmer he'd seen down at the grange hall, he slid the gun into the holster on his daddy's belt, and it fit just fine. *Daddy's gun*, he thought. And he knew it had to be true. This was the gun his daddy had taken to war.

All serious now, no smiles, Teddy backed up from the closet, right hand hovering over the gun as if he were about to draw. Partly he wanted to be a gunfighter, and partly a soldier like his daddy. He turned toward the front door, ready to face off against an imaginary enemy.

The cowboy's ghost stood just inside the door, daylight streaming through him, not much more to him than if he were made of spider-webs.

"Oh" Teddy said, in a very small voice. He stared, eyes wide, mouth open. He knew he had seen the ghost before, but they were up close now, maybe ten feet apart. "Are you…what are you doing here?"

The cowboy narrowed his eyes.

"Wait," Teddy said, realizing that he'd known all along. "You opened the closet."

The ghost nodded at him in grim approval, the way Mr. Graham next door always did. Then he turned, gestured for Teddy to follow, and walked out of the house, passing right through the screen door.

Teddy blinked a few times. Seeing it up close like that kind of made his eyes hurt. His lips felt dry and he wetted them with his tongue, unsure what to do next. The ghost wanted him to follow, and if he understood right, had something to show him. At least that was how it seemed. He knew he shouldn't go running off without telling ma, especially after some ghost, but she wouldn't be waking up for at least half an hour or so. Not if today was like every other day. And if he didn't follow, gosh he would always wonder what it was the ghost had wanted to show him.

"Damn," he said, but only because nobody would hear.

Teddy swallowed hard, then hurriedly put the Christmas cookie tin back into the closet, grabbed the old sweater from its hook, shut the door tight, and rushed outside, careful not to let the screen door bang behind him.

«««—»»»

It felt like the kind of thing you ought to keep secret, partly because it seemed special and Teddy wanted it all to himself, and partly because he didn't want anybody to think he'd lost his marbles. So as he followed the ghost around the side of his house and through the Mariottes' backyard, Teddy tried to look like nothing at all out of the ordinary had happened today. He pulled on the ratty old sweater, realized immediately it had to have belonged to his daddy, and smiled to himself. The mothball smell didn't bother him. The sweater hung low enough to cover the gun hanging in its holster. Combined with the sweater, it made him feel really grown up.

The ghost ambled sort of leisurely, like he wasn't in any hurry, but Teddy knew the cowboy was hanging back to make sure he could keep up. Every couple of minutes the specter glanced over his shoulder, then sort of nodded to himself as he kept on, leading Teddy out onto Navarro Street and then onto the dirt road that led out to Hatton Ranch. When the ghost walked in sunlight and Teddy looked at him straight on, he could see right through the fella, like he was cowboy-colored glass. But whenever the gunslinger passed into the shadow of a tree or a telephone pole, he seemed more *there* somehow, like in the dark he might fill in entirely.

Only one car went by on the dirt road, kicking up dust that swirled right through the ghost, obscuring him from sight for a few seconds. The car—a brand spanking new Thunderbird—kept on going. The old, jowly fella behind the wheel did not so much as glance at the cowboy, but he gave Teddy a good long look as he drove by. Teddy's face flushed all warm and the gun weighed real heavy on his hip, but the car kept on going and soon even the dust of its passing had settled again.

The cowboy had stopped up the road a piece, leaning against the split-rail fence that marked the boundaries all around the huge spread of the Hatton ranch. He waited while Teddy caught up.

"Where are we going?" Teddy asked, keeping his voice low and glancing around. If people like the porky old fella in the T-Bird couldn't see the ghost, anyone watching him would think he was talking to himself. He didn't want stories like that getting back to his ma.

The ghost didn't answer, though. Instead, he nodded in an appreciative way, wearing the kind of expression Teddy remembered on his daddy's face now and again. Then he cocked his head, indicating that Teddy should follow, and hopped the fence.

Teddy hesitated. He licked his lips. His whole body felt prickly, like his hands or arms sometimes did if he laid on them wrong. Ma would say his hand had fallen asleep, but Teddy knew it had to do with the blood inside him not flowing right 'cause of the position he'd been in. Rachel had told him that, and it was just the sort of thing the Beddoes girls had always been smart about.

It wasn't that he had suddenly become afraid of the ghost. Heck, that gunslinging specter had to be the coolest thing he could ever have imagined—and it *had* occurred to him that he might be imagining it. But trespassing on the Hatton ranch, well, that could get him in trouble. Old man Hatton had run Teddy's daddy off his land dozens of times in the old days, at least according to Ma, and Teddy didn't like the idea of being run off.

The cowboy turned, cocking his head like a bird. This time when he beckoned, there was a little impatience in him, and suddenly none of this seemed as much of a lark as it had a few minutes ago. Something in the cowboy's face, what little Teddy could see of it, considering the sun passed right through it and all, told him they had serious business on the Hatton ranch.

Teddy swallowed hard, looked around to make sure no one was watching, and then threw one leg over the fence. Then he was on the other side and running like hell after that cowboy, toward a stand of trees fifty or sixty yards from the road, and a giddy ripple went through him. So what if old man Hatton ran him off? He'd run Daddy off, and Teddy liked the idea of being like his daddy. He liked that a lot.

Heck, the old guy hadn't killed his daddy. The Koreans had done that.

"What's your name?" he asked the cowboy, when they were on the other side of a tree-lined rise, walking across open graze land that looked more like scrub than field. No wonder there weren't any horses around when this part of the ranch gave them nothing to nibble on.

The ghost gave him a strange look, then, half-smile and half-frown. Teddy got that look a lot in town, especially from folks in McKelvie's store. Ma said people didn't know what to make of

Teddy, but she didn't say it like it was a bad thing. She said it proud, like it mattered to her. She said he was smart and grown-up for his age, and folks weren't used to little boys who could speak for themselves. One time Mrs. McKelvie overheard Ma saying something like that, and said children ought to be seen and not heard, and Ma had said that someday the whole world was gonna hear from her Teddy.

He'd beamed for the rest of that day. She'd even bought him licorice.

They didn't get over to McKelvie's store much lately. Most of the time, his ma said she was too tired to walk that far. Teddy would have liked some of that licorice, but he never complained. With everything Ma did for him, he knew it would be ungrateful, and Mr. Graham always told him that was one thing he ought never to be.

The cowboy didn't talk at all. Teddy had sort of figured that out, but the questions kept coming out of him, like he had no control over his mouth at all. Finally he managed at least to turn his babbling into just plain talking. He told the ghost about all the books he'd read about gunslingers and whenever he played cowboys and Indians, he pretended he had a pair of Colts strapped to his hips. He even demonstrated his technique, drawing invisible guns and firing, making the pa-kow sound with his mouth. As soon as he heard himself, he stopped. Out there alone on the rough land of the Hatton ranch, it sounded kind of childish. And the gun—the real gun—banging against his hip seemed to get heavier.

Teddy hitched up the gun belt, and his pants, which had started to slide down from its weight.

"Are we almost wherever it is we're going?" he asked. "We're awful far from home and I oughta be there when Ma wakes up. Or at least home for dinner. I don't want her to worry."

That's when they came to the fence. Maybe the Hatton property kept going beyond it, and maybe it didn't. On the other side was a stretch of woods he couldn't see the end of from here, and there were empty beer bottles scattered on the ground on either side. Some pop bottles, too, but mostly beer. Teddy looked at them, wondering who would come all this way just to drink beer. Then he thought of Artie and the goons he palled around with, and he had a pretty good idea.

When the ghost picked up a couple of bottles, one in each hand, Teddy's jaw dropped. Ma would've said he was trying to catch flies, and he did feel like a dope just standing there like that, but he couldn't believe what he was seeing. The ghost—barely there at this angle, the sun bleaching him out like the yellow scrub grass—actually touched the bottles, picked them up and set them on the fence rail.

"How did you do that?" Teddy asked at last.

The ghost winked, but kept going, picking up more bottles and gesturing for Teddy to do the same. Between the two of them they set up more than two dozen empty beer and pop bottles, all along the rail, and by then Teddy had figured out just what they were up to out here.

Target practice.

The ghost led him a dozen paces back the way they'd come. Careful, nice and easy, not like some high noon gunfight, the cowboy took out his phantom pistol, cocked it, and pulled the trigger.

Teddy flinched, waiting for the gunshot, but it did not make a sound.

The last bottle on the left shattered, glass showering to the ground.

"Wow," Teddy whispered.

The cowboy gestured for him to try it. Teddy's hands shook as he took off his daddy's old sweater and drew the old Army pistol. He had seen enough movies and read enough books to understand the basics—which end the bullets came out of and how to pull the trigger—but aiming the thing took a bit of getting used to. For a few seconds he just tried to get used to holding the gun straight, realizing that if he supported his right wrist with his left hand, he could just about keep it steady.

He pulled the trigger.

Nothing happened. The gun did not kick in his hand the way the cowboy's had. No glass shattered. Disappointment flooded through him. All this way, standing there with a ghost, and he didn't have any bullets.

The cowboy held out his hand. Teddy flinched, afraid the ghost would touch him. It never would have occurred to him if he hadn't seen the cowboy pick up those bottles, but now the idea of being touched by a ghost—a dead man, though he felt sort of sad thinking of his new friend that way—gave him the shivers.

If the cowboy noticed Teddy's reaction, he didn't let on. Warily, Teddy handed him the gun. The moment when the ghost lifted its weight from his grasp made him catch his breath, smiling nervously.

"You're really here," he said.

The ghost shook his head with that same indulgent smile. Teddy missed his daddy something fierce when he saw that look, but still he was glad he had met the ghost and that they were out here having this adventure. He had already decided he would tell Sedesky about it, but not Rachel. A girl wouldn't understand. And he bet Rachel Beddoes didn't even believe in ghosts, but Sedesky did. Ghosts scared the crap out of Mikey Sedesky. Teddy would have to tell him there wasn't anything to be scared of.

The ghost opened up the gun—Teddy didn't really see how he'd done it—and slid out the cylinder where the bullets went. All of the chambers were empty. But the cowboy didn't seem at all surprised. He just lifted the gun up to his face, pursed his lips, and blew into the empty chambers, not like he was trying to clean dust out of the cylinder, but nice and easy, like breathing.

Then he snapped the cylinder shut, gave it a spin, and handed the gun back to Teddy.

The metal felt cold, the gun heavier than before.

And this time, when Teddy pulled the trigger, the gun kicked in his hands so hard that all the bones in his arms hurt. But like the cowboy's gun, his daddy's old pistol fired quiet bullets.

Of course, Teddy's shot didn't hit much more than a few leaves in the trees beyond the fence. But the cowboy demonstrated how he ought to stand and hold the gun, and sight along the barrel, and Teddy did his best to mimic the ghost.

It took over an hour, but he managed to shoot two of the bottles right off the fence, and all the while, the gun never ran out of bullets, and never made a sound.

When Teddy looked over and saw the sun sinking low, a little tremor of panic went through him. He slid the gun into its holster and tugged the ratty sweater back on to cover it.

"Tomorrow I'll do better," he said as he turned to bid the ghost farewell, but the cowboy had vanished in the twilight.

Teddy was alone.

Hitching his pants up, he ran all the way home.

《《—》》

That night, Teddy lay in his bed, staring at the ceiling without really seeing it. It seemed almost as if the images in his mind's eye were projected on that blank surface, and he played out the day's events over and over. A ghost? Thinking about it now, it amazed Teddy that he had not run away screaming, but in the moment, with the cowboy right there in front of him and so *real*, he had known he had nothing to fear. The gunslinger had kind eyes.

Now he couldn't sleep. It felt like Christmas. Not the excitement of Christmas Eve, knowing that Santa would be coming within hours, but the following night, after spending an entire day opening presents and celebrating and running over to Sedesky's so they could compare notes about what they'd gotten.

There had been no comparing notes with Sedesky tonight. He had to think about what he wanted to say about what had happened to him today. Maybe if he tried to arrange for Sedesky and Rachel to come over tomorrow, and the ghost came back, they would see him, too. If not, he knew they would never believe him. They might wish they could see a ghost themselves, but if they weren't going to get to see one, they weren't going to allow the possibility that Teddy had, either. Sedesky and Rachel were his friends, but fair was fair. He understood that.

Teddy yawned. His eyes burned, he was so tired. Really, it wasn't so much that he could not have gone to sleep, as that he did not want to. No matter how excited he might be, if he just closed his eyes and turned over, he knew he would drift off eventually. But the events of the day were crystal clear in his mind—fully real. And he worried that if he slept, when he woke in the morning the hours he spent with the ghost would have blurred some, and started to seem like maybe they were a dream. He hated that idea. Teddy wanted to hang onto the certainty of the memory as long as he could.

Yet amidst the nearly giddy aftermath of his day, something else lingered, niggling at the back of his mind, and that gave him another reason to stay awake. If he drifted off to sleep, he knew his thoughts would turn in that direction, and he did not like the troubling things that waited there.

After target practice at the Hatton ranch, Teddy had rushed home as fast as his legs could carry him. Twice he'd had to halt and drag up the gun belt before its weight pulled his pants down to his knees. In the gathering dusk he had raced along Navarro Street as lights came on inside some of the houses, families sitting down to dinner. He had cut through the Mariottes' backyard and into his own. Breathing hard, more than a little frantic at the idea of going in through his front door wearing his daddy's old ratty sweater and carrying his gun, Teddy had looked around for a hiding spot. He'd pulled off the sweater and wrapped up the gun and belt, then tucked the whole package behind the coiled up garden hose before rushing inside.

He needn't have worried. Ma had still been asleep. It had been a simple thing to retrieve the gun and return it to its rightful place, and all the while she hadn't stirred. It worried him.

The radio voices still filled the house, and there his ma lay, curled up on the sofa, snoring lightly. The last of the day's light filled the room with a blue gloom, and after he'd put the gun away, Teddy went and clicked on the floor lamp by the sofa. He knelt beside his ma and shook her gently awake.

"Ma, you're still sleeping," he told her, and the words sounded so dumb to him. "Sorry I'm so late. I was out with Mikey and we kinda lost track of time."

Such a weak excuse, and he hated to lie to her. It made him feel ashamed. But Ma had smiled sleepily and then, as she sat up and saw the darkening windows and realized the time, she had frowned deeply.

"Look at the time," she said. "You must be starving, and I haven't fixed anything for dinner."

"How about breakfast for dinner?" Teddy had suggested.

Sometimes, as a special treat or when they were in a hurry, his ma would make bacon and eggs for dinner. They always made a big deal out of it, like they were getting away with breaking the rules somehow.

Tonight, it had not seemed so special. His ma had barely touched her eggs and only had a couple of pieces of bacon. Teddy had been famished, but the weight of guilt slowed him down and when the eggs got cold he stopped eating. His ma had asked him to clean up the dishes, apologized, and then gone back to the couch, and when Teddy asked if she was okay, all she would say was that she was a little under the weather.

"I'll be right as rain, tomorrow," she had promised.

By the time Teddy finished up with the dishes, she had fallen asleep again. He had left her with her radio voices and gone out back to retrieve the sweater and the gun belt, quickly returning everything to the painted-over closet in the front hall.

Now, lying in bed, he could still feel the weight of the gun tingling in his hands, and he could still hear the low murmur of radio voices drifting up to him from below. His ma had slept on the sofa before, but she had never been asleep when it was time for Teddy to go to bed, not even when she had the flu. Tonight he had brushed his teeth and put on his pajamas and gone down to say good night, but he had not wanted to wake her, so he had kissed her softly on the cheek and gone upstairs.

He didn't like sleeping upstairs all by himself, but if his ma had the flu again, he wanted her to get the rest she needed. She had promised she'd be right as rain come morning, and he hoped she was right. But deep down he doubted that, and it made him wonder if she doubted it, too.

《《——》》》

Teddy opened his eyes slowly, only vaguely aware of the hiss of static from downstairs. The radio station had gone off the air for the night. As that bit of information formed in his mind, he realized with no little surprise that he had fallen asleep after all. Quickly he remembered the ghost, and almost as quickly he wanted to see the cowboy again. As he had feared, already the image had lost its sharpness in his mind, and he could not summon a complete picture of how the ghost had looked when he had first seen it, out on the street in front of his house.

He sighed with disappointment, but knew he could do nothing to get that moment back. His eyes were heavy and even now he had not come fully awake. Sleep called him to return, and though he knew the memory would retain little clarity come morning, he began to succumb.

A sound halted his eyelids at half-mast, and a slight frown creased his forehead. Tick-tock, tick-tock, but it wasn't a clock. Teddy listened with half an ear, trying to sort out the origin of that familiar sound. It grew louder, though still muffled, and he opened his eyes fully and stared at his bedroom window. He did know that sound. Not a tick-tock, but the clip-clop of a horse's hooves.

His bedroom lay draped in indigo darkness, enough light provided by the streetlamp in front of Mr. Graham's house to silhouette the furniture, but not enough for him to make out the time on the clock by his bed. Who rode a horse down his street in the middle of the night?

A terrible possibility rushed through him—*Mr. Hatton.* Had the rancher learned of his trespassing and come to confront him? Teddy's heart pounded in his chest for ten full seconds before the absurdity of that idea made it crumble apart. Mr. Hatton might be the only one living around here who kept horses, but the old man would not come riding up in the middle of the night just to scare a fifth-grader.

Don't be stupid, Teddy, he thought to himself, and smiled.

But the clip-clop sound began to slow, and curiosity dragged him out of bed. If not Mr. Hatton, then who could be out riding so late? It occurred to him as he went to the window that, since he didn't know anyone else who owned horses, maybe someone had stolen one from Mr. Hatton. Teddy might be able to get a look at the thief and tell the police. He might even get a reward!

On the book shelf next to the window was a little lamp, but Teddy didn't turn it on. If he managed to get a look at the horse thief, he didn't want to be spotted. Instead, he crouched beside the window and peered around the edge of the dusty curtain. A quarter moon hung low in the sky and the street lamp down in front of Mr. Graham's flickered a little, like maybe it would go out soon, but despite that illumination, for a few seconds he didn't see anyone out there at all.

Then movement caught his eye, and he heard the slow clip-clop of hooves again. Teddy narrowed his eyes as he saw the rider—all dressed in black and astride a black horse—and then he blinked and his eyes went very wide. With his black cowboy hat pulled low over his eyes and the long black coat he wore, the man on horseback looked even more like a gunfighter than the cowboy's ghost.

Holding the horse's reins loosely, the man in black sat up high in the saddle, and his coat fell open to reveal the moonlit gleam of black metal at his hip. He watched as the rider urged the horse forward at an achingly slow pace. The man in black studied the Grahams' house as he passed, and then glanced across the street at the Sullivans', like he might be searching for a certain house but didn't know the exact address.

The thought froze the breath in Teddy's throat. He stared, eyes widening further as the man passed through the dome of yellow light from the street lamp, and he realized he could see right through both horse and rider.

Shivers went up his spine and he bit his lip. From downstairs he could hear the hiss of the radio, the sound it made when the world had stopped broadcasting.

Clip-clop, clip-clop, the rider came on, more and more slowly. Right out in front of Teddy's house, he seemed to pause a moment and tilt his head slightly to the side, like he was listening for something.

"No," Teddy whispered, there alone in his darkened room. "Keep riding."

For another breath, the black rider hesitated and then, almost reluctantly, spurred the horse onward. The animal's hooves clacked on the pavement, and Teddy felt pretty sure it had picked up the pace a little. Still, he stared, watching as the black rider and his horse moved on, past the Hesses' house and then the Landrys'.

Teddy's lower lip trembled and his eyes began to fill. He slid down and leaned against the wall, taking long, steadying breaths, unable to put together even just in his own thoughts why such fear had gripped him. A single tear traced its way down his cheek and he sighed with relief.

"You should have been here," he whispered into the dark, thinking of the cowboy, and then realizing that the words had not been meant for that ghost, but for his father. His heart hurt his chest.

Then he froze once more.

Outside, the clip-clop had ceased. Teddy rose up to his knees and peered out the window, hoping for a moment that the black rider would have simply vanished, the way the cowboy's ghost had earlier in the day. But no, the figure remained. The rider had come to a halt in front of the Landry house, but wasn't looking at the Landrys' or at the Mansurs' across the street. The black rider hung his head, hat tilted almost straight down. He seemed almost to have fallen asleep in the saddle.

Then, without looking up, he tugged the reins and the black horse turned. Slowly, the rider raised his head, facing Teddy's house, and though the brim of his hat covered his eyes, Teddy knew the dark man was looking right at him, that the rider could see him despite the darkness in his bedroom.

With a tug on the reins, the black rider started back toward Teddy's house. Clip-clop, clip-clop. His coat hung wide open, and in the moonlight, the black metal of his gun seemed to wink.

"No," Teddy whispered. "I won't let you."

The rider snapped the reins and the horse leaped into a gallop, and then Teddy was up and running. His bare feet squeaked on the wood floor as he raced into the hallway and sprinted for the steps. The hiss of the radio grew loud in his ears as he gripped the banisters and half-ran, half-slid down the stairs. His face burned with the desperation of tears he refused to shed, and he tried to steady his heart the way that his hands had steadied his father's gun that day.

And he knew why the ghost had visited his house.

At the bottom of the steps he came face to face with the front door, and he heard the thunder of hooves right outside, could practically feel it shaking the floorboards as he turned from the door and ran down the front hall. In the room on the left, he could hear his mother coughing in her sleep. It was an awful sound, almost like choking, and the wheeze that went along with it seemed to match the static hiss of the radio.

Teddy grabbed the handle of the door under the stairs and yanked hard. Thick with old paint, it stuck.

The sound of hooves had stopped, but now he heard the tread of boots on the front stoop, and the doorknob rattled. The frame creaked as the rider tested its strength.

The little pantry door under the stairs gave a shriek of warped wood as he forced it open. Desperate, he snatched the old cookie tin off of its shelf, popped off the cover, and let the tin clatter to the ground as he hefted the weight of his daddy's gun.

As all fell silent at the front door, he twisted around to see the black rider step right through the door, just as easily as the ghost had passed through the screen earlier, his head still dipped, face half-hidden behind the brim of his hat. Hands shaking, Teddy nearly dropped the gun, but he managed to lift it and take trembling aim.

"I won't let you," he said, and somehow his voice did not quaver, and then his hands went still.

The rider lifted his head as though taking notice of him for the very first time, and Teddy nearly screamed. Where his face ought to have been there was only emptiness, darker than the darkest night and deep as forever.

The rider went for his gun, and Lord he was fast. Teddy pulled the trigger three times. His daddy's gun bucked in his hands but made not a sound. The rider staggered backward and fell through the door, like it wasn't even there.

Whispering silent prayers, and sometimes private thank-yous to a gunfighter whose days had passed, he stood with the gun aimed at the front door for as long as he could keep his arms raised. When he could no longer hold them up, he sat on the floor and leaned against the frame of the open pantry door, the gun cradled across his lap, listening to the hiss of nothing on the radio.

«‹‹—››»

Ma woke him in the morning, flushed with color, eyes bright with anger and confusion, wondering what he thought he was doing sleeping in the hallway.

Teddy caught hell for playing with his daddy's gun. Even got grounded for a week, which meant he had to spend every second he wasn't at school right there in the house with his ma.

He didn't mind at all.

HAVEN

KEALAN PATRICK BURKE

"I t's your mother. I'm afraid she's passed away."
Yes, yes. Old news. Never once has he stopped to think about how odd it is that he is so certain. The knowledge was just *there*, shortly before the phone rang, manifesting itself as an ability to breathe unrestricted, to straighten his shoulders and not meet the resistance of her eternal gaze, to dust off a genuine smile and use it without feeling it ephemeral.

Gone, and the days that follow are among the most wonderful he's ever had. Scarcely had he dared to imagine the release could be so full, so overwhelming, allowing him to tread with lightened step and floating heart. He encounters strangers and rather than showing them the top of his head in a cowl of cowardice and shame, he beams at them and bids them the sentiments in accordance with the age of the day. That these greetings are seldom reciprocated bothers him little, for his resolve is growing ever more formidable now that he has only one shadow trailing behind him.

Gone, and the nights exude peace, the mattress accepting his tired bones like clay in the hands of a potter. His dreams are golden, exorcized of the heavy cloying darkness that was the signature of life with Mother. There is no doubt that he loved her, but she molded him into a creature of indifference, isolating him in his own little box of shadow where there was never room for any kind of feeling.

He suspects what little grief he feels at her passing stems from his being accustomed to her constant presence rather than any true emotion on his part. This suspicion in turn ignites guilt, but guilt is something he has learned to master and, aided by his newfound happiness, it is soon beaten into submission.

The celebration of her death is a tawdry affair and Tom finds himself at the hub of a ring of people he doesn't know, or care to. The minister is a patrician man at least twenty years his senior, all practiced smiles and Bible passages as he leads them in a chorus of emotionless verse that rises like startled ravens above the gloomy fall graveyard. The air smells of cold earth and dying leaves.

Tom weathers the condolences, secretly wondering what it is about death that leads people to the assumption that they can immediately insinuate themselves into the lives of the grieving. If anything, he finds a note of condescension in those voices, powered by the look of *there but for the grace of God* in their eyes. It sickens him and reinforces his need to leave as soon as this stunted procession of sympathy is over.

When the last bleak face has moved away, he stuffs his hands into the pockets of his dark overcoat and rounds the church, the sympathizer's last words to him carried on ill-formed tendrils of autumn wind, falling just short of his desire to hear them.

Grumbling, he slips through the wrought-iron church gate, the spire of St. Andrew's like a chiding finger at his back, reminding him who might be watching his disregard for all things sacred. The image weighs on his shoulders like the memory of the woman he has left behind him in the ground. A woman he scarcely knows.

«««—»»»

He has come home to the house on Marrow Lane.

As expected, his mother complains about the length of his hair, how much weight he has lost and asks him why he has bothered to come visit her after so long an absence. Her frequent wincing and moaning about her incessant headaches render his excuses meaningless.

"They steal my sleep and it's getting harder to keep anything down."

"You need to eat to keep your strength up," he replies, feeling achingly redundant and thinking: Who is this woman?

Her dramatics are almost certainly a cry for attention, a trait not unknown to her and worsened by age. He delivers the customary platitudes and takes his leave of her, ushered out on a cloud of protest only silenced by the thick oak door of the house.

«««—»»»

Now, standing before that very same door, running a trimmed fingernail over the cracks and ridges in the wood grain, he ponders the irony of her death.

An aneurysm. If it's any consolation, I doubt she felt a thing. It would have been very sudden.

I see.

Had she been complaining about headaches or dizziness lately?

No. At least, not to me...

Realizing he might have been able to save her had he taken her histrionics seriously brings to mind a far darker question: *Had you known, would you have done anything?*

Brushing the thought aside, he opens the door of the two-story memory vault he used to call home. As he steps into the hall his senses hone in on the smallest, the slightest

(Tommy, is that you?)

of sounds. He waits, the dust settling around him in the chorus of quiet, ears attuned to the soundtrack of the old house. Eventually he straightens, exhales heavily and continues down the hall until he comes to the living room.

From the doorway, he sees the familiar sight of the old 10" television set in the corner opposite. A miniscule and fog-shrouded representation of himself is all that's showing on the vapid eye of the screen as he enters the room.

The beige carpet knots itself beneath his shoes and he resolves to have it torn up as soon as he moves in proper. He suspects that foul, vomit-colored layer of shag is older than himself and he has hated it for as long as he can remember.

The same goes for the sofa, a bloated brown semblance of intestines passing itself off as Naugahyde. The upholstery is ripped, yellow foam winking lewdly at him from elliptical eye-sockets. *Gone*, he thinks, relishing the thought of being rid of these particular harbingers of memory.

His double shadow bids him look up and he nods at the imitation gold chandelier, missing two of its four bulbs, then down to the once white wallpaper, curling from the mildewed plaster beneath...*Gone*.

The photographs, sepia-toned and black and white depictions of stern-faced young men cradling even sterner looking women in their burly arms, people he has never met but who he assumes are his relatives...*Gone*.

Gone, gone, gone. All of it. Anything not immediately pertaining to *his* life will be dumped and with an abandon impervious to the wheedling pleas of sentimentality. It is, after all, *his* castle now.

Grinning, he makes his way down the hall to the kitchen.

This room seems smaller than he remembers it and he wonders if it has shrunk in on itself after years of absorbing the auras of subconscious misery from the inhabitants of this place.

The lemon-hued walls seem to sag as he wanders around the room. He sniffs at the leaky radiator with the small plastic bowl beneath the tap to catch the water and shakes his head at the grease-smeared range, the picture on the wall above it speckled with spots so that the faces of the two watercolor children look positively leprous. A foul smell drifts to his nose from the trash compactor beneath the sink. He decides to investigate that some other time.

Against the far wall stands a simple pine table with three chairs and it is here his gaze stalls as the bloated corpse of memory rises to the surface of his mind.

You're a dreamer Tommy, you'll always be a dreamer and a man who spends too much time in his own head never gets a goddamn thing done.

Don't talk to him like that.

I don't remember anyone asking your opinion, Agnes. It's a sweet life for both of you, living in your daydreams while I'm out busting my ass to put food on the table.

Tom stems the flow of recollection, feels it swell against his resistance. The surface of the table is pitted with scratch marks and tiny holes where knives have been used to make a point. Coffee rings on the left—his mother's side of the table—stare up at him like blinded eyes. On the right, paler circles where his father lost himself in the liquid utopia of liquor.

And in the middle where Tom used to sit there is nothing.

He can almost see himself now—a young boy, eyes permanently narrowed in anticipation of a blow that could come at any time, skin sallow, devoid of the youthful glow typical of a child his age, sitting in a chair that only emphasizes his diminutive frame, his parents flanking him like birds of prey, always watching and waiting as if they expect something profound to trickle from his small tight-lipped mouth. But Tommy remains silent as much as possible. It is safer.

Shrugging off the memory, Tom shuffles over to the range and the bulbous white kettle, the base blackened by time and negligence, the handle loose, screws rattling. He opens it and angles it toward the naked bulb behind him. To his surprise it appears moderately clean. Nevertheless, he rinses it until he is sure nothing untoward will end up in his cup, fills it and lights the gas ring beneath, the thought of piping hot coffee staving off the unpleasant chill reminiscence has brought in tow.

Suddenly the blue flame beneath the kettle sputters as the kitchen door drifts open. He turns as it groans wide, allowing him to see down the length of the hallway.

Damn it.

The front door is standing open. He figures he must have for-gotten to close it when he came in so drawn was he by the familiar. He stomps down the hall, grabs the door handle and is pushing it closed when a faint shuffling gives him pause. He listens, glances at his wristwatch: almost eight. Not an odd time for people to be out wandering, surely?

Peering around the edge of the door and out onto the cracked pavement reveals nothing except the lazy onset of twilight; the air is heavy, stars twitch into life in the vermillion canvas that hangs above Marrow Lane. A neighborhood dog yips and growls, yips and whines like a violin with ill-tuned strings. Someone yells: "Shut that damn dog the hell up," and is ignored.

Tom frowns and shivers at the autumn chill insinuating its way through the fabric of his coat. Just as he is about to shut the door, he catches sight of an old woman standing by the streetlight a few feet down from his house, her hair a wild halo of sodium fire. She is dressed in nothing more than a housecoat and slippers and appears to be staring right at him, sending an unwelcome spark of unease through him and he backs away from the door, starts to ease it closed.

The old lady moves.

He pauses, one eye peeking through the inch-wide space between door and jamb, watching though now he feels as if he has donned a coat of snakes, his skin crawling as the shadow-faced woman moves along the sidewalk with short, stiff steps, the orb of fuzzy darkness hiding eyes that may or may not be fixed on him. She shuffles closer still and he realizes this is the sound he heard earlier. *Shhhnick! Shhhnick! Shhhnick!*

He wants to close the door, an action that will leave his sudden inexplicable fear outside with the old woman, but he is powerless to do anything but watch.

She reaches the mailbox—a simple black tin semi-cylinder staked in Tom's garden but jutting out over the pavement—and stops, cocks her head and brings a gnarled hand toward it.

Is she pilfering the mail or what? he wonders, his unease no less potent as the idea of confronting her is rapidly abandoned.

He hears the soft scraping sound of the mailbox door being opened and watches in disbelief as the old lady stoops down and peers inside. After a moment in which he imagines he can feel the victory radiating in icy waves from her skeletal frame, her hand emerges clutching a small white rectangle. Clutching the letter to her chest, she swivels on her heels and shuffles back up the street, passing through the orange glow from the streetlight much quicker than she had on her way to steal the mail.

I should have done something. He watches the shadows swallow her. *That letter might have been important.*

The kettle shrieks and jars the thought from his head.

«««—»»»

Later that evening, he stands at the threshold to a time capsule, held in place by a feeling of unreality that almost makes him dizzy.

Over the last few years his visits to this house have been infrequent and he has never stayed, had in fact come armed with a plethora of excuses should such a thing be suggested. As a result, he has never come upstairs and seen his old room.

He is shocked to find it is exactly the same, from the crimson toy chest at the foot of the bed to the Mickey Mouse wallpaper. His old teddy bear Rufus, now missing an eye, sits atop a once white pillow, arms splayed in frozen greeting. The carpet whispers as he advances further into the sanctuary of his childhood, head pounding, eyes wide with the strain of trying to absorb the sudden rush of familiarity.

A small oak desk, rescued from the local dump and restored to nothing like its former glory by Tom's father in one of his rare charitable moods, stands solemnly before the small white-framed arched window overlooking the neighboring rooftops.

Through one of the four panes, a thin crack like mercury lightning streaks an eternal path in the glass from top to bottom. Beyond that, the darkness rolls over the silent neighborhood, dampening the sounds of life and nodding its ethereal assent to the night creatures and the hunters waiting for their time to shine.

Tom shakes his head, looks down at the pockmarked surface of the desk and remembers... *Just as his father jabs the kitchen table with his knife or fork or the stub of his carpenter's pencil, so Tommy waits until he is alone and punctuates his own confused anger with the corner of a ruler, or pen, or...*

"Did I hate him?" Tom asks the empty room. "Did I hate them both and not know it?"

He kneels down before the desk as if it is the armrest in a confessional, his knees quickly growing sore on the threadbare carpet. He studies the indecipherable doodles and unfinished scribbles printed on the table. Only one is clear and etched with an angry hand into the wood:

HAVEN

This one he understands, even if he can't quite remember carving it.

In here, in this room, he had been permitted to believe the misery wasn't endless, that someday his father would arrive home wearing a smile in place of his ever-present scowl and smelling of wood and sawdust instead of whiskey. In here, solitude had provided the perfect movie screen for the illusions his hope projected and as long as he stayed here, nothing could break the spell imagination wove around him. Here was peace, love and happiness. Out there, over the moat and a million miles away, were misery, hate and pain.

Tom lifts his head and looks out at an encroaching darkness unique to the season. He pictures the dying leaves caught in a maelstrom, spinning round in a mindless vortex like lost souls and he realizes nothing has changed.

As he gets to his feet, he sees himself again, youthful body hunched over the desk, hiding the bruises on his face, weeping as he mourns the death of another fantasy at the vicious hands of reality.

He decides then that he will not stay here tonight. Even though he has long since dismissed the idea that adolescent fantasies can soften the edges of life, he doesn't want to sleep in a place where that very belief died.

This room is haunted, but not by ghosts. He can sense his childhood self here, the child that has stayed in this room, poring over the marks on the table, still hating the Mickey Mouse wallpaper, still trying to figure out why his daddy beats him while his mother watches with tears in her eyes. He is still angry and probably still dreaming of a better life he will never get.

"But my life did get better," Tom tells the silent room, surprised by the lack of conviction in his voice. The taste of stale coffee clings to the back of his throat as he swallows and turns to leave.

Stop lying to yourself. This was the only safe place.

The voice in his head is devoid of malice but filled with determination. He ignores it for it is just another unwanted memory and one he has the luxury of dismissing.

With a rattling sigh he slowly makes his way back downstairs and wonders if it might be better to put the house up for sale, to let someone oblivious to the horrid memories make it their home, someone immune to the tapestries of pain fashioned from the dust itself and the sting of sharp tongues still lingering in the air.

He thought it would be different coming back here, that his mother had been the only remaining anchor to a past too dreadful to contemplate. A foolish assumption.

If anything, her presence had allowed him to think only of her part in the shadow play that had been his childhood. With her gone, the curtains were thrust open, every room a set upon which the dramas of a miserable youth waited for an audience.

But the fact remains that he has no place else to go.

He supposes a few weeks here won't hurt, just until he comes up with something better. Perhaps an extended vacation, to clear his head and relax for the first time in as long as he can remember.

He stops at the bottom of the stairs; sure he hasn't heard what his brain is telling him he has. A few moments of listening yield nothing to confirm there has been any noise and the tension begins to ebb from his muscles. Then it comes, softly, seeping under the door like floodwater: *Shhhnick! Shhhnick! Shhhnick!* He doesn't move; waits instead for what he is now certain will follow.

A brief scratching like nails on a garage door.

Or an old mailbox being opened.

This is crazy.

It takes a great deal of effort for him to swallow the knot of inexplicable fear that has lodged in his throat but he is suddenly tired of being afraid, can't remember the last time he hasn't been, and a surge of uncharacteristic resolve brings him to the door, makes him wrench it open, propels him down the garden path and delivers him to the mailbox and the old lady standing before it.

She is peering once again into the bulbous darkness inside.

"Excuse me," he says, his voice brittle in the cool air.

She ignores him, apparently too intent on her felonious task, but this close he can see that she is a lot older than he first thought, the myriad lines in her sallow face retaining the shadows as if they are an intrinsic part of her. The black pools of her eyes are curved at the behest of a toothless smile as she retrieves her second prize of the night from his mailbox.

It occurs to him that he has seen her somewhere before but is not altogether surprised. Marrow Lane is a small neighborhood.

"Excuse me but what do you think you're doing?" He wants to tap her on the shoulder, to grab her elbow or anything that might bring her focus round to him, but for some reason he senses that touching her would be a dreadful mistake.

She is holding the small white envelope up to the streetlight and he has almost conceded, is in fact formulating a parting caveat when she suddenly turns and says: "You always had a great imagination,

Tommy" before once again shuffling off into the shadows, leaving him helpless to do anything but watch.

"Wait, who are you?" he cries after her and she looks back over her shoulder at him, her face a creamy blur in the darkness but then even the shuffling ceases and the sounds of night rush back in.

Only the soughing of the wind answers him.

Frowning, he goes back inside.

How did she know my name?

«««—»»»

In the hallway, Rufus sits against the wall.

Tom stands paralyzed, the door clicking shut behind him, muting the wind.

"Hello?" he asks the hallway and thinks that if the teddy bear turns his head in response he will most certainly drop dead of a heart attack. While the old lady was bizarre, she certainly wasn't beyond rational explanation. This however, is dancing on the boundaries of sanity.

He clearly remembers seeing the toy seated on the bed in his old room. He hadn't moved it, would recall if he had. How then, has it ended up down here?

Horrible images of the teddy bear carefully navigating the stairs while he was outside flash behind his eyes and he scoffs, a little too casually and feels his hackles rise.

"To hell with it." He rushes forward and scoops up the stuffed toy, then marches up the stairs, the loud clumping of his boots deliberate and reassuring. If someone else is here, they will know he is coming and that he isn't happy.

He reaches the landing and takes a deep breath, steels himself for whatever he might find in his old bedroom. With his heart chiseling its way through his ribcage, he stalks into the room. And comes to a dead halt.

A little boy, sallow-faced and sheet-white, has replaced Rufus on the bed; an ugly bruise purpling his left eye and most of his cheek. He is dressed in Mickey Mouse pajamas, *Tom's* old pajamas and as Tom watches, the boy raises his hands to receive the bear. Despite the surrealistic feel reality has draped over its shoulders, Tom tosses the bear to the child and tells himself to remain calm.

"Who are you?"

The boy looks at the bear as if he's addressing not Tom, but the toy. "You know who I am. Who do I remind you of?"

In truth, this is a question Tom has been hoping the boy doesn't ask, because the answer is something he is not prepared to face so he says: "I don't know."

The child looks amused and Tom feels his nerves fraying at the edges, unraveling. "How did you get in here?" he asks.

"I'm the one who makes stuff up, not you. So stop pretending you don't already know these things you're asking me."

To accept what is presenting itself as the truth, as reality, as normality is to Tom, opening the door wide to insanity. So for now, he will keep on pretending that the child sitting on the bed is not a younger version of himself. He carefully makes his way over to the desk and sits down, his finger absently tracing the striations in the surface of the table that form the word: HAVEN.

"I couldn't do it you know," the boy says, fingering Rufus's eye. "I couldn't bring her back."

"Who?"

"Mom. I guess I thought I'd be able to. After all, I was able to make Gramma come back."

Tom feels his skin grow cold and the old lady at the mailbox flashes before his eyes. She had seemed familiar. Now he knows why and it brings to mind the sepia-toned pictures of smiling strangers down in the living room.

Without thinking, he blurts: "But she isn't dead. She's in a home in Harperville."

The boy nods. "She found her own safe place. I brought her back here where she belongs though, just like I thought I could bring Mommy home. Just like I brought *you* home."

Tom rubs a hand over his face and leans forward. "And who do you think *I* am?"

"Still pretending you don't know? You're me, the part of me that went on and left me behind, the part of me forced to leave the safe place. You're what escaped."

Tom chuckles at that but it is a sound so far from mirth it frightens him and his face draws tight with worry. "This is madness, you do see that don't you? This is like a literal translation of what shrinks mean when they talk about people talking to them*selves*. I'm expecting to wake any moment in an asylum."

The boy looks at him, his coral blue eyes glistening. "You've often thought there was something missing in your life, haven't you?"

Tom says nothing.

"So have I." For the moment, the stuffed toy is forgotten. "I thought in here nothing could touch me and for a while it worked. I got to stay where it was safe while you carried on living in the real world, forgetting the make-believe and acting like everyone else. I tried to bring Mommy back when she died but it didn't work. Gramma came back and you came back, even though you still won't believe."

"What do you want from me?" Tom asks in a voice little more than a whisper.

The child looks back to the toy. "My safe place is crumbling. I can't be here on my own anymore."

"Why? If you've been here this long..." *What the hell am I saying? Am I actually buying this?*

But what the child says next dismisses all doubts because in the instant the words reach him, he is once more afraid, a fear that transcends all others.

"Daddy came back."

It is irrational, but by now Tom is coming to expect nothing less. He gets to his feet and looks down at the boy, at the fear etched on his face, a terror so suddenly familiar and personal that he believes everything without question, simple as that. Denying this reality any longer will drive him mad.

"He hurt you?"

The child nods. "He slipped through once, when I fell asleep and forgot to close the door all the way. I woke up and saw him standing over me, just a large shadow with gleaming white teeth. Now, I keep the door closed." He looks toward the door and Tom follows his gaze.

"Will you stay with me?"

"I don't know." His eyes are fixed on the door. It's open just a crack, but that crack is now as deadly as a yawning abyss.

"There is nothing out there for you. You know that. You've felt it ever since you left."

Tom mutters agreement but can't look away from the door or the shadows crawling up the walls of the stairs beyond.

"Please."

He thinks of the word scratched into the desk, the word he carved there all those years ago when he believed it to be true. Now he realizes it still can be.

Three paces and he is across the room and slamming the door closed.

The boy looks at him and smiles. "We might not be able to keep him out forever."

Tom walks to the bed and sits just below the boy's slippered feet. "We'll see."

His eyes are on the door.

"I missed you," says the boy.

Tom tries to ignore the creaking of the stairs.

BRAVE GIRL

JACK KETCHUM

"Police operator 321. Where's your emergency?"

"It's my mommy."

The voice on the other end was so small that even its sex was indeterminate. The usual questions were not going to apply.

"What happened to your mommy?"

"She fell."

"Where did she fall?"

"In the bathroom. In the tub."

"Is she awake?"

"Unh-unh."

"Is there water in the tub?"

"I made it go away."

"You drained the tub?"

"Uh-huh."

"Good. Okay. My name is Officer Price. What's yours?"

"Suzy."

"Is there anybody else in the house, Suzy?"

"Unh-unh."

"Okay, Suzy. I want you to stay on the line, okay? Don't hang up. I'm going to transfer you to Emergency Services and they're going to help you and your mommy, all right? Don't hang up now, okay?"

"Okay."

He punched in EMS.

"Dana, it's Tom. I've got a little girl, can't be more than four or five. Name's Suzy. She says her mother's unconscious. Fell in the bathroom."

"Got it."

It was barely ten o'clock and shaping up to be a busy summer day. Electrical fire at Knott's Hardware over on Elm and Main just under an hour ago. Earlier, a three-car pile-up on route 6—somebody hurrying to get to work through a deceptive sudden pocket of Maine fog. A heart-attack at Bel Haven Rest Home only minutes after that. The little girl's address was up on the computer screen. 415 Whiting Road. Listing under the name L. Jackson.

"Suzy?"

"Uh-huh."

"This is Officer Keeley, Suzy. I want you to stand by a moment, all right? I'm not going to put you on hold. Just stay on the phone. Sam? You with me?"

"Yup."

"Okay, Suzy. Your mommy fell, right? In the bathroom?"

"Yeah."

"And she's unconscious?"

"Huh?"

"She's not awake?"

"Unh-unh."

"Can you tell if she's breathing?"

"I...I think."

"We're on it," said Sam.

"Is your front door unlocked, Suzy?"

"The door?"

"Your front door."

"I don't know."

"Do you know how to lock and unlock the front door, Suzy?"

"Yes. Mommy showed me."

"Okay. I want you to put the phone down somewhere—don't hang up but just put it down somewhere, okay? and go see if the door's unlocked. And if it isn't unlocked, I want you to unlock it so that we can come in and help mommy, okay? But don't hang up the phone, all right? Promise?"

"Promise."

She heard a rattling sound. Telephone against wood. Excellent. In a moment she heard the girl pick up again.

"Hi."

"Did you unlock the door, Suzy?"

"Uh-huh. It was locked."

"But you unlocked it."

"Uh-huh."

I love this kid, she thought. This kid is terrific.

"Great, Suzy. You're doing absolutely great. We'll be over there in a couple of minutes, okay? Just a few minutes now. Did you see what happened to your mommy? Did you see her fall?"

"I was in my bedroom. I heard a big thump."

"So you don't know why she fell?

"Unh-unh. She just did."

"Did she ever fall before, Suzy?"

"Unh-unh."

"Does mommy take any medicine?"

"Huh?"

"Does mommy take any medicine? Has she been sick at all?"

"She takes aspirin sometimes."

"Just aspirin?"

"Uh-huh."

"How old are you, Suzy?"

"Four."

"Four? Wow, that's pretty old!"

Giggles. "Is not."

"Listen, mommy's going to be just fine. We're on our way and we're going to take good care of her. You're not scared or anything, are you?"

"Nope."

"Good girl. 'Cause you don't need to be. Everything's going to be fine."

"Okay."

"Do you have any relatives who live nearby, Suzy? Maybe an aunt or an uncle? Somebody we can call to come and stay with you for a while, while we take care of mommy?"

"Grandma. Grandma stays with me."

"Okay, who's grandma? Can you give me her name?"

Giggles again. "*Grand*ma, silly."

She heard sirens in the background. Good response time, she thought. Not bad at all.

"Okay, Suzy. In a few minutes the police are going to come to your door..."

"I can see them through the window!"

She had to smile at the excitement in her voice. "Good. And they're going to ask you a lot of the same questions I just asked you. Okay?"

"Yes."

"You tell them just what you told me."

"Okay."

"And then there are going to be other people, they'll be dressed all in white, and they're going to come to the door in a few minutes. They'll bring mommy to the hospital so that a doctor can see her and make sure she's all better. Alright?"

"Yes."

She heard voices, footfalls, a door closing. A feminine voice asking the little girl for the phone.

"'Bye."

"'Bye, Suzy. You did really, really *good*."

"Thanks."

And she had.

"Minty, badge 457. We're on the scene."

She told Minty about the grandmother and when it was over Officer Dana Keeley took a very deep breath and smiled. This was one to remember. A four-year-old kid who very likely just saved her mother from drowning. She'd check in with the hospital later to see about the condition of one L. Jackson but she felt morally certain they were in pretty good shape here. In the meantime she couldn't wait to tell Chuck. She knew her husband was going to be proud of her. Hell, *she* was proud of her. She thought she'd set just the right tone with the little girl—friendly and easy—plus she'd got the job done down to the last detail.

The girl hadn't even seemed terribly frightened.

That was the way it was supposed to go of course, she was there to keep things calm among other things but still it struck her as pretty amazing.

Four years old. Little Suzy, she thought, was quite a child. She hoped that when the time came for her and Chuck they'd have the parenting skills and the sheer good luck to have kids who turned out as well as she did.

She wondered if the story'd make the evening news.

She thought it deserved a mention.

«««—»»»

"Incredible," Minty said. "Little girl's all of four years old. She knows enough to dial 911, gives the dispatcher everything she needs, has the good sense to turn off the tap and hit the drain lever so her mother doesn't drown, knows exactly where her mother's address book is so we can locate Mrs. Jackson over there, shows us up to the bathroom where mom's lying naked, with blood all over the place for godsakes..."

"I know," said Crocker. "I wanna be just like her when I grow up."

Minty laughed but it might easily have been no laughing matter. Apparently Liza Jackson had begun to draw her morning bath and when she stepped into the still-flowing water, slipped and fell, because when they found her she had one dry leg draped over the ledge of the tub and the other buckled under her. She'd hit the ceramic soap dish with sufficient force to splatter blood from her head-wound all the way up to the shower rod.

Hell of a thing for a little kid to see.

Odd that she hadn't mentioned all that blood to the dispatcher. Head-wounds—even ones like Liza Jackson's which didn't seem terribly serious—bled like crazy. For a four-year-old she'd imagine it would be pretty scary. But then she hadn't had a problem watching the EMS crew wheel her barely-concious mother out into the ambulance either. This was one tough-minded little girl.

"What did you get from the grandmother?"

"She didn't want to say a whole lot in front of the girl but I gather the divorce wasn't pretty. He's moved all the way out to California, sends child support when he gets around to it. Liza Jackson's living on inherited money from the grandfather and a part-time salary at, uh, let's see..."

He flipped through his pad, checked his notes.

"...a place called It's the Berries..."

"I know it. Country store kind of affair, caters to the tourist trade.

81

Does most of its business during summer and leaf-season. Dried flower arrangements, potpourri, soaps and candles, jams and honey. That kind of thing."

"She's got no brothers or sisters. But Mrs. Jackson has no problem with taking care of Suzy for the duration."

"Fine."

She glanced at them over on the sofa. Mrs. Jackson was smiling slightly, brushing out the girl's long straight honey-brown hair. *A hospital's no place for a little girl,* she'd said. *We'll wait for word here.* The EMS crew had assured them that while, yes, there was the possibility of concussion and concussions could be tricky, she'd come around very quickly, so that they doubted the head-wound was serious, her major problem at this point being loss of blood—and Mrs. Jackson was apparently willing to take them at their word. Minty wouldn't have, had it been her daughter. But then Minty wasn't a Maine-iac born and bred and tough as a rail spike. Suzy had her back to the woman, her expression unreadable—a pretty, serious-looking little girl in a short blue-and-white checkered dress that was not quite a party dress but not quite the thing for pre-school either.

When they'd arrived she'd still been in her pyjamas. She guessed the dress was grandma's idea.

The press would like it. There was a local tv crew waiting outside—waiting patiently for a change. The grandmother had already okayed the interview.

They were pretty much squared away here.

She walked over to the couch.

"Do you need us to stay, Mrs. Jackson? Until the interview's through I mean."

"That's not necessary, Officer. We can handle this ourselves, I'm sure."

She stood and extended her hand. Minty took it. The woman's grip was firm and dry.

"I want to thank you for your efforts on my daughter's behalf," she said. "And for arriving as promptly as you did."

"Thank you, ma'am. But the one we've all got to thank, really, is your granddaughter. Suzy? You take good care now, okay?"

"I will."

Minty believed her.

«««—»»»

Carole Belliver had rarely done an interview that went so smoothly. The little girl had no timidity whatsoever in front of the camera—she didn't fidget, she didn't stutter, she didn't weave back and forth or shift out of frame—all of which was typical behavior for adults on camera. She answered Carole's questions clearly and without hesitation.

Plus she was pretty as all hell. The camera loved her.

There was only one moment of unusable tape because of something the girl had done as opposed to their usual false stops and starts and that was when she dropped the little blonde doll she was holding and stooped to pick it up and the dress she was wearing was so short you could see her white panties which Carole glimpsed briefly and promptly glanced away from, and then wondered why. Was it that the little girl acted and sounded so much like a miniature adult that Carole was embarrassed for her, as you would be for an adult?

It was possible. She'd done and thought sillier things in her life.

The piece was fluff of course but it was *good* fluff. Not some flower-show or county fair but a real human interest story for a change. Unusual and touching. With a charming kid as its heroine. She could be proud of this one. This one wasn't going to make her cringe when it was broadcast.

It occurred to her that they could all be proud of this one, everybody involved really, from the dispatchers god knows to the police and EMS team to the grandmother who'd no doubt helped raise this little wonder and finally, extending even to her and her crew. Everybody got to do their job, fulfill their responsibilities efficiently and well. And the one who had made all of this happen for them was a four-year-old.

Quite a day.

They had down all the reactions shots. All they needed now was her tag line.

"This is Carole Belliver—reporting to you on a brave, exceptional little girl—from Knottsville, Maine."

"Got it," Bernie said.

"You want to cover it?"

"Why? *I said I got it.*"

"Okay. Jeez, fine."

What the hell was *that* about? *Bernie had just snapped at her.* Bernie was the nicest, most easygoing cameraman she'd ever worked with. She couldn't believe it. It was totally out of character. He and Harold, her soundman, were packing their gear into the van as if they were in some big hurry to get out of there. And she realized now that they'd both been unusually silent ever since the interview. Normally when the camera stopped rolling you couldn't shut them up.

But the interview had gone well. *Hadn't it?*

Was it something she'd said or done?

By now the print media had arrived, some of them all the way from Bangor and Portland and they were talking to Suzy and her grandmother on the front steps where she'd taped them earlier. Flashbulbs popped. Suzy smiled.

Bernie and Harold looked grim.

"Uh, guys. You want to let me into the loop? I thought everything went fine here."

"It did," Bernie said.

"So? So what's the problem?"

"You didn't see? You were standing right there. I thought you must have—then went on anyway. Sorry."

"See what?"

"When she dropped the doll."

"Right, I saw her drop the doll."

"And she bent down to pick it up."

"Yeah?"

He sighed. "I've got it all on tape. We can take a look over at the studio. I want to know it wasn't just my imagination."

"It wasn't," Harold said. "I saw it too."

"I don't get it. What are you talking about?"

She glanced over at Suzy on the steps. The girl was looking directly at her, ignoring the reporters, frowning—and for a moment held her gaze. *She's sick of this*, Carole thought. That's the reason for the frown. She smiled. Suzy didn't.

And she had no idea what all the mystery was about until they rolled the tape at the studio and she watched the little girl drop the doll and stoop and Bernie said *there* and stopped the tape so that she saw what she hadn't noticed at the time because she'd looked away so abruptly, strangely embarrassed for this little girl so mature and adult for her age so that they'd simply not registered for her—the long wide angry welts along the back of both thighs just below the pantyline which told her that this was not only a smart, brave little girl but perhaps a sad and foolish one too who had drained the tub dry and dialed 911 to save her mother's life.

Which may not have been worth saving.

Nobody had noticed this. Not the cops, not EMS. Nobody.

She rolled the tape again. Jesus.

She wondered about the grandmother. She *had* to know. How could she not know?

"What do you want to do?" Bernie said.

She felt a kind of hardness, an access to stone will. Not unlike the little girl's perhaps. She remembered that last look from the steps.

"I want to phone the reporters who were out there with us, kill the story. Dupe the tapes. Phone the police and child welfare and get copies to them. I want us to do what her daughter evidently couldn't bring herself to do. I want us to do our best to drown the bitch."

They both seemed fine with that.

DEALING WITH MAMA LILA

SANDY DELUCA

1.

I fell in love with Marko Lovel when I was twenty, swept away by his good looks and sweet-talking style, unaware of his blood-thirsty nature and his family's lust for darkness; and fearing that he'd learn about my stretch in prison, but the Lovels were natural-born grifters and thieves, living without apology or morality—a family after my own heart—and people who sometimes practiced their twisted deeds beyond the natural world.

Mama Lila Lovel was sixteen when Marko was born and she kept her figure later on, donning fitted jeans and sweaters that showed off her shapely breasts. Her hair was black and shiny; her eyes a startling shade of green and her lips were full and pretty. Sometimes I'd catch my brother, Nando, checking her out, and I'd tell him, "She's too old for you."

Nando said, "What's age got to do with anything? She knows how to shuffle those cards."

Mama told fake fortunes and performed bogus séances, scamming desperate women, who willingly drank Mama's herb tea, and then claimed it gave them bad dreams. Once in a while somebody filed a complaint against her, but nothing ever stuck. She might have been a fraud, but she knew how to play with magic—the real kind—the kind that got her off the hook, but nothing ever has a one hundred percent guarantee.

The mojo rubbed off on Marko, and he locked himself in our basement every morning, reading from a book passed down from Mama Lila's grandmother. He memorized the words, hoping he'd have as much success as his predecessors. And every night he met with dangerous dealers and hustlers, planning robberies, scams and revenge on those who betrayed them.

Marko got shot, robbing a gas station, by a dirty cop who claimed my husband was packing a loaded pistol and pointing it at his Sergeant. I should have been there, waiting out back in my car, but the gas gauge was broken and I thought Marko had filled the tank. I'd circled the block a few times, knowing he would be emerging from an alley door, but I ran out of gas a half block from the robbery.

Marko wasn't armed that night, but Internal Affairs covered up that fact. Mama Lila put a curse on the entire police force—and she cursed me, too. Nothing happened right away, but I've learned that you shouldn't underestimate the power of a gypsy curse.

«««—»»»

Two weeks before Marko died, he sat in our parlor, lost in thought and gazing in a mirror, another family heirloom; one he claimed predicted the future—most likely an item bartered or stolen during a phony gypsy card reading.

I looked into the glass and saw my own reflection, but Marko claimed he saw other images, and he told me, "Hey, if I die, can you go to my grave, dig me up and get the things Mama buries me with?"

"Stop kidding around, okay?"

"My jewelry—my valuables—should belong to you, not buried six feet under. Might sound crazy now, but...just do it if it happens, all right?"

"You're asking me to be a grave robber now?" I chuckled, and then told him. "You're not going anywhere for a long time."

He tapped the mirror's gilded frame, thought for a moment, and then said slowly, "I deal with a lot of bad people and you just never know what could happen."

"You sound like a crazy man."

He took my hand. "Just do it, okay?"

His words chilled me, and a dark feeling churned in my gut.

He winked at me, then laid the mirror face-down on the coffee table. He rose from his chair, walked away with his hands tucked in his pockets, whistling, and saying something unintelligible. I turned the looking glass over, gazed into it, and for a split second—a flash—I saw blood splattered on pavement.

I lost it after Marko died, couldn't function, and Dr. Gill gave me sedatives, and sleeping came real easy. Mama Lila identified Marko's body, made the plans for his burial and brought me a bottle of Jack and some weed, telling me she knew how much I was hurting.

We buried Marko at night, in an olden graveyard—deep in thick woods—where the Lovel family had gone for generations. Despite my protests, Mama Lila tossed my husband's belongings in his casket—things promised to me.

I always get what's mine—at least I used to—and on a rainy October night, when forecasters predicted record floods, Nando and I visited Marko's grave. We loaded a shovel, pry bars and plastic bags in the back seat of my car.

We parked under a row of trees, where leaves tumbled, swirling within spiraling mist, and rain speckled the landscape. Nando popped open a pint bottle of Merlot he'd grabbed from under the seat.

"Have one," he told me, reaching for another and handing it to me. "It's damn cold outside and I got a feeling we'll be here for a while."

The wine filled me with warmth, giving me a slight buzz and when we finished, Nando grabbed our gear, I snatched my umbrella from the dash and we began our trek to the grave. Nando mumbled something about bad luck when a flock of black birds circled overhead and I told him to get a grip.

Someone had laid a bouquet of roses, in the shape of a hand, over Marko's gravestone; and beaded rosaries hung on a low-hanging tree branch nearby—gypsy customs—probably left there by Mama Lila. The petals washed away in muddy water and the beads clicked and clattered as rain battered the ground.

Nando shot me a sidelong glance. "Can't we come back on a clear night?"

"It's now or never. Just start digging."

Nando grimaced, and then began to shovel.

Fraudulent checks and scamming old women were his specialties. He got caught; and I took him in when he made parole.

He owed me and worked diligently, piling dirt next to Marko's headstone. Sweat beads broke out on his forehead, despite the chilly night. He cursed and complained about aching muscles and a sore back. I shook my head, remembering what Marko asked me to do.

"At last," Nando said, when the shovel struck the casket. He looked upward, a smile flashing for a moment, and then a scowl emerged. "You won't be happy until I come down with pneumonia."

"Open it," I ordered.

He tossed the shovel aside, brushed away mud with his hands, and then unbolted the lid with a large pry bar.

He shook his head, peering inside the box; breathless, cold-air mist escaping from his lips, and he told me, "You owe me, Angel."

"I thought it was the other way around." I tipped my umbrella to the side. "Anyway, you know I'm good for the loot."

I climbed into the hole he'd dug, cursing because the cuffs of my jeans were soaked and the spindles of my umbrella had ripped through the fabric.

"Is everything here?"

"You tell me."

I grasped Nando's elbow, steadying myself, and staring at the corpse. I sobbed, and then repulsion filled me.

My handsome lover was abhorrent and unrecognizable; his head was a withered skull, with thin rotting skin attached to decayed bone. Brittle hair fanned out on a black velvet pillow, bony hands were folded on a skeletal chest. A Tarot deck lay beneath dry-boned fingers. A small oval mirror lay above Marko's head. His white shirt had turned gray. A canister of oil and a pouch of herbs were at his right, feathers from a black bird at his feet, and a robe to his left. Bones poked through ruined flesh, worms crawled from orifices.

I sobbed louder; contemplated closing the casket, burying the hideous corpse once more, but we had to grab Marko's valuables.

Mama Lila talked about gypsy resurrection when she did her con-job séances, telling women who buried dead spouses, "It's possible for them to return to you…if love is strong enough." She'd hand them mirrors, bought at a dollar store, herbs plucked from a window box in her kitchen, and oil she stole from tables at local restaurants. And she'd tell those women to say chants she'd written on yellowed pages—words I'd seen in my husband's book—things I'd memorized.

Mama Lila was a fraud, but she'd buried her son with the same props, telling me on the day of Marko's funeral, "What I tell those women is a scam, but sometimes the ritual works. You just never know."

I nodded, "Marko...he..."

She handed me a glass of whiskey, waved her hand, and then wiped a tear from her eye, her bangle bracelets clicking, as dark clouds covered the sun and crows screeched in bare-limbed trees. She pouted, and whispered, "I resurrected Marko's father. He died at thirty—got shot, just like Marko. I got him back...for a while..." She eyed the whiskey glass, and told me, "Drink up. You're going to need the strength."

I guzzled the drink, placed the glass on a windowsill, and then clutched her shoulder because I'd never met Papa Lovel. "Where's your husband now?"

"He had an accident right after I brought him back. He was never right after that."

"What are you telling me, Mama?"

"Be careful. I know about the things Marko told you."

My brother's gruff voice broke through my reverie. "Stop daydreaming. Let's hurry the hell up. Cops find us here and I go back to prison."

"Relax. Nobody—not even cops—come out here at night. We've got to make sure everything is done right and we get what we came here for."

Mama buried Marko with a gold ring, speckled with rubies and diamonds, handmade in the sixteenth century, and worth a lot— enough to live the good life for a while longer. I slipped it in my pocket, and then removed a gold chain from his neck.

"Italian gold," I whispered to Nando.

"You can't hold on to it like you did those paintings, antiques and other crap you got laying around the house. Cash that stuff in and we're golden for a long, long time."

"Told you before, authorities have been looking for the Kandinsky and Cezanne for five years...same with the Degas. They're too hot to unload now. The boys in New York will let me know when the time's right. Now get me some bags."

"Marko had balls going into the museum, carrying the art out like that—in broad daylight, man." Nando shook his head.

"That was his style," I told my brother. "The bags?"

Nando grumbled and did what I asked.

I gathered gold coins scattered in the casket, things Marko stole from the Greenborough Museum of the Civil War. An easy score because he'd simply reached into a display case while I flirted with a young security guard; coins worth more than the ring and chain combined.

"Benny Ricci will pay us good for these," I told my brother. He cupped his hands and I filled them with the booty, and then he carefully poured them inside a plastic bag.

We did the same with Marko's ruby earring, his gold wrist bands, the gold chain and a velvet bag filled with jewels he'd heisted over the years.

I removed the cards from beneath Marko's hands, gently laid them on the ground with the mirror. I lifted the robe, shook out dust and worms, and put it beside the other objects. I found Marko's leather-bound book under his left foot. I opened it, reading aloud and Nando rolled his eyes.

SUMMONING THE DEAD
Say these words with caution and only think of your beloved...
"I call you from the well of death, with spirits of the night,
and angels by your side and hope my love is strong enough
to bring you back."

I held my breath, squeezed my eyes shut for a moment, and then slowly opened them, and for a second I thought I saw Mama Lila standing in swirling mist, but the vision dissipated and I realized the corpse had not changed. Nothing was there but rot and death. A night owl called out amid rushing wind and rain. I felt powerless, foolish, so I wept awhile, my tears splattering on the ruined body and the book. I repeated the words several more times, waiting a few minutes, but my attempt was futile, so I wept more—telling myself I'd never see my love alive again, reminding myself how silly my attempts had been and remembering how mindless Mama Lila sounded when she'd told me she resurrected Papa Lovel.

"You all right, Angel?" Nando's voice was soft.

"Yeah. Just cover it up. We're done here."

Nando slammed the coffin lid, picked up the shovel and began his tedious task.

We left Marko there, buried under muddy earth, and then Nando and I slid back into the Escort. I'd thrown the book, mirror and cards in with the jewels for old time's sake. Nando revved up the engine, and I turned to him, told him softly, "I'm such an idiot."

I wanted Marko by my side again, watching December snow, dancing to old jazz music we'd heard years before in Harlem. My longing burned as rain continued to fall.

"I'm going to catch a cold," I whispered to my brother. "You got more wine?"

He nodded, telling me, "You'll feel better once we get the dough for the stuff we dug up."

"Yeah, yeah..."

We toasted the booty we'd gathered, and then drove home in silence and I drifted to sleep, dreaming of Mama Lila scurrying around her kitchen, boiling a pot on her olden stove, stirring bones bubbling in the water, and she sang, *"I call you from the well of death..."*

She stopped singing, then spun around on her heels. *"You should have died instead of Marko..."*

I awoke when Nando turned the Escort into my drive, but Mama Lila's words still echoed in my head.

2.

Rain and wind pummeled the house and lights flickered on and off. I inspected windows, making sure they were shut tight, and then I set out candles and flashlights in case we lost power. I continued to pace, from floor to floor, and from room to room. The floorboards creaked when I made my way to my bedroom, and then Nando stepped out of shadow. He cocked his head to one side, and said, "Hey, despite my bitching, I hope everything is okay."

"You did fine—as always," I told my brother.

"Anything else?" Nando's eyes were bloodshot, rimmed with dark circles.

"No, just take care of bringing the stuff to Benny after you get some rest."

Nando nodded, then receded back into gloom and shadow.

I retreated to my room, washing my hands in the attached bathroom, then changed into sweat pants and shirt. I didn't bother with shoes. I had to rest, but longing for Marko filled me again as I lay on my bed, listening to the tick of my clock, and the wind. The chill of night hadn't left me, and my muscles ached from dampness.

I drifted to sleep, dreaming of Marko—his body twitching in darkness, his eyes opening and his lips forming a silent scream. Then bony hands pressed against the coffin's lid, pummeling madly, and suddenly bursting through dampened wood, as splinters burst upward. He let out a groan, and then clawed through earth, working his hands and gnarled fingers until he broke free. He climbed upward slowly, his body bent, his blood-drenched fingers moving madly, as he rose to a standing position. In misty night he walked up the hill to our home, his eyes fixed on lights shining in upstairs windows.

Marko approached my door, turned the knob and entered the house. He looked around, torn rotting flesh more evident in the glow of the chandelier. He moved through the corridor, and up the stairs— mouth forming a crooked smile when someone laughed, and then hummed, behind one of the closed doors—most likely my brother entertaining one of his women. Marko stopped for a moment, listening to those sounds. He moved forward, walking awkwardly, until he reached my bedroom door, and then my eyes flew open.

"Marko?"

There was no light, but for a streetlamp shining beyond my window. Its yellow glow revealed falling raindrops and storm sounds—swirling rain and fierce wind—echoed in the night, but something was off. The bedroom walls slanted inward and the ceiling was higher. The room was cold, despite a blazing fire I'd lit earlier. There was a thump; something dragged across the floor, and then a hand emerged, clutching the foot of my bed.

A figure rose, a dark thing with no eyes or face, and I screamed, awakening myself from a dream within a dream, lying there shivering, and the haunting images still with me. The clock said six. I stretched, then looked through my window. The streetlamp burned yellow as in my dream. Snow now fell in a murky landscape. I needed coffee, maybe something stronger. I climbed out of bed. My mirror was lopsided; drops of moisture trickled from its frame. There were streaks of mud and snow on the floor.

Had Nando come to my room during the night? Was there an unwanted intruder lurking in shadow? I slipped my handgun from my bureau drawer, making sure it was loaded. Five rounds would do, but I normally hit my target with the first shot. No doubt that gun had saved my ass countless times.

I made my way through the hall. The small Cezanne and Kandinsky were still intact. The Degas ballerina stood undisturbed on the Art Noveau end table, but there was sludge on the expensive Oriental rug I'd recently finagled from a downtown antique shop. I cursed as I descended the stairs, where streaks of grime continued. Who had dirtied my home and invaded things sacred to me?

Once again something dragged across the floor, as I flicked on the light at the edge of the stairs. A shadow floated over the floor, and then it vanished—a penumbra—a trick of light.

I ran upstairs, pounded on my brother's door. He opened it, eyes sleepy and hair tousled. He looked over his shoulder at a woman who slept soundly, tangled in satin sheets, black hair spilling on a pillow. I strained my eyes to see. No time to judge him or whoever shared his bed.

I turned my attention back to my brother. "Marko…somebody was in the house."

He shook his head, "Sorry. I got drunk with a friend. She wandered outside, around the house…I…"

"Are you going to clean it up? I hope—"

"Not now, Angel." And my brother closed his door, leaving me in darkness and with a million questions flickering through my mind.

3.

The dreams continued, but no ghostly intruders visited me and I realized that heebie jeebie words, written in ancient books, were powerless. It wasn't long before Nando and I went back to doing what we did best, and Mama Lila became an accomplice.

Our last job was at a jewelry store in the city. Tilling's Fine Diamonds. I'd met the owner, Barry Tilling, in a bar, immediately learning about his loneliness, and his need for female companionship. He began to trust me, even before I started bringing him homemade lunches and walking with him each morning in the park.

And sometimes I'd see Marko, jogging along a bike path, or standing in line for coffee through the window of the local donut shop. But Marko was dead, and it was ridiculous to believe that my graveyard spell had worked.

Barry Tilling didn't believe in a security system at his smalltime jewelry shop. After weeks of playing him, feeding him and making promises I'd never keep, I found out where he kept his safe, and where he hid other valuables.

I resigned myself to the fact that dealing with Mama Lila would remain a fact of life, and on the night of the robbery she watched the door at Tilling's Fine Diamonds, holding a handgun, telling us every few minutes, "Hurry. Cops patrol the area at midnight." And then she whispered chants in Romani, her gaze on the pitch-black sky as the safe lock clicked and Nando threw open the door. Piles of cash and a couple bags of diamonds were scooped up.

After one of the regular fences paid us for the jewels, we split everything, over bottles of white and red wine—courtesy of Mama Lila. She counted her share, and then stared me in the eye. "You're not hiding anything from me are you, Angelica?"

"No, everything is split even. Why would you say that?"

"Maybe I'm not talking about this job. I've been having these dreams...about Marko."

"I dream about him all the time, too," I whispered.

«««—»»»

Nando and I decided to lay low for a while. I'd stashed away enough loot to get through the next year, or so.

Things were going pretty good, and on the morning the cops arrested a transient for the jewelry shop robbery, I wondered if Mama Lila's Romani chants had anything to do with it. It didn't matter because the heat was off us, despite the TV meteorologist predicting more bad weather.

I showered, changed into jeans and a white knit sweater. I gazed at myself in my bedroom mirror. I looked tired, thinner than before. I blamed too many sleepless nights and the stress of recent events. I'd rest later, but now I had to grab some cash we'd hidden in a vacant attic room.

I exited my bedroom, moved through the back hall and up the attic stairs, slipping my hand in my pocket for a key. The lock clicked when I turned the key, and I pushed open the door. I flicked on the light, and gasped.

The room was empty. Gone was a suitcase we'd filled with dough. I'd hung Marko's ring on a hook by the window, but it had vanished, too.

"Nando," I called. There was silence, but for the sound of rain rushing in from an open window. I watched it splatter onto the hardwood floor and soak billowing curtains, as wind wafted inside.

I stood there, cursing my brother, asking myself if he'd bailed with one of his late-night visitors.

I flinched when a car door slammed outside and muffled voices sounded. I quickly moved to the window. Nando was there in the rain, bending down, dragging away what looked like a burlap sack, most likely filled with cash and treasures.

"Nando!" I called out.

He looked upward, fury burning in his eyes, and then he looked to my Escort, its engine revving a few feet away.

"You bastard!" I screamed. I'd left my shotgun on the dresser downstairs. "You won't get away with this."

I ran to the door, turned the doorknob, but it was locked. I kicked splintered wood, rattled the handle, but it did no good. I slammed the door with my shoulder, screaming in pain, realizing my attempt was futile. I ran back to the window, climbed onto the ledge and looked downward.

I watched, with rain soaking me, and anger burning as Nando sprung open the trunk, where he'd packed the Kandinsky, Cezanne and Degas, and other treasures that had graced my home. A cackling laugh erupted. Mama Lila stood beneath a stretch of trees, her handgun pointed at my brother, and her gaze flickering upward, smiling cruelly when she aimed her gun.

And then my husband stepped out of the shadows—whole and beautiful—alive, taking Lila's arm as she pulled the trigger. Nando screamed, high-pitched and terrifying, his blood exploding from his chest. That's when I closed my eyes and jumped.

I shrieked as I sailed downward, realizing I might die, and then my hip, and already bruised shoulder, slammed against the ground. I looked up and Marko was standing over me, eyes cold, and a wicked smile curling on his lips. I wanted to ask him who really got killed on the night of the gas station robbery—who did Mama Lila really bury in that secluded grave? He pointed his old Magnum at me, shook his head, and then slipped the gun in his belt. Maybe he had pity on me, or maybe he thought I was already as good as dead.

I heard his boots sloshing through water when he left my side, the Escort speeding away and its brakes screeching when it turned down the drive.

I closed my eyes and darkness shrouded me. I'm not sure how long I'd lain there in the pouring rain, but I'd only broken a leg and sprained my shoulder; and there were worse things to deal with, because I lost everything that night—the love of my life, my double-crossing brother, and the loot I'd worked so hard to accumulate.

The rain hasn't stopped since that day, and every now and then I see a vision—like a flash of lightning—like a dream in Marko's looking glass. Spiked whiskey and wine and a gypsy curse are a potent blend. Mama Lila's grift got me good.

HUSBAND OF KELLIE

T.T. ZUMA

A solitary figure, that of a frail young woman, stood with her head bent low in the snows of an old New Hampshire corn-field. Her exposed hands were sepia tinted and numb, and they trembled from a combination of the biting north winds and the weight of the cold steel resting in her arms. With glassy eyes, she once again read the inscription hastily painted onto the weathered oak board before her.

CRAIG COOK
HUSBAND OF KELLIE
1975 - 2013

The woman shuddered. Memories, blunt as rusty ice picks, punched themselves into her thoughts.

Her husband, smiling as he walked out the door, telling her not to worry, that with the new government protocols enacted to fight the epidemic, he was guaranteed to come home to her safely. Then hours later, when embracing him at their front door, she realized his return was due to instinct, and not any promises he had made her.

A motion below her feet pulled her back into the present. She blinked softly and focused on the ground. It was barely perceptible at first, but yes, there it was. The snow was breathing.

She took a cautionary step backward and paused. Even though it was expected, when the ground in front of her erupted, she screamed.

Two fists thrust up through the ground like twin volcanoes, creating a scattershot of debris that turned the surrounding snow black.

The young woman stood her ground and watched the resurrection in despair as a set of arms followed the fists. Moments later a head followed. Then, the rest of her husband rose up from his grave.

He stood before her, his eyes locked onto hers.

The young woman stared back. She was seeking recognition, but all she found in his eyes were hunger. She braced herself and then weakly raised the shotgun that had been nestled in her frozen hands. As the woman aimed, her arms trembled, and her thoughts once more flashed back to her husband's explanation of the new protocols.

He spoke casually, telling her that the virus had mutated, that reanimation of the recent dead wasn't instantaneous anymore. That it was now delayed for 36 hours. For those that lived outside the cities, the dead bodies were to be buried in a shallow grave without a coffin. He told her that it was plenty of time to bury the dead and then terminate reanimation. Then, he added somberly, that after the 36 hours had passed, someone from the Government or a relative must be present to insure termination. He assured her that the plague of walking dead would soon be over. Kellie saw herself nodding her head in agreement with him as he walked out the door wondering aloud how a family member could cope with doing something so hideous to someone they loved.

The young woman's thoughts were chased away when she heard grunting. Concentrating on the sound, she was momentarily startled when she realized that he was calling her name.

Her husband began to shuffle awkwardly towards her with his arms outstretched, his eyes wide, and his mouth opened impossibly wide.

Kellie pulled the trigger.

With tears flowing, she lowered the shotgun and mouthed the words, "I love you, Craig."

Then, Kellie turned slowly to face the east entrance of the cornfield. Gazing toward a large ash tree at the perimeter, she began to speak once more, "And I love you too, Da…"

A second shot echoed through the graveyard, penetrating Kellie's heart and exiting through her back. Streaks of red accented the black and white palette of the gravesite. Kellie's body slipped slowly to the ground as if she were a blanket covering and comforting her husband.

A man, middle-aged and dressed in hunters' orange, lowered his high-powered rifle and leaned it against the ash tree. His shoulders sunk low to the ground and his chest tightened as he struggled to control the sobs racking his body.

Grabbing the tip of the rifle barrel and then dragging it along behind him, the man walked to his pickup truck, parked twenty feet farther down the road. The snow parted in whispers as he forced his boots ahead of him, the butt of his rifle leaving its own wake. Upon reaching the truck, he placed the rifle into the rack in the back seat and then picked up a shovel out of the bed.

Walking toward the gravesite, he remembered the phone call from his daughter three days ago.

Kellie had told him how Craig had come home early from an errand, bloodied, bitten, and incoherent. She didn't think twice about attending to his wounds and risking infection. When it was apparent that he would soon die, she had kissed her husband one last time before he passed. Only after Craig had drawn his last breath did she call him, and then only to ask if he would finish this for her. Kellie spoke of her mother, about how much she loved her, and how she didn't think her mother would understand what needed to be done.

As the man approached his daughter's body, only one question now occupied his thoughts: How would he tell his wife what he had done?

How, she would ask, *how could a father do something so terrible to his own daughter?*

And then he wondered what his wife would say to him when he told her he would have to do it all over again, only 36 hours from now.

OBEDIENT FLIES

GREG F. GIFUNE

I t was the blood that caught her attention. Sizzling and popping, melding to the fry pan as wafts of thick smoke billowed up, only to be sucked away by a fan over the back burners. Whatever remnants of life it had once sustained, now trapped in that smoke; filtered through the twirling blades before being released back into the open air outside her apartment. Dust to dust, born of nature only to be returned to it in a bizarre ritualistic manner. She poked at the slab of meat with a spatula. The heat was too high, the steak had already burned, and the blood—*juice* she had been taught to call it as a young girl—had all but evaporated.

With a frown she switched off the stove and dumped the entire pan into the adjacent sink, watching it spit and spatter like a still living thing until most of the smoke had gone. The smell—so distinctive and primitive—conjured feelings of prehistoric impulse, and she imagined life on an open plain, clad in furs and bones, huddled in caves amidst the tortured screams of nature, interrupted, reborn, mutated by the sudden emergence of Man. A disease, she thought, a destroyer…an arrogant corrupter of beauty and natural order.

From a duffel bag on the kitchen table she removed her camera, focused on the contents of the sink and fired off several clicks, photographing it from numerous angles. Inhaling the pungent aroma of charred flesh, she felt at one with her newest piece of art and allowed a slight smile to purse her lips. The losers at the ad agencies she'd once freelanced for had never understood—couldn't even begin to comprehend—this work that was so dear to her.

Commercial photography had paid the bills, as insipid as it was, but had also allowed her to spend free time focusing on the artistic expression her camera allowed. As much a physical extension of herself as a painter's brush, for Lydia, the camera was her tool, her eyes, her witness to the world in which she moved and lived and would eventually die. It was her soul, really, the prism through which a piece of her would live forever, if only within the pages of an ignored and insignificant portfolio few would ever see.

She put the camera away, ran cold water over the pan then dumped the meat into a tall wastebasket beneath the sink. It had never been her intention to eat it.

Before she'd stopped taking work, before Devon had moved in, before he'd gotten sick, Lydia would have spent the evening at *The Spine*, camera in one hand, a drink in the other. A club a few blocks from her apartment where local rock and roll wannabes played, often sharing the stage with self-appointed poets who smoked clove cigarettes and recited embarrassingly pretentious white-angst verse, it had provided her with a relatively safe place to hide and burn away the hours. But those days were over now. Life had changed, and frivolous diversions were no longer an option.

Devon was dying; they both knew it.

Dragging the camera along, she moved from the kitchen into the den, ignoring the windows fogged with condensation and the light snow swirling about, tripping through the beams of streetlights and draping the city in white. Transformation no longer held the fascination for her it once had. She leaned against the foot of the threadbare couch, focused on Devon and snapped off a few shots.

He smiled up at her, swaddled in moth-nibbled blankets, his head propped against two pillows stained with sweat. "Hey," he said, his voice reduced to a raspy gurgle, always on the verge of erupting into the hacking cough they had both grown accustomed to. "Is it still snowing?"

Lydia nodded. "Didn't think you'd care."

He blinked some perspiration from his eyes and shifted his position a bit, downplaying the pain with a muffled grunt. "Wish we could go for a walk. I always loved walking in the snow."

"Shameless romantic."

"Yes," he answered quietly, swallowing with difficulty.

Lydia put the camera down on a coffee table and sat on the arm of the couch. "It's bad again, Dev. I'm going to have to pick up some work or they're going to start shutting things off. They already disconnected the cable and the gas."

Eyes wet, he looked away. His sunken features bathed in sweat, body wracked with uncontrollable bouts of shivers, convulsive coughing fits, and the terrible flesh wounds no longer wielded the power over her they had initially. Like all else around her, Devon was becoming art, teetering between reality and the subjective—something his weary expression signaled he had accepted somewhere along the line as well. "I'll be dead soon," he told her.

"I know."

"Just another series in your portfolio."

"Yes."

He forced another smile. "I'm honored."

Lydia remembered the first time she'd seen him. A gay club she frequented, a place where a woman could go and dance and observe without having to worry about anyone trying to pick her up. Visions of a strong and healthy Devon dancing atop a small platform near one of the bars in a turquoise g-string, his wiry body, tight and strong from hours of swimming at the nearby YMCA gyrating in time to the music. She remembered their first drink together, how she'd asked if she could photograph him, and how he'd giggled and blushed like a flattered school kid. Not at all what she'd expected from a man who earned his living shaking his ass.

"If you helped me," he said, "I could go to the park."

"I'm not doing that."

"They'd find me in the morning. Covered in snow, peaceful. Then you'd be free of me. You could get on with your life."

Lydia glared at him. "Don't be an idiot, Dev."

"I've heard freezing to death isn't that bad. Only at first—that's what they say—but then supposedly you get all warm and drowsy, and it's just like drifting off to sleep."

"Shhh."

"You could photograph it," he offered. "Think of it from that angle. The imagery, the—"

"Just rest now, you—"

"Besides, if they shut the heat off we'll both freeze to death anyway."

They realized Devon needed to be in a hospital, but it would only be a temporary solution, an impersonal and sterile rest stop, and Lydia couldn't bring herself to do it. Deep down that wasn't what Devon wanted either. Not really. Not anymore.

"Pain..." An exhaling rush masked as fragile laughter broke free of him.

Lydia gave an understanding nod. Even now, slowly fading away, it was not physical pain he was referring to, rather something more. The pain born of death, separation, longing, love and hate, that often-elusive feeling that the soul had been torn from the body and there wasn't a goddamn thing that could be done to prevent it. Somewhere on the way to Heaven even Jesus had stumbled. Three times, the Bible said. A man—a human being—bearing the internal pain of a world gone mad in order to transcend it, to become something better, something pure and good. The crown of thorns, the bloodied and devastated palms and feet, the punctured side—all of it as real as anything else, yet still black window dressing—a simplified visual even a child could comprehend. But His agony—like theirs—had been something far more profound, with greater depth and meaning than what could be experienced merely through the flesh. Lydia's camera—the things it recorded—had never been intended absolutes, only gateways, like the allure of the ocean's surface, tempting the beholder to explore it further, to venture beyond it, to see what may or may not lie beneath its simplistic exterior.

She looked at the empty audio rack where the stereo had resided until a few weeks prior, when she'd loaded it in her arms and carried it to the pawnshop on the corner. It had afforded them another month with heat, a few rolls of film, and a bit of food. Now silence ruled, interrupted only by the sounds of her clicking shutter, small talk, and Devon's illness.

By the time she'd turned back to ask him if he needed anything, he'd fallen asleep.

In the ten years since she'd fled Potter's Cove with four years worth of waitressing tips, a bag of clothes, the beginnings of a portfolio, and her camera, for what she perceived as the ambiguous safety of the metropolis, there had been other brief relationships but nothing of value. A small town girl who had embraced the city, Lydia soon learned that the city did not embrace one back. It existed instead as a living entity with its own needs and desires, its own will, its own wrath.

A welcome isolation followed, along with a sense of freedom she had not enjoyed in some time. Freedom to resume her portfolio, to pursue her art, her passion without the false hope and fleeting promises of perpetual strangers masked as friends or lovers occupying space and ripping away chunks of her she only realized were missing once they'd gone. Expending the energy to reconstruct herself from scraps like some urban scarecrow was pointless. Open wounds and bleeding hearts healed, but only to a point. That was, after all, what scars were for.

And then she found Devon, with his small but sinewy frame, shock of spiked, bleached blond hair and the greenest eyes she'd ever seen. They sat together in the center of her living room floor on throw pillows, surrounded by candles while a James Taylor CD played softly from the stereo speakers. They had left the club together just after closing, stopped at an all night Chinese dive for noodles then settled at Lydia's apartment. Devon had a few joints, and together with a bottle of cheap wine they got hammered there on the floor, talking about everything and anything, sometimes laughing, sometimes teetering on the verge of tears.

Lydia had photographed him that night; occasionally snapping a shot here or there as the night wore on and gradually became morning. Like Lydia, he had left home early and abruptly, already aware of his need to escape the restrictive confines of small town life. But for Devon, with little education and no job skills, he had turned to hustling, then dancing, then a combination of the two. Yet he still maintained a child-like demeanor—innocence almost—from the way his eyes blinked to his quiet laugh to his soft voice and unconscious mannerisms. He'd also been fascinated with her photography. It made most people uncomfortable, her constant need to lug the camera around, but Devon had thought it enchanting from the start, and so she opened up to him and discussed things she had never spoken about with anyone.

The decision for him to move in had been an easy one. He'd been staying with an older man, a regular patron of the club who had taken him in, but Devon had grown tired of the tradeoff and welcomed the chance to live with someone who wanted nothing more from him than loyalty and genuine friendship.

Once exposed and drawn deeper into the true essence of Lydia's art, he'd asked, "How did it start? Where did it all begin?"

And it was then that she did something she never dreamed she could. She showed him the portfolio.

Lydia slammed shut the door on those memories and found herself back in the present, moving toward her bedroom. She went to the closet, and from a shelf retrieved the lock box containing her portfolio. Once on the bed, she unlocked it with a key she wore around her neck on a delicate chain, flipped open the lid and stared down at the leather bound photo album.

There was no need to open it just yet. Arranged in chronological order, she knew each piece it contained by heart, down to the minutest detail. The early entries were Polaroid pictures she had taken with an instant camera, a gift from an out-of-town aunt she seldom saw but received gifts and cards from on holidays. A present for her thirteenth birthday, Lydia had at first been disinterested in the gift, but over time, experimenting now and then, she soon began to understand its potential.

And then its power.

Slush and snow painted the bedroom windows, reminding her of how it had clung to tree branches that day so many years before. The forest behind their home transformed into a frosty landscape of ice and snow—barren, silent, still, pale. Like the dead. A day when school had been cancelled and children took to the streets to build snowmen, to sled, to ice skate on nearby frozen cranberry bogs, and a day when she had decided to venture into the forest with her new camera, hoping to capture it on film. A day when she had positioned herself on a large boulder, and, inhaling the crisp fresh air, scanned the surrounding trees in search of her first shot.

How did it start? Where did it all begin?

Lydia set the album aside with a sigh and stared at her hands. Rings on nearly every finger, nails natural and void of polish or color, ashen skin stretched tight over bone. Narrow wrists cloaked in countless silver bracelets, which led to thin arms and delicate shoulders. She slowly brought her hands to her face. Where had the time gone in those twenty years since her thirteenth birthday? Glancing at the portfolio, her question was answered. A quiet moan seeped in from the living room but she ignored it. Devon, still only twenty-two, would never experience a moment like this, a moment where one still felt relative youth and vibrancy while afforded the luxury of gazing back over the course of many years. But she had given Devon a gift of greater depth and lasting value. "We know the truth," she said softly, fingers tracing the edge of the album. "Don't we, Dev."

«««—»»»

Footsteps crunching the snow and leaves beneath echoed through the forest, the sound intrusive in an otherwise hushed atmosphere. Sitting on the boulder, cradled by a ring of birch trees, spindly branches stripped and weighted with frozen snow, Lydia cocked her head, watching, listening and even then knowing there was something about the sound that signaled urgency. She held her position, her hiding place, and focused on two indistinct forms darting through a dense patch of trees in the distance, their breath escaping them in bil-lows of rolling steam. The smaller of the two, the one in the lead, stag-gered into the clearing, nearly lost his footing then looked around in a frantic spinning motion. Lydia squinted through watery eyes at Kyle Watson, a boy from the neighborhood two years younger than she. Even at a distance of perhaps fifty feet, she could see the fear in his eyes and the frenetic rise and fall of his small chest. From behind him emerged the second figure, and Kyle made a break for it, but caught his foot on something and lurched forward, face-first into the snow.

Todd Mantrich grinned and sauntered triumphantly toward his fallen prey. A boy she had grown up with and gone to school with, Lydia knew Todd as the violent and sadistic bully he had always been. Held back twice, he was fifteen while the rest of his class had just turned thirteen, and Todd lived on the wrong side of town, the poor side, where the houses were not neat and proper and presentable, with manicured lawns and paved driveways. His home was more a shack, with a dirt patch for a front yard. His clothes bore none of the designer labels the rest of the children of Potter's Cove wore like badges of honor, and his parents didn't frequent the yacht clubs or private golf courses most others did. His father pushed a broom for a living and his mother drove a school bus. There were rumors, always spoken in hushed voices by adults at cocktail parties and children in the school cafeteria, that his parents abused him. They were alcoholics, and Todd had "problems" which accounted for his low grades and constant suspension from school for fighting or smoking or brutalizing other students.

Lydia knew him as the boy who always called her "Skinny Lydie", the boy who had cornered her one morning in the hallway just outside the boy's bathroom. The boy with breath like cigarette smoke and eyes like she had never seen before, eyes that appeared calm and controlled at first glance—almost lifeless—but that harbored something else. Like snake eyes, just before the fangs are exposed and it lunges for you. There was gleeful rage behind those eyes, something she had seen firsthand when he'd pinned her against the wall and run his hands first across her breasts and then around to her back.

"Shit," he'd laughed quietly. "Your shoulder blades are bigger than your tits, Skinny Lydie, may as well walk backwards."

And upon seeing the tears fill her eyes he had walked away, satisfied.

Lydia didn't tell, never mentioned it to anyone because even then she realized Todd was capable of much more than mere intimidation, a cheap feel, and dirty words.

And that morning, safely hidden and watching him slowly circle little Kyle Watson, she saw that same dead look in Todd's eyes.

"Get up, you little prick," he said, pushing the smaller boy with his boot.

Kyle rolled over, his padded snowsuit making maneuverability difficult, and pushed himself further away, still on his back, his body forming a trough in the snow. "Quit it, Todd!"

"You think you could outrun me, you piece of shit?" Todd put hands on hips and laughed, an odd hollow sound, void of joy. Reaching down, he grabbed Kyle by the front of his snowsuit, yanked him to his feet and shook him so violently Lydia feared he might snap the boy's spine. A punch to the gut followed, and as he released him, Kyle gasped, doubled over, and sank slowly to his knees.

Lydia felt herself shrink, as if hoping the boulder would absorb and hide her. Breathing carefully, slowly through her nose, she clutched the camera in her lap, eyes trained on the scene playing out before her.

Todd ripped the knit cap from Kyle's head, tossed it aside, then pulled the boy to his feet and slapped him twice. Still crying, Kyle tried to break free, but Todd clamped a hand around his throat and leaned in so close their faces nearly touched. He spoke, but in a softer tone, and Lydia could not make out the words. Still holding him by the throat, Todd grabbed the zipper and ripped it down until the front of the snowsuit was open. That laugh echoing through the trees again, he spun Kyle around, and with one violent tug, pulled it down. He released the younger boy, shoved him to the ground, the suit tangling around his feet as he fell. Todd dropped the snowsuit and placed a boot on the small of Kyle's back.

"Quit it!" He struggled to rise, face pink, cold and streaked with tears. "I'm telling! I'm telling!"

Todd slid his boot to the back of Kyle's head and pushed down, grinding the boy's face deeper into the snow. "You're not gonna say shit, pussy boy."

Lydia wiped the moisture from her eyes with the back of a gloved hand, careful to move slowly, and no longer certain the tears had been caused by the chilly air alone. Her heart pounded in her chest and her mouth had gone dry, palms sweating beneath the knit gloves as shivers which began at the nape of her neck fanned out across her back and shoulders. *Do something.*

Todd stepped away, and his eyes searched the nearby trees. With a purposeful stride he closed on one small tree in particular and snapped free a branch. He broke it over his knee, chose the shorter of two lengths and threw the other aside. Moving closer, he slapped the stick against his thigh, the sound mingling with Kyle's sobs. Eyes wide, like that day in the hallway, Todd cocked back his arm and swung the stick down across the back of the boy's legs. "Your mommy's not here to save you this time, is she? *Is she*, pussy?"

《《—》》

Lydia reached out with a steady hand, slid her fingers beneath the album cover and flipped it open. Her eyes found the first series of photographs. The earliest traces of what would become her life, her art, stared back, a bit faded; corners brown with age but still potent beneath plastic sleeves.

«‹‹—››»

Todd had hold of Kyle's shirt collar. He jerked the boy to his feet and shoved him toward a tree stump. As he fell forward, flopping onto the rotted bark, a fine spray of snow exploded around them, joining the flakes still descending so gracefully. And then he was whipping the boy again and again with the stick, harder it seemed, with each arching swing as cries and laughter became one. Todd suspended his assault long enough to catch his breath, and then suddenly the waistband of Kyle's long thermal underwear was in his free hand. Tugging them down, the pants were quickly around the boy's ankles, the backs of his thighs and tiny rounded buttocks streaked with crimson blotches and scratches already spotted with blood.

Lydia was certain, even after all these years, that Kyle never uttered another word. Even his crying had stopped, and silence returned to the forest. Only this silence was no longer natural, no longer one of peace and uninterrupted solitude.

Her eyes locked on Todd's right then, until a shrieking howl fractured the stillness and she found herself choking back bile and trying desperately to remain still, even after her eyes had left Todd and focused on the stick now protruding from Kyle Watson's backside. And as the boy whimpered, his body shaking but still bent over the stump, Todd staggered back and steadied himself against a nearby tree. He shivered, his body quaked, stiffened, then slowly went limp, and he leaned his full weight against the tree before sliding down into the snow on the seat of his pants, his face slick with perspiration, enveloped in clouds of labored breath.

They remained frozen for what seemed an eternity, these three, until Todd finally forced himself to his feet and crouched down next to Kyle. He touched his back, tenderly at first, then seemed to realize it and instead grabbed a handful of the boy's hair, yanking his head up and back so he could look into his eyes. "You tell anybody about this, you little faggot, and I'll fucking kill you."

Todd released him, regained his feet and ran back through the forest, vanishing into the cluster of trees from which he'd come. Kyle Watson remained where he was, the slow rise and fall of his back the only indication that he was even still alive.

112

Lydia felt a rush of relief, and granted herself permission to cry. But no tears would come. She slid off the boulder and moved cautiously through the trees.

The boy lifted his head slightly, found her, and began to cry.

She sensed movement, and for a moment thought she was falling, fainting dead away, but she had only crouched down next to him. Her hand touched his wet red cheeks—so cold—as she studied the branch, still inside him. "It's okay, Kyle," she heard herself say. "It's okay. I won't tell."

"Get it—" the boy gagged—"get it out."

Lydia pushed forward onto her knees, realizing only then the camera was still in her hand. Slowly, she lifted it to her eye.

It spit free a photograph, and she pulled it loose, watching as the blank gray square gradually formed a picture, as if by magic, as if she had willed it to do so. Then she took another, and sat next to him in the snow, studying the results.

Kyle's sudden movement distracted her. He had reached back for the stick.

She placed a hand on his back, and his hand fell free, flopping lifelessly next to him. "It's going to be all right, Kyle," she whispered, not even certain he had heard her. "We won't tell anyone about this. It's not that bad, it's—it's not that deep—you'll be all right."

Now convinced that the boy had been more humiliated than physically injured, she rubbed his back for a time, studied his bare buttocks then returned the camera to her face. With her other hand, Lydia grasped the stick.

«««—»»»

She turned the page.

"My God," Devon mumbled when she had allowed him to flip through her portfolio for the first time, "are these…are these *real*?"

She sat watching his reaction as he dug deeper into the album, moving beyond her early pieces to those she had created upon arriving in the city. She smiled, able to see the portfolio clearly in his lap, recognizing the shift in maturity evident in her photographs, the progression of style and depth and skill. The shots of a homeless man she had taken while sipping her coffee, huddled beneath sweaters and a heavy winter coat. Her use of the single light from the street adjacent to the alley was masterful, cutting the shadows where the man lay draped in tattered and soiled clothes, toes exposed through makeshift shoes of plastic bags taped to his ankles, riddled with frostbite and black as the night sky. She had watched him for days, returning each night once she realized he had grown too sick to move, and had recorded with detached poignancy his gradual death.

Next came pictures from the park she took after purchasing a wonderful night scope lens. Nights spent cruising for her next subject, shots of muggings and beatings and even a gang rape captured from the relative safety of nearby shrubs or from beneath one of the footbridges connecting the series of park streams and ponds.

"Please," Devon had said, looking up from the portfolio with tears in his eyes. "Please tell me these aren't real. Tell me they're staged, that these are actors or models or—please, Lydia, *please* tell me they're not real."

"I'm just a witness, Dev. That's all. An artist, nothing more, nothing less."

"No, you could have done something to prevent these things," he said. "You could have helped these people."

Still a bit hazy from the wine they had consumed that evening, she watched him through eyes now blurred. "What are you saying?"

"The world's in flames and you just sit back and watch it burn." He dropped the portfolio as if it were some rotting, maggot-infested thing, and stared at her. "And it turns you on, doesn't it? *Doesn't it?*"

It was night, and since Devon had first moved in, she felt alone. Again.

"My God, that—that first one is just a child, he can't be more than—"

"I only recorded it." She blanched, having never heard him even raise his voice.

Devon struggled to his feet, blinking rapidly, looking like an animal cornered and aware that its days of freedom were over.

"Do you know why Todd did it?" she asked.

"Why does anyone do something so brutal?"

"Because his father was doing the same thing to him." Lydia took the portfolio in her arms, cradling it tenderly, like an infant. "That's what we do, isn't it, Dev? We learn."

He shook his head as if hoping to dislodge her words from his ears. "If this other boy was abused by his parents then I'm sorry for him, but—"

"I did the same, Dev, no different."

"What are you talking about? You came from a good family—with money—you never wanted for anything."

"I learned to accept, to be obedient. I did what my parents taught me."

He staggered back a bit, nearly tripped and then settled. The silence between them was deafening until, after a fitful swallow, he whispered, "What did they do to you?"

Lydia's eyes died, and she wondered if at that moment they looked like Todd's had that day in the forest, that day he'd cornered her, that day she'd seen his picture in the local newspaper after he'd been arrested for slitting his parent's throats while they slept. "They overlooked me."

«««—»»»

The wind picked up, and the old apartment building creaked and groaned. Lydia closed the portfolio, carefully returned it to the box and locked it shut. After putting it away in the closet, she hesitated near the window and watched the empty street for a time, a profusion of thoughts spinning through her mind like the snow squall just beyond the foggy pane.

It was time, there was no avoiding it.

The living room was quiet, the soft light from a nearby lamp framing Devon's prone and sleeping form in shadow. Watching him, she breathed slowly, waiting to see if her presence would cause him to stir.

The faint touch of something foreign caught her attention. She raised her hand and glanced down to find a large housefly squatting atop it. Bringing her hand closer, she peered at the creature, watching it move in a gradual circle across her skin, its tiny legs barely registering sensation. Turning her wrist slowly, she opened her palm and allowed it to crawl to the center. Lethargic and subdued, it had lived far longer than it should have, and like Devon, was approaching death. The result seemed unnatural and pointless, beings reduced to something other than originally intended.

115

«‹—›»

He had stormed off, leaving Lydia behind as he ran to his bedroom and began to pack, muttering incoherently, slamming things, frightening her.

Lydia made for the walk-in closet just off the hallway she had converted to a makeshift darkroom a few years prior. Once inside she scanned the recently developed photographs dangling from a cord strung from one corner of the room to the next, the trays and bottles of chemical solutions…and something else she kept there.

Devon had been so distraught he hadn't noticed the razor when Lydia entered the room and threw herself at his feet. Begging him to understand, to stay, to just listen and to let her explain, she wrapped her arms around his legs, feigning tears.

Ignoring her, he continued stuffing his belongings into a suitcase. "You need fucking help."

Tightening her grip, she drew the blade quickly—deeply—across the back of his ankles. His Achilles' tendons severed, Devon collapsed even before he'd had the chance to scream. Then she was on him, pummeling him with her fists, releasing a rage on his small frame that had been trapped within her for decades.

«‹—›»

Lydia, her new companion still perched on the soft flesh of her palm, shifted her eyes to the roll of duct tape on the floor. She'd sealed Devon's mouth with it in the past, but over the last few days it had no longer been necessary. He barely had the strength to raise his head, much less muster a scream or cry for help. Despite it all, she still loved him. He had taught her that a true artist was not a silent voyeur, rather a creator—an instigator—a god, in a way. She carefully reached out with her free hand and pulled the blanket down.

His ankles were still wrapped in gauze, but the skin beneath and around it had turned a peculiar shade, and the stench was overwhelming. Although she had done her best to dress his wounds, the others were even worse. The area of his inner thigh, where she'd extracted a piece with a carving knife days before was still leaking blood through the dressing. She sighed. It had stained the couch.

After two days of photographing the changes in his flesh as it sat on the kitchen table, she'd made the decision to cook it, but what had earlier been such a compelling new series for her portfolio, now seemed a waste of time. Darkness had closed on her these past days, hampering her perception, and now she wondered if this final chapter of her portfolio would ever be completed. "Maybe it doesn't matter."

Devon's head lolled to the side, his eyes glazed and distant. Drool clung to the corners of his mouth, and a wheezing sigh escaped him. "Lydia."

"I didn't mean to wake you," she said, only then aware that she'd spoken aloud. Glancing down at the fly, she wondered if he was watching too.

"No more," he whispered. "Take me down to the snow. Please, I...I don't want to die here."

Slowly, Lydia curled her fingers into a fist. Inside, the fly offered little resistance.

"We'll see," she said. "We'll see."

EXIT STRATEGY

TIM WAGGONER

The first thing you're aware of is darkness.

You're not sure if your eyes are open, so you reach up to check. You quickly draw your hand away, blinking furiously, eyes watering. So, two things established. Your eyes are definitely open, and you're surrounded by absolute darkness. Unless, that is, you're blind. Really, how would you know?

It's a frightening thought.

You're lying naked on a wet, spongy surface, and there's a foul, acrid smell in the air that makes your stomach twist with sudden nausea. You sit up to get your nose farther away from the stink, your body moving easily enough. It doesn't appear you're injured, so that's good news. It's warm in here—wherever *here* is—almost too warm. You're glad for your lack of clothes. It would be stifling in here otherwise. Although sitting up was no problem, standing is another matter. The spongy ground gives beneath you, almost as if you're inside a children's bouncy house, but you manage to get up and stay on your feet. You have to keep shifting your weight from one foot to another, though, as if standing on the deck of a ship at sea.

You stand there for some time, trying to decide what to do next. You have no memory of how you came to be in this place and no knowledge of what this place might be. You have no knowledge of your identity, not even your gender. You let your hands explore your body, and after a few seconds, you settle the gender issue. You don't

119

know your age, but you're an adult, and probably not too old. Your skin is still smooth enough.

How big is this place? You can't see walls or a ceiling. You could be in a structure the size of a broom closet or one that stretches outward in all directions toward infinity. You can't tell. You consider shouting. Maybe the echoes, if any, will give you some idea of this place's dimensions. But just because you're currently alone doesn't mean there isn't someone else here with you. Maybe many some-ones—and there's no guarantee they'd be friendly. So you remain silent, and—unable to come up with a better plan—you start walking, your bare feet making soft slapping sounds on the wet spongy ground. No matter how large this place may be or how small, there has to be a door or exit of some kind, or else how did you get here in the first place?

You have no idea how long you walk. How can you measure time in a place like this? You wish you'd thought to count your footsteps, but you didn't and it's too late to start now. Eventually, the tender flesh on the bottom of your feet starts to sting, and your throat becomes raw from breathing in the acrid air. At least the stink no longer nauseates you. That's something. You do, however, feel a different sensation in your stomach. It's not hunger, and it's not exactly pain. More like an itching, crawling sensation. Whatever it is, you decide to ignore it. You have bigger problems to deal with right now.

You walk for some time longer, long enough for you to consider taking a break and resting, although you're reluctant to sit. You don't like the idea of plunking your bare ass in the strange fluid covering the ground. A few steps farther, and you smack face-first into some kind of barrier. You're not walking fast enough for there to be much impact, so you don't fall backward, although you have to do a little jig to keep your balance on the spongy ground. The barrier is covered with some thick, sticky substance which is now smeared all over the front of your body. In addition, you feel a sharp pain in your stomach. It causes you to take in a hissing breath of air, but you barely notice, so disgusted are you by the slime slathered over your face, chest, arms, and legs. You shake your body and run your fingers over your skin in an attempt to get off as much of the goo as you can. It splatters to the ground in large gloppy chunks, but you can only remove so much. It's too thick, too sticky.

Doing your best to ignore the remaining slime coating your skin, you step forward and slowly extend your hands toward the barrier. Its surface is coated in a thick layer of goo, but when you press harder, you can feel the spongy material beneath. It feels a lot like the ground. You experience pressure in your abdomen again. You stop pressing on the barrier, and the internal pressure eases. You push again, and the pressure returns. Frowning, you make a fist and punch the barrier as hard as you can. You let out a cry of pain and double over, hands pressed to your abdomen. You stand like that, crouched over, teeth gritted, breathing hard, until the pain subsides. When it's diminished to a dull ache, you stand upright once more.

It's not possible, of course, but you know deep down in your gut—no pun intended—what's going on. You are trapped inside your own stomach. How you got here isn't important, and neither is the precise nature of "here." Your feet hurt because you've been walking for God knows how long in gastric acid, and you don't know how much longer you can go on before the flesh is eaten down to the bone. You need to get out—now.

A memory comes to you then, the first you've had since becoming aware in this place. It's a memory of a diagram you saw once in an old book when you were a child. You can't remember where you got the book from. Maybe it belonged to one of your parents, or maybe you stumbled across it in a library. Whichever the case, you remember the illustration—a man's head and throat, cut in half long ways to reveal the inside. A progression of three pictures showed the tip of the man's tongue arcing back toward the opening of his throat, going down and dragging the rest of the tongue along with it until it's pulled tight, blocking his airway and killing him. Beneath the picture, a simple description: *A man swallows his tongue.*

The idea terrified you, and ever since—even into your adult years—you've slept on your side so that you won't swallow your tongue in your sleep and suffocate yourself. Even when you became an adult and learned tongue swallowing was impossible, a kind of medical urban legend, you continued sleeping on your side. Why take chances? Now you wonder if you finally did it, rolled over onto your back one night, swallowed your tongue and—like a cartoon vacuum cleaner sucking in its own cord—swallowed yourself out of existence.

Screw it. The why doesn't matter. All that matters is getting *out.*

121

You spring forward and begin hitting and kicking at the barrier—at the inner lining of your stomach—clawing at it with your fingers, tearing at it with your teeth. The pain inside your gut is excruciating, but you don't stop. If anything, you redouble your efforts. You tell yourself it's like birth. Yes, there's a hell of a lot of pain, but in the end, it will be worth it.

Tissue tears and blood gushes like a broken water main, splashing your eyes, filling your nose and mouth, but still you don't stop. You keep digging until you make a large enough opening, and then you begin wriggling, clawing and chewing all the way, making a soft slick tunnel as you go, screaming in agony as the smaller you inside also tries to dig free. As does the you inside *that* you, and the you inside *that* you, and the you inside *that* you…

Even though you're in so much pain you can barely think, you realize that you had the wrong metaphor when you thought of cartoon vacuum cleaners. A nesting doll is more like it.

You keep digging, and you keep screaming.

Every last one of you.

ABATTOIR BLUES

JAMES A. MOORE

Where to begin, that's the catch here. I mean, I could start at the beginning, of course, but where is that? Do I start with my birth? No, because, really, I'm not important to the story, I'm just the witness. Do I start with the state of the world? Do I tell you about the women who seemed so much a part of it, Katie or the other girl, Brittany? Or do I start with the scariest bastard I've ever met, Bryce Darby?

It's not an easy thing to do, but I suppose I'll just start and see where this goes.

First, it was back in the bad days. The really bad ones, the ones other old bastards like me refer to when they talk about how easy everyone has it now.

The world as we knew it didn't end in a global war. The greenhouse gasses didn't screw everything up beyond repair, and we didn't nuke ourselves into the next Stone Age. Instead, I think we just got lost in the paperwork. It all came down to money, and the acquisition of the stuff was the end all be all for almost everyone.

And then one day there wasn't any money. Companies that had been spending like there was an endless flow of cash suddenly started crying about not being able to pay anyone. Guess what? Nobody was willing to do the work without being paid. One thing led to another and before you know it, everything turned to shit. My father was an investment banker and that was what he always said; everything just turned to shit.

Let me clarify that for you, because it's not easy to express. Everything that we had come to take for granted vanished, basically overnight. The restaurants couldn't get the food they needed to cook, so they went under. Even if they hadn't, no one had the money to pay them. There were a lot of shady people already on the streets, pimps and drug dealers who thought they understood how the world worked, but they learned otherwise damned fast. See, civilization wasn't nearly as civilized as we thought it was. The bad guys thought they ruled the streets, but as soon as things started getting tight, the people who needed drugs became the weakest link in the chain, and most of them got their fool asses killed. It's one thing to mug somebody who's being careless and a whole different story to take the food or money from someone who's actively looking to feed a family and is just as hungry as you are, and in better control of their faculties. Dead junkies were as common as shell-shocked businessmen who couldn't understand what the hell had happened to their world.

The first thing that happened was riots. The stores ran out of food, and all the calm, caring people who called themselves neighbors all started looking out for number one, taking care of their own and damn the consequences. Oh, there were a few exceptions, but not that mattered all that much in the major cities. I remember watching whole neighborhoods burn down, blasted by fire and gunfire alike.

Mostly it was the richest neighborhoods that burned. How's that for irony? All those rich snobs with their expensive cars and their hired help became targets as soon as the police went on strike or started taking care of their own instead of the job. I know, because I was one of the survivors. My family wasn't as lucky. My father took the easy way out and ate a bottle of pills that were supposed to help him sleep. My mother.... When they came for the food they took her and my sister with them. I found my mother's body a few days later, naked and shot to hell. I never found my sister's body. She was twelve when they came. I guess they decided she had her uses beyond just a quick lay. That was around the same time that selling women really became a great method for bartering.

You know who does best when savage times come around? Savages. Animals. Killers. Civilized minds aren't adaptable. They have all sorts of notions about how things are supposed to work, and most of the truly civilized people fell hard and fast. Lawyers? No good at all without laws. Doctors? They can be useful, true, but a lot of what they depend on is medications made by pharmaceutical companies. No money meant no drugs. Doctors still had a purpose, but their demand wasn't what it had been. Better than lawyers and politicians, sure, but not at the top of the heap.

Soldiers, cops, thugs, they all became higher up on the food chain. They had the advantage, you see. They were ready for combat, and the best of them understood strategy and command without the need for firepower. It all changed. All of it. Feudal states came around, many of them forming around the remains of the big cities, but a good number growing in the middle of nowhere, where farm land was still viable and the farmers could gather together in numbers to take care of their own and their property. The strongest barriers did nothing if there wasn't any food. The best weapons meant jack and shit against animal cunning.

Armies rose and armies fell and in due course, the world calmed down again. It didn't settle completely, but it became less volatile. And in most cases, it was the animals that figured out how to rule the best. They made their deals and they kept their peaces when they had to. The greedy ones got stupid and counted on their weapons to handle everything. Guess what? Guns don't do shit without bullets. A lot of the smartest ones hid the ammunition and waited patiently until the over-eager types had wasted their supplies. There was one man in Alabama who managed to build one hell of an army, his name was Sullivan as I recall, and he had a grip on all of the southern states that lasted right up until the time he ran out of bullets. He had some, sure, but most of his soldiers ran out in the surge to take as much as he could claim for the country he was trying to build. He never considered running out of bullets. He thought the factories in some of the states would still be running and that he could just take what he needed, but the money problem took care of that. Most of the workers had taken what they could when the plants closed their doors and others had done the same. So the conquering hero ran across broken down, ruined factories without even the supplies to start again if he could have found people with the knowhow to assemble the required parts.

As I heard it, the man who took down Sullivan carried his head on a broom handle for a couple of weeks, until the stench was too much and the face was no longer recognizable.

It went on that way for a while and then the new leaders emerged, the patient ones, the careful ones. The real predators.

You know how leaders keep their followers? There are a lot of methods, but the ones that work the best for the longest involve making sure your people are fed and then keeping them amused. For a few years there was too much violence going on to worry about much of anything, but once everyone started settling into their new routines, their new lives, the need for entertainment came back with a vengeance. It wasn't movies or music or books that made the difference. All three are still around, of course, and in some places they have enough juice to make some of the old devices work, so people can still enjoy the old movies and the recorded music, but mostly the leaders decided to go a little old school when it came to entertainment.

They cleared their fields, baseball diamonds, football stadiums, and they set the rules and then, by God, they brought in the gladiators. It wasn't like it had been in the old days. Most of the people who'd lived past the Fall weren't the sort to go down gently, if you get my point. It's hard to make slaves of survivors and harder to get them to fight for your amusement if there's nothing in it for them. So the rules changed a bit from state to state and city to city, but mostly the fighters were there for the glory and the prizes. I heard that in Atlantic City the fights were normally for women. In Manhattan they fought for property granted by the Sheik of the area. In Providence the normal prize was food and fuel and occasionally a functioning and loaded weapon. In Delaware they came closer than a lot to the old ways; they fought for freedom after they were dumb enough to break the rules. Life or death depended on winning a series of fights that took place once every ten days.

And then there was Boston. That one was unique. The field of battle was called the Pit for some occasions and the Abattoir when things got serious. The fighters worked for a different type of survival. The King of Boston was an Irishman named Herlihy, and he was one of the rare breed that was in power before the Fall and stayed in power after it was all said and done.

And Herlihy was a genius, let me tell you. Herlihy took over the hospitals when the Fall took place, and he kept them running, and kept them stocked with doctors and with medicine. I don't pretend to know how he did it, but he did. He had fully functioning hospitals when most of the known world was dealing with diseases damned near everyone had forgotten even existed. Boston held through the worst of the Fall, basically because Herlihy would not let it collapse on itself.

Think about it. It doesn't matter how big or bad you are, sooner or later you're gonna get sick. And if you wanted to get patched up and sent on your way, you paid Herlihy's rates because there was no other option. There wasn't even a black market, because he ran that too.

Boston was the only town that had matches every single night. Each day after the sun set, you could pay your rates and get a seat to watch the fights and, if you had the stomach for it, you could stay for the Abattoir matches. Early in the evening the bouts were just sort of a warm up, more comedic and pathetic than anything else. You wanted to get a broken arm fixed at the hospital, you could pay dearly for it or, if you were bolder, you could fight for the right. No weapons except staffs, but you could take on somebody in the same sort of shape and whoever was standing when it was done got tended to. More than one person left the fights in far worse shape than they had been when they got there. More broken bones and a few missing teeth were their reward and the only chance they had to get patched up was to try again. Comedy for the new Dark Ages, boys and girls. Everybody got a laugh for the cost of admission.

Above that, and slightly more brutal were the cases where the Pit worked for mediation. Herlihy had a sense of humor, you see, and a lot of complaints got handled in public displays of violence. Your neighbor killed your guard dog, raped your mother and stole your canned ham? You could demand justice in the Pit, and if you won you not only got the satisfaction of beating the shit out of your neighbor, you got to return whatever favors you claimed he had committed. Those were the meat and bones of fight nights. Once the comedy was done, you got the warm ups for the big matches, blood was shed, but no death got dealt.

And finally there was the Abattoir. Medicine and medical knowledge took a lot of resources. The only way to get tended to was to have something to barter with. If you didn't it was either fight yourself or have a champion take care of it for you and if you could win, the medical problem got fixed. And if you failed, you died. No halfway point. All or nothing. Believe me, it was a popular sport and a lot of people came from other parts of the country to participate.

When it came to the early part of the night, there were no substitutions allowed. When things got serious, the rules changed. That's how I met Bryce Darby. I had a neighbor almost a decade back named William Pratt who liked to make accusations. It was easy for him, because he was a soldier and he was a fighter and he picked his targets carefully, knowing exactly who he could take on and how much he could get out of them. Pratt pointed his finger at the house next to his on the left and swore that the man living there had stolen his food supplies. His neighbor was overweight and obnoxious and had all the right connections, so when the charges came down, he took on Pratt, certain that he would win. Pratt beat him down and cleaned out his larder. The neighbor got a lot skinnier, because Pratt followed the letter of the law and left him alive, but he maimed the poor bastard in the process. What little he had left was used to get himself mended and after that the downhill descent was fast and complete.

The neighbor on the next road over had a wife that Pratt fancied. So he claimed that the fellow had raped his wife, Betty, and Betty was too well beaten down by her husband to deny the charge. The man got his wife back after the fighting was said and done, but not until Pratt had forced himself on her repeatedly. The system wasn't fair, but for a man like Pratt it was pure heaven on earth. He was a very capable fighter and he knew how to pick his targets.

And one day he picked me. One of his previous enemies burned one of Pratt's houses down while he was off celebrating a victory—and believe me, Pratt celebrated because with as often as he was in the fights he had developed a certain amount of celebrity—and when he came home to find his house was ruined, he took a look around the neighborhood and picked me as the latest in a long line of people to offend him.

I was accused before the local Magistrate and within hours the enforcers came and took me from my home, locking the doors behind me, because I was innocent until beaten in combat. I was dragged before the Magistrate in chains and had my choices explained to me, crying and trembling the entire time. I'm not a weak man, but I knew my limits and I had no desire to lose my worldly possessions to a vicious bastard who was also a trained killer.

The Magistrate read the formal charges and asked if I would represent myself or if I would have an Advocate. I chose to be represented in combat, unlike most of my neighbors.

I need to explain that. You see, there were a few souls out there who worked as the new version of attorneys. They were mercenaries, and for the right price they would fight your fights for you. The cost was never light, but if you felt your chances were bettered by having one of them fight for you, it was a chance to keep what you believed was yours or at least to walk away from the combat in one piece.

I had seen what Pratt did to his opponents in combat. I wasn't really much for the fights, but when neighbors were involved I normally watched, so I had been there to see him mete out his form of "justice." Yes, he took his neighbor's wife when he was done with the fight, but in combat he'd also ruined the man's left knee and stomped him repeatedly in the testicles, until they were effectively so much shredded meat. He'd crippled a man over imagined food theft and it seemed that every time he had a dispute he got more deliberately violent, whether he was trying to prove a point or merely increase his growing fame I don't know, but I knew I didn't want to be the recipient of his new found fury.

So I chose an Advocate from the seven men that were in the Magistrate's offices that day. I had never seen any of them fight, but I took my time and chose carefully. Want to know how you choose an Advocate? If you ever run across the need for one, look for the one who's the hungriest. Not the biggest, not the most scarred, but the one who looks like he wants it the most. There's all sorts of fanaticism, and I think the hungry ones are the deadliest fanatics of all, because they'll do damned near anything for a win.

Bryce Darby looked absolutely ravenous. I mean he was a terror. I took one look at him and seriously thought about fighting Pratt on my own, because I wasn't sure I wanted to catch Darby's attention, not ever. He was a big man, but not a giant, and he was just plain ugly. He had short red hair and a broad face that looked incapable of smiling or anything that even vaguely resembled mercy. He was not the largest Advocate, and he was younger than most of them, but when I looked in his eyes and did my best to read his soul, I knew he was the only choice for me. I knew he was the one who would do the most damage to Pratt, and that was important to me.

"What's your fee?" I had to lick my lips before I asked him, because I was a nervous wreck just thinking about what he might charge.

Darby looked me over from head to toe and back and the expression on his brutal face never changed. "What have you got?"

We bartered. It was short and sweet. He got a lot for his troubles, but only if he managed to win arbitration. If he failed, he got nothing. I made that clear from the very beginning. The way I saw it, he was the one who would take the beating either way, and if he won the fight he was entitled to what he earned.

We didn't shake hands. He never once broke a smile, but the deal was made in the Magistrate's office and when it was done the Magistrate himself looked at me and told me that I'd made the right choice.

At that point Bryce Darby had been in a total of six conflicts. He'd won every last one of them. I settled back with that knowledge and I awaited the scheduling of the court case. And while I waited, I listened to the horror stories about Bryce Darby. Here's a few of them, to maybe get clear to you just how much the man was already capable of. According to the tales I heard, he was a monster before the Fall took place. Rumors claimed that he had taken on a grown man at the age of fourteen and beaten him half to death with his bare hands. Others claimed that he had actually curb stomped a poor bastard that outweighed him by close to a hundred pounds. Still more stories had him taking on cops and beating them down when they tried to arrest him. Those are just the ones I can remember clearly, but there were more. A lot more. Bryce Darby was apparently a natural killing machine who was incapable of feeling pain.

Worked just fine for me, especially since he was on my side. When the date was set for two weeks later, I talked over the rates with him one more time. You see, if Pratt were to win, I would lose everything to him. If he lost, he would lose one of his homes and all of its contents to me. All I truly needed to know was that for the next two weeks my house was locked away from me and from everyone else. I could not sleep there, nor take from the place any of my possessions. Pratt was in similar straights but he'd been prepared for it. He had a place to stay set up. I was out on the street. I made a side offer to Darby. I told him if he ruined the man for life, I'd double what he was supposed to make.

He never even blinked. He just nodded his head and left it at that.

Two weeks after I was locked out of my house I went to the fights and watched another man enter combat as my Advocate. By that point

I was furious and desperate to see William Pratt broken and wrecked. I watched the boards and saw people placing bets on Pratt as the favorite and wondered if I had just lost everything I'd ever fought for or owned.

I want to explain that. I said that Bryce Darby was hungry and I meant it. He was a big man. He wasn't a giant, but he was in amazing shape and he was as cold a bastard as I had ever met. Back before the Fall he was exactly the type that gave sociopaths a bad name. And William Pratt? He was worse as far as I could tell. He was a scarred, muscular giant, covered with tattoos and scattered with earrings, studs and spikes. He was an animal and he was a hardened killing machine. I feared him for a very real reason.

Bryce Darby looked at the man without so much as flinching. I didn't know if that made him very brave or very stupid.

The Pit and the Abattoir took place in exactly the same spot. The only difference was the Pit left both opponents alive. The stone circle stood ten feet taller than the ground around it, and was surrounded by barbed wire and sharpened steel posts that aimed into the center of the arena. Two walkways with stairs led from the sides to the battle-field, and those were elevated as well. And all around the combat zone the recessed area sat and reeked, covered with dead bodies, with bones, with stacks of ruined weapons. Only the actual battle zone was cleared of debris. The rest of it was left as a reminder of how very serious the fights could get.

Darby stared at Pratt. Pratt looked at the younger man for all of a second before he started preening for the crowd. His audience ate it up. Darby just kept staring. Despite myself, I felt a smile grow on my face in that moment. I knew I had chosen right, you see. Darby was hungrier than Pratt.

The battle began with the usual gong of the bell, and ended a few seconds later. Pratt hit Darby exactly once, his fist slamming into the younger man's jaw and leaving an angry red mark. He was still thinking about things the wrong way. He was thinking that his opponent was human.

Darby changed his mind quickly. I had told him to ruin Pratt and that was exactly what he did. He started with the wrist just above the fist that struck him in the face. I can remember the sound of Pratt screaming as Darby bent his arm into an unnatural shape. A moment after that he destroyed the man's elbow and then his shoulder. That should have been enough. There was no way that Pratt was going to fight any longer, and I think everyone knew it. Instead, Darby continued the carnage. He dropped Pratt to the ground with a brutal sweep of his steel-toed boot that broke the man's kneecap. Pratt fell down and cried out, his face pale and shocky, and he tried to crawl away. Darby watched him for a moment and then kicked the man in his ribs and flipped him onto his back like a turtle too weak to right itself. When he was down and bloodied and gasping, Darby stomped down on his jaw, shattering the mandible and sending bloody teeth through the air.

My God, the crowd went crazy, screaming, stomping, cursing and cheering. I hate to admit it, but I cheered too. I roared my approval and watched him as he worked with all the skill and finesse of an artist. I watched him mutilate the older man with his hands and his feet until there was simply no chance that Pratt would ever fight again.

By law I won all that Pratt had accused me of taking from him. I awarded the man's remaining house and almost all of the contents in it to Bryce Darby as compensation for services rendered. I never heard from Pratt again. I have little doubt that he died from the injuries he sustained. I sincerely doubt he could have afforded medical attention.

I didn't see Darby again for years and I was fine with that, but I heard about the man. Tales of his savagery made the circuit the way stories of the old football and boxing heroes had in the past. You'd get to the market and people would be talking about the devastation he'd dealt out to another person or in a few cases to several people at once.

Almost four years after he'd worked as my Advocate I saw the man on the street, just in time to watch him wreck a gang that was out to do him in. I think it was that day that I started believing all of the old tales about him.

I had married by then. My first son had been born and a daughter was on the way and so I worked my ass off, handling work for Herlihy and taking care of collecting for some of his managers. Everyone had to pay Herlihy and somebody had to work for him. I didn't mind the work and most of the smart ones never considered arguing about what had to be paid.

I was coming home from work and stopping at the market place for supplies when I saw the men approaching. I knew the type, of course. Call them marauders, thieves, whatever you damned well please, but they were a gang of thugs, pure and simple. They took one look at my uniform and decided to leave me alone: there were distinct advantages to working for Herlihy and that was one of them. Take on one enforcer and you take on all of them. No one wanted to deal with Herlihy's army. Everyone else, however, was fair game.

The women were easy targets. They were both lookers and they appeared to be alone. One was a brunette, a fair skinned woman with a good physique and light scars to show how much she had been through in her life. The other was younger, and absolutely striking. She had flame red hair and the natural grace of a dancer. She was also exactly the sort that would cause a man to get stupid. Everything about her said she was trouble and I for one preferred to admire that sort from a distance and avoid the burns that would come from getting too close.

The gang didn't seem to share my idea of common sense. Five young men, all of them on the prowl and trying to prove themselves to the people around them, looking to make an impression on the world that would let them get ahead.

They decided to take what they wanted from the women. I could see it on their faces, in the way they moved, and I started in the direction of the women to prevent things from getting bad. I was cocky, I admit it. I had grown comfortable in my uniform and the security it provided. I walked over to the women with a swagger of my own that was only partially for show. The baton on my hip and the taser in my holster made me confident in my ability to handle whatever situation came up. You see, I'd forgotten about hunger. I hadn't read those men the right way.

They weren't afraid of my uniform, just respectful of what it meant.

"Ladies, I think you should be on your way." I looked toward the redhead and the brunette as I approached, and I called out loud and clear, sure that they would get my point. I suppose they did. They started loading the baskets of food they'd picked up into their car all the faster. That they had a car spoke volumes. Most people walked to market, because fuel was costly and cars were even more of a luxury. The rebuilt muscle car couldn't have been easy to come by. I had grown accustomed to having a car, and I didn't think about how desperately some people would want to take one that wasn't marked, like mine was, as being the property of Herlihy.

The men looked my way and then looked at the two women. One shield against five men, with two women, a week's worth of food and a vehicle on the line. I never had a chance.

One of them started to say something to me, harsh and insulting. I reached for the baton as I listened to the tone of voice, and while I was preparing to break a head or two, one of his partners tried to jump me from behind.

I heard the redhead's voice call out, loud and clear and desperate. She screamed the name Bryce and backed up as a few of the men got too close for her comfort.

Darby came from the direction of the market at a hard run, his legs eating the distance even as he looked from one person to the next and assessed the situation. Everything I had seen in him four years earlier was still there, but magnified. He struck like a tidal wave, slamming into the men and breaking them. That's the only way I can put it. He hit and they fell, screaming, terrified, because as much as I represented the potential for punishment, Darby was the personification of that concept. The first man he hit was snarling as he tried to defend himself. Darby grabbed the man by the sides of his head and yanked, dragging the startled face down to meet up with his knee in one violent, fluid motion. The man's face shattered, nearly imploded, and Darby was letting him go and moving on to the next in line before they knew what the hell was happening. The second and third were knocked down and bleeding seconds later. The fourth caught on. Maybe he was a fan of the fights, maybe he was simply quick enough to see what had happened to his friends, but he tried to run away. Darby kicked him in the small of his back and knocked him into the side of his car. Metal bent, flesh and bone took on a new shape, and Darby, seeing that his car was damaged, beat the man all the harder.

All that while I was trying to get the man swinging at me subdued. I finally cracked him on the skull hard enough to get his attention, and while he was trying to retreat, I cracked the back of his head for extra measure.

Sounds brutal, I know, but I also know they'd planned a lot worse for the women and possibly even for me.

I knocked one man senseless. In the same time, Bryce Darby

either maimed or crippled four opponents, and I had a head start on him. He looked at me just exactly long enough to assess whether or not I was a threat, and then he went to the women. I was panting, adrenaline made my legs and arms jitter and my pulse race furiously. Darby didn't look like he'd even given thought to the idea of sweating. In that moment I was reminded that there are some people who are more animal than man, and that they can have a serious advantage. I hadn't completely forgotten that fact. If I had, I'd have been dead before then. Still, he brought it home.

While I was recovering and calling in the attack, Darby checked on the women with him. When I was done with the call he came over and looked me over. I knew what was going through his mind. I could read that much easily. He was puzzled. He didn't get it. There was nothing in it for me, you see. I went in and risked my neck for two women who meant absolutely nothing to me and I hadn't negotiated a price for assisting them. He would have in the same situation. That was what took him off guard.

The two women with him thanked me. I nodded my head by way of saying it was all right and Darby crossed his arms over his chest and looked the area over while the exchange took place. One of the assailants had recovered a bit and tried to get up. Darby walked over and stomped down on the man's back with one of his scarred combat boots. The man let out a yelp and stayed still after that.

When the women had said their thanks and I had accepted them—and even that was awkward at the time. I wish I could explain it better than to say civility was just making a comeback—Darby led them back to the car and helped them put their supplies away. As I was climbing into my own vehicle he came over and put a hand on my shoulder. The hand was heavy, callused and very strong.

"Listen. Thanks." That was all he said, all he intended to say.

"I owed you." I didn't expect the words to come out of my mouth. They fairly jumped out on their own.

Darby's blue eyes looked into mine and studied me and I held my breath. I was in a uniform that gave me a certain amount of automatic respect, but the stories I'd heard in the past reminded me that the man in front of me didn't have much need for authority.

He shook his head. "Bullshit. Didn't know I was the one that saved your house when you helped them. So thanks."

He walked away before I could say anything else.

I thought about him a lot after that. Not because I wanted to, but because he was a puzzle. By all rights he should have been dead, or in charge of one of the gangs that still roamed around and took what they wanted. He managed a strange harmony with the new, violent system that came up after the Fall. He kept himself fed and safe and at the same time he meted out violence like a savage. He *was* a savage, but he'd figured out how to turn it off and on and believe me, that was almost unique. Half of the people I went up against were the ones who couldn't manage to do that very thing and the other half were the ones who simply wouldn't.

We met again one final time, on the day when he came to the Magistrate's office not to look for more work, but to ask for medical services. As with almost all cases for the Pit and the Abattoir, the Magistrate had the final say. Herlihy was far too busy to dictate prices.

The Magistrate working that day was a man named Tate Rodriguez. Tate was a hard man, but considered himself fair. Most times I agreed with him.

He was working as the Magistrate and I was working as one of his five assistants. Assistant Magistrates were basically bodyguards. A lot of people took the decisions made by Magistrates poorly and Herlihy wanted his business administrators protected. No one ever got too comfortable in the job. Sloppy work meant someone died. Let the wrong person die and you found out the hard way why Herlihy was in charge of Boston.

Bryce Darby came into the room and walked to the right instead of to the left. The left doorway led to the room for Advocates. The right door led to the much longer lines where people waited to either press charges, accept charges or plead for medical assistance. The line was almost three hours long. I'd clocked it.

Bryce Darby met up with the Magistrate after seven minutes. Tate lost the bet. He didn't think Darby would cut in line. I knew better.

Long story short, Darby needed medical assistance for three different people. The names meant almost nothing to me. Kate Sullivan, I learned, was the brunette I'd seen him with. Brittany Corin was the redhead. The third person was a man named Corin, either the redhead's brother or husband. He could have paid for the medical assistance, but it would have cost him everything he had. Instead Darby chose to offer himself to the Abattoir, which made him the first person I'd ever heard of who was willing to fight to the death rather than fork over the goods to make his life easier.

Less than five minutes after Darby made his decision, Tate closed down his office and had all of us escort him to Herlihy. Fame has its price, you see. It wasn't just anyone asking for medical assistance and it wasn't just for one person. Bryce Darby, who was as close to a celebrity as anyone in the Pit, had just offered himself up for a death match in the Abattoir. From a business sense, it was too big to ignore. Three people had to be treated and tended to, but in exchange the King of Boston got the equivalent of the first ever Super Bowl of Bloodshed.

Three hours was how long they discussed exactly what they wanted to do. Normally the choice of who a man fought in the Abattoir was decided simply by random situation. This was different; this was huge. They wanted to make sure they got everything they could out of Bryce Darby's death.

The news was monumental. Everyone wanted to attend the Abattoir that night. Want to know how to make money? Take the very best you have and offer them up as a sacrifice in the name of entertainment.

I knew what they had planned. I couldn't very well go out of my way to tell Darby. It wasn't technically against the rules, but it would be frowned on. Instead, I went to the hospital and found Brittany Corin.

She hadn't had her surgery yet, but she'd been prepped for it. Like all three of Darby's friends, she was treated with care and respect. No one who went in for serious surgery was mistreated. It was well known that the rough cases cost dearly and sometimes cost lives. So, yes, the people were treated well. The friends of Bryce Darby? They were treated like royalty.

She was a beautiful girl. Even lying in bed and being prepared for surgery—it was her appendix that was in danger of rupturing—she was lovely. I told her what I knew, and she in turn thanked me for that with a smile and a promise not to tell anyone where the information came from. I wished her luck with her surgery and left behind a teddy bear as a get well wish.

Then I made sure I had my tickets for the greatest show the Abattoir had ever produced.

Nori, my wife, was not much for the Abattoir. She had as little interest in it as I did, but on that occasion she made an exception. She wanted to see the man who had saved me before we were married. Four months pregnant with our daughter and I led her through the crowds and down to the seats I'd gotten us near the front. Rank has its privileges. The Magistrate who'd arranged the whole affair had extra seats and didn't hold a grudge after losing his bet. He was there with his wife and his ten-year-old son. The very notion of taking a child to see the show was abhorrent to me, but the world had changed since I was born and I had to accept that.

The Abattoir was filled to capacity and even Herlihy was there, along with his entourage. There was a live band to play between fights, and there were concession stands, complete with food, snacks and T-shirts with Darby's likeness on them. I was amazed. The world had ended years ago and people starved on the streets, but we had T-shirts. If he could have managed it, I think Herlihy would have produced program books.

There were other fights, of course, but they were precursory. A few moments of violence to whet appetites. The sky was red; I remember that. The fires that blazed around the place lit the clouds above us with a scarlet hue that perfectly suited the attitudes of the audience, myself included. Civility was pushed to the side for a few hours, and everyone wanted to see blood and death. Screw the warm-ups, and damn the musicians as failures; they merely delayed the fight that was still to come.

And then it was time. The small feuds were done and the time for carnage was there and damn me with the musicians, I was thrilled to see it. My pulse raced and my limbs surged with adrenaline and I stood and cheered along with everyone else when the announcer called out that this was the fight to end all fights.

Bryce Darby, the undefeated champion of dozens of contests in the Pit was going into the Abattoir for the first time ever. It's one thing to know a man is capable of violence and another entirely to see him commit murder.

Everyone was told the situation: Bryce Darby wanted medical assistance for three people in desperate need of that help. None of the situations were minor. In exchange for that assistance he would have to fight for the privilege against not one or even three opponents, but against six in unarmed combat to the death.

Each of the men was introduced. Each, as well we knew, also sought medical assistance for someone else. Each of them wanted to save someone dear to them. Life and death not for the fighters, but for the people who meant the most to them. Really, what better way to guarantee a show?

The men were all formidable. A few of them had been in trouble with Herlihy before and that was what I knew that Darby wasn't supposed to know. The public story was that they fought for their loved ones and that was true enough, but they also fought to get back in the King's good graces. They were desperate and they were hungry.

When they'd all been introduced, Darby stepped out from his entrance and stopped, allowing everyone to see him. The applause was riotous. People stood up and stomped their feet, they called out for blood and cheered for the redheaded brute who stood to get himself beaten to death by the other six men in the arena.

Herlihy himself struck the gong that day. He rose from his spot and walked along the narrow walkway, grabbed the heavy club used to strike the seven foot wide metal disk and bashed it with all the force he could muster.

Before the vibrations had ceased, Darby had killed the first of his opponents. In the past he had always let the aggressors come to him, but not that day. He charged at a muscular ape of a man whose wife had heart troubles and who had fought hard to get more medical attention than he could afford, and heaved the man out of the arena before he knew what was happening. The man screamed as he rose through the air and only stopped when the metal guard spike drove through his chest and neck.

Half of the audience cheered even louder. The rest sat stunned. They were expecting combat, not slaughter.

Bryce Darby didn't care about showmanship. He cared about surviving the next few minutes.

There was no organization. The men had not been given time to prepare for fighting against one opponent. Instead they simply charged, determined to kill their enemy as quickly as they could. The odds were still in their favor, five to one. It should have been an easy win for them, but like the audience, they weren't as ready as they thought they were.

I need to remind you that most of the people who were in the audience could have told you horror stories about their lives during and after the Fall. Nori had been attacked on several occasions—she was beautiful and exotic and more than one man tried to have his way with her—and she had been forced to do unpleasant things to a few men, up to and including castration, to make her point. And she was not a fighter. The men in the Abattoir were picked for their abilities. They were chosen by Herlihy himself to fight against Darby. They were brutes, powerful and deadly in their own rights and even as a seasoned fighter I'd have probably chosen a good Advocate rather than fight any one of them.

Darby hit the second opponent in the throat with his left hand. I remember that, because the man was trying to dodge from the right hook he'd thrown and instead he took the blow that destroyed his windpipe and knocked his Adam's apple into a new shape. The audience watched as the man fell flat and clutched at his throat, trying to somehow claw breaths from his ruined airway.

Darby didn't waste the time. He moved on to the next target and shifted his body enough to absorb the first few blows the man threw his way. The third opponent cheated. He intended to keep his life and to end Darby's and to that end he wrapped his hands around rolls of quarters or maybe it was metal posts cut down to size, but either way, his fists were even deadlier than usual. He smashed himself into Darby with all the frenzy of a tidal wave ramming into the breakers. They traded blows with unsettling fury and even the most energetic members of the audience stopped to watch. I won't claim the auditorium was silent, but it was definitely quieter, enough so that I could hear the slam of fists into flesh and the ragged breaths of the two men as they did battle.

The man was good and he was fighting for his life and in the end, it didn't matter. He slipped up first, and Bryce Darby wrecked him for his weakness. Darby ducked a hard swing at his face and as he moved out of the way of the blow he slashed his fingers across his enemy's eyes, blinding him. To this day I don't know if he was lucky, cheating or just amazingly good, but his fingers came back bloodied and the man stopped fighting and screamed as he cried crimson tears.

Darby didn't give him a chance to recover. He knocked the man sprawling and stomped down in his neck, grinding the heel of his boot into flesh until something deep inside broke and the wound bled black.

The fourth man tried to run. That's maybe what I remember the very best. He tried to escape from Darby and without so much as hesitating the redhead drove him down to his knees and then flattened him. By the time the poor bastard's face hit the ground he was already dead.

Darby's face was a bloody mess by then. His lips were swollen and busted by the last man he'd fought, and trails of blood ran from his nose as well. His cheek was swelling, his jaw was bloodied and his body was already reddening. He looked like a monster. He acted the part, too.

The fifth man tried to plead. He opened his mouth to speak, and Darby twisted his head to the left until his neck broke. Do you have any idea how hard that must be to accomplish?

There was one man left. I watched. I cheered along with everyone else as he grabbed the last of his enemies and ruined him. There was no showmanship, nor any finesse. Every move he made was slower than before and he was aching. Even with most of his opponents killed quickly the fight had taken its toll and the last man died the same as the first, screaming as he was thrown into the spikes that surrounded the Abattoir.

I watched and so did everyone else. That was the last time Nori ever asked to go to the Pit and the last time I went as well.

I wish I could give this a happier ending. In the end, Bryce Darby got what he came for. His friends, his family, whatever they were to him, they got their medical attention. Three people were given another chance at life, and in exchange six were murdered and six more were turned away from the aid they needed.

Bryce Darby was hailed as a hero, and I suppose he was in some ways. And at the same time something changed in Boston. I don't even think anyone was conscious of it at first, but something vital was stolen away by the fight.

Herlihy lost favor among his people. He'd fought to keep Boston intact and had done an amazing job when all around him the country fell into chaos. To be sure, there was death and violence in Boston during the Fall, but next to the other big cities the worst events could almost been seen as minor. Still, something changed. The people stopped thinking of their leader as benevolent and realized that he was less than perfect.

He held on for a while, but his powerful grip started slipping. Change was painful, and I'd be lying if I said I was proud of everything I did in the name of the king. In time I and most of my peers were called on to kill, and we did it in an effort to keep the peace.

I heard about it when Bryce Darby was killed. He was shot down by men in uniforms exactly like the one I wore until the day I retired. He was killed over nothing, really. He chose not to listen to suggestions that he might prefer to lose a pit fight. Nothing fatal, just a skirmish in a court of law. A few people wanted to place bets, and he was stubborn and foolish to the very end.

You see, bullets were harder to come by, but they weren't impossible to find. He won his last fight and as he headed for his house and the people he cared for, three men in uniforms took aim and fired.

I understand he actually killed two of them before he dropped, but that might just be a rumor. I like to think maybe it's the truth though. It seems fitting that he died in combat, which was the way he lived most of the time.

Is there a moral here? No. Just a reminder of a different time, when lives weren't worth much except as entertainment. These days the hospitals run again across the country, and there's food enough to let people eat and in some cases grow fat. The gladiatorial pits are gone, mostly, or used for different forms of entertainment.

You know all of that, of course. You live here, after all.

I don't miss the Abattoir. I could never feel bad for the loss of that sort of hell pit. But these days I find I miss the likes of Bryce Darby. He was not kind and he was not a good man, but he was honest. I think that's missing a lot more than most folks understand.

I hear he has a son that strongly resembles him. I understand he's one of the men who took down Herlihy and replaced the old government. Somehow I find that fitting.

CANNONBALL LYCANTHROPE

JANET JOYCE HOLDEN

"That's a nice ride."

"Thanks."

He gestured toward the unleaded pump. "You get the heads redone?"

"Yep."

"Some other modifications, too, I bet. You traveling across country?"

"Yep."

"It's a cool car, man."

He left it at that. He figured he'd gotten what he needed and he'd already spotted the girl in the passenger seat, fast asleep, her head propped up on a huge bed pillow. As for her companion, sure—they could take him, no problem. And they'd follow the original plan, keep going until it was dark and they all had to pull in for gas once more. In this surreptitious chase across country the timing couldn't have been better. They were stronger come nightfall, while she was at her weakest.

He walked across the forecourt, passed by the front of a Hostess delivery truck and approached the silver 5 Series BMW hiding in its shadow. Cally had finished at the pump and was already in the driver's seat, fingers rapping on the steering wheel while Ed was walking back from the store, loaded up with chips and cola. Dan shook his head and saw indigestion in his future. He climbed inside and buckled up.

"So?" Cally was leaning forward, staring at the delivery truck as if he could see through it.

"Relax. He's just a guy."

"Yeah, but those shoulders, man. Not to mention we're having a hard time keeping up."

Dan couldn't argue with the latter. He'd been doing the math along the route and so far their average speed was just under 90 and on some of the open stretches they'd had to push their vehicle well over the 150 mark. Nonetheless he shrugged. It was important to keep a lid on Cally's anxiousness, bottle it up until it became useful. "Our vehicle can handle it, and the guy hits the gym once in a while. So what?"

"Yeah, well, when the time comes, maybe you should take him and I'll go after the girl."

"Don't be stupid, and don't forget who she is. We stick with the original plan. You'll be fine."

Ed arrived in a fanfare of plastic bottles and chip packets, all of it dumped on the rear passenger seat. "The car is sweet. Is it a '69?"

Dan grinned, couldn't help it. "Yeah, and there's a chrome wolf's head on the stick shift." He glanced over his shoulder at the detritus in the back. "Couldn't you have gotten me a sandwich?"

"From a gas station? Hell, no. You'll get food—"

The throaty eruption of a nearby engine brought the exchange to a halt.

"Okay, he's rolling," Cally announced. "Time to go."

«««—»»»

Movement in his peripheral vision. The girl had woken up and was stretching. A moment later she was leaning over the back, looking out of the window. It had been two hours since they'd pulled in for gas and for the thousandth time he checked the Charger's gauges; temperatures looked fine, a quick calculation using the trip and they were still on target to arrive at the West Coast at noon the following day. They were also half way down on fuel, which was to be expected, but the needle still taunted him and reminded him those bastards would more than likely try something at the next stop.

"Still there?"

"Yes," she said. "Maybe half a mile back, it's hard to tell."

He nodded. They both knew what was coming, ever since the other vehicle had gotten bold and joined them way back on the I-70 at Columbus. A quick glance at the rear view mirror, but his eyes didn't linger. Hard to look at that boiling wall of cloud in their wake, hanging heavy and painting the sky black. No doubt the locals would put it down to an incoming storm, they were used to such sights as this. But this was no mere storm. Winter was on their tail, pushing them to their absolute limit.

He sensed her attention shift toward him. All that threat of ice, wind and rain, it was nothing compared to the power behind her eyes. And now she was staring at him while her fingers played with the talisman around her neck—a five-pointed star and a tiny bundle of twigs the color of gray bones, tied together with a jolly pink ribbon.

"We'll be fine," she said.

Her voice made him believe, and he attempted to relax as they sped toward the inevitable. Nothing to do now but let the car eat up the road and watch the horizon shift color as the sun went down. Another hour and it would be dark, front and back.

Subconsciously, he began to go over the odds and what was at stake. He hadn't paid much attention during the briefing; he'd been in the midst of withdrawal, flushing out the drugs. Consequently, most of the stuff they'd told him he'd forgotten, which was probably for the better after one of the assassins had shown his face at the last rest stop. Something about the guy...

We'll be fine. The words sang loud in his head like church bells at a wedding. They papered over his disquiet and made light of the monster inside. Because those boys back there weren't alone in their menace. Did they know whom they were up against? Maybe they did, and had planned accordingly. He never ceased to be amazed at the different methods people tried in order to get the better of him. Or maybe they were going in blind. It brought a smile to his face until he considered he was operating under a similar delusion.

At least the girl had faith.

The car got on with the real business and swept them across the plain. He fell into its powerful rhythm and let it soothe him, let it carry him and his precious cargo toward the failing sunset. And in no time at all twilight arrived and brought with it a horde of birds and insects. Bugs hammered the windshield and fogged the view. He'd driven this route before, albeit under different circumstances, but he'd never seen it as crazy as this. It was an extension of what had begun as soon as they'd left the cities; flora, fauna, they had all reached out toward his passenger, had stretched out wings, claws, leaves and roots in worship and accolade. It was a riot out there and it wasn't until complete darkness arrived that the cacophony subsided.

Twenty or so minutes from their destination, he could see the headlights of their pursuer in the mirror. "Why this place in particular?"

"It's quiet," she said. "It's somewhere we can finish this."

"You know, once it begins..." But her attention had left him. It was back out there in the silent fields, dancing in the dark with the wheat and the moths. And left alone he looked at his hands, thick fingers wrapped around the steering wheel. Part of him was already listening to his own siren song. A rallying call that silenced some fears and aroused others; that despite the drug-induced dormancy, his body hadn't forgotten, and that events would follow the usual course and people would get hurt. He took another look in the mirror. Hopefully it would be the right people.

«««—»»»

"So, what's the record for the Cannonball Run?" Ed's breath wafted over the back seat, carrying the sour aroma of half-chewed corn chips.

"Across country? No idea." Dan's stomach rumbled.

"Thirty-two hours and seven minutes," Cally said. "Nineteen eighty-three, Diem and Turner, in a Ferrari 308. And it's not the Cannonball anymore."

"Nineteen eighty-three?" Ed laughed. "A hundred bucks says it's already been beat. Hell, the speed we're going, we've already got it licked. "

"Don't be stupid. No way anyone could do it now. Cops, radar, helicopters, congestion—"

Dan sat back and shut out the banter. For the past half hour, something undeterminable had been rising in his gut. Hunger, he surmised, having stayed clear of Ed's smorgasbord of indigestibles. And yet it

146

felt more like a warning, one that had yet to reveal itself. Better hurry up and show your face, he thought. It's almost time.

He settled in the front seat, took comfort in the thick darkness traveling in their wake; a cold wall from which he gathered strength. That and the artifacts lying in their precious box in the trunk. No way that little girl could put up a fight against those. And she was the real threat, despite Cally worrying over her companion.

"Lights up ahead. I think they're pulling in."

"Easy, easy." Dan waved his hand. "Don't get too close."

"Is this it?" Ed was already checking his guns and knives, his beloved packs of chips forgotten.

"Yes. You remember the drill?"

"Let's just get it over with." Cally's anxiety was cranked up again, but he brought the car in smooth and parked a good three lengths behind the Charger, over at the next pump.

"Shit. They're already out." Ed opened the rear door.

Dan saw the girl and her companion heading toward the store. He leaned over, grabbed Cally's keys and popped the trunk. "They're splitting up. He's hitting the restroom."

"That means they don't know we're coming." Cally looked relieved. He was reaching under his seat. A knife. A shotgun. They both emerged.

"Now?" said Ed.

"Yes, now." Dan got out and approached the rear of the car. He watched his companions leave the vehicle and cross the forecourt, carrying their weapons in the open, making no attempt to hide their intent. A quick look around. Lights in the overhead canopy lacked luster, as if this particular gas station didn't care one way or another if it was ignored by passing traffic. And no other vehicles, except for their target. Perfect.

He raised the trunk lid and reached for the box. Condensation dulled its surface and dampened his fingertips as he twisted the locks. And just for a second, he paused. He'd got that feeling again. Nothing he could pin down, so he lifted the lid.

The weapons appeared carved from ice. Opaque, pale, they seemed too delicate to be of use. Dan stared in awe. Jack's own precious blades. Entrusted to Dan because old Jack still held the North in his cold embrace and wasn't about to give it up. Not yet. He gripped the handles, felt the charge of deadly cold vibrate through his wrists. A stark contrast to the vehicle crouched on the forecourt like a fire dragon on wheels, breathing intolerable heat after carrying them across the plain at such high speed.

Wielding the blades, Dan stepped back and headed for the store. He could see the girl inside, talking to a guy behind the counter. It wouldn't be a problem; he'd take them both. Off to his right, the shadows paled. Clouds in the east were shifting, and a fraction of the moon was beginning to shine through. He looked through the window once more. The girl had her hand raised, finger pointing, still talking to the man but her eyes were looking beyond the glass, out toward the sky. He dipped low. No need to announce his presence just yet.

To the left—a grunting noise, followed by a sharp hiss of pain. No sign of Ed, or Cally. They'd gone around the side of the building, but the sound told him the fight had already begun. He smiled and increased his pace. Until movement from that same direction forced him to look.

It was Ed, stumbling forward, his arms wrapped tight across his waist. The man fell to his knees and blood spattered. He relaxed, his hands came away from his abdomen and his guts writhed forth and spilled across concrete. "You never—" he began, and fell forward.

"Where's Cally?" Dan crouched alongside. With the blades in one hand, he hauled on his companion's shoulder. "What happened?"

Ed laughed, regurgitated blood. "—never told us it was a full moon."

Dan stood up. Nothing he could do. His companion was fading rapidly, life and heat expanding into the night air. He wondered about Cally and hoped he was keeping their assailant busy. Must have been armed with one hell of a knife to draw a man's guts like that. It gave him pause, but only for a moment. The girl's protector was stronger than he'd thought but there was still a job to be done.

His stride resolute, he approached the store and threw open the door. The enemy had shown its hand and the time for stealth was over. Shelves to the left and right. The counter was to the rear and he saw the girl, no sign of the proprietor. He switched one of the weapons to his left hand. Ten paces. That's all he needed to close the distance. She was smiling at him, not in the least bit afraid.

Movement. A round object like a soccer ball bounced down one of the aisles and arrived at his feet. It was accompanied by a sour, musky odor that turned his stomach. He looked down. One eye in Cally's severed head was staring at him, while the other was missing, replaced by a gaping socket. Wreckage at the throat suggested the head had been bitten off, rather than cut. Not a knife, then. Teeth. And Ed had said something about a full moon.

A low growl from the end of the aisle made him look. But despite the horror it was a distraction. He had to get to his target. But when the monster lowered its shoulders and got ready to charge he knew he had no choice; he'd never make it to the girl in time. He turned and faced it. It was the shape of a man, but the face, ah, the face...

Purely on instinct he brought both blades to the fore and watched the monster pause, saw the head shift and the eyes glitter with cunning. A bitter grin escaped him. He let the weapons fall open to either side, offering up chest and head as a target. A recognizable feint to those with any skill, but to a creature such as this—

"What are you waiting for?" He shifted his balance, better able to fend off a frontal assault. "Come on, you fucker. Taste the spirit of Winter!"

«««—»»»

The collapse of the man's guard inspired opportunity and he was already powering down the aisle before the words were done. He slammed into the guy a fraction of a second after those nasty-looking blades snapped back, front and center. One skewered his sternum like a pile driver. The other slid into the flesh of his neck and exited close to his vertebrae. But his jaws were already wide, and although they didn't achieve their ultimate aim, the damage was more than enough.

Stapled together by the blades, they fell in unison and slid along the aisle. He could see the girl's shoes. Any closer, he mused, and she'd be bowled over like a ninepin. The thought drifted on a sea of pain. The blades radiated cold; they chilled muscle and turned blood to sleet. Funny, how extreme cold always felt like burning.

The man underneath him was gasping, struggling for his last breath through a ripped throat. He wondered if he'd share the man's ultimate fate. The cold was extending, burrowing in. He feared he would die and it all seemed such a waste. "All this?" He swallowed; it hurt to speak in this guise, "For just a few more weeks of winter?"

The guy stared, hands too weak to grip his weapons and abruptly the cold bond between them collapsed. A smile, and the man was gone. Meanwhile, the cold traveled into his gut and his shoulders felt numb, and in a fever of pain he saw the girl's shoes, closer this time.

"Quickly," she said, entirely unafraid of the horrors at her feet. She gave him a push and deftly retracted the blades. The weapons folded in her hands, or so it appeared through his filmy eyes. The cold disappeared but the burning remained. *Quickly*, she'd told him, and so he did his best.

In a fetal position he went through the bitter throes of change. Regaining his humanity was slow, for the lunar orb still had him and her grip was strong. When it was done, he slowly regained his feet. Three men dead and it was only by the grace of the moon he hadn't joined them. He looked to the counter. No sign of the proprietor and he wondered if the girl had killed him.

He watched her fingering the talisman around her neck although he doubted she'd ever need such a thing against the likes of him. She bore a faint smile, a beatific aura of success. It seemed at odds with the carnage until he considered she was entirely indifferent. In their annual tugs of war, the seasons invariably killed thousands. Winter might well have lost his battle out here on the plains, but further north he was still burying the unwary in snow or just plain old freezing them to death, while Spring's subsequent thaws would no doubt follow and drown those he'd missed.

He saw movement by the counter. It was the proprietor, waking from a deep slumber. She had been merciful after all. At his feet, the body of the creature he'd killed was already turning to water. Just another casualty of Equinox.

The girl beckoned and he followed her outside. The wall of cloud had disappeared and the air felt warm and seductive. Insects danced under the dull lights, and the moon still shone and bathed the surrounding fields in silver. But his lunar mistress was keeping her distance, her grip on him now softer and more benevolent. She'd had her fun and was now content.

The gas station guy joined them. He was scratching his head and staring out into the dark. "Funny," he said. "One hell of a storm brewing earlier. And now it feels like spring is in the air."

He left the proprietor and the girl chatting about the weather while he filled up the Dodge. He looked toward the restroom. No sign of the other bodies and he didn't quite understand why. They'd tasted human enough, but all that remained was their silver BMW parked at the next pump, and as he waited for the tank to fill he wondered what she had done with those lethal blades.

He paid the man, and he and the girl jumped back in the car. He gunned the engine, saw her face light up as it roared. "No need to go so fast, now," he began.

"Oh, but you must," she said. "I enjoy the speed."

He shrugged, put the vehicle in gear and rejoined the narrow asphalt road that stretched toward the western horizon. Sixty, seventy, eighty and up, the engine took it all in stride while Spring rode alongside him with a bold grin on her face. Her mood was infectious, but ultimately it was a strong sense of relief that bore his spirit from the depths and made him thankful of his own gifts and the good grace of the moon.

They passed beneath a bridge, where swallows were diving in the early dawn. Behind them, master of them all, the sun was on the rise, spinning webs of light through thin cloud. It was going to be a beautiful day.

THROWING MONSTERS

JONATHAN JANZ

Sarah Slover told her three-year old son, "Put the brick down." The brick remained poised above Daniel's head. His bland gaze didn't waver. She forced herself to maintain eye contact, to for God's sake not lose a staring contest to a toddler, but she felt her resolve weakening.

Daniel peered into her eyes, his little body as moveless as the brick above his head.

Breathe, she told herself. *Breathe.*

"Daniel," she said with a calmness she didn't feel, "you'll hurt yourself if you don't put it down."

Or worse, she thought, *you'll hurt me.*

Daniel held her gaze a moment longer.

Then he let the brick fall.

It landed an inch from his feet, gouging the ground and coming to rest on its side. She glanced up and down the country road, but of course there was no one there. There never was. It was one of the few things she still liked about the country: no one was around to witness her crappy parenting.

She crossed the sidewalk, bent, and grabbed his shoulders.

Alarm bloomed in his little face. "I didn't throw it, Mommy."

"I know that," she said and struggled to quell her anger, "but it was still dangerous."

"I put it down."

"No," she said. "You held it above your head and dropped it like a bomb from an airplane."

Daniel wouldn't meet her stare. "It's just a brick."

She resisted an urge to shake him. She said, "It could have broken your foot. Another inch and it *would* have."

A red pick-up rumbled by. Fascinated, Daniel watched it pass. God, she thought. To be three again, to be able to let something as simple as a pick-up truck scatter a stressful moment like wind-blown dust. As Daniel watched the red truck recede, she remembered something she'd read about discipline in a parenting magazine: *Hit 'em where it hurts.*

Sarah said, "Do I need to take your fire truck away for you to listen to me?"

"No, Mommy," he said, still watching the pick-up's rusty bumper, the purplish exhaust belching from its rusty muffler.

"The next time you throw something, I *will* take it away. Are we understood?"

"I didn't throw it," he said absently.

Sighing, she straightened and moved toward the house.

"Come inside," she said. "It's nearly lunchtime."

But instead of following her, Daniel stood in the yard, alone, and watched the red truck disappear into the forest.

«««—»»»

Daniel threw two more things while she cooked lunch. A toy bear and the remote control. The battery lid fell off the remote, and when she tried to replace it, she found it wouldn't slide into place. Lips a thin line, she tossed the remote aside and returned to the macaroni, which was boiling over.

Sarah reached out to turn off the stove and hissed as steam burned her forearm. "Dammit," she said and rubbed her throbbing flesh. "Damn, damn, damn."

A voice from behind her: "That's a bad word, Mommy."

Sarah bit her lip.

After lunch it was the same thing, Daniel hurling sand from his sandbox, lobbing an empty cup across the kitchen to clatter against the back door. When he purposely bounced his favorite red ball down the basement steps, she said in a tremulous voice, "Go get it."

154

Daniel paused in the basement doorway, a finger pressed to his lips.

"I'm not telling you again," Sarah said, fists balled at her sides. "Get the goddamn ball."

A reply, barely audible.

"What?"

"The monster will get me."

She swept a lock of long brown hair out of her face with an irritated hand. "What are you talking about?"

"The monster," he said. "In the basement."

Sarah's eyes widened. She wasn't a bit surprised Daniel thought there was a monster in their basement. The goddamned place was like a dungeon. She'd gone down to do laundry last week and had discovered a dead mouse at the foot of the stairs. Not only did the thing stink, but the sight of it had been awful. Like it had been gnawed on, the back legs shredded to bloody ribbons. She was sure it had been H.P.—their cat's name had been her ex-husband's idea; he loved all kinds of weirdo stories—but she hadn't seen the cat down there in ages. Like H.P. was even more frightened of the basement than her son was.

Thinking hard, Sarah moved up next to Daniel. She peered down at the sooty basement stairs, snaked an arm around his narrow shoulders. "I'll make you a deal," she said.

His body tensed, his tone suddenly wary. "What kind of a deal?"

"I'll get the ball for you if you promise not to throw things anymore."

He scowled. "*No.*"

"Alright," she said lightly. "But the monster won't be happy."

Daniel glanced quickly up at her. "He won't?"

"The monster only eats little boys who throw things when they're not supposed to. That's why he's called the Throwing Monster."

Real alarm showing in the boy's face. It tugged at her conscience, but she'd battled with this stupid issue long enough. An opportunity like this might never come again.

Daniel inched closer to her. "Will he eat me if I stop throwing stuff?"

"Of course not, honey. He only eats little boys who don't listen to their mommies."

155

Amazingly, it worked.

Two days went by, the calmest period she'd had since Daniel began walking. Sarah was certain the problem had been solved when she stepped into his bedroom and caught him chucking matchbox cars at the cat.

"Uh-oh," she said, hands on hips.

Terror flooded his little face. He backpedaled, nearly tripping over H.P. "I didn't mean to, Mommy. I didn't mean to."

She sighed. "I don't know…"

He dashed over to her, fastened himself to her legs. "Please don't let the monster get me, Mommy! *Please!*" When he looked up, the tears in his eyes made her question her tactics.

But only for a moment.

If letting Daniel endure one nightmare would ensure household serenity, so be it. She'd already lost enough sleep for two lifetimes worrying over when she'd lost control of him.

"You'll make him stay in the basement, Mommy?" he asked in a breathless little voice. "Promise?"

She eyed him. "You won't throw again?"

A tear slipped down his cheek. "Uh-uh."

"Then you might be safe."

«««—»»»

The next morning, Saturday morning, they were in the cramped living room, Sarah on the couch sipping her coffee. Daniel was watching cartoons when he suddenly spat at the television screen. In silence, she watched the saliva crawl down the glass.

She set the coffee on the stand beside her. "Daniel?"

"Sorry," he replied in a toneless voice. In the screen's reflection she could see his little face and what might have been the ghost of a smile.

She willed her heartbeat to slow, her jaw to unclench. "You need to get a towel and wipe that off."

No answer.

"Daniel, I mean it. *Now.*"

"You do it," he said.

"One…," she said, "…two…"

In the reflecting screen she could see he was definitely smiling now.

She sat forward. "...three...four..."

Daniel yawned. She stood up.

"Five," she said.

But Daniel didn't even turn around. She glared at his back in mute fury. Then she remembered she hadn't assigned a consequence to her count. *Moron!* she thought. She'd done that several times this week, counting like an idiot while her son ignored her.

Then, she remembered. A wicked grin spread on her face. "Okay, honey. I'll clean it up for you." On the way out of the room she added, "But the Spitting Monster won't like it."

Her mental count only reached two before he burst through the doorway after her. "The what?" he asked, panic stitching his voice.

She kept her tone matter-of-fact. "The Spitting Monster. He lives in the basement with the others."

"Others?" he asked in a tiny voice. He glanced toward the basement in dread.

She hadn't meant to plant the idea, but she could see her words working on imagination, conjuring ghastly creatures and generally scaring the shit out of him.

"Yes," she pressed on. "The Hitting Monster. The Screaming Monster. The Throwing Monster, but you know about him."

Daniel nodded, absolute faith and unfathomable terror at war in his big brown eyes.

Eric's eyes, she thought.

As her son thought it over, Sarah gazed down at him and remembered.

Remembered six months ago when it all crashed down around her, Eric re-entering the picture to claim paternity. Of course it was true, she'd known that all along. But Tom was such a good man, where was the harm in letting him think Daniel was his? Tom was steady and Tom was good. Tom loved Daniel and Tom was shattered when the doctor told him Daniel wasn't his biological son, the boy had been sired by Eric after all. Then Tom moved out, started the divorce proceedings, and every goddamn person in town turned against her. She hated the women at the supermarket, the ones who cast furtive glances at her in the produce section. Eyeing her like she was Hester Fucking Prynne. Watching her the same way the bastards at the bars did, like she was easy pickings now that Tom was gone. Like she couldn't survive without a man between her legs.

She hated herself for humiliating Tom, for letting Eric ruin everything.

And now, she supposed, she was suffering for her sins.

"Mommy?" Daniel asked.

She blinked a moment before answering. "Yes?"

"You won't let the monsters get me, will you?"

A kiss. "Of course not, honey. Not if you behave."

«‹‹—›»›

The phone rang that evening around nine.

It was Eric.

"Put Danny on," he said.

She drew herself up. "Daniel is already in bed."

"Jesus," Eric said, "it's still light out."

She put him at about four drinks, maybe five.

"His bedtime is eight-thirty," she said. "He needs his sleep."

In the dead air between them she heard a band playing in the background, like he'd stepped into the parking lot to call.

"So you're free for a while," he said and she could almost see him standing there, a horny grin peeking through his black goatee. His shaggy black hair would be pushed back by his sunglasses or a do-rag. He'd be wearing a muscle shirt, his tall sculpted frame like someone on a romance novel cover. Despite herself, she felt the old stirring.

"I don't know," she said. "It's getting late."

Soft laughter. "Make sure the porch light's on."

He arrived a half hour later, the Harley loud enough to shake the house. She tiptoed to her son's bedroom door and strained to hear movement from within, but he seemed to be sleeping peacefully.

Hammering on the front door.

She jogged down the hall to silence it, opened the door and said in a harsh whisper, "Come in before you wake Daniel."

No apology. Eric never apologized. It was a point of pride for him.

He swayed as he moved past, a fog of beer attending him.

"How many have you had?" she asked.

Making his way toward the kitchen. "A few. Got any popcorn?"

"In the cupboard."

Instead of going for the popcorn, Eric opened the pantry door and rummaged around. "No booze?"

Sarah shrugged. "I don't like whiskey like you do."

Sighing, Eric went over, opened the fridge, and peered inside. "Still drinking that fruity shit?" He brought out a wine cooler.

She knew he wouldn't get her one, so she reached in and got one herself. They stood in the kitchen drinking a moment before he said, "You've lost weight. Everywhere except your tits."

She rolled her eyes but was unable to suppress a smile. He moved closer and nuzzled her neck. He smelled like aftershave and beer. His long arms encircled her, reached down and groped her ass. She knew she should be throwing him out, all the trouble he had caused her, but it had been weeks since she'd been with anyone.

She surrendered to it, the feel of his beard on her neck, her shoulder. He lifted off her shirt and pushed down her bra to lap at her nipples. She took a long, sweet drink of raspberry wine cooler as he reached between her legs and massaged her sex. She helped him get her blue jeans off and somehow they were on the living room floor, Eric thrusting into her so feverishly she had to bite the back of her hand to stifle her cries. God, but the man could make love. Though her heart was with Tom, her body had always been Eric's. In high school. Fifteen-years-old in the back of his Mustang. On the football field at midnight. In his apartment while Daniel was at the sitter and Tom was at work.

And now, at twenty-five, here she was on the floor of her living room gripped by that same maddening itch, consumed by that quivering white haze that no one else could conjure. His muscular body tightened, his face a dark mask of lust. Then he slumped on top of her, his warm musky smell drowsing over her.

They lazed there a moment, Eric going slowly limp inside her. When he got up and went to the fridge for another wine cooler, she lay there naked and sweating.

Sarah frowned.

She was suddenly certain she was being watched. Gasping, she fumbled for a throw pillow and covered her breasts with it. She glanced down the hall, sure she'd see Daniel standing there, but her son had apparently slept through her and Eric's lovemaking.

Slowly, she exhaled. When Sarah rose and turned toward the kitchen, she realized the basement door was open.

Funny. She was certain she'd closed it. She strode over and pushed it shut, and as she did she caught a whiff of something rotten. Another dead mouse, maybe. Or moisture seeping through the single dingy window. God, how she hated it down there.

Frowning, Sarah went to the bathroom to clean up.

When she stepped out of the bathroom her breath caught in her throat.

Daniel's door was open.

She hurried around the corner hoping the cat had pushed it open, but there was Eric, standing over her son, something approaching tenderness in his face.

Too bad he wanted nothing to do with the boy when he was sober.

Careful not to awaken Daniel, she seized Eric's elbow. "Come on."

"He's got my chin, too." Eric shook his head. "God*damn*, that's a handsome boy."

Daniel stirred. Despite the murk of the bedroom, she could see how badly her son's hair needed a trim. For some reason, this added to her anxiety.

"*Come on*," she said, tugging Eric's arm.

She half dragged him out of the bedroom and elbowed shut the door.

"How dare you?" she demanded.

But Eric had lost interest. He ambled down the hallway and into the kitchen.

She followed after him, calling, "If you'd pay some child support, you could see Daniel every day."

Eric grabbed another wine cooler and left without saying goodbye.

Sarah closed her eyes, leaned against the kitchen doorjamb, and listened to the Harley's engine recede. Then she crossed to the fridge and got herself a pair of wine coolers.

Maybe getting drunk would help her sleep.

160

«‹‹—›»»

The next morning Daniel was under her skin from the moment he climbed into her bed at just before six.

The only time the boy was really affectionate was when she wanted to sleep. Burrowing into her neck, kissing her closed lids. She might have welcomed the closeness had she not been hung over. As it was, his attentions reminded her of a persistent puppy.

At breakfast Daniel wouldn't sit still, insisted on getting into the pantry instead. The child lock on the knob had long since disappeared, which meant Daniel had a world of dangers at his disposal: cleaning solutions, bleach, old mops, even a set of steak knives she never used. She needed to carry it all to the basement, where the quarantine pile already included several glass jars, a hammer, rat poison, and a set of andirons Daniel kept using as baseball bats, but she didn't feel like doing it. She never felt like going to the basement, which was probably why they so rarely had clean clothes.

She was eating cereal at the kitchen table when everything grew quiet. Sarah waited, her spoon poised above her cereal. Silence was always a bad sign. When Daniel grew silent, he was either pooping or getting into trouble. Since he was mostly potty-trained and had his big boy underpants on, she was betting on trouble.

"Daniel?"

Silence from the closet.

From where she sat, the open door blocked her view of what he was doing. She could see the open basement door across the hall. She pictured her son backing out of the closet with a steak knife, getting closer and closer to the basement stairs until the ground dropped away behind him. He'd tumble into darkness and either break his neck or impale himself.

And she'd get thrown in jail for neglect.

Sarah was across the kitchen in a second. She jerked open the door and stared down at her son.

Sucking on a bottle of window cleaner.

It wasn't Sarah slapping the bottle away and seizing Daniel by the shirt. It wasn't Sarah dragging him bodily to the kitchen sink and hoisting him toward the faucet.

Daniel screamed and spluttered as she shoved his open mouth under the faucet. He bellowed and slapped at her and thrashed to get away. Several times he nearly flopped out of her hands like a game fish evading capture. Finally, Sarah gave up washing his mouth and started pounding his back, forgetting in her panic one could not dislodge liquid the way one could a solid. When his feet again touched the linoleum floor, Daniel squirmed free of her grip and stumbled away. Sobbing, he bolted down the hall and out the front door.

She didn't know whether to pursue him or call poison control.

She called poison control.

The woman listened calmly to her story and asked her how much Windex Daniel had imbibed.

Sarah had no idea.

"Were you watching him?"

A beat.

"Of course I was watching him."

"How much did you see him drink?"

"I didn't see him drink it."

"Where were you when this was happening?"

"Goddammit, quit grilling me and tell me what to do."

"Miss, I can't help you if you don't give me specifics."

"Damn it." Covering the phone. "*Daniel.*"

"Miss?"

"He just…I don't know where he went. *Daniel!*"

"If you're not certain, you better take him to the emergency room."

"*Thanks a lot.*"

Sarah hurled the phone against the wall.

She exploded through the front door and saw Daniel on the sidewalk looking up at her.

He retreated a step.

She said through clenched teeth, "Don't you run from me."

His bottom lip quivered.

"Daniel Thomas Slover, you come right up these steps so I can talk to you."

Daniel didn't move.

"*Now.*"

Reluctantly, he approached. The old guilt surged through her at the way he flinched as she reached out to draw him closer. She never hit him, but a couple times—okay, a *few* times—she'd shaken him by the shoulders. If he'd only *listen*.

Speaking directly into his wet, red face, she said, "Tell me how much you drank."

He wouldn't meet her stare.

"Look at me, Daniel."

He did, but only for an instant.

"How much did you drink?"

"Nothing," he said, only it came out *nutting*.

"Look me in the eyes."

He did.

"Are you lying to me?"

"It wouldn't come out," he said. "I couldn't get the blue water out."

"Oh Christ," she said and squeezed him to her. God, she thought. She loved him so much, but why did being a mom have to be so *hard*?

"Why did you put me in the sink?" he said, sobbing harder. She breathed in the scent of his hair, which had gotten oily. She hadn't given him a bath in how many days? Could it be four now?

She brushed away the thought, told herself to focus on the issue at hand. "Because you did a bad thing," she said. "You should never, ever get in that closet."

She felt his little body tense.

Sarah took a breath. "Do you know why?"

"Because of the monsters?" The plea in his voice tore at her, but her heart was still hammering.

"That's right."

"Which monster is it?"

She considered a moment. "The Closet Monster. He's the worst of all."

His brown eyes filled with dread. He seemed to shrink from the house.

"It's okay," she said. "We'll keep the door shut so he can't get out."

"But what if he does?"

She stroked his hair.

"He won't get out, Daniel. And if he did, he'd go for me first." She smiled. "I'm bigger, right?"

They went to the store that afternoon and bought new child locks and doorknob covers.

«««—»»»

That night Eric tried to kill her.

He showed up just before midnight, a fifth of Jim Beam in his hand. He didn't have money for child support, but he always had whiskey. He'd awakened her from the bar, the sound of some woman giggling into the phone like she was right there next to him.

"Don't call me again," she said. And hung up.

His Harley rumbled up the road soon after, as she knew it would. She met him in the yard.

"You've got five seconds," she said. "Then I call the cops."

He grinned at the cell phone in her hand. "You won't call shit."

He brought the whiskey bottle to his lips. Sarah dialed 911.

Before she hit Call, he smacked the phone out of her hand. It sailed through the darkness and disappeared into the immense Yew bush beside the porch.

Her hand felt as if it had been scalded. She stared at him in shock. Eric smirked, proud of himself.

Without thinking, Sarah slapped him hard across the bridge of the nose. He staggered back, the whiskey bottle shattering on the sidewalk. They both stared at it in stunned silence. He fingered the cut on his nose and inspected the blood on his fingertips. He glowered at her, teeth bared.

With a cry she stumbled toward the porch, but he reached the front door first. She spun, meaning to evade him, but he grasped her around the waist and heaved her off the porch. Though the grass was soft where she landed, she didn't land well. When she got up and sprinted for the backdoor, her right ankle wouldn't work. Limping, she heard Eric leap off the porch and hustle after her. She didn't get far before he hauled her down from behind. She writhed his his grip, elbowed him in the throat, but he flipped her onto her back and belted her across the face. A billion white stars filled her vision. He grasped a handful of her long hair and dragged her toward the forest bordering the yard. Sarah howled, the roots of her hair ripping like yanked weeds. She did her best to gain traction, to move with Eric so he wouldn't tear her scalp off, but his steps were so rapid she could only hold onto his hand and blunder along.

Sarah threw a terrified glance at the approaching woods.

Never had she felt so isolated, so alone. She loved the privacy of living on the outside of town, and until now, she'd believed the seclusion would somehow protect them from harm.

But their nearest neighbor was a quarter mile away. If she screamed for help it would only wake her son. Then he'd be in as much danger as she was.

The woods were upon them. Three feet away was the drop-off that led to a nasty deadfall of branches, the place where Sarah discarded her yard waste.

Desperately, Sarah sank her nails into Eric's hand. He seized her by the throat, lifted her in the air. She battered his arms, but it had no effect. He pivoted and hurled her toward the deadfall. She pinwheeled her arms as she fell backward through space. Sarah opened her mouth to scream, but she hit the snarl of branches and the air was driven out of her. Pain seared her lower back. Something had savaged the nape of her neck.

The rest of her body was numb.

After a time, Sarah opened her eyes. The sky above her was a black, moonless pool. No sound broke the stillness of the woods. She strained to sit up, but her legs were higher than her shoulders, and she hadn't the strength to move. She expected to hear Eric gloating or perhaps even climbing down the decline to finish her off, but if he was still there he was keeping it a secret.

After several moments had passed, Sarah rolled over and saw that safe ground was only a few feet behind her. Carefully, she crawled over the jagged branches and lowered to the earth. She kept expecting to see Eric's leering face appear over the rim of the drop-off, but each time she looked up she saw only the inky sky. As she clawed her way upward she became aware of an icy pounding in her right thigh, a dull throb in her chest. She made it to the edge of the yard and collapsed on her back. Eric was nowhere in sight.

She was safe.

Sarah gasped and sat upright.

Daniel.

Despite the pain in her ankle, Sarah reached the house in seconds. She scrambled down the hall and sucked in breath when she beheld Daniel's door open. She burst through the door and saw him sitting up in bed. She wrapped him up and asked him what was wrong.

"I saw him," Daniel said.

She squeezed her son, thankful he couldn't see her face.

"Saw who, Honey?"

"The Throwing Monster," Daniel wailed. "He smelled bad, Mommy. He breathed on me. He *laughed* at me."

She couldn't speak.

"He was in my room, Mommy! You were right, he's gonna get me!"

She rocked her son and mentally vowed to call the police.

«« — »»

She called Tom instead.

It was late, but Tom was a light sleeper. As it rang, she gripped the phone tighter and willed her hand to cease trembling. She sat alone in the kitchen, in the dark. *Please Tom,* she urged. *Please pick up.*

He answered, his voice open and friendly as always.

"Hey, Tom. It's Sarah."

A pregnant silence. She could almost feel the rage baking out of the phone.

"It's one in the morning," he said.

"I know. Sorry for waking you up."

Another lengthy silence, Tom waiting for her to state her business.

"Is your mom doing alright?" she asked and immediately regretted it. The woman had been closer to Sarah than her own mother before the bombshell dropped. She hadn't seen Tom's mother since.

"She misses Daniel," he said.

She swallowed. Jesus, her wounds had begun to ache. "How are things at the plant?"

"What can I do for you, Sarah?" he asked, and though she knew she deserved his iciness, his tone still made her wince.

"I don't know," she said. She bit her lip. "I really don't think there's much you can do to help."

Tom's voice went tight. "Nothing's wrong with Daniel is it?"

His concern for her son was unbearable. He'd been the perfect father before he discovered he wasn't a father. At least not by blood. Sarah closed her eyes. Why had she been so awful to him?

"He's okay," she said, her voice suddenly thick. "He misses you though."

No response.

"I miss you, too," she added.

He was quiet a long time before saying, "I think about Daniel a lot. I love that kid."

She could have killed herself at the way Tom's voice broke.

"Daniel really misses you," she said. "Maybe you can take him out for ice cream soon."

"Maybe," he said. A shuddering sigh. "I really have to get some sleep. I'm due at the plant by six."

"Please don't go."

"Sarah—"

She shut her eyes. "It's Eric. He was here last night."

Tom's voice hardened. "Did he hurt Daniel?"

She considered lying. It would get him here in a heartbeat.

Sarah exhaled. "No," she said. "He didn't hurt Daniel."

Tom was quiet a moment. Then he said, "I've got to go."

He hung up.

Sarah set the phone on the table and pushed to her feet. Her robe hung open, and though the cool night air chilled her naked body, she didn't have the strength to cover up.

She paused between the basement and the pantry.

Both doors were open.

Sarah squinted into the gloom and saw that, yes, both white doorknob covers were still in place, the ones that were supposed to be childproof.

Had Daniel figured out a way to open the doors anyway?

Angry at the way her hands shook, she reached out and shut first the closet door, then the basement door. There. She probably forgot to close them earlier, though she hadn't been in the basement for days. Lord, but she hated going down there. Yeah, she was behind on the laundry, but wearing dirty clothes was better than spending five minutes in that tomb with only the one window, too small to climb through and scarcely big enough to let in any light. Yes, being in the basement was very much like being in a tomb. The stench was getting worse, too. Even with the door closed the scent of rot was inescapable. She was sure now there was something dead down there.

Sarah cinched her robe against the chill. She'd ask Daniel about the doors when he awoke.

«««—»»»

Her son said very little throughout the day. He didn't cause her any problems, but he didn't smile or laugh the way he normally did either. When she asked him what was wrong, he said *nutting*, but deep down she knew what he was thinking about. A dark figure standing in the doorway of his room. Maybe even looming over his bed.

Had Eric touched her son? Threatened him?

Sarah stood at the kitchen sink and turned on the water just to hear something other than silence. Jesus, what a difference being single made. When she and Tom moved out here, when Daniel was just an infant, Sarah only saw the positives. More solitude, no barking dogs left out all night by irresponsible neighbors. The beauty. Some of her best memories were of evening walks with Tom and Daniel down Country Road 450, the asphalt under the stroller cracking a little but smooth enough. They used to walk after dinner, when Daniel was the crankiest, and the country air, redolent with lilacs, pine needles, and the faintest tinge of cow manure from a farm miles away, never failed to mollify her son's cries.

But now she was alone. Well, nearly alone. When she reflected on it, she realized that in many ways being out here with a small child was worse than being all by herself. Not only was there fear for her own safety, there was Daniel to think about.

Sarah shut off the water, leaned over the sink. No twenty-five year-old should have so much responsibility. If only Tom were still here. If only she hadn't given in to Eric, mortgaged a good life and security for a few fleeting moments of passion.

Who was she kidding?

Eric was Daniel's father. He was as inextricably linked with her and Daniel as Tom was. In many ways, moreso. And last night he had almost killed her.

And she stood here and did nothing.

Take control, she told herself. *Right now.*

She was preparing to call the sheriff's office when Daniel screamed.

For a moment she was paralyzed with confusion. It was nearing sunset and Daniel never left the house after supper, but the scream had come from outside. She'd been sure Daniel was playing quietly in the living room, but apparently he'd gone out the front door and made his way around to the back yard.

Mother of the Year, she thought. *Christ. It's a wonder the kid's still alive.*

Sarah burst through the backdoor and scanned the yard for her son.

Movement near the woods caught her eye. Peering through the gloom she could just make out a red shirt, a pair of khaki shorts. She approached and saw him standing close to the drop-off. He was biting a fingernail. Behind him the cicadas were droning out their idiots' chorus.

She did her best to keep her tone level. "What are you doing out here?"

When he didn't answer, she said, "You know you're not allowed out after supper."

"I saw him."

A whisper of fear on the nape of her neck.

"Saw who?"

"The Throwing Monster," he said. "The one from my room."

"Daniel…"

"I *saw* him," he said. "He was looking through the window."

The buzzing of the cicadas seemed to grow louder.

Sarah's heart began to thud. "What window?"

"The window over the TV," Daniel said.

"Honey, I've got to tell you something about the monsters."

She peered into Daniel's eyes, ready to tell him everything, to confess how terrible she'd been, how she wasn't the mother he deserved, but that she really did love him. More than anything—

Sarah paused, a question burning through her guilt. "When did you see him, Daniel? When did you see the Throwing Monster?"

"Just now," he said. "That's why I came out here."

She lifted him and hugged him tight. Carrying him away from the woods, she said, "Don't say a word, honey. We're going inside."

They hurried toward the house, and though she could sense the question in Daniel's tense body, he didn't try to squirm out of her arms. She remained watchful as they climbed the back porch steps, searching the left corner of the house, the tall evergreen bushes, for movement. If Eric was still around, he'd be lurking there. Clutching Daniel tight, she drew open the screen door with her free hand.

Movement against her ankles made her cry out and nearly topple off the back porch with Daniel in her arms.

Just the cat.

H.P. had burst through the opening door as if attempting to outrun some carnivorous beast. The thought caused the lump of dread in her belly to expand. Heart hammering, Sarah stepped through the doorway, and eased the door shut behind them. Its pneumatic wheeze and metallic click made her wince, and knowing Eric might have heard the commotion back here too, she swung closed the heavy wooden backdoor, twisted the lock. Still holding her son despite the growing numbness in her shoulder, she snatched the cell phone from the table and crossed to the front door. She locked it and carried Daniel down the hall to his room.

She set him on the floor, and got on her knees before him. "I need you to hide, Daniel."

"From the monster?"

"He's just a man, honey, but he's not a good man like Tom." She cupped his chin. "Mommy needs you to hide under the bed."

"Mommy, I—"

"Right now."

"Are you hiding with me?"

The plea in his voice made her eyes well up. "I can't, baby. I have to call the police."

"Mommy—"

"*Now, honey*," she said and led him over to the bed. "Lay down on your back."

"But the monster—"

"*There's no monster, Daniel. I promise you.*"

She got him under the bed and stood erect. Straining to hear Eric's footfalls, his breathing, she crept out of Daniel's room and made her way down the hall. She dialed 911 and glanced at the front door. Still locked. Waiting for someone to pick up, she stared at the window above the television, the one Eric must have been peeping through when he scared the hell out of Daniel. Poor kid. Of all the fathers in the world he could have had—

"What's your emergency?" an older woman's voice asked.

Sarah jumped. Then, a hand on her chest, she willed herself to remain calm, to choose her words carefully. "Someone is trying to break into my house. He's trying to kill us."

The woman asked questions and Sarah gave answers. She told the woman the name, age, and description of the perpetrator, the urgency of the situation. The woman told her someone would be right out, and to lock her and her son in a safe place. Sarah said she would.

She hung up, acid boiling in the pit of her throat. She turned, meaning to find some weapon, something to protect herself, and discovered that the pantry and basement doors were ajar. Though panic threatened to overtake her, Sarah kept her head, marched over to the doors. So Daniel had figured out how to beat the child locks. So what? She pushed shut the closet door and froze, breath clotting in her throat.

The kitchen window was open. Its ivory curtain fluttered in the early evening breeze.

Eric was already inside.

Sarah opened the pantry door and selected the largest knife she owned. A chopping knife, thick and sharp. At the cold feel of its handle, a wave of lightheadedness rolled through her. *Breathe*, she told herself. *Breathe*. Protect Daniel. You can make up for an awful lot of mistakes if you can do that.

She stood in the shadow of the closet door and considered.

Eric must have come in while she and Daniel were in the bedroom. He couldn't have snuck past her as she called 911.

But he still might be in the kitchen. Holding the knife before her with both hands, she moved along the half-wall and readied herself for an attack. If Eric was there, on the other side of the counter, he'd leap out at her with all his fury. She had to be ready to meet him.

Sarah stepped around the half-wall.

Nothing.

Which meant Eric could only be in two places. She drew in a shallow breath, faintly hopeful that the first possibility was true, that Eric had, upon hearing her call to 911, escaped the way he had come, had slipped out through the kitchen window. She wanted to believe the danger had passed.

But she knew it hadn't.

Eric could only be in the basement.

171

The police would be several minutes in coming. Unless a cruiser happened to be patrolling this part of the boonies when her call came, it would take a policeman ten minutes to arrive. Maybe longer.

She could go to Daniel now, gather him in her arms and make a run for the car, but if Eric really was in the basement, he'd emerge and run them down before they got halfway across the yard.

Sarah compressed her lips.

It was up to her.

She made her way through the kitchen and stepped through the basement doorway. The lights were off down there, but that didn't mean anything. Eric preferred the dark.

Sure at any moment a hand would dart between the stair slats, batten onto one of her ankles, Sarah descended into the tomb. The stench had grown worse than ever, a fulsome, repellant cloud that thinned her breathing, nauseated her to the point of dizziness. The handle of the chopping knife was slick in her palms. She kept the tip tilted down just in case she tripped and skewered herself. The thought brought on an insane urge to laugh. Here she was, facing death, and she was on teetering on the verge of laughter. Maybe she really was going insane. Maybe—

The sound of laughter, real laughter, made her freeze.

She whimpered aloud. Oh, Christ, what the hell was it? If it was Eric down there, what was wrong with his voice? The laughter was meaty, wet. A throaty gurgle, so different than his normal voice. Was he hopelessly drunk, too impaired to realize what his breaking in here had forced her into doing? Sarah supposed she could scamper up the stairs, throw shut the door, somehow bar it and hold on for dear life until the police arrived, but it had still only been how long? Two, three minutes since she called 911?

She only had one step to go before she reached the landing. Then it would be three more steps to the basement floor and her confrontation with Eric.

The laughter swelled, drifted up the steps to her, filled the basement with its ghastly echoes.

Goddamn you, Eric. Goddamn you for scaring me this way. For wrecking my life, for giving my son nightmares. You son of a bitch.

Sarah rounded the corner and trod the final few steps to the basement floor. She strained to penetrate the darkness, but her eyes weren't fully adjusted yet. There was a pullstring bulb a few feet away, above the washing machine. She'd believed she'd be safer in the dark, where her familiarity with the layout of the basement would work to her advantage. But now she longed to see the look on Eric's face just before she plunged the chopping knife into his throat. She sidled over to the pullstring, reached out.

Grinning savagely, Sarah yanked the string.

And screamed.

In the corner of the basement, where the light from the dim yellow bulb hardly reached, Eric's remains lay in pool of blood. His ribs had been spread apart and left jutting in all directions. She saw a glistening rope of intestines strung out like something run over on the highway and a trail of blood that disappeared behind the furnace. It was from that direction Sarah heard the smacking sounds, the hungry laughter.

From above she heard someone hammering on the door, a man's voice calling out Daniel's name. It was Tom, she realized, Tom who'd gotten here before the police. He'd probably been worried sick since last night's call and had driven over to check on them.

Maybe Tom would save her, maybe he'd forget what she'd—

A bestial roar shook the basement.

Sarah clapped a hand over her mouth, too horrified by the sound to move. Then the wall beyond the furnace darkened, shifted. The shadows gathered there and swam along the wall toward her, and as she turned and watched the hulking black shadows pass behind the water heater, the boxes of Daniel's infant clothes, she realized the thing wasn't shapeless at all, was a larger version of Eric. It had his muscular body, his strong jaw.

But when it rounded the corner and scuttled along the wall, defying gravity and chortling maniacally, she discovered it was more than Eric's features that comprised the creature's face.

It had Sarah's eyes. And not only were the blue eyes hers, but the straight white teeth gleaming out of that bloody black face looked like hers as well.

Except for the fangs.

Sarah shrieked as it bounded toward her. A suffocating, sickly sweet odor enveloped her as the creature lunged.

From above she heard the front door bang open, both Tom's and the policeman's voices calling out their names, and in the moment before impact she heard Daniel's footsteps scamper down the hallway toward the front door. Then the creature was on her, ripping her apart, its pulpy body slamming her to the musty concrete floor and pinning her like a lover. She opened her mouth to scream, but its mouth closed over hers, its fangs shredding her cheeks, chewing, slurping.

Sarah plunged the knife deep into the creature's side, but its laughter merely grew louder. The edges of her vision blurred, the pain exquisite as the claws plunged into her torso, punctured her flesh. Blood sprayed around the creature's razor talons. Sarah bucked beneath it, but it wormed its fingers deeper inside her and with a sudden wrenching motion, pried open her ribs. The life gushed out of her as the creature buried its face in her organs and fed. The last thing she glimpsed before the world went black was the sight of Daniel's little legs passing the basement window, side by side with Tom's legs. Moving away from the house and leaving the monsters behind.

THE FIERCE STABBING AND SUBSEQUENT POST-DEATH VENGEANCE OF SCOOTER BROWN

JEFF STRAND

"So, Mr. Galen, how many times did you stab Mr. Brown?" "I don't recall."

"Really? Surely you'd recall such a thing."

"It's not like I was counting every single stab."

"Of course not, of course not, but I think you can at least give me a ballpark figure."

"I dunno. Twenty?"

"Try forty-three."

"Forty-three? Really?"

"Yes, Mr. Galen. You stabbed the victim forty-three times."

"Wow. That's a lot of times to stab a person."

"It certainly is. So would you mind explaining to me why you felt it was necessary to stab him that many times?"

"Well, I was trying to kill him."

"That much is obvious, Mr. Galen."

"I thought it was obvious, too, but you're the one who asked. I wouldn't have asked, myself. Seems like common sense."

"My question was not about whether you wished for Mr. Brown to live or die. My question was about quantity. If you stab a man once, twice, or perhaps even three times, then your motive may have been murder. But when you stab him forty-three times, one must surmise that there's a deeper issue."

"No, I just wanted to make sure he was dead."

"Where did your second stab occur, Mr. Galen?"

"In the van."

"Do not try to turn this into a madcap comedy routine, Mr. Galen. You know perfectly well that I was asking about which part of his body received that particular stab wound."

"Oh. I forget."

"Do you, Mr. Galen? Do you?"

"His neck?"

"His *throat*. You plunged the knife directly into his throat."

"Ah, yeah, that's right. Got him right in the Adam's apple."

"Are you proud of that?"

"No, sir."

"So tell me, Mr. Galen, how many people do you think can survive having the eight-inch serrated blade of a hunting knife slam into their throat?"

"I'd think that somebody has, at some point. It's inevitable."

"Perhaps so, perhaps so. But do you agree that delivering another forty-one stabbings after that could be considered excessive?"

"They weren't all in his neck."

"No, they weren't."

"I know at least one got his finger. You aren't going to die from that."

"Of the forty-three stab wounds that were received by Mr. Scooter Brown, exactly two of them were on his fingers. What do you think about that?"

"He should have held up his hands more to defend himself."

"Are you taking this seriously, Mr. Galen?"

"Very much, sir."

"It doesn't sound like you are."

"I'm just saying that if somebody is stabbing you repeatedly with a hunting knife, that you should maybe put your hands up a bit more. That's all."

"Are you suggesting that Mr. Brown had suicidal tendencies?"

"No, not necessarily. All I'm saying is that if *I* were being stabbed, I'd make more of an effort to block the knife. That's all I'm saying."

"Is it possible, Mr. Galen, that once the blade entered his throat, that his mental faculties may have been compromised, making it difficult for him to determine the proper method of defending himself?"

"Yes, that's possible."

"Because I consider myself well above average in the art of self-defense, and yet if I am truly honest with myself, I have to admit that arterial spurting would create difficulty for me in making the best judgment calls."

"I already agreed that it was possible! You don't have to keep bitching about it!"

"Why are you being antagonistic, Mr. Galen?"

"I'm not."

"Do you mean to say that you used the b-word in a non-antagonistic manner?"

"I'm just trying to explain what happened, and you keep judging me!"

"Give me an example of where I judged you."

"You accused me of saying he was suicidal just because I said that I'd put up my hands more if I were being stabbed."

"You're right. I did. And for that I apologize."

"Thank you."

"Where were we before that?"

"I forget."

"I remember now. You stabbed him forty-three times, but, as we've discussed, even somebody with no formal training in medicine and/or anatomy would know that the second stab was going to be fatal to Mr. Brown. And yet you continued to stab him over and over and over. Why?"

"I guess I have a bit of a rage problem."

"A bit?"

"Yes, a bit."

"Come now, Mr. Galen, certainly we can both agree that such a high quantity of stab wounds counts as more than 'a bit' of a rage problem?"

"Why do you keep bringing that up? Aren't one stab wound and forty-three stab wounds the same amount of rage? Let it drop, for God's sake."

"No, I don't believe I will. Because you know where I'm headed with this, don't you?"

"Nope."

"I think you do."

"I really don't."

"How much time elapsed between the first stab and the final stab?"

"I don't remember."

"Interesting."

"I didn't look at the clock."

"How convenient."

"Do you always look at the clock before you start doing something and when you finish doing something? How long did it take you to shop for that pair of pants?"

"Stop trying to change the subject. My pants are irrelevant and you know it."

"I'm just saying."

"What are you just saying?"

"That you don't know the time of every single thing you do in every single day."

"Fair enough. I suppose I will accept your challenge, Mr. Galen. It took me approximately fifteen minutes to shop for this pair of pants, if you count the time spent in the fitting room and the time spent in the checkout line. During that time I believe I also purchased two or three shirts. So, fifteen minutes is my answer. What's yours?"

"I'm not sure."

"Really?"

"I guess it might have been about fifteen minutes."

"Are you seriously trying to convince me that you believe it was fifteen minutes?"

"About that."

"Please do not lie to me, Mr. Galen."

"It might have been longer."

"How about two hours and thirty-six minutes?"

"Was it that long?"

"It was indeed."

"Wow."

"And how long did it take him to die?"

"Fifteen minutes?"

"Two minutes, Mr. Galen."

"Oh."

"Two short minutes for Mr. Brown to bleed out. And yet you continued to stab his corpse for quite some time after that. Do you believe that's indicative of a healthy psyche?"

"I suppose not."

"Is it not, in fact, appropriate to say that you are a sick and deranged human being?"

"It depends on your definition of 'sick.'"

"Are you making light of the situation?"

"No, sir."

"Did you truly believe that I was using the definition of 'sick' used by today's youth, the one where it means 'awesome' or 'really cool?'"

"Maybe."

"Mr. Galen…"

"Okay, no, I didn't truly believe that."

"There is nothing 'awesome' or 'really cool' or 'groovy' about your recent behavior. It was, in fact, quite disgusting. It was not admirable, nor noble, nor even particularly clever. It did not make you seem macho. If you'd killed him with your bare hands, then perhaps I'd admire it—not from a moral standpoint, of course, but purely in terms of skill. But what you did made you seem like nothing more than a drooling psychopath."

"I didn't drool."

"Still lying, Mr. Galen?"

"I only drooled a little."

"You wiped your mouth on seven different occasions."

"That doesn't mean I was drooling!"

"You also made slurping noises."

"Some blood got in my mouth!"

"One does not slurp when blood from one's victim sprays into one's mouth. One slurps when the drool of excitement spews from their salivary glands. You repulse me, Mr. Galen. You repulse me to the very core of my being. In fact, I wish that you were not in my office, because your presence causes my skin to feel like it's covered with dirt and insects."

"Should I leave?"

"No, you're already here. We might as well get this over with."

"Are you sure? You seem irritable."

"No, no, it's all right. The ability to gaze into people's memories does make me cranky, but I'll be fine. So you want me to bring Mr. Brown back to life?"

"Yes, sir."

"Why?"

"To apologize."

"Is that so?"

"Yes."

"Are you sure?"

"Yes."

"You won't stab him some more?"

"No, sir. I'm done with that. It was wrong to do it in the first place, and I've learned from my mistake."

"I'd like to believe you, Mr. Galen. I really would. But I find it rather disturbing that you didn't even know Mr. Brown before you went on your stabbing spree."

"I understand your concern."

"If he had wronged you in some way, even a minor way, like cutting you off in traffic, I might think to myself, 'Well, that was a disproportionately violent reaction, but at least I can pinpoint the motive.' But when you lure a gentleman into your van under the guise of needing medical assistance for a non-existent wife who is having a heart attack, and then proceed to stab him to death, and then continue to stab him for more than two hours after he is dead, I am forced to conclude that you are mentally ill."

"That's fair."

"I'm not trying to be rude. I simply believe, based on the information I have retrieved both from our conversation and directly from your brain, that you mean this man further harm."

"No, I just want to apologize."

"I don't believe you."

"Can't you read my mind?"

"Yes, but my psychic abilities are more about memories. Specific images. Not emotions. I know, for example, that you vigorously masturbated on Tuesday evening but not how you felt about it."

"Oh. Uh, sorry about the image."

"No need to apologize. I've seen worse. Now, I do have the ability to probe deeper with my abilities, to know if you are telling the truth, but it requires that I caress your eyeballs."

"Caress my eyeballs?"

"Yes."

"That sounds awful."

"It is."

"Okay, do it. Go ahead."

"Are you sure?"

"Yes."

"Very well, then. Keep them open wide."

"*Ow!*"

"You knew that it would hurt, right? That couldn't have been a surprise."

"I didn't know it would hurt *that* much!"

"Well, now you do. Hmmm. Okay, I now have to apologize for expressing doubts about your intentions, because I can see that you truly do wish to tell Mr. Brown that you're sorry. For some bizarre, demented, unfathomable reason, his acceptance of your apology is important to you. Very, very odd."

"I told you!"

"Don't act like my suspicion wasn't justified, Mr. Galen. You are a savage beast."

"But you can bring him back to life?"

"Yes."

"When?"

"He's already alive again. I don't care to waste time."

"Scooter...?"

"*You!*"

"I just want to say I'm sorry."

"*Fuck you!*"

"And he's dead again. Sorry. My power to reanimate the dead is not long-lasting."

"He...he...he rejected my apology!"

"Yes, he certainly did. Nothing wishy-washy about his response."

"But...I paid five thousand dollars so he could accept my apology!"

"You might have mentioned the expenditure while he was still alive. Personally, I would have opened with that, but since I've never stabbed a man to death, I can't honestly say that I know how I'd behave."

"That selfish bastard!"

"He was rude, but you can understand his point of view, right?"

"He was supposed to ease my conscience! Now I'm going to have sleepless nights for the rest of my life! The scorpions that live under my skin will never stop their incessant stinging! I can feel them now! Their pincers slice through my veins! I can see the blood in his eyes! So much blood! So much blood!"

"Is our business here finished, Mr. Galen?"

"So much blood!"

"Please close the door on your way out. Thank you very much."

THE HOUSE IN CYRUS HOLLER:
A WILL CASTLETON ADVENTURE

DAVID BAIN

With thanks to Mike Arnzen
for the instigation...

1. Incident on a Country Road

"Really, Will? Do we have to?"

Will scrolled through the old time radio show mp3s on his phone. "Come on, Sam. Stormy night like this, the atmosphere's perfect. How about *The Phantom Hitchhiker?* Or here's one you'll like. *The House in Cypress Canyon.* A true classic—a haunted house werewolf story, fun twist ending. Utterly crazy. Or this other one, *Three Skeleton Key*, about bad guys trapped in a lighthouse full of rats. Riveting. You'd love it. Or, no, *On a Country Road.* Just where we are now. Stars Cary Grant. Timeless. An escaped killer, a couple stranded in the boonies. You *like* Cary Grant."

Samantha sighed, gripped the steering wheel of Will's Jeep harder as she rounded a mountain curve. "I like his *movies*, yes, but this is stupid."

183

"Fine," Will said. "What would you *rather* listen to instead? You can get maybe three stations out here in the hills, and they all seem to play country older than these radio shows. Wait, here's one. *End of the Road.* Car salesman takes this dangerous dame for a test drive. It's killer, both literally and figuratively. You *know* you love this murder stuff."

He hit play.

"You know what's stupid, Will? It's not your damned hundred-year-old spooky radio stories."

"They're not quite a century old yet—mid-1930s to late 1950s, most of them."

She ignored him. "What's stupid is your insistence on no fast food, no chain hotels, no for God's sakes *four-lane roads* this trip. This *real America* crap. What's stupid is the fact that *I'm* the one driving through this storm on Kentucky's backwoods mountainside version of Lombard Street! *Without railings,* I might add."

"So pull over and I'll drive."

"Pull over *where?* On the berm? Because I don't *see* any berm, Will."

Will looked at the side of the road, dim in the downpour. She was right.

On the radio, which was wired into Will's phone via the electric outlet, an announcer was promising that this show was "well calculated to keep you in … *suspense!*"

"Okay, just stop the Jeep. I'll drive."

"Stop in the middle of the road?"

The old timey radio announcer went into a spiel for Roma Wine—"That's R-O-M-A!"

"There's been no one behind us for—"

At least one of the front tires exploded and Samantha fought the wheel.

Will saw a tall figure in the road, but wasn't sure Samantha had— in a flash, imprinted on Will's brain before the darkness: a hulk of a man, sharp, vile weapon in one hand—a huge Bowie knife, maybe— other fist raised high as if in victory.

The Jeep went up on two wheels, a tumble down the Appalachian hillside already inevitable.

And everything came to a halt.

184

Their GPS, a pen, Will's Glock, Samantha's Diet Coke, a cupful of change, various other vehicle detritus stopped mid-scatter.

Silence.

A roll of thunder above.

Will realized his head had knocked hard against the passenger-side window in Samantha's initial swerve. Blood trickled down the right side of his face. He had to swipe it out of his eye. He didn't *think* he had a concussion, felt some pain but nothing extraordinary. Even superficial head wounds, he knew, bled like bastards. The mere presence of blood was hardly the way to gauge an injury.

Wait. *No sound.*

But Samantha was mid-scream, in the middle of an attempt to wrench the wheel left, away from the imminent spill down the verdant countryside mountain.

Outside, the thick forest trees and shrubby overgrowth posed mid-sway in the headlights.

Raindrops floated immobilized in the humid air.

Time had stopped.

Will registered this fact for about a second before something grabbed the collar of his jacket and hauled him *through* the door of the Jeep.

And he understood in an instant at least part of what was going on.

The Ghost World.

The first few times he'd been pulled into this netherworld between the living and the dead he'd thought he was going crazy. Physics, gravity, cause and effect, logic itself. The rules weren't the same here in The Ghost World. In fact, they seemed to vary each time he was sucked into this realm. Sometimes they weren't even consistent during the same damn visit.

Will felt himself hurled headlong by a powerful hand. He tumbled ass over skull and skidded along the macadam, knocking his knees painfully against the pavement, his elbows scraping through the thin skin of his jacket, his cheek on the receiving end of a nasty case of gritty road rash before he finally slid to a stop and managed to lift his throbbing head.

Will's huge assailant, large as a bear and just as ugly—twisted nose, snarling, snaggle-toothed visage, matted locks which might as well have been fur clinging to both sides of his jutting jaw—advanced on him. With thunder shaking the mountain, it was almost as if the raging, wind-ravaged rural geography shook with each of the behemoth's steps—*thunder and yet no lightning? With the rain stopped midfall?*

No time to think about this.

Will scrambled to his feet.

The man did indeed wield a knife. It was huge, serrated. The handle looked strange, bones or spines that were supposed to represent claws sticking out on the hilt below the grip, all pointing the same general direction, almost like a comb. Will noted this as he barely dodged a swing that came inches from gutting him. He felt the weapon scatter hanging raindrops as it swept past his middle. The blade, gripped in his attacker's swinging fist, left a hole in the rain, an empty swath while the rest of the rain glittered bloodily in the red of the Jeep's brake lights.

Stepping backwards to avoid the giant's advance, Will slipped on the slick pavement.

The killer leapt at him.

Will scrabbled backwards, doing an awkward crabwalk, but Big and Ugly caught his legs, wrapping his arms about them and slicing the back of Will's right calf in the process. The wound instantly burned like a thin strip of fire.

Will tried to kick out from the man's grasp, but the grip was strong as a bear's.

The man released one arm and raised the knife.

Will screamed despite himself—there was no doubt this butcher was aiming for Will's crotch.

Straining, contorting into a half-assed sitting position—but also moving more swiftly than he'd thought possible—Will caught the man's wrist in his hand for a split second. It was just enough to deflect the swing into the pavement and allow Will an instant to get a leg free.

Or, at least free enough for a lurchy, awkward, sidekick at his attacker's knife hand.

A kick that was totally ineffective.

The monstrous ghost—for surely this was a ghost despite its physicality here in The Ghost World—recovered enough to slice the blade's edge along the outside hind quarter of Will's right thigh.

186

He cried out in agony, but then, as the monster grinned at the small victory, Will simply grabbed the fur above the man-beast's face and punched the monster as hard as he could, squashing his large, slightly bulbous nose.

The too-solid specter roared, instinctively brought a hand to his nose.

Will used the moment to scramble free and stagger to his feet.

So did the freak, free hand still on his schnoz.

Pain raged in both Will's leg wounds.

He'd never had to kill a ghost. How to do this? What were the rules? Were there even any? Why had this ghost pulled him here? How?

Too many questions, no time. The killer was already up and plowing toward him, linebacker-style, blood pumping out his broken nose, oversized knife pumping in his ready fist.

But this, an attacker running toward him, was home territory for Will. A knife attack at close quarters is one of the most dangerous situations to be in, whatever your training, but his martial arts, his time as a bodyguard found him at least marginally prepared.

First rule: get out of the line of attack.

Second rule: Strike, and keep striking, remaining out of that line of attack.

Will easily sidestepped Ol' Big and Ugly.

One hand deflected the knife hand at the wrist.

The other jabbed Big and Ugly in the face, part of Will's fist crunching into the giant's already damaged nose.

Big and Ugly keened, a sound between a grunt, a growl and a whine.

Will kept jabbing.

Big and Ugly tried ineffectually to swing, went down—fell forward, crumpling at the knees due to the pain in his face—funny how that worked.

Will managed, despite the pain in the sliced spots in his legs, to add a roundhouse kick to Big and Ugly's rear as he fell, sending the gigantic man sprawling.

The knife glittered in a flash of lightning as it skittered across the black, slick macadam.

In his experience, you got rid of ghosts by helping them move on, through compassion, by solving their murder, by loving them into

187

The Light. Although he had been dealing with ghosts for years—had, in one case involving the ghost of a Native American foster child, actually gone to therapy with a ghost—he understood relatively nothing about their world or existence. He'd woken up "slightly psychic"—just psychic enough for it to cause a multitude of problems in his life—after a near-death experience of his own, except he'd experienced only the tunnel and the Light, the usual story most NDE survivors report. He had no specific psychic abilities—his visions, his encounters happened differently every goddamned time.

Will had a feeling Big and Ugly here was the sort of spirit who abjectly refused The Light. He doubted this abomination would've been a willing participant in any twelve-step program in life, much less post-death.

Will's training told him apprehension, capture, incarceration, the legal system—*life*, even if it eventually meant the death penalty—was always the first priority. But there was no apprehending a malevolent preternatural entity such as this. The creature—maybe it had indeed once been human, but Will doubted it had ever had human *empathy*—emanated pure evil. He, Will, was not an empath, receptive to emotions, as his sole psychic friend Mazie claimed some of their ilk were, but he sensed nonetheless that there was no good, no caring, no love in the specter splayed out on the pavement before him.

What had happened to this spirit, back in real life...?

The monster clambered to find all fours.

Will walked over to where the knife lay, picked it up.

The freak was on its knees, would find its footing within seconds.

Will walked over, straddled the monster, grabbed a handful of its hair, pulled its head back, put the knife to its throat.

He wouldn't have been able to bring himself to slit its windpipe back in the real world.

But this was The Ghost World. The rules were different here. This was half-life vs. hellfire.

Good vs. Evil. Simple as that. A gladiatorial arena. Kill or be killed.

And, he realized—already knew, in fact, from experience as a Marshal, from experience in the field of personal protection—that this sort of thing, kill or be killed, too much of it, was exactly what broke soldiers, what took fresh-faced boys and transmogrified them into angry men incapable of true inner peace.

You adapted, had to. Some men became stone killers. Some didn't.

But Will knew this much: The Ghost World was inner as well as outer—even if the scars faded, the wounds in his legs would never fully heal; he would remember this battle, brief as it was, with literally every step he would take from here on in.

And if he were to slit this beast's throat in cold, vengeful blood, it would be a scar far worse than those on his legs. He served justice, not whatever infernal masters claimed this demon.

Not knowing he was going to say it, Will said, "I've bested you. It's time for you to move on to your eternal reward, whatever that may be."

There was a miserable mewling sound deep in the giant's throat, a sound filled at once with reproach, dread and a sort of ineffectual rage. Will felt the giant's body grow suddenly warm, then fever-hot.

He stepped back, had to let go because of the heat, but kept the knife at the ready.

Flames started licking through the Goliath's clothes, and Will suddenly realized Mr. Ugly's very flesh was on fire *from the inside*. The mewling turned into a wailing cry of utter pain, despair and anguish, echoing across the mountain hills.

Then there was nothing but ashes which quickly melted into the rain-soaked pavement.

2. The Phantom Hiker

He had no time to wonder how he had attracted Big and Ugly's attention. Most likely just a fluke—a ghost who happened to be at just the right place at the right time.

Will tucked the knife into his belt, turned to run back to the Jeep—stopped.

He was being watched.

Here in the Ghost World, knowing he was being watched wasn't just a feeling. It was a fact.

This same someone, he now realized, had, in fact, watched the entire battle. It had been evident in the hairs on the back of his neck, but he'd been too preoccupied fighting for his life to notice.

There, on the other side of the road from the Jeep.

A woman.

A ghost.

She wasn't wearing a flowing, spectral gown—that was just the aura she gave off. She was, in fact, despite her transparent state, wearing khaki shorts and a dark, possibly red, flannel shirt. Hiking boots, thick socks. An abundance of hair, the style a bit retro—Rita Hayworth or maybe even Marilyn. She was beautiful.

She locked her gaze on his, serious, beckoned with a hand.

This wasn't an enemy. Will understood that simply from the earnestness in her eyes, the sober cast of her countenance.

"No," he said. He pointed to the Jeep. "Samantha, my girlfriend," he said. "I have to stop this accident."

The pretty hiker shook her head. Beckoned again.

"I have to do what I can. I can't leave her."

The spirit pointed to her wrist. There was no watch there, but Will got it. Time had stopped. Samantha, the Jeep, weren't going anywhere.

Will hesitated. "You want to show me something."

A well-duh question if ever there was one, Will understood the second after he said it, but the spirit nodded.

He glanced at the Jeep again, then at the ghost. She was already turning away from the road, heading into the thick underbrush.

Hating to leave Samantha, but resigned to the fact that he was perhaps here in the Ghost World for a purpose other than merely dispatching a demonic soul, Will followed.

The female hiker's ghost did not leave a trail in the stalled raindrops. Will did, however, the mystically hanging water gently imploding on his clothes as he jogged over to where the ghost had stood.

She hadn't disappeared into the woods. Rather, there was a scant trail through the forest. She walked, but also seemed to float. Foliage and darkness obscuring his view of her boots, Will couldn't see if her feet touched the ground, but he wouldn't have been surprised to find they didn't.

She looked over her shoulder as she walked. Will glanced over his shoulder to look at the mid-crash Jeep.

What if time were to start up again a minute from now?

The ghost stopped, turned toward him up there on the trail, her visage imploring him to come. She waved him toward her.

Will took a breath and followed.

Now, as he jogged to catch up, pain burning in his still-open but coagulating knife wounds, he realized this wasn't just a path, but a seldom-used driveway or road. It was overgrown, grass in the ruts even, but it was obvious a vehicle sometimes made its way through these overgrown twists and turns.

She moved on ahead, unhindered by darkness, rain or vegetation. It was all Will could do to keep up as the road wound on, sometimes rising, sometimes falling in the shadow-shrouded night.

Will's ribs ached from the fight earlier. His face and butt hurt from where the madman had tossed him around on the pavement. Normally this hike would have been nothing to him, but he found his breathing labored.

A rickety wooden sign was posted at the top of a particularly steep hill maybe three-quarters of a mile or more from the main road. This was apparently where the small road ended.

3. The House in Cyrus Holler

CYRUS HOLLER, the sign read in a dark paint that had run slightly before drying.

Beyond, seen through a sheen of suspended raindrops, was a weedy, unkempt lawn leading to a large, ramshackle cabin. There were tall, ragged crosses at random intervals across the grass, decorated with numerous animal skulls—Will recognized deer, cows, pigs, bears, rabbits, all manner of rodent from groundhog to squirrel to mouse, the latter dangling like Christmas ornaments from ratty ropes tied to the lengthwise beams of the crosses. Some of the crosses bore strange amalgams of different animal bones rearranged, perhaps grafted or, hell, who knew, maybe even superglued together to mimic the structure of a human body—for instance, the nearest had a bear skull at its head but the rib and hip and leg bones were unidentifiable to Will—they were certainly far too large to be human. He caught a glimpse of a pick-up that looked like it had maybe been drivable back during the Dust Bowl parked alongside the house. As for the building itself, the original central cabin, which looked fairly sturdily built, had been added to haphazardly. Awkwardly constructed wings and side rooms branched like mismatched body parts drunkenly attached to the wrong sockets on a Frankenstein monster. Will could imagine the entire structure coming to life, the central cabin rising on the branching side rooms as if these were spider legs, the door and boarded up windows forming a face which would chase you down, devouring your soul, which would then wander those strange, spindly halls forever.

The woman was standing only a few feet from him.

"What is this place?" he asked.

She only raised an arm, pointed to the house. She looked oddly mournful as she did this.

Ol' Big and Ugly had roared and grunted throughout their battle, but Will realized this ghost was utterly silent.

"Can't you speak?"

She lowered her hand, her gaze never leaving Will's.

She opened her mouth wide, making a large O.

She had perfect teeth.

But she had no tongue. It had been severed.

And now, as he watched, he saw scars rise on her face. Then fingers disappeared, and next an entire arm. Her torso beneath her flannel shirt began to lose its shape in awful ways.

"He tortured you, the guy I fought back there?"

Her point made, her wounds sunk back into her spectral body. She nodded, then pointed to the house again, this time emphatically.

"He lived there."

She looked at him like he was an idiot, then nodded slowly and pointed again.

"You want me to go in there with you?"

She nodded again, her look again suggesting he was a simpleton.

Then, without beckoning, she turned and started walking through the skull-bearing crosses toward the house.

She walked onto the porch—her feet did indeed seem to soundlessly touch the surface, though she left no impression in the water collected there. Will was dripping wet as he stepped out of the hanging rain.

She stopped at the closed wooden door, stared at it a moment.

Someone had painted KEEP OUT! on it in the same runny paint.

The hiker looked at this warning, then, to Will's surprise, gave it the finger.

Then she *stepped through* the door, leaving Will alone.

So now what?

Will stood staring at the door, reached out to see if the ancient, old-fashioned iron latch was locked.

And, of course, his hand passed right through it.

The hiker's ghostly hand emerged from the door, beckoned him to follow.

Will had never been a ghost in the Ghost World before.

He took a breath and walked through the door, his vision briefly going dark as he passed through the wood. He'd expected a physical sensation of some sort, but there was none.

The skulls outside hadn't prepared him for the interior of the cabin.

A bear skull, poised as if roaring—or perhaps screaming—sat on a small dais as the centerpiece on a long dining table. Other, smaller skulls, some most certainly human, topped with half-melted black candles, currently unlit, were arranged in a circle around the screaming skull. Gallon jars half full with a thick, perhaps amber, viscous-looking substance, sealed, sat in front of two huge chairs at either end of the table.

Animal skulls as bookends for what looked like a collection of ancient, moldering photo albums. A human skull that had been somehow grafted to the lid of a large ceramic urn standing in a corner. A skull of an unidentifiable mammal—some sort of fanged, taxidermic amalgam of bear and mountain lion?—on top of an antique stand-alone radio. A human skull on top of a monolithic old boxy television set with a gigantic curved screen. Spread out on an end table near a chair was a huge stack of magazines...no, comic books that seemed to be from the same retro era as the TV and radio. They were probably worth a mint.

Will saw openings to various hallways, shrouded in darkness, and wanted to know what was down these, but the woman stood pointing to the gleaming white skull on top of the TV.

"You...you want me to...turn on the TV?" Will said.

She rolled her eyes. Pointed to the skull, then to her face, then back at the skull.

"It's...you mean? *Holy God,*" Will said.

She nodded.

She walked to a glass-fronted wooden cabinet, pointed to that.

Will walked over, looked in. Tiny, dusty ceramic garden gnomes were frozen in place, capering, dancing, mugging behind toadstools. They looked to Will as if they too were victims of time's temporary stoppage, as if they would come to life the second time resumed. Interspersed among the dwarves were more skulls.

"Skulls and knickknacks," Will said. "Nice."

She pointed again, more dramatically, at the third shelf down.

"There's a little box there," Will said. "Mahogany, looks like."

She nodded. Will reached to open the cabinet, but his hand passed through the wood and glass.

She held up a finger, her sadness becoming stern. She looked like a grave schoolteacher, wanting her student to take note. She pointed repeatedly at the floor, at the center of the rug in the living room.

"Something under us?"

She nodded rapidly. She pointed to the box in the cabinet, to the floor, and repeated this cycle twice more for emphasis.

"A key in the box?" Will said. "A basement where he did these things to you?"

She nodded.

"Why are you showing me all this?"

She rolled her eyes again. She pointed back in the direction of the road.

"Yes, time to go. I understand. But what about *you?* Am I supposed to help you move on? Am I supposed to help you somehow?"

She shook her head furiously, her hair shaking around her head. She pointed toward the road again, looking angrily at him.

"I…" Will began. "You want me to just get back to the road."

She shook her head again. She obviously didn't care if he got back to the road just yet. She pointed to herself, then toward the road, repeated this emphatically.

"He took you from the road? He…he caused an accident? Took you here?"

She nodded, pointed toward the road again, pointed at him.

"He…caused *our* accident?"

She shook her head and walked over to the photo albums, pointed at them.

"He…?"

She pointed again at the albums.

"My God," Will said. *"Someone else who still lives here caused the accident! Is Samantha safe?"*

The ghost's expression became sad again. She hesitated, then slowly shook her head in the negative. She emphatically pointed once more at the photo albums, then at him, then at the photo albums, but Will bolted from the house, sprinting past the ragged crosses and through the wet forest, hurtling headlong into the night, ignoring the pain in his side and legs, ignoring the labor of his lungs.

When he got back to the road, his Jeep was still balanced in mid-overturn, Samantha still frozen in futile battle with the steering wheel, the same scream, the same utter panic still filling her face.

The hiker was already standing there, directly in front of the Jeep, having somehow arrived before him despite his speed. If the Jeep were still in motion, it would've mowed her down.

"But…," Will said.

The ghost's hands had been solemnly clasped in front of her. Now she pointed at the Jeep.

Will walked over to the vehicle. He tried to pull it back to the ground, but his hands passed through the metal. He tried to push it, tried to move it in any way, but he remained non-corporeal.

Desperate, he turned once more to the hiker's ghost.

She remained solemn, sad. She pointed at his seat in the Jeep.

"What?" Will said.

She didn't move, just stood there pointing.

"No," Will said. "No, there has to be something I can do."

She was a statue, pointing at the passenger seat.

"I can't just get back into that Jeep, lady! If nothing else, I'll just stay out here forever, keep Samantha from ever getting hurt by this."

The ghost, still pointing, started to fade.

"No," Will said. "No, come back. There has to be *something* I can do!"

But he was already alone.

«««—»»»

Will lost all sense of time.

It didn't take him long to discover the improvised stop sticks—long nails, twisted together into makeshift caltrops—placed across the road several yards back from where the Jeep now leaned, mid-accident.

At one point he went back to the cabin, remembering the ghost had wanted him to see something in the photo albums.

But his hand was solid now when he touched the door's iron handle. He searched for another entrance, but everything was locked or boarded up. When he tried to break a window or pick up an object with which to break the window, his hand became non-corporeal.

He considered walking to the nearest town, maybe trying to somehow communicate with someone there—but how, if time was stopped with the Ghost World determined to make his body solid or spirit at its whim?

Will stood in the hanging rain, that thunder rumbling across the sky, lightning flashing though the storm otherwise never moved. He stared at Samantha, wanting to somehow reshape her scream, her terror, into the beautiful, peaceful face he woke up to each morning.

Perhaps it was only hours, perhaps it was years, decades, maybe even an age before Will finally, forlornly climbed through the metal of the yellow passenger side door and back into the Jeep.

4. End of the Road

He lurched for the wheel, fumbled to somehow reach the brake—as if any of this would help—but the Jeep was instantly solid around him and instantly back in the full velocity of motion, physics tossing him as if he'd never exited the vehicle.

Up was down. Right was left.

The roaring and tearing and screaming rage of metal rending his eardrums.

Samantha's scream.

Shattered glass.

Fireworks of pain exploding throughout the shell of his body.

An infinite sky of bruised black.

«««—»»»

Will smelled the woods all around him. It was alive with the sounds of insects, wind, the soft patter of rain after a storm. He was camping, ten years old, the world bigger than infinity. But the wicked flames he'd been staring into caught him.

Wait, what flames?

The flames inside him. His life, fading, burning, raging at the latest conflagration, flaring red and yellow and orange. The pain in Will's ribs as he groggily came to was the color of a blazing bonfire.

There were minor blazes in various other parts of his body as well. Blood trickled over them, thickening, but still trying to quench the fires.

Will heard himself moan, and the moan served to more fully wake him.

He was in a fetal position.

Legs unnaturally together.

Wrists bound behind his back.

He groggily called Samantha's name.

There was no response.

His consciousness fully returning now, Will managed to twist and wriggle his wrists enough to understand he'd been bound by ropes.

Will twisted and turned, glanced down at his ankles. Thick cord there too.

No panic. If he could wriggle his wrists like this, he could, likely, given time, get out.

The Jeep was up the steep hill from him, a mangled wreck.

He could see the driver's seat.

No sign of Samantha.

He called her name again.

No answer.

He called her name again. Louder.

Nothing.

Then he noticed the flattened grass.

Someone had been here and left.

Dragging something.

Obviously whoever had come hadn't been a good Samaritan.

Unless the binding was a pro job—and Will could already tell this wasn't—the trick to freeing yourself when tied up with rope is flexing. It's what magicians did—usually flexing all their muscles

197

even as they were tied up to give them slightly more range of move-ment, though Will obviously hadn't had this luxury. Still, this felt like rather cheap twine. All the better. Whoever had done this had taken a quick precaution, but hadn't really planned on him coming to.

He had carried all his wounds from the fight with Big and Ugly back here to the real world. His face felt raw with road grit. His ribs sang with a feeling like broken glass grinding together—he'd broken a rib while fighting a serial killer back when he'd first received his psychic "gift" and he knew at least one rib was now, at best, cracked there in his chest. The knife-slices in his legs flared with slits of orange hot fire with every movement, but he had to do this—he was no help to Samantha unless he worked his way free.

Will writhed, trying to pry off his boots as he flexed and unflexed his arms, putting pressure on the ropes at his wrist. His boots made his feet much thicker; he'd have a lot more wiggle room with them off. Will tried to dig his heels into the ground to give himself leverage, but the mud was far too wet and slippery.

Mud was also slipping in between the rope and his wrists and he twisted and turned on the ground, the oozing slime slicking down the twine. It would help him in the short term, but the mud would actu-ally *constrict* the rope, should it start to dry.

Will continued flexing, gritting his teeth, wishing he hadn't slacked off on his training regimen as he and Samantha's vacation had approached.

He tried to hump along the ground, his goal to maneuver himself next to a tree. He found the motion actually aided his flexing. The rope around his wrists was indeed growing ever so slightly more loose.

He managed to get close enough to a large maple to start rubbing his boot against it. He was trying to wedge the heel against the bark in order to help him slide his foot out.

Mud in his nose, his mouth, his eyes. Rain pelting.

He was on a slight incline, and it was all he could do to fight gravity, stay against the tree.

The ropes around his wrists loosened further, but still he could not free his hands.

His left boot finally slid off.

This loosened the twine around his ankles considerably, but the bony protrusion of his ankles refused to work their way through.

He flexed, grunting, spitting mud, cursing.

He could only imagine what was being done to Samantha.

He flexed again, hard, while trying to wedge the other boot up against the tree.

And, doing so, he slid down the hill in the small crater of mud he'd dug for himself as he writhed.

But the other boot caught on the trunk as he slid.

And his other foot pulled free.

His feet slipped out of the ropes in a few kicking motions.

From there, he managed to stand.

He wedged a low, thin but strong tree branch in between his wrists and, using that leverage, managed to further loosen the ropes.

His red, abraded, throbbing hands and wrists were soon free.

«««—»»»

The sun began to rise as Will scrambled up the hill. He was covered with dirt and mud, his hair caked to his head, mud squishing both inside and out of the boots he'd put back on.

It was rough going, brambles and brush and twigs tearing at him, everything wet. Every step forward, he slid half a step back.

His muscles burned, his head ached, the cuts on his leg wounds pulsed white hot, his ribs were swords digging into his side.

Will's mind raced as he fought the hillside. The ghostly hiker had pointed to photo albums. *Family* albums, likely. So this was possibly a family endeavor, and Ol' Big and Ugly had been just one member who'd passed away—a head honcho, hopefully, but who knew what he might be up against back at Cyrus Holler.

Halfway to the Jeep he found Ol' Big and Ugly's knife, glinting in the soft rain, the emerging sunlight, looking wicked as ever. Below the hilt the bone handle had been carved, on the same plane as the blade, into talons with what looked like actual claws from something ursine.

Thunder rumbled in the distance. The worst of the storm was definitely past. There was a pink edge to the receding dawn clouds, like blood on cotton swabs.

It struck Will that if Ol' B&U had been a ghost, then this was an artifact from The Ghost World.

How the hell had it come back with him?

199

Best not to worry about the hows and whys of the supernatural realm. At least he had a weapon.

Will tucked the blade into his belt, continued fighting the hillside. He made it to the Jeep. Found Samantha's cell phone.

Smashed.

Found his own cell.

In the same condition.

Wait!

His Glock!

No sign of it.

He continued making his way up the mountain—hill or mountain, he wasn't sure which this was officially, but it sure as hell felt like a frigging mountainside as Will struggled to reach the road. How the hell had they—whoever *they* were—managed to drag Samantha all this way?

One thought struck him as he climbed: Maybe this wasn't a family affair after all. Or at least not a big family. Or maybe just not a particularly bright one.

Because...*why had no one stayed behind to guard him?*

Obvious answer: Because the whole happy family wanted in on the festivities with Samantha.

Will redoubled his climbing efforts, adrenaline now blocking most of the pain.

«««—»»»

Morning had fully broken by the time Will reached the road. Humidity clung to his sweating skin—he had abandoned his jacket on the hillside in favor of freer movement. Leaves rattled and hissed in the slightest of breezes.

The air smelled green with a hint of rot, as if the entire forest had gone to mold. Streaks and odd blotches of mud stained the road from near where Will had emerged onto the pavement to the spot where the Cyrus Holler path began. Puddles, drips from the overhanging limbs and dew had conspired to obscure any details, but this must have been where their assailants had dragged Sam. Some of the clumps of mud didn't make sense for merely dragging a body, though. They were too large, not smeared enough.

Will soldiered on into the forest, deciding after a moment to approach the house indirectly—they might be watching the path—but he soon found there was no need. His tracking skills weren't the greatest, but it was obvious they had plodded down the main path—it looked like there might be a small army of trolls involved, given the obviousness of their passage. The grass which had stood tall last night was utterly trampled.

He had been watching for blood—Sam's—but could see no trace.

Until he got to the yard.

5. Four Skeletal Keys

Three of the crucifixes had tumbled. The bones that had been affixed to them had been scattered, some of them crushed. There were swaths of blood on the lawn.

Will approached cautiously, knife in hand.

He was only a few feet onto the lawn when he came within earshot of the muffled noises deep inside the cabin.

Roaring. Bestial.

And screaming.

Samantha's.

《《—》》

Will sprinted to the porch.

It was slick with blood, a trail of which led inside the door.

The door was locked, of course.

Will wished he were a ghost again, that he could simply walk through the thick wood of the portal as he'd done before, but he was going to have to get in some other way.

Now, as he thought desperately about how to gain access to the interior of the cabin, he noted another sound—a mewling cry, maybe combined with a growl, just behind the door, the sound of a dog in intense pain. The monstrous roaring and Samantha's pleading were somewhere deeper in the building—probably in whatever lay under the living area the ghost had shown him.

As awful as the inhuman noises in there sounded, Samantha's screams were worse.

How to get in?

He could race around the house, look for an alternate entrance.

No time—and there hadn't been any evidence of any during his time in The Ghost World.

The windows were boarded.

The door too thick to break down.

But the door was also ancient.

And so was its antiquated lock.

Will could pick locks.

If he had the right tools.

Will turned and examined the yard.

Bones.

If he found one the right size, the right length...One that wasn't too brittle...

Will grabbed what looked like a femur. He used Big and Ugly's knife to quickly, crudely whittle a tool the approximate size and shape he thought would work.

Samantha's muffled cries sounded both enraged and terrified. Will could make out no words.

He could not imagine what sort of creature would make those awful whining, growling half-howls, half-moans of pain behind the door, much less what Samantha could possibly be facing.

And yet he had to force his breath to come slowly, had to force his fingers to work carefully despite the lock being a relative gaping hole, as locks went.

The bone, untreated, was brittle. He could feel the tension in the tenuous calcium structure of the bone tensing, so pliable, against the old, solid, possibly rusted metal inside the close iron quarters of the lock.

Sweat, awash with grit and his own dried blood, ran into Will's eyes, stinging as he worked the tight mechanisms of the ancient latchwork, trying to ignore the whimpers of the beast on the other side of the door, the roaring of whatever had Samantha in the basement, the horrific cries of the woman he loved. He tried to blink the sweat away, but in the end he had to take a second to use his forearm to wipe it off.

He could feel the last pin giving way. His eyes were staring at that stupid runny-painted "KEEP OUT" on the door, but that's not what he was *seeing*. He could picture the structure of the lock in his mind, now, forced himself to focus only on that, imagining the bone sliver working it, moving it, ignoring the awful, gut-rending cacophony in his ears.

The bone wasn't going to hold.

He was putting too much pressure on it, had to.

The bone snapped.

A millisecond after he opened the lock.

Will stood, threw the door open, already wielding the knife.

«‹‹—›»›

He was expecting maybe a dog, thinking perhaps Samantha had put up a fight, injured a guard animal. He had, after all, taught her some self-defense.

A sickly-sweet odor, pervasive in the room, flooded his olfactory senses, but Will had no time, initially, to discern its origin.

What Will saw crouched in the corner of the main room on the wooden slats of the cabin floor, however, was...if not a woman, a female. She was partially disemboweled, a gaping gash in her side. She was holding a coil of guts into an oddly pulsing stomach wound. One side of her hirsute face was covered with a congealing mass of blood from a horrendous slash. She was covered in coarse hair—she looked like old time pictures of hair-covered sideshow freaks—and now—though her feral, inhuman eyes seemed only half-aware, crazed, taking him in—she started...*barking?* It was hard to make out through the wound, but she had *a maw.* Will was sure of it. Her nose and mouth jutted out in a misshapen snout, albeit one not fully formed, more like her hairy nose and mouth were stretched by a ball stuck under the skin of her face. Will's mind wanted to deem it a werewolf—it was definitely human-like; it had *breasts*, for god's sake. But he also saw...bear? Its still-shifting, elongating snout was roundish, its paws thick and heavily padded, its claws larger, more fearsome than any canine's.

Will also saw in a glance that whatever melee had started out on the lawn had continued in here. The long table had been pushed askew. The skulls which sat on it had tumbled to the floor, some shattering. The large jars with the viscous contents—honey? *Honey jars?* Yes, the source of the sickly sweet odor—had smashed to the ground.

The book shelf had been knocked over and some of the photo albums had been knocked to the floor. One was indeed a photo album, though he didn't have time in the mere millisecond he had to glance at the destruction to make out any details. In that same glance, however, he understood that at least two of the books were most definitely *not* photo albums. There was some sort of ornate writing and bizarre illustrations on the random open pages—and without actively reading or even actively *seeing* what was there, what he glimpsed nonetheless hurt his brain. Will knew it instinctually, the way an almost unperceived odor might warn a small animal away from a predator's cave, that the language used to write those books would challenge his brain's very *conception* of language, that the illustrations would challenge his mind's perception of the solidity of time and space.

All this, and more, in a glance, in a fraction of a second:

Huge, bloody tracks—the tracks of a giant more animal than human—led to the spot where the carpet had been flung aside, revealing a trap door, a huge lock in its center, beneath which something savage, beyond human, beyond animal roared and Samantha screamed in anger and rage and protest and fear.

The knife flew from Will's hand.

The strange books had done it. Will thought this even as the werebeast's snout—was it already longer than it had been mere seconds earlier?—made for his throat, as his head hit the hard wooden floor, as the creature's slablike claws hugged him, their bodies a jumble of screaming and snarling, of hair and flesh, it's large, hairy breasts smushing into his chest, its claws ripping at Will's back.

Will's hands found the creature's neck—it felt thick as a tire—all his strength focused on keeping those slathering jaws from his carotid artery.

Even though the thing had appeared somewhat slight while crouched in the corner, it was at least twice as heavy as he'd imagined it *could* be. Will couldn't roll, couldn't turn the two of them on their sides, the creature having the total upper hand above him. It roared and issued odd, excited yipping sounds from its scarred, bleeding jaw as it fought his hands.

The creature's hind legs scrabbled for purchase on the already blood-slicked floor and Will used the opportunity to bring his own feet up and in—his injured rib crunching, sending bright sparklers of pain throughout his torso, the partially coagulated cuts on his legs ripping open anew. He managed to bring his boots clumsily between them, kicking at the beast's hips, stretching its already injured abdomen, finally managing to at least partially throw the thing sideways so its entire weight was no longer on him.

How to fight this thing? Standard techniques might not work.

And it apparently had relatively quick regenerative abilities. It had definitely healed some since Will had first glimpsed it. The wound in its face was not as...*gashy* as it had been.

Yes, but what about the rip in its stomach?

Will had only an instant—keeping one hand on the beast's throat he reached down with his other and grabbed a slippery, rubbery loop of gut and tugged. He realized that some of its intestine had unspooled behind it when it had leapt at him, and now his tugging merely uncoiled more of it.

The thing lurched its head back and its gore-streaked neck slipped free of Will's hand.

Will instinctively brought his hand that was holding the creature's guts up in a defensive move and the beast's sharp teeth, just missing Will's flailing hand, snapped into and through its own intestine. Black blood and even darker bile spurted from the new opening in the tube-like organ, a vile odor also spraying forth into the air, mixing with the copper aroma of blood, the cloyingly sweet stench of honey.

The knife, Will saw, was within reach on the floor, near the awful books, if he could have a free instant in which to retrieve it.

The beast roared, its maw opening wide.

Not thinking, Will stuffed a fistful of the thing's own intestine deep between those ferocious teeth.

This cut the howl short. The beast started gagging, helplessly chewing on its own innards. Will felt it growl desperately, deep in its chest, as his body lay atop its. He stretched across the floor, reaching for the knife.

This time there was no mercy, as there had been with ol' Big and Ugly.

Partially masticated chunks of bowel fell free as Will decapitated the damned thing.

It did not regenerate.

《《《—》》》

Will smashed in the glass in the cabinet front and retrieved the hardwood box, knocking aside skulls and shattering gnomes.

Inside the box was an old-fashioned metal "barrel" key, about two-thirds the length of his hand. The part one gripped was fashioned into three grinning skulls.

Despite the fact that it was relatively huge compared to a modern key, there was no way this key would fit the gigantic latch in the floor. He put it in his pocket.

He didn't think he could find the patience to pick another lock, not with the noises from below.

"I'm coming, Samantha!" he yelled.

He hoped he wasn't lying.

Will heard Samantha scream his name in response over the monstrous bellows.

In addition to all his other wounds, his back blazed in pain with every movement from the werebeast's clawing.

The sun was finding ever more cracks in the windows now, and Will saw that the lock in the trap door appeared strangely curved.

It reminded him of something, but he couldn't place it.

The curve looked like a comma, like a...*like a claw.*

Will, mud-covered, blood-streaked, bile-soaked, hardly able to stand his own stench, reached into his belt and pulled out the knife.

The bone handle.

With the strange talons.

He gripped the knife gently by the blade.

He knelt by the lock.

The handle slipped in like a hand into a glove.

Will twisted the blade, feeling the lock give.

《《《—》》》

The wooden stairs beneath the trap door led down to flickering lights, shifting shadows and an uneven earthen floor.

There was no room for caution in this instance. Will leapt down the stairs.

A huge basement.

A thousand candles—how had there been time for them to be lit?

A bizarre altar of bones against a wall in the center. Bones set in the wall in surreal spirals and unreadable but obviously blasphemous runes.

A torture area at one end, hundreds of sharp, twisted, evil instruments. Samantha shackled to a rack. The huge werebeast, wearing a black cloak, did not appear to be torturing Sam, at least not yet. It was, instead, yammering in some animalistic language, reading from another of the damned books, this one gigantic. The book would have been difficult for the likes of Will to hold in both arms, but the beast held it in one huge, wickedly clawed paw while its free mitt traced strange sigils in the air.

The roars he'd heard all the way out on the lawn were not coming from the were-priest.

The roars were coming from the end of the basement opposite the torture chamber.

The demonic creature nailed to the cross of bones there was itself partially skeletal.

And yet bulges and bubbling ripples of white, mottled flesh were forming on it even as Will watched.

He recognized the creature.

Ol' Big and Ugly.

Except thrice as huge.

And thrice as ugly.

His skin, what there was of it, looked dead, desiccated. Green and blue and black-red veins throbbed and pulsed on the surface and beneath. His maw was fully bearlike, his ears protruding in flopping triangles, his hands shifting between talon claws and dead-white bear mitts. He was bound to the bone cross—if by physical or some sort of spiritual bounds, Will could not discern. He had no sex organs, his legs coming together in a smooth, hairless joining of gray skin at their union point. *His eyes.* His eyes burned red with literal flame, literal wisps of fire more hellish than any red hot poker he could imagine torturers using on victims of the rack to which Samantha was bound. Looking at the flames in Ol' Big and Ugly's eyes hurt in the same way merely glancing at those infernal books upstairs had hurt.

There was a heap of something at the base of the cross to which Ol' Big and Ugly was affixed. It appeared to be a mass of hair and …

flesh? Yes, *flayed*, prepared flesh, free of bone, apparently treated in some manner because there was no accompanying stench. An offering. Samantha, a human, was surely to be the final sacrifice. Will inferred this much before he took action: He had stumbled upon this scene *in media res*. These were still initial prayers in a larger ritual. Samantha's blood would surely be the sacrifice which would bring Big and Ugly fully back from The Beyond, more powerful and wicked than ever, to wreck who knew what havoc upon the mortal skin of this earth.

The were-priest's red eyes—inhuman, but not truly infernal, like Ol' Big and Ugly's eyes—glaring from beneath its cowl, had noticed him now. There was drying blood on its claws and snout, surely from whatever altercation had happened with the now-dead creature upstairs. It shrieked in rage, a keening higher than Will would have imagined it capable of. It was apparently enraged that he had interrupted its infernal preparations.

Forget the logic, the hows and whys, this was *happening*.

There was only action or doom.

Will clenched the knife, expecting the creature to rush him.

Instead it threw the book at him.

With amazing force.

Later, Will would swear the book *flew* at him—that its covers and pages flapped like the wings of an enraged bird as it rocketed into his head, impossible to dodge. Will was knocked blind to the ground, losing the knife again, incomprehensible words from the book raging through his brain, setting it afire with their fiendish syllables.

Will had to fight the words in order to come to. As a distant part of his consciousness heard a jumble of Samantha yelling for him to get up, the were-priest's growly verbiage and Ol' Big and Ugly's demonic roaring, the core of his mind heard iniquitous consonants and vowels not of any language spoken on this planet since recorded time.

But there was also *information* in the book. Ol' Big & Ugly, had, during life, performed rituals which turned his very bones into a key. With the proper rituals, with the proper spells and sacrifices proffered unto this key, Ol' B&U would become a portal, allowing incomprehensible twistings of reality far more malicious and unfathomable than mere lycanthropy or demonic reign to spread like a plague.

Will retreated into innocence in order to survive, to wake back unto himself. There had been, he realized for the first time in more than two decades, a time when he'd thought words were literally magical—and, the truth, he realized is that they *are*. Nursery rhymes. Songs from kindergarten. Poems he'd memorized during a lit class in college. Classic rock tunes. Words that fit together magically, innocently, *perfectly*. These rhymes—he sang and recited dozens at once as the otherworldly words stormed and thundered around him—were things that *should* be, that were *meant* to be—while the insane vocabulary with which the book bombarded him and creatures like the were-priest and Ol' Big and Ugly's infernal incarnation were the antithesis of *meant to be*. *Mother Goose, Boston's first album, Wallace Stevens' "The Idea of Order at Key West."* These were the words that might save the world.

It felt to Will as if he did battle with the book for longer than he had spent avoiding getting back into the Jeep back in the Ghost World, but when he finally came to it was apparently only seconds later. His head was throbbing anew. The book lay on the earthen floor—but it was now just a book, whatever powers it had now suddenly utterly spent, gone.

Samantha was still shackled, still screaming for Will to get up.

The were-priest was desperately throwing skins pell-mell from the heap at Big and Ugly—and Big and Ugly was *absorbing* them. The skins would stick to B&U's veiny white viscous skin then slowly sink in, and he would grow more solid, more flesh bubbling forth on his huge skeletal frame with each atrocious sacrificial pelt.

Only action or doom.

The were-priest noticed that Will had roused himself.

Will turned, found the knife.

When he spun back around, the were-priest, cowl unfurling behind him like a supervillain's cape, was leaping upon him.

The knife slipped between the roaring creature's wide-open jaw, entering the soft, red flesh of the palate, the force of the beast's lunge and Will's thrust pushing the silver, blood and gristle-flecked blade up and through the side of the long muzzle. Will yanked with all his might and tore the weapon loose, the incredibly (preternaturally?) sharp edge cutting through bone and tooth, fur and skin.

The were-priest howled in agony.

Will's next thrust entered the were-priest's eye, aiming for the brain.

The creature began fluxing back and forth between inbred behemoth and outright monster, between mutant redneck and its wolfbear form, snarling wheezily all the while through its terrible oral wound.

Big and Ugly raged, pulling with all his otherworldly might to free himself from the boney cross.

Will twisted the knife once it was deep in the were-priest's head.

Gore spurted in spastic eruptions of yellow, gray, white and red fluids.

The beast flailed at him, but the claws were receding, becoming more and more human, and Will only suffered minor scrapes and scratches before the were-thing was, at last, dead.

He turned toward Ol' Big and Ugly just in time to see the devil, now bigger and fleshier than ever, rip its arms free. The behemoth had to crouch in the basement, looming over Will, wicked claws scraping the ceiling in approximation of that victory fist-pump Will had seen him perform as Samantha hit the caltrops on the road.

There was evil glee in those burning, hurtful eyes and B&U roared directly in Will's face, simply for the effect, to emphasize that he was now the default victor, that Will was too late despite all his efforts.

"You're not yet fully formed!" Will yelled back in its face. "And I'm *alive*. So *I* win!"

The demon's skin, this close, smelled like death.

Its skin. Not fully formed.

Like death.

It needed dead, prepared skins.

Acting on impulse, Will leapt at the creature, embracing a thin point around its stomach where he could just clasp his hands behind its spine.

"Absorb me, you bastard!" he yelled. *"Absorb me!"*

Ol' Big and Ugly was a skeletal key, yes, but he was also now partially a portal to an insane world infernal entities were intent upon unleashing on our plane of existence.

The portal was not yet completely open, not enough to release anything, but Will found his way in through a crack.

On the other side of the psychic door was what Will could best describe, in human terms—though there were really no words, no language for it—as an infinite desert plain. There were stars, but they were so, so distant and few.

A thousand unreal entities, all of them insane, whining, whooping, howling, waiting for the portal to be fully opened for them, swirled in the air above, tense, watching, snarling prayers and praise for Ol' Big and Ugly, their champion.

Here, in this place, Will found himself a knight, all his armor gone. He was wearing little more than a loincloth, his body broken and bloodied beyond all the injuries he'd suffered back in Cyrus Holler.

He leaned on his sword, could barely stand.

His sword?

Yes, it was an elongated broadsword version of Ol' Big and Ugly's knife.

It was as if there were a weight on him, an unbearable, crushing load, its mass in the very pain of his countless wounds.

And Big and Ugly was even bigger here, at least three or four times Will's size.

Oh great, Will thought. *Brilliant move, coming here.*

Wherever *here* was.

The hulking monstrosity, all bone and deathly flesh, was already advancing.

Will tried to lift his sword. He got it off the ground but just barely.

He was so weary. So much pain. He had been carrying this body for so long, through so many journeys. He'd screwed up so many times along the way, taken so many wrong paths...

Will wanted to lift the sword high over his head and smite the charging, ogreish giant, but he only managed to lift it halfheartedly to waist level.

He slashed at the thing as it came.

Way too early.

The sword, a weight heavier than that of his wounds, slung ineffectually through the air well in advance of Ol' Big and Ugly's stampede, the monster clopping him upside the head, more stars appearing in Will's head than there appeared to be in the skies of this universe.

Will's body clattered to the ground.

He wasn't sure he could get up.

The pain was…just more pain.

Pain itself was nothing; pain was his old, old friend.

211

It was the *weight* of the pain that kept him from standing.

What *weight*, god damn it? He was wearing rags, was barely dressed!

The laughter bellowing forth from the skeletal colossus sent ripples of rage through Will.

It was a gleeful evil, a *celebration* of hate. The weird spirits swirling all around joined in with their own malicious mirth, sending shivers of dread and regret through Will's soul.

Wait.

Regret?

This was the sort of regret a ghost carried, slogging around the afterlife, miserable with the weight of the life it's left.

Was this place anything more than just another, strange, outré, distant Ghost World?

The rules were different here—they always were in the Ghost World—but there *were* always rules.

Regret. Regret was part of the weight, here, in this place.

That was a rule.

And Ol' Big and Ugly didn't know regret. Not in the least.

These hooting imps and phantoms, they didn't know regret, either.

Will stood.

Big and Ugly leapt, shaking the ground, and roared in Will's face, just as he had in the basement, the bellow of a smug conqueror claiming his prize.

Will lifted his sword, amazed to find he could lift it not only past his shoulders, but over his head.

For now, quite suddenly, Will found that he *himself* was transforming, transmogrifying into a full-blown demon.

Big and Ugly, all the whirling non-corporeal beings prattling and babbling their insensate, chortling harangues against sanity and order, were the utter embodiments of evil, hatred, corruption, malevolence, wickedness.

But, Will realized, as he found his demon self and allowed it to gain flesh, as he gathered all the guilt in his soul and let it heal his wounds and gather bulk on his body—something he knew was only possible here, in this realm—big evil was actually *small*. He had won against the infernal book by retreating into innocence. But that would not be allowed, here on this plane. Not part of the rules here. Here you fought evil with evil, hatred with hatred, anger with anger. Demons, monsters, hellspawn like Ol' Big and Ugly, they were an *easy* sort of evil. They were *overt, obvious.* Uncomplicated sin incarnate. They were spiritual simpletons.

Will, on the other hand, found himself gathering every one of his smallest sins unto himself, layering it upon his body here in this extra dimensional Ghost World like the multiple skeins of an onion, his bulk growing exponentially as his body grew, as his height unfurled, as he soon towered over Ol' Big and Ugly.

Small evils are the hardest to combat, the hardest to beat. The human soul could combat the urge to kill, the thrill of rape, the thirst for instant revenge. We choke these down, do not act on them. But what built grotesque layers on the soul were the petty insults executed, the small hurts dealt out to loved ones—*Samantha, all their paltry, vicious arguments*—the snide comments uttered out of earshot, the noble gestures not taken, the "professional" posturings, all the lies and subterfuge perpetrated in pursuit of legal tender, the small, lazy oversights that weren't oversights at all.

Ol' Big and Ugly was but a gnat to Will now, cowering far below.

And he smote his enemy down into an unrecognizable pulp, demons mourning and lamenting, screaming and reeling away in the wake of Will Castleton's wrath as he stepped back through the fading crack between this reality and that.

《《—》》

"Will?" Samantha said as he used the three-skulled key to unlock her chains.

"Suppose God were hanging out at your house," Will said to her.

Ol' Big and Ugly lay as an unrecognizable white, veiny heap of pulp on the other side of the room.

"Will, you're not making sense."

"Would you treat your kids or spouse or friends or parents differently?"

"Will, I don't understand."

"Suppose God were in the car with you. Would you say what you say to other drivers?"

"Jesus, Will! What the *hell!* Just let me *out!"*

"Jesus?" Will said. "Suppose Jesus were on a walk with you downtown. Would we—you and I, that is, on a stroll in downtown Chicago with Jesus, not far from our apartment, not far at all—ignore the homeless person the way we do when we don't expressly feel God with us?"

"Why are you asking me this?"

Will blinked. Once. Twice. He made a sound that might have been a laugh, but it was totally without mirth. "I don't know. *Jesus.* Are you okay?"

Samantha started crying, clasped at Will's clothes, kissed him endlessly.

He drew her close to him, held her, kissed back.

«‹—»›

"What did they argue about on the way up here? Were they in human form or..."

"I don't know. I was barely conscious. It was like a dream. A horrible dream. I remember huge shapes, guttural voices. I remember thinking I should get away, barely aware enough to crawl. I didn't get far before the bigger one had me again and took me downstairs."

«‹—»›

Will found several five-gallon containers of gasoline in the garage. He no longer had the heart for exploring the extraneous hallways of the place. He took the old, mint-condition comics, laid some of them on top of the old radio, others on top of the old television.

He stood there in the damned living room, full of toppled skulls, the nude were-creature, now just a mongoloid-looking nude human, already entering rigor mortis.

Every wound he had experienced that night sat like a stone, a weight deep inside his body—no. He couldn't think of it that way.

He spread the gasoline on top of the comics, retrieved a candle from the basement. Lit the house as they left it.

If the conflagration started a forest fire, *fuck it.*

«««—»»»

They stood, silent, and watched it burn.

The woods did not catch fire. It was as if the house and lawn were a small, contained reality unto itself, the surrounding vegetation immune to the flames consuming the offensive property.

«««—»»»

They said nothing in particular to each other, waiting an hour or more, holding each other by the roadside, neither strong enough to attempt the walk to the nearest town before the first vehicle came along.

The guy's name was Earl. He was a skinny kid in black skinny jeans and a black wifebeater, drove a big, gleaming, night-black Ford F150, had been on his way back home from work at Angelo "Havoc"'s Garage in Easy Corner, the next town down the holler.

"Have a little trouble, looks like?" he asked.

"Yeah, just a little," Will said, pointing at the spot where the Jeep had gone off the road. "Happened during the storm. We both got beat up pretty good, but we're alive."

"Damn," Earl said. "And just right here, too. Fuckenstance, that."

"A fucken-what?"

"Term me and a few homies use. A weird co-inky-dink, like."

"Oh, what sort of coincidence?"

"Well, if I'm right—and I think I am—that holler, one that starts right behind you, I don't think you wanna know too much about it."

"You don't say," Samantha said.

"Damn straight," Earl said. He got out a smoke, lit it, burnt a good suck of it, spoke. "Place back there, burned down back in the Thirties, Forties, something like that. They found a fuckload of weird shit in the remains, scared enough of the populace to make it a local legend, yo."

"The Thirties or Forties," Will said.

"Yeah, ancient Kentucky secret." Earl sucking on his cig, blowing a couple smoke rings. "Good and covered up, back in the day, what I hear. All sorts of atrocities—whatever awful haint you

215

want, if you can imagine it, someone says it was there, back in them woods. Bullshit, right? Listen, I'll give you a ride back to Easy Corner, get you set up. Glad you folks're alive in the first place, a crash like that in that rager of a bruhaha we had last night, thunder and lightnin' like you would not believe...Doubt more than me and maybe three other fellers drive down this stretch on a good day, if that. Lucky it's even paved. Cyrus Holler, they call it."

COOKED

JONATHAN MABERRY

-1-

Billy Sparrow was high.

Almost high.

The 'almost' part was a bitch. It was a heartbreak.

He needed to get high enough to fly away, like Cooter promised they could do.

But he wasn't high enough for that.

For Billy the high used to start before he even clicked his lighter to smoke the ice. Meth was always like that, you even think about it you get a tingle in the balls and a flutter behind the eyes. High before you're high, that's what Cooter used to say.

Cooter used say a lot of stuff.

Cooter was pretty funny. He had Billy laughing the first time they smoked meth. Called it methandfriendofmine. That was funny.

He and Cooter would smoke so much they'd get pipe-drunk and then everything was funny. Peeling wallpaper was funny. A cockroach swimming in his cereal bowl was funny. Even watching Carla, that scratchity-ann crank hoe, pick at her blisters was funny.

That was a long time ago.

The anticipation wasn't the same.

The high wasn't the high anymore.

Now, when Billy popped a lighter under the quartz all he felt was bad stuff. His stomach was full of bees and there were thorns in his head. Even when he sucked in that first lungful and the world fell off its hinges. That used to be epic. That used to be the fucking *it*.

Now it was like opening a door into a haunted house.

Cooter was in that haunted house, too.

Sitting there, grinning at him with crooked teeth surrounded by charred skin, staring with eyeballs that had been boiled white in the fire.

If Billy smoked too long he could see Cooter die all over again. It was like a big DVR playing the scene over and over again in his head. Surround-sound and everything. No amount of smoke could bury that, and the deeper into the high Billy went to hide from it, the clearer the picture got.

-2-

They'd come in a couple of Escalades. Farelli and his posse of six wiseguy wannabes from Newark, rolling up to Cooter's little place on DeFrane Street. White boys dressed like they thought the *Sopranos* was on the Fashion Channel. Pointy shoes and tight pants and shirts open to show Neanderthal hair on their chests. Acting tough, hoping to be noticed by guys who *are* tough. Talking trash.

Carrying baseball bats and gas in red plastic cans.

Billy was in the attic, huddled over the last fumes in a pipe. He heard the shouts, but at first that didn't mean shit to him. You get high, you hear stuff. Some highs are good, some highs blow. People steal shit from each other. There are fights. It's no big deal.

But then the shouts turned to screams.

Screams weren't part of it. Meth doesn't take you down that avenue. Billy staggered to his feet and looked down the attic stairs. There was no doors anywhere. Billy remembered he and Cooter taking them off, but he couldn't remember what that had been about.

The screams were loud enough to poke holes in the envelope of his high.

He crept down to the second floor and leaned over the banister.

There they were.

The dickheads from Seventh Avenue. Farelli's thugs were like a pack of dogs. Billy lost count of the number of times they beat him up. Rubbed his face in dogshit. Kicked him in the balls. Always laughing about it. Always grabbing their own nuts and yelling "Eat me!" every time they saw Cooter. Always calling Cooter faggot or nigger or other shit.

Worse than a pack of dogs, Billy thought. Dogs won't fuck with you for no reason.

Billy Sparrow didn't hate very many things, but he hated Farelli and his crew.

Farelli lived in the house with all those statues of the Virgin Mary on their lawn. The virgin and a bunch of dumb-ass plastic pink flamingos.

Billy had a vague memory of him and Cooter stealing some of them the other night. Or was it last night? What the fuck did they do with them?

They stole all sorts of shit. Flamingos, those goofy little lawn gnomes, a statue of a black guy dressed like a jockey. That one really pissed Cooter off. Billy didn't know why. Sure, Cooter was black but he wasn't a jockey. But it pissed Cooter off, and when Cooter gets pissed he gets funny.

Billy remembered what they'd done with the stuff they stole. The gnomes and flamingos were all on the front lawn here, with the Virgin Mary and the lawn jockey snuggled down in the crab grass together. Cooter couldn't take their clothes off—they were statues, after all—but the way he laid them down said it all. With the gnomes and pink birds watching. It was fucking hilarious.

Afterward, when they were about to get high, Cooter said that he'd have to move that shit before his uncle saw it. Uncle Conch Boukman was a hard-headed, short-tempered old man who moved to New Jersey after his village in Haiti was destroyed in that earthquake. Cooter was his only relative, but to Billy they were so different that it was hard to tell that there was any connection.

But Uncle Conch brought a little money with him, and he paid the mortgage off on Cooter's pad.

The screams from downstairs punched Billy in the head and it shook him out of the memories of last night.

Farelli and his goon squad were all there. So were a whole mess of Cooter's friends. Couple of kids Billy knew, too. Maybe ten people, hanging out, getting high. One guy—the uptown kid who brought some quality ice with him—with the shorts down around his knees so Carla could give him a courtesy BJ. But Carla wasn't blowing him. Or anybody. Billy looked at her and saw her face burst apart as a baseball bat hit her.

She screamed and then the bat hit her and she couldn't scream anymore. Carla fell back and she fell weird, like she had no bones in her neck.

That's when it all went crazy.

That's when Farelli's thugs went apeshit. Bats and chains.

Farelli stood in the center of the living room and even from upstairs Billy could see that there was a bulge in Farelli's pants. He was rock-hard watching this shit. Billy knew about that. His old man had been like that sometimes. Getting serious wood because using a belt on Billy and his sisters felt that good. Made him feel that jazzed.

That's when Billy heard Cooter come crashing into the room, swinging a mop handle and catching Farelli's cousin, Tony, right across the forehead.

There was a moment when Billy thought it would all be over right there and then. Everyone and everything froze solid. Even the screaming stopped for just a second.

Billy wanted to scream a warning. He wanted to shout at Cooter and everyone else. Tell them to run, tell them to get the fuck out.

While there was still a chance.

-3-

But there was no chance.

Cooter knew it when he came charging out of the kitchen with the mop.

Farelli and his goons knew it before they loaded into their Escalades. They knew it when they stopped at the Lukoil to fill up their red gas cans.

Even the zoned-out stoners knew it. Carla probably knew it, too, right up until the bat knocked her head loose on her neck.

Billy knew it. Billy knew that all of them—greaser or meth-head—were born into this. Into this moment, like they were all bowling-balls thrown down polished wood alleys but all the alleys were designed to converge into one spot. No pins. Just a bunch of bats and a gas can and a mop handle.

The moment became unstuck when Farelli laughed.

The right kind of laugh will do that.

Cooter looked at him and Farelli looked back.

Billy screamed then.

Nobody heard him, because everyone was screaming. The bats went up and down and around and around, and somebody kept painting all of the drowsy, doped-up, screaming faces with red.

Cooter tried to run.

They splashed him with gas.

Farelli flicked a cigarette at him.

Cooter made it all the way to the second floor. Billy tried to help him. Swatting at the flames that were wreathed around Cooter's face. Billy shoved him into the bathroom, knocked him down with burned hands into the tub. Turned on the water.

But by then there were flames coming up through the floor.

The water filled the tub, but fire reached up with long yellow fingers between the floor boards and drove Billy back. From the bathroom doorway he watched the inferno heat boil the water in the tub. Where Cooter was.

When Billy dove through the second floor window, he saw three things.

The Escalades driving away, laughter tumbling out of the open windows.

The faces of pink flamingos and lawn gnomes and the mother of Jesus staring up at him with plastic eyes.

And then the hedges reaching up, tearing at him with a thousand green fingers.

-4-

Billy got out of the hospital the day they buried Cooter.

He was the only one at the graveside. Billy and the priest, who didn't even look at him. And a brass urn full of ashes.

Billy's hands were burned. He had bandages around his face and under his clothes. Billy felt the fire still burning in his skin and the screams still burning in his head. They would have kept him in the hospital but despite everything they say about providing medical coverage if you don't have money, they will kick a meth head out after a couple of days. He didn't have any money, so he walked home. Back to Cooter's.

The house was a blackened shell. The fire department had been able to save the front steps. The rest was cinder.

Billy sat down on the top step, rested his elbows on his knees, hung his head, and cried until there was no moisture left in his body. The urn sat next to him. No one had claimed it, so they'd given it to him, and he carried it all the way back.

He stayed there all day, talking to Cooter in his head.

Cooter didn't say shit, though.

Two days later Billy bought some rock. Smoked it. Saw Cooter. They slopped on the couch and played video games. They talked about living and dying. They hung out.

When the rock was gone and the high broke apart into little pieces of reality, Cooter went back to sleeping in his urn. Billy went back to the burned-out house, sat down on the step next to the ashes. And cried.

That was life.

That was every day.

On the sixth day after the funeral, on the long downslope of a high, Billy sat on the step with his head in his hands. He heard a car pull up and stop, but he didn't look up.

"You that white boy," said a voice.

Billy looked up slowly. Moving fast hurt. It broke blisters. So, Billy moved like he was old. Uncle Conch stood on the soot-covered little bit of pavement that ran between the two halves of the front lawn. He wore a black suit and a shirt the color of snow. His hat hid most of his face so that only his chin and mouth were in the light. He had dark lips and cigarette-yellow teeth.

"You that white boy," he repeated, his thick Haitian accent making everything sound like a song. "You was friends with Cooter."

"I guess," said Billy. He realized that his nose was running and he sniffed. Tasted some tears, so he wiped his eyes.

Uncle Conch looked down at the urn. "That my Cooter?"

Billy nodded. "You weren't at the funeral, so they said I could have his ashes."

"Yeah," said the old man, "I'm too close to the grave my ownself for me to want to visit a boneyard."

That made sense to Billy, and he nodded.

After a while, Uncle Conch said, "You and Cooter always doing the drug."

He never said 'doing drugs' or 'smoking meth'. Doing the drug.

"I guess."

Uncle Conch stepped a little closer. He had bad legs and leaned heavily on a cane that was carved with snakes and skulls.

"Why you do the drug?"

"What?"

"The drug. Why you and my Cooter always do the drug? Where it take you?"

Billy thought about that. "Away, I s'pose."

"You suppose? You don't know?"

"Away."

Billy stared down at the lawn. The heat had withered the grass to brown strings, and the fire hoses had turned that to clingy seaweed. The tendrils were wrapped around the legs of half-melted flamingos and the throats of charred gnomes.

Another shuffling step closer. "Tell me," he said.

Billy squinted up. "Why do you want to know about that stuff?"

Uncle Conch lowered himself down to the step. It took a long, painful time for the old man to do it. Billy tried to help, but he was too badly burned. When he was down, Uncle Conch took a minute to catch his breath and he produced a spotless white handkerchief and mopped his brow. Billy was pretty sure he'd never seen anyone use a handkerchief before, not outside of a movie.

"Tell me, boy," wheezed Uncle Conch, "why you and my Cooter always want to go away? What you want to get away from?"

Billy looked past him to the street, but what he was seeing was the open mouth of the grave before they lowered the box. The mound of dirt was a brown heap that they didn't bother to cover with one of those green AstroTurf mats. Nobody gave enough of a shit even for that.

"I don't know."

"Tell me, boy. I got to know."

Billy looked at him. "Why? What does it matter now?"

"It matters to me. Cooter may not be a saint, but he all the family I had left. Tell me what he wanted to do. Let me carry that for what time I got left. Give me that much so I don't bury his dream, too."

Billy stared at Uncle Conch for almost a minute before he could answer. "You were in Haiti when we were growing up," he said. "Cooter and me were always getting kicked around, you know?"

"No, I don't know. Tell me."

"I don't know...I saw Haiti on the news and stuff. I know that you guys had it worse down there than we had here..."

"Poor is poor is poor," said Uncle Conch. "Kid starving in the street don't measure his hunger 'gainst some other kid he never met. Kid still hungry. Kid still cries when he hungry."

"Yeah, but it wasn't just that. Cooter's mom was pretty cool—she was your daughter?"

Uncle Conch shook his head. "My sister's daughter. Only one of us to leave Haiti in a hundred years."

"Until you."

The old man shook his head. "I live here, boy, but I ain't ever left Haiti. Haiti is home. I'm a Boukman—you know what that mean?"

Billy shook his head.

"My great-great-many times-great granddaddy was Dutty Boukman, a *houngan* from Jamaica who settled in Haiti. Let me tell what a *houngan* is," said Uncle Conch. "That's a sorcerer, a priest of the old religion. Dutty led the first slave revolt in Haiti. He that strong. He that fierce a man. Once Dutty shucked off his chains no man could put them back on again. Them French they had to shoot him a hundred times to bring Dutty Boukman down. Why so many times? Because Dutty was filled with the *loa* of Kalfu—and that is one powerful spirit. Kalfu is the *loa* of the crossroads and every slave who ever died had to stand before that spirit and tell Kalfu how they died and who killed them. Kalfu got so angry he looked for the right man, the right slave, to open a doorway in his soul, to let him come through. That's what Dutty Boukman did. Dutty's heart was so filled with hate for the slavers that he opened up the door in his soul and let Kalfu come walking through. Oh, now Kalfu is not Casper. You know Casper, the friendly ghost? Like on TV? No, Kalfu not like that. Kalfu controls all the evil forces of the spirit world. He bring bad luck and hard justice. Dutty was filled with that dark magic and when he told all the other slaves to rise up, they rise up. That was 1791. By 1794 slavery was abolished in Haiti. That's how strong Dutty Boukman was. That's the blood that flows right pass the crossroads. The river of dark blood that flows over the years from him to me." He paused and sadness filled his eyes. "And to Cooter. And that river of blood end with Cooter, but it don't make the little boy strong. All that river did was wash him away, and up in heaven his mama is singing a sad song."

The birds in the trees seemed to echo that music.

"I live here, but Haiti is in me." Uncle Conch touched his chest. "When I die here, my soul will be buried in Haiti."

Billy nodded. That was something he could understand. "Cooter and me always wanted to find a place that we could call home. My mom died when I was two, so I never got to know her. Cancer. Sucks, but I was over Cooter's all the time. His mom was so great, you know? She was always singing songs."

"Little Bird," said Uncle Conch, and there was a smile buried down inside the wrinkles on his face. Sad, and deep and real. "That's what we called her. Little Songbird."

"She was great. She was the best. But…you know, she died, too. A bus hit her. I mean, how random and fucked up is that? How does God allow a bus to hit someone like her? Fucking bus should have hit my dad. Or Cooter's dad. Those two assholes should have had a fleet of busses hit them. Fuckers."

Uncle Conch nodded. "I didn't know that about her husband. Not until I get a letter and she tell me. I was putting money together to come here and talk to that man when I get the other letter. 'Bout the bus."

They sat and thought about it.

"You didn't come, though," said Billy. It wasn't an accusation. He was putting it out there to see what it looked like.

Uncle Conch nodded. "I didn't come. Not 'til after the quake."

"Yeah."

"I think the quake was a judgment on me."

Billy looked at him. "What?"

"The *loa*—they know what kind of man I am."

"Cooter said you were a priest, too," said Billy. "They said in your village back on the island people thought you could magic and stuff. Tell the future, cure all sorts of diseases and raise dead people. He said you were a good guy."

The words were kindly meant, but Uncle Conch looked sad. "What Cooter know? All he knows is what his mama, Little Songbird, tell him, and what she know? Over here her whole life, just hearing 'bout things in letters. No…it's the *loa* who know the truth. They know that I carry Boukman blood—hero blood—and they know I studied the ways of the *houngan,* but they also know I ain't done much with it 'cept make myownself happy. Drink and pussy and some deviltry to make the long nights scream. Yeah, you can fool your family but you can't fool the *loa.*" He paused and Billy did not interrupt. "Maybe I'm a bad man, white boy. Maybe I'm a bad man like Cooter's dad. Like your dad."

Billy said nothing.

But then Uncle Conch shook his head. "No, not like those cock-roaches. I don't put my hand on a woman and I don't put my hand on a baby. Even so…I'm a bad man. I done bad things." He nodded to the rhythm of his own thoughts. "Haiti a bad place. Hard place to be a good man. Easy place for a bad man to be a bad man. Bad is more fun."

"I—"

Uncle Conch laughed. A deep, rumbling laugh that had no humor in it. "Don't worry, white boy, I ain't going to do bad things to you."

"You weren't bad to Cooter."

The old man sighed and ran his fingers along the outside of the brass urn. "I wasn't good to him, neither."

"You paid his bills, man. You gave him a place to live."

Uncle Conch turned and looked at the charred walls behind him. "All I gave that boy is a place to die, and I think he was dead before they cooked him in there."

But Billy shook his head. "No, man, that's just it. Cooter and me…we could always get free. We could get away anytime we liked."

The old man's brows knitted. "How? How you and my Cooter get free?"

When Billy didn't answer, the old man nodded.

"The pipe," said Uncle Conch.

"I guess."

"That got you away?"

"Yeah."

"All the way away?"

Billy thought about it. "At first, yeah."

"What happened at first?"

"At first, man, we'd light a pipe and take one hit and we were gone. Really gone. We were flying." He closed his eyes to summon the memory, and his body swayed as if he was gliding on the winds, riding the thermals, high above it all. "That's how we escaped, man."

"Escaped?"

"Cooter's dad. Mine. When Cooter's dad went to jail, we sailed so high that night. Oh, god, we were all the way up. Flying like birds."

When he opened his eyes, Uncle Conch was not looking at him. Instead he was studying the soot-blackened flamingos.

"That why you got these birds all over the lawn?"

Billy sniffed back more tears. "That was Cooter's idea. He said that maybe if we got high enough we'd fly way up in the sky, like the flamingos. You ever see them? They soar up there, not a care in the world, just floating on the wind like nothing beneath them matters. Nobody can touch them up there. They're so high. And so free." He looked at the melted wings of the pink plastic birds. "Now Cooter's gone and all the flamingos are dead. Cooked, man. It's all cooked."

A sob broke in Billy's chest and he hugged his ribs with bandaged hands as he wept for Cooter.

Uncle Conch laid a hand on Billy's trembling shoulder.

"Why'd they have to do that?" sobbed Billy. "Why'd they have to do all that? So we stole their yard stuff. So we took some stupid pink birds and stupid gnomes and that other stuff. If they were mad about it, most they should have done was mess us up a little. They done that plenty of times. All they had to do was knock us around a little and take their stuff back. And, look, man, they didn't even take their shit. All that stuff's still here. What was it all about, man? What's the point of anything if they didn't even take their stuff back?"

He kept crying and his voice crumbled beneath the weight of it. The only word he could manage was, "Cooter…"

Then Uncle Conch bent close and whispered in his ear.

"Now you listen to me, boy," he said, "I told you once that I'm a *houngan* and the blood of Dutty Boukman run through my veins. Told you that my many-times grandfather got so mad, so damn mad, that he opened up a door in his soul and let something evil come right on through."

"Kalfu," said Billy.

"The *loa* Kalfu, lord of the crossroads, bringer of hard justice." Uncle Conch picked up the urn. "I just 'bout pissed on everything good there was in the Boukman name. I left my Little Songbird to get knocked around by a weak, bad man. I let her boy die trying to fly away from this shithole. I done that. I could have changed it, but I didn't, so I done that."

Billy shook his head, but Uncle Conch was staring at the urn. He opened it and looked at the soft gray nothing that was Cooter.

"I done this," he murmured. "I got no one else alive on this earth who is blood kin to me. The Boukman name, proudest blood of my people, dies when I die. And if I die this moment, right now, then that blood turns to piss that ain't worth hosing off the street."

He drew a long breath.

"But I got me a little breath left and a little blood yet, and I got me a heart that is so full of hate that it wants to burst open and break the world. So what you think I should do?"

Billy said nothing. His eyes were huge and round.

"You 'member Cooter said I could magic, white boy. Pretend I'm a genie in a bottle and you can ask one wish. What that wish going to be?"

Billy looked at the urn and down at the melted flamingos and then up at the endless blue sky. "I guess I'd want two wishes," he said.

"What wishes, boy?"

"I'd want to see Cooter again. He's my best friend, you know? He's the greatest, Cooter's the king. I'd want to see him again. Not with burns on him, though. Like he was last week. Laughing and happy, singing to himself like the way his mom used to. That's what I'd wish for."

A tear broke from Uncle Conch's eye and wandered over the million seams and lines in the old man's face, burning like hot silver.

"And what's your second wish? You want me to burn those boys who burned Cooter? You want me to raise the devils of hell to burn them? Or how about I call the *loas* of vengeance and we turn these melted gnomes into a pack of monsters to hunt *that* pack of monsters. I could do that. That's dark magic. I call Kalfu and I could do that."

But Billy shook his head. "No…if I only had one more wish after that, I'd want Cooter and me to fly out of here. Far away. Like flamingos, but not melted ones. Not fly like we're smoking ice, but really fly. All the way into the sky. That would be the shit, man. That's what Cooter would want."

Uncle Conch stared at Billy for a long, long time.

"That's all you want? You can have all the revenge you want and instead you want to fly away with my Cooter like a couple of birds?"

Billy closed his eyes. "Big pink flamingos, man. So high...so free..."

-5-

Billy thought he said more to Uncle Conch, but he couldn't hear his own words. Another sob hitched his shoulders.

But it wasn't a sob, of course. He knew that. When he opened his eyes, he knew that much.

Far, far below the Passaic River curved along the edge of Newark, but from up here it looked like a blue ribbon. Billy turned to say something to Uncle Conch, but it wasn't the old man. It was Cooter. Big and pink and riding free. Billy called out to him, but his voice sounded different. It didn't sound like his voice. And it didn't sound wrong. It sounded right. It sounded so right.

Billy closed his eyes and he laughed in that strange new voice as he and Cooter flew free.

-6-

Uncle Conch took his time getting to his feet. He was old but parts of him were even older, used up before their time. He braced himself on his cane and began lumbering toward his car.

In his chest, his heart hammered like old drums. Fast, insistent, powerful. Pain darted up and down his left arm.

But he hummed as he walked to his car. He knew that he wasn't going to die in the next five minutes. Not that soon. When he got to the curb he turned and looked at the debris in the yard. The flamingos were gone, and that made him smile. For just a moment. It would be the last of Uncle Conch's smiles to touch that face.

Then his eyes fell on the little singed and half-melted gnomes. Nasty looking little things. Stupid things. White man's idea of what looked good on a man's lawn.

The eyes that looked on the gnomes was Uncle Conch's for one blink longer. Then with the next blink the eyes changed from dark brown to fiery red. The smile on the old mouth changed, became broader, brighter. No longer the pained smile of a dying man but the vital smile of something far more powerful. In his chest the old heart began hammering to a rhythm that was many times older than the body around it. A rhythm many times older than the pavement beneath the scuffed shoes. Many times older than the country in which he stood. As old as hate, and that was so very old.

"Rise up, my brother spirits," said the voice that was no longer Uncle Conch's. Nor was the language English, or French or Creole.

On the lawn, there was a small sound, a tiny groan, a rasp of plastic. One of the lawn gnomes raised its singed and sooty head. The white beard was streaked with ash, the eyes were melted holes. The mouth was stamped into the plastic. But then the plastic lips trembled and the whole body trembled with effort and finally there was a *popping* noise as the mouth opened. Broken, twisted plastic in a zigzag gash. The little creature smiled, and its wide and wicked grin was exactly the same as what was now stretched across Uncle Conch's mouth. The mouth that had belonged to Uncle Conch, when there had been an Uncle Conch.

"Rise up, brother spirits," repeated Kalfu, using Uncle Conch's borrowed mouth. Each word was exhaled on a hot breath that blew through the open door of hate in the ancient body. "They are serving dinner on Seventh Avenue. White meat, served rare. All you can eat."

One by one the melted gnomes opened empty eyes and ripped open jagged mouths. Hungry mouths. They rose unsteadily to their feet, tottering toward the open car door beside which Kalfu, their brother, waited.

MIZ RUTHIE PAYS HER RESPECTS

LUCY A. SNYDER

Andrew Dockholm straightened his navy blue JROTC uniform and stepped through the automatic doors leading to the Hillsonville Regional Airport's baggage claim area. He spotted a tall, silver-haired woman in an ankle-length black dress by the lone conveyor belt. She clutched a leather purse and a bouquet of yellow roses and white lilies in her left hand, and was leaning over to try to catch a small blue suitcase with her right. The woman looked just like her pictures on Facebook, except for the black dress; she was mostly dressed in flowery hippie clothes in those.

"Let me get that for you, Miz Ruthie!" Andrew shouldered his way through the sparse crowd so he could get to the light suitcase before his cousin did.

"Oh! Andrew. Hello there. I could've gotten that, but thank you." Ruthie blinked at him, looking surprised, then glanced past him, her expression darkening. "Is your mother or your father with you?"

"No ma'am. I got my regular driver's license last week, so I just came on out here in my truck after drill practice." Andrew beamed at her.

"Do your folks know you're picking me up?" She looked a bit worried, and maybe a touch suspicious.

"Not exactly, ma'am...I got the feeling they don't cotton to you much. Don't know why 'cuz you seem like a real nice lady in your emails, and you always give me good loot in Mafia Wars, and we're family, right?"

Andrew's folks had never made the cause of their disapproval clear, although once when his pa had too much Wild Turkey and had gone on a drunken rant he'd called Miz Ruthie "That Frisco witch." His pa never had much compunction about calling women the b-word, so the witch thing had made Andrew curious, but later his pa denied having said it and went silent as a lowcountry clam about their cousin. Miz Ruthie had posted stuff supporting Obama on Facebook, but Andrew supposed he could turn the other cheek on that because women usually had stupid ideas about politics. And she'd posted stuff about doing Tarot readings, which his grandpa preached was Satanic, but Andrew had seen a Tarot deck at a gaming store once and as far as he could tell it was just paper and ink like a regular playing card deck. He didn't see what was so bad about it besides that one devil card. It wasn't like she was a Muslim or something.

"It's only right you want to pay your respects to my grandpa," Andrew continued. "The whole county came out for his funeral last weekend. It wouldn't be right to make a lady like you take a taxi or somethin'."

After all, Miz Ruthie had to be at least fifty, practically as old as his own grandma, but he knew better than to tell her that. Old ladies didn't like you pointing out that they were old. Andrew figured he wouldn't be much of a man if he didn't step up and offer to take his cousin out to the family graveyard. Besides, he liked showing off his new truck, a Dodge Ram with a hemi V8 engine. He'd worked three solid years of weekends and summers down at the sawmill to save up for it—had to get his pa to lie about his age to the owner at first—but at fourteen Andrew had been as big and strong as any sixteen-year-old. And besides, like his pa and grandpa had always said, all those labor laws were just dumb government meddling.

Ruthie still looked worried. "Well, I wouldn't want you to get in any trouble...."

"I ain't gonna get in no trouble! I stay out late all the time, and my pa don't care as long as I do my chores."

"What about your mama?"

Andrew blinked at her. "What about her? She don't wear the pants."

Despite Miz Ruthie's gentle protestations, Andrew insisted on carrying her suitcase out to his truck. He took a moment to pop the hood to show her the engine, clean and pretty as a prom queen's pussy, and tell her how fast it went up the road to Table Rock Mountain. And then they were off, speeding down the highway toward the turnoff to the old stone church where all their kin were buried, including Andrew's grandpa, the Reverend Robert M. Dockholm, who'd presided over New Bedrock Baptist Church for over thirty years.

"So are you going into Air Force ROTC in college?" Miz Ruthie asked, gesturing toward his uniform.

"No ma'am, I'm gonna be an Army Ranger. I already got it all worked out with the recruiter. I'm only in Air Force JROTC 'cuz that's all they have at my high school."

"What about college?" she asked.

"College? I already got a job, I don't need no college."

"Ah."

Andrew pulled his truck into the gravel parking lot in front of the old stone church; since it didn't have electricity or indoor plumbing, the congregation only used the 180-year-old building for weddings and funerals in good weather. The lights of the New Bedrock Baptist Church were visible on the hill beyond. The evening sky was a solid ceiling of gray clouds, and the piney air hung moist and heavy. Thunder rolled somewhere in the distance.

"Well, I'll do my best to keep this quick so you don't have to wait out here too long," Miz Ruthie said, glancing out the window at the ominous sky.

"Oh, I'm gonna go into the cemetery with you."

Miz Ruthie bit her lip. "It would probably be better if you just stayed here."

"No ma'am! It's getting' dark out there, and what if you was to trip on a root, or twist your ankle in a gopher hole? I'd be failin' my duty if I didn't escort you proper."

"Okay." She frowned; clearly she was turning something over in her mind. "But I need to pay my respects in my own way, and I want you to promise you won't interfere with me."

"Sure, I promise." He drew an X over his heart with his finger. "Soldier's honor."

"All right then." She opened her door and stepped out onto the gravel with her funeral bouquet, then gave him a sharp look. "You better remember your promise; if you don't like something, don't look."

Andrew squinted at her, wondering what she meant, and followed close behind as she made her way up the path into the graveyard. The first part of the cemetery was the oldest, some graves dating to the early 1800s. They walked among the mottled, decaying marble stones, some so worn that he could barely make out that there had ever been inscriptions on them. The ground was a patchwork of velvety dark moss, gravel-embedded soil, and short green grass.

Andrew ran his hands over the tops of the headstones as he walked, the worn stone rough and gritty. Some of these people were born before the nation had its independence. All had died before it was torn by the War Between the States. He felt a surge of pride; he and his JROTC squad had spent several weeks after school cleaning up the cemetery, clearing brush and weeds away from the old markers and headstones and crypts. His grandpa had told him they'd done a right fine job.

Old stones gave way to newer markers and crypts. The inscriptions became recognizable, and so were the family names. Hillson. Harris. Keller. Smith. Calhoun. Dockholm. Andrew watched as Miz Ruthie went to her mother's grave, pulled three lilies from the bouquet, and laid them on her headstone.

But then, instead of heading to the Reverend Dockholm's freshly-mounded grave near the edge of the trees, Miz Ruthie went to a headstone tucked back amongst the graves of townsfolk who weren't their kin, except maybe by marriage. She knelt at the forgotten grave, laid the bouquet down, and spent several minutes kneeling there with her head bowed.

Andrew tried to stand at easy attention while she paid her respects to whoever it was, but just as he was starting to feel really antsy she got up and headed toward his grandfather's resting place, her hands empty. Shouldn't she have some flowers to pay proper respects? Frowning, he followed her over to the grave.

She held up her hand. "Remember, you promised: no interfering."

She pulled a travel pack of Kleenex out of the pocket of her long black dress—

That's good, she's going to have a big ol' cry over him like my momma did, Andrew thought.

—which she shoved down the front of her dress, apparently into her cleavage. And then she unzipped the dress from neck to hem. Andrew felt his face flush crimson as she shrugged out of the dowdy old-lady garment, revealing that she was wearing a short stoplight-red cocktail dress and gartered fishnet stockings beneath. Miz Ruthie had a really nice ass, and Andrew felt his blush deepen as he realized he'd gotten a rubbery boner at the sight of her in the clingy satin. She was old enough to be his granny, for sweet Jesus' sake!

Miz Ruthie folded the black overdress and set it on a nearby headstone, then strode to the Reverend's grave and began dancing, sweeping the flowers off his headstone with her lean legs.

"Miz Ruthie, what are you doing?" Andrew was aghast.

"Paying all the respects I owe your grandfather." Her skirt rode up with each Rockette kick, and he saw a sterling silver flask strapped to the outside of her left thigh. "Remember, you promised. Crossed your heart and promised."

Once she'd cleared the headstone of flowers, she stood facing the headstone with her legs on either side of the grave, did a half-squat and hiked her skirt up to her hips. She wasn't wearing any underwear. Andrew watched, horrified and hard, as she made a V with her fingers and pulled up on her pussy, and suddenly she was peeing in a strong arc right on the headstone, urine spilling down the words "In Loving Memory of the Reverend Robert M. Dockholm."

Andrew was rooted to the spot, unable to move or speak in his shock. A thousand thoughts crowded in his head, which was about 999 more than usually occupied the space. She was defiling his grandfather's grave! Vandalizing it! And she. Could. Pee. Standing. Up! Andrew had never heard of women doing such a thing. Was she one of those freaky chicks with a dick? He couldn't see anything like a penis, not even a little Cheeto-looking one like that kid in gym class had. No wonder his pa thought she was a witch!

Ruthie's pee stream faltered, stopped, and she swiveled around and did a deeper squat so that her ass was nearly touching the soil. And she began to shit, the poop coming out of her in a long, smooth coil, mounding in perfect circles like soft-serve on the grave. As she grimaced in concentration, gritting her teeth, grinding her hips in circles to squeeze out the poop *just so*, he began to suspect she'd been practicing. And also probably eating a whole lot of prunes on the plane ride from California.

Andrew's vision was starting to darken at the edges, his legs shaking beneath him, so he went with it and fell to his knees, shutting his eyes against his cousin's abominations and loudly repeating every prayer and psalm he could remember.

As he spoke, "The Lord is my strength and shield; my heart trusts in Him and I am helped," inside he was praying, *Dear God, strike this wicked witch down with your Almighty wrath, please dear God, oh please, strike her down.*

His hair rose on end, the air going electric, and a heartbeat later there was a sudden crack of lightning in the trees nearby and one of the tall pines shrieked as its trunk was sundered near the roots, and Andrew could hear it falling—

"Andrew, get out of the way!" Miz Ruthie shouted.

He opened his eyes to see the pine tree plummeting straight down toward his head, no time to stand up. He frog-hopped forward, but the tree slammed down on his right leg, pinning him to the mossy ground, the pain a bright blue spark arcing from his ankle right up into his spine.

Miz Ruthie was still in full squat, but was vigorously wiping herself clean with a handful of the Kleenex she'd stashed in her bra; she dropped the crumpled tissues neatly around her poo-swirl, completing the first-glance illusion that it was some kind of ice cream dessert. Then she stood, pulled her flask out of her thigh holster, unscrewed the cap, and poured the liquid inside over her shit sundae. Andrew smelled strong whiskey. She stepped aside, pulled a packet of matches out of her bra, and lit up her pile, filling the air with the stench of burning feces.

Miz Ruthie strode over to him and squatted near his head, frowning down at him. He tried not to stare at the dark furry fringe peeking beneath the hem of her dress.

"Is your leg broken?"

"No, ma'am, I don't think so." His voice was a dry croak. He'd broken his leg when he fell off a pile of logs at the mill once, and aside from the initial pain his leg wasn't hurting nearly as badly as it had back then.

"Did you pray for God to strike me down?" Her sharp blue eyes bored down into his, daring him to tell her a lie.

He tried to shrink back into the tree's branches. "Yes, ma'am. I did. But...but you deserved it for what you done to my grandpa!"

She laughed at him. "Oh, I did, did I? Let me tell you a little something about just desserts, boy. Let me tell you a little something about that dead old bastard over there that you hold in such high regard.

"Dear ol' Uncle Bob there took over the church when I was about your age, still in high school. My best friend in the whole world was a girl named Jenny; she was the finest fiddle player in the whole state, sweet as orange blossom honey, smart. Would have made a hell of a doctor some day. One afternoon, one of her older cousins offered her a ride home from school, only he didn't take her home; he drove out to the old bridge and raped her. She was so wrecked she wouldn't even talk to me about what he'd done to her, but when she realized she was pregnant, she went to Uncle Bob for help. She thought he surely knew *everything*, and would make things right. And Uncle Bob, ever the student of Christ's wisdom and forgiveness, cussed her out for telling lies about her choir-boy cousin and accused her of being a whore. Jenny left the church in tears, went to her room and wrote me a letter, then went out to the woods behind her family's house and killed herself. Her father passed her suicide off as a hunting accident so she could be buried over there in this rusty old cemetery."

Ruthie nodded toward the headstone where she'd left her bouquet, then pointed a shaky finger at his grandfather's grave. "The Reverend Robert M. Dockholm might as well have loaded the shotgun, put it to Jenny's head and pulled the trigger. As far as I'm concerned, he murdered that girl. Bob deserved to be broken like he broke Jenny, deserved a load of buckshot right between his sanctimonious eyes, but instead he got thirty more years of respect as the pillar of the community, thirty years of ill-gotten wealth by spiritually blackmailing all the sick old folks in the county into signing their worldly possessions over to his church. Jenny's cousin at least had the decency to pick a fight in a biker bar and get his head caved in with a tire iron the year after he assaulted her, but that Bible-waving sack of shit over there got to enjoy a nice life and a nice quiet death.

And so tonight he got me paying my respects the best way I know how."

Miz Ruthie stood up and put her fists on her hips, glaring down at Andrew. "There's a whole lot more you need to know about this fine little town and the people who live in it, but it's up to you whether you want to open your eyes and get a clue about the world, the *real* world, and get out of that nice warm pile of small-town bullshit you've been wallowing in. And here's clue number one: God isn't your personal hit man. I learned that a long time ago, because believe me, I prayed for Him to take out your grandfather. You pray for anyone else's death ever again, boy, you best be prepared for your own."

She inhaled like a diver preparing for a plunge. "So. You've got two choices here. Your first choice is to close your eyes and start praying again, pretending I'm not really here, and I'll call a cab to take me to the airport and call the VFD to come get this tree off you. You'll never have to hear from me again. Your second choice is you take my hand, I'll get the tree off you, and I'll get dressed and we'll go down the road to the Steak and Shake. I'll buy you a malt and tell you all about the skeletons in the family closet.

"So what's it gonna be, Andrew?"

The boy stared up at her, took his own deep breath, and held out his hand.

LETTING GO

MARY SANGIOVANNI

They blurred sometimes so Hank Swanson couldn't see them. They rushed by his ear and made angry sounds that he could no longer attribute to the wind shouldering through the cracks in the house. They were getting stronger. The day before, they moved the toaster three whole feet across the counter. And he suspected that one had learned how to break light bulbs. He'd found two already that week in egg-shell shatters on the floor in the front hallway. They were angry. Maybe getting dangerous.

There were four of them in the house, although they rarely all convened together. Sometimes they were lured by the sound of *Law & Order* from the television set. Quite often, he caught them from the corner of his eye while reading the newspaper. Mostly, though, he felt them late at night, when he was alone with his thoughts. They stood behind him, surrounding his easy chair, charging the air with heat and cold and tension and thin noise. They had never tried to hurt him physically.

He suspected that was going to change, though, now that they could act on things in the house.

These certain memories haunted him—powerful ones. Ones he couldn't let go. But he'd discovered that when one held onto such things long enough and hard enough, they took on lives of their own, lives of discontent and disapproval. They were stuck there with him, unable to rest in the dust of the past and the graves of resolution. And they hated him for it.

He stood in the first floor bathroom, studying a worn and tired face. Thin lines fanned from the corners of blue eyes that had seen too much. Set grooves around his mouth spoke not of years of smiles, but of grimaces and bared teeth. That scar above his left eyebrow remained from when, in a flurry of fear, Linda had scratched at his face.

Hank had done so much he wished he could take back. The lusterless gray of his hair reminded him of the overcast sky on the day Linda left. The DUTY HONOR FIDELITY tattoo on his right bicep was the same dark color as that little Vietnamese girl's eyes...

Upstairs in his bedroom, Abuse howled like a battered woman. Like Hank's wife had. Like his mother had, all those years ago. It was, perhaps, the most volatile of all the memories. Its explosive temper mirrored what his own had once been. He remembered that, every time Abuse threw an angry tantrum.

He flinched when he heard a wooden crash upstairs, heavy, like his dresser had been knocked over. He turned away from the mirror to find Nam standing behind him.

It grinned. Its sweat-slick tanned body rippled with muscle as it stepped casually out of the way. Hank brushed past, and felt steamy jungle heat from its skin. Hank believed that the memories' physicality was an effect of what Linda might have called personification. She was an English teacher, and although he'd paid little attention to English, it seemed to fit, that word *personification*. He'd suspected even then that the memories could take shape from the blurs of light and shadow they used to be. They seemed now more physical than ever. Now, they had faces. Patchwork pieces of faces from recollections in his head.

Nam's eyes were like that little girl's. Its arms were like the Viet Cong he'd clipped in the back of the head. Its laughter was like the old woman's before he'd burst her throat open. He didn't acknowledge the memory, but it followed him into the kitchen. He felt its eyes on him as he made a sandwich at the counter.

It spoke to him in Vietnamese. "We have come to a realization. A consensus."

He answered in English without turning around. "Oh yeah? What's that?"

Its reply, also in English, came halted and awkward. "If we kill you, you will then must let us go."

"How so?"

"No one take memory with him when he die."

Hank stopped, turning slowly, the mayonnaise knife in his hand. "That would only be true if consciousness ended with death. How can you be sure that will happen?"

"Because you believe it."

"What if I'm wrong?" He turned back to the sandwich. "Then you'd be stuck with me for eternity."

"Not necessarily so, Hank." A third voice frosted the air between them.

Hank paused, mid-bite. Death in the Family was, by far, the most cool and collected. It scared him more than the others. He put the sandwich down and turned around. The memory—a first from his childhood—sat at the kitchen table. It wore a neat cream sweater which made the pale bluish boy-features of its face and hands more prominent. Its colorless lips pressed together. The black hair, rumpled like a child's, recalled the windsweep of racing Schwinns and the sweaty hairlines of baseball and tag in mid-summer. It sat otherwise reserved, Sunday-best neat, its lean, pre-teenaged limbs poised. After a moment, it unfolded its hands and dusted an errant piece of fuzz from its sweater. "Really, Hank, give us some credit for a degree of forethought."

It looked up, and its pupiless white eyes managed the semblance of focus on him. He felt cold down his back. "Let's say you take with you into the afterlife whatever you remember of this one. Then it simply becomes a matter of eradicating the part of your physical brain which harbors memories. Now, we've mastered physical contact. It's a matter of time before we master force."

It paused to let him soak up this information. Hank wasn't sure that Death in the Family spoke the whole truth. There seemed to Hank to be a huge leap between wiggling light bulbs out of their sockets to crash on the floor, and wielding a baseball bat to brain him in his sleep.

Death in the Family continued. "You hardly seem as hung up on the good memories as you are on us, so we believe the cost to be relatively low. I see from your expression that you don't buy that. Consider for a moment if the Judeo-Christian concept of Heaven and Hell exists. Your soul—your energy—either seeks God and God alone, and leaves memories behind, or is sent to Hell for eternal torment, where memories will be the least of your concern. Or, for the sake of argument, let's say it turns out that the soul is home for the memories that construct your sense of self. Then the afterlife is buoyed by memories. If we simply disconnect you from us, you'll go to the sweet peaceful oblivion you wanted anyway. No judgment, no reconnection with your angry dead. No hell." It winked at him. "And we'll be put to rest. There is no one else to keep us here. No one who cares enough to keep your memories alive. You're alone."

Hank snorted. "Alone."

Death in the Family gave him a wide, crocodile smile. "Alone with us."

"There are holes in your theory. What if my version of hell is being forced to relive each and every one of you every day for the rest of time? Or what if I'm left a ghost in the afterlife, to haunt the earth where all my memories of violence and pain keep me chained?"

Leaning in the doorway, gleaming with sweat in the kitchen light, Nam cast an uncertain glance in Death in the Family's direction, but the other memory seemed unperturbed.

"Hell, Hank—any true form of hell, I'd say—would be more than that, by its very nature. In either scenario, you're describing your life exactly as you live it now, on Earth, day to day remembering us, day to day chained to this house. Hell, by its connotations, would constitute more than the mere mechanisms of your daily life."

"You're guessing. But you don't know for sure."

The memory shifted in the chair, folding its hands on the table again. "Hank, really, it doesn't matter. Crushing your skull would give us some satisfaction at least, even if nothing else were to change. And the potential risk is worth it to us, since the possibility that it will work in our favor seems higher than it working in yours."

"No single one of you can do it, anyway. You can't kill me."

Death in the Family regarded him with a cool stare, eye to glassy eye. "That's not true, generally speaking. Single memories drive the life out of people all the time. What about your Linda's Death of a Child? The one you beat out of her. Remember that one?"

Hank felt anger rise in waves of heat beneath his arms and around his neck. "That was an accident." He cringed at how much he sounded like his dad, when his little brother Robbie had died. An accident, his father claimed.

The memory seemed to read his thoughts. "Seems to be a popular refrain among the males in your family." After a pause, it added, "Ask Abuse if that's true, that it was an accident. See what she says."

"Screw you."

Death in the Family gave him a patient smile. "All of this conversation is of no real relevance. All of us together can do this. All of us together can overwhelm you."

"Why are you telling me all this? Giving me a running head start, are you?"

"Common courtesy. You created us, after all. It changes nothing, though, for you to know. You've proved that there is nowhere you can go that we can't find you. And face it, Hank—you've stopped running."

«««—»»»

The night passed with little more than thumping in the upstairs hallway—they were practicing, evidently, but hadn't quite worked up to smashing his skull in yet. They made their presence known, though. They wanted him to be afraid, to maybe force some soul searching that might let them go.

Wasn't going to happen. Those bastards were his to hold onto, his to wallow over if he chose. He owned them.

Not to be deterred, though, Shot in the Leg gave him a hard time the following morning.

From the open window, he felt that outside the air was humid, thick with unspilled rain. The sky blew down and swallowed his neighborhood in fog. In the distance, he heard the hungry rumble of thunder.

Oncoming storms always made the pain in his knee worse, right on the outer meniscus, which a bullet had nearly severed years ago. Even though he'd had surgery, the knee never felt quite right—not after those occasional nights in the bottle, and definitely not before storms.

Shot in the Leg leaned casually against the wall by the TV. It wore the same flippant tousle of blond hair and the same cocky smirk as the punk from the convenience store who shot Hank. Its legs were mottled with scars beneath the rips in the jeans. One was large, thick in the thigh like his partner's had been. The other was skinny, like the guy in shorts from the convenience store, the one who'd covered his girlfriend from the spray of glass and flying bullets. Both looked shaky. Shot in the Leg did not look phased, though. Its legs always shook. Hank wondered if it felt anything beyond hate—like pain. Throbbing ligaments. Strained muscles. Buckling knees. Now that they could think on their own, he wondered what the memories remembered. What they thought about when they were alone.

The memory folded its arms across the blood-splattered chest. The clerk's chest, the one the punk kid shot before shooting Hank. At the time he'd been Officer Henry Swanson, working his way up to a spot somewhere in the Tactical Division of Morris County's Major Crimes Unit.

He was now Mr. Swanson-down-the-street, ex-vet, ex-cop, ex-husband, full-time asshole.

"So you ready to die, officer?"

Hank tried to ignore it. On TV, Michael Strahan was making Kelly Ripa smile. He liked to see Kelly smile. Sometimes she looked so pretty. Sometimes she looked like Linda.

"You can't ignore me. Not today."

Hank felt a twinge in his knee, and he rubbed it absently.

From the corner of his eye, he saw Shot in the Leg shove itself off the wall. It sauntered, as best as it was able, in front of the television set, crossed around the coffee table, and sat down on the other end of the couch. It kicked up dirty worn sneakers and propped them on top of an old issue of Penthouse.

The woman on page 12 of that issue looked like Linda, too.

"Hank, do you want to die?"

He didn't turn his head. "No."

"Do you want to live?"

"Haven't given that much thought." Hank watched the Kelly-Michael banter without really hearing it. Michael was a snappy dresser. Kelly could be beautiful sometimes.

"Just let us go."

"Leave me alone."

Shot in the Leg laughed. "We'd like to. Let us go."

Hank sighed. "You think I like having you here?"

"I think you keep us to fill up that space. Somehow, we're easier to hold onto than your wedding, or birthday parties, or making the force."

"Nothing to them. I can barely remember those things."

"Consider recalling them a project then."

"I'm in retirement. I'm not looking for new projects."

Shot in the Leg gave him an exasperated sigh. "Look, I'm trying to keep you from getting little sharp broken pieces of skull all stuck in your nice, clean brain. But there's no love lost if you won't listen. We hate you, and we know you hate us."

That was not entirely true. What Hank hated was to admit that, of the four of them, something about Shot in the Leg seemed okay. He'd been trying to be good the night he was shot, trying to Serve and Protect, to save lives. He'd failed, of course, as he'd failed at his marriage, as he'd failed as a son and a big brother, but for that one memory, he could at least honestly look at himself and know he tried.

His knee ached in little pulses. That he tried to be good—that was not entirely true, either. A clusterfuck of a situation, the shooting had been. Protocol ignored, hair-trigger Dirty-Harry hijinks ending with people getting shot. A barely-cleared IA investigation. A bum knee.

But if any of the memories ever cut him a break, it was Shot in the Leg. He thought that warranted a certain degree of honesty between them.

"You four are all I've got."

"How about no memories at all, then? A clean slate. A new beginning."

"Too old for that. Too late. Now if you don't mind, I'm watching this. Go practice moving toasters." Hank scowled and turned up the volume. Sometimes Michael looked waxy and Kelly looked plastic. A cranky thought, and one, for some reason, that reminded him of Linda.

She looked waxy when her eye swelled. And plastic when she put on extra make-up to cover a bruise.

He felt bad about both. Sometimes Linda was so pretty. So pretty. He missed her.

Shot in the Leg got up. "Suit yourself. Kitchen appliances, nothing. I've learned the fine and dexterous art of loading a firearm. You know...in case the toasters don't work."

‹‹‹——›››

Abuse rarely confronted him head on. When it did, it usually sported something sprained, mildly fractured, or in need of stitches. He hated those rare occasions when he ran into it in the upstairs hallway, not so much because of the sight of the physical injuries, but because of the guilt. He'd taken to avoiding it as often as possible. When it went on one of its tearing fits in the bedroom upstairs, he slept on the couch. When it tore up the kitchen, around seven most evenings, he went out to China Wok down the street.

He was nearly certain Abuse learned to move the toaster first.

The memory used to remind him of weak and beaten women, women whose fragile inner beauty and relentless outer beauty drove the awful sinking feelings of possessiveness, helpless mistrust and blind anger. The beauty that struck chords of remorse after.

Nowadays, he saw the purest and most intense rage of all the memories in Linda's swollen eye. It glared at him from beneath the long blond hair, stringy with blood in the front, his mother's split lip puffed out in an angry pout. There was even some reclamation of power in the broken wrist, the cracked rib that bled out underneath the pale and papery skin, the dress he'd nearly twisted Linda's arm off for wearing one night. These things reminded him of the horrible mistake he'd made. He'd hurt her, again and again in ways she could never forgive. In ways he couldn't forgive himself. And Abuse reminded him every chance it got.

Hank climbed the stairs that evening to right whatever Abuse had knocked over in the bedroom. In the upstairs hallway, he listened for its crying and hearing nothing, he crept to the bedroom.

He froze in the doorway when he found it in a fetal curl on the bed. Its blood seeped into the cotton of the comforter and spread out across the quilted diamonds. To the left of the bed, the dresser lay splintered face-down. A number of casualties in the form of underwear and socks had tumbled out toward the foot of the bed. The lamp that formerly stood on top, as well as the silver picture frame with Linda's picture, lay in pieces just where the comforter brushed the floor.

Hank's mouth opened, then closed. Cool sweat ran from beneath his arms, and his chest felt tight. The memory had done that. The memory had toppled something that even Hank would have had trouble moving.

He took a careful step back into the hallway.

Abuse shot up and glared at him. The shredded silver rags it wore snapped outward as if up in arms. It moved off the bed and swooped to the doorway so fast that Hank cried out. He backed up further into the hall until he felt the hard wooden post of the banister thump against his back. He was cornered. Abuse swam up to him, hovering inches from his face, the gash in its forehead leaking watery blood over the crusted black around it.

It smelled like Linda's perfume. The scent made him feel sick.

"I've been waiting for you to come upstairs."

"Please don't do this." He'd gotten used to the plaintive whisper his voice took on any time that particular memory cornered him. He hated it, but he slipped into the whisper every time, all the same, like familiar slippers.

"I wanted to see your face when I told you I can kill you now, if I wanted to. Almost every one of us can. We're close, so close to where I want us to be. But we agreed to do it together. All of us."

"You can't do anything, you lying—"

His sentence was cut off by a sharp crack to the mouth. The force of it turned his jaw. He felt Linda's long red nails graze his cheek. His face stung in the wake of the palm, shocking him into silence.

It could touch him. Physically touch him.

"What should I break today? I can do fingers, maybe, or toes. Something little. Something delicious. I can fuck you up, you egotistical bitch."

It laughed, a wild woman's cackle.

And Hank realized then that he was in serious trouble.

He took a chance and pushed it away, hard. His hands sank into the soft chill of it, and it felt like wet sand—like silt, really. Cold, a little slippery, and soft.

But he'd caught it off-guard and an inch or so in, he felt something solid—the part of it, maybe, that had solidified enough to allow physical contact with him in the first place. And he managed to move it. It staggered back a foot or so before recovering and lunging forward, but it was enough time for him to slip away and down the stairs.

He turned once near the bottom, surprised that it hadn't caught up and tried to push him down already. At the top of the steps, it seethed, its bruised knuckles tight as it clenched its fists, restraint arresting its chase. Fury shone bright and wet in its one unswollen eye, its split lip bleeding over bared teeth and down its chin. It howled, not in fear or pain as Linda had done, not in frustration as his mother had. It was angry. It did not want to wait for the others; it wanted to kill him right now.

Death in the Family came up behind it and took hold of its arm, gentle but commanding.

"Get the others," Death in the Family said to it. "It's time."

«««—»»»

Hank went out to the garage and got the broom. The bristles stuck out in odd directions like bed-head, but the wood felt good and sturdy in his hands.

The memories had to be solid to hurt him, and if they were solid, he could fight back. Let them try and kill him.

He owned them. His death was not their call.

Hank Swanson knew he wasn't any better than anyone else. But he didn't think he was pure evil. After all, people bought, sold, traded, stole and borrowed memories on which to build a sense of self all the time. In his retirement, he never gave much thought to a conscience. He'd always assumed that he let his wither and die. Years of exposure to murder, greed, rape, callousness, and stupidity did that to a person. They made a guy realize that evil is plainly and simply impure. Mussolini made the trains run on time, and all that. The Devil had been God's favorite angel, according to Linda's faith. So what was conscience but personal judgment? Who was he to judge anyone's acts? A person "in good conscience" couldn't righteously hate something that wasn't pure evil, and frankly, no one was an absolute either way, good or bad. He never thought of himself as being in good conscience, but he knew one thing. Shot in the Leg was wrong. He didn't hate those memories. Not that he felt no sense of justice; he'd always suspected a part of him kept the memories around to punish himself, in a way. But he simply didn't feel that he could pass sentence anymore, even on himself. It wasn't for him to decide. And his encounter with Abuse upstairs made him realize that extended to the memories, as well.

They had no right to condemn him, either. He wanted to live.

He made purposeful strides from the garage to the den, testing out the swing of the broom handle, listening for their approach: the whisper of feet that weren't really feet and the dull hum of their anger.

In the center of the den, he waited. He heard the crash of broken glass from somewhere upstairs.

He considered leaving, but it wouldn't matter. Train station, hotel room, deep in the woods, on a sunny beach—they'd always know where to find him. They were part of him.

He could reason with them. Suggest therapy. The thought got squashed fast, though. Therapy was like Neverland magic—one had to believe in it in order for it to work. And he didn't. Never had. Even if he would consider it, therapy took years, if it worked at all. The memories were fed up *now*. They were out of patience. He didn't have years.

Hank heard them on the stairs. He actually heard their footsteps on the stairs. They meant to intimidate him with the physical thud of their footfalls.

He swung the broom handle at the air in front of him. It made a satisfying whizz sound.

They entered the den together, the four of them, their expressions blank. Their eyes watched him, solemn and somehow peaceful. This was going to be their death, too, and they were ready for it. They were just riding it out, seeing it to the end. Their desperate resolve frightened him.

He swung the broom handle out in front of him. "Stay away from me."

They drifted closer, not quite tentative but cautious, like jaguars moving in on their prey. Each held a weapon.

Death in the Family smiled. "That's all we want, Hank." It held a baseball bat. Where had it dug up that old thing? The force hadn't had a company game in years.

Nam held a rake from the shed. In Vietnamese, it said, "If you hold still, we'll make it quick."

"Fuck you," he responded in English. "Fuck all of you."

Abuse had a broken wine bottle by the neck. Hank kept a wary eye on it. The jagged end looked to him like a gaping, hungry mouth, salivating in the den light.

He tried to think of good memories—something, anything to weaken their hold. But the bad memories had a much further head start. They'd grown strong over time—time he didn't have to build up good ones.

Still, he tried to think of a birthday party as a kid, something fun, something enjoyable. He remembered instead the fight his father had gotten into with his mother on his little brother's birthday. How angry his father was when he left the house with Robbie. His mother's baby. Her favorite.

Robbie looked up to Hank. Robbie didn't want to go river fishing with Dad. He was always scared when Dad got that look in his eyes and ground his teeth and clenched his fists like that. When he focused straight ahead and refused to look at anyone.

His dad claimed he'd dozed off while they were waiting for the fish to bite. Robbie had gone off by himself, slipped on a rock, and fallen into the water. Robbie couldn't swim. He never liked the water. He never liked going anywhere alone with Dad. The splashing woke up his father, but not in time to reach Robbie. Or so he said. There were no fishing trips after that.

Hank hadn't been there, because he'd caught attitude that morning, and endured the smack-around and the grounding to get out of going on the trip. Hank had saved himself.

No happy memories there. Death in the Family grinned at him, again seeming to read his thoughts.

"Bastards." He glared at them all, and made a half-arc with the broom handle. The memories snapped back out of range.

Abuse lunged at him and he swung again, but the memory was quicker. It brought the broken glass down on his hand, and back up along the inside of his wrist, slicing it open. He dropped the broom handle. Where the bottle had bitten through his skin, tiny drops of his blood smeared the jagged teeth.

He bent to pick up the broom with his left hand. He wouldn't be able to swing it as well, especially with the pain pumping out bloody squirts down his stronger arm, but he'd make do. He looked up, and saw Death in the Family standing over him with the bat.

He crab-scuttled back and stood on shaky legs. The jerky movement sent a light patter of blood across the carpet. They closed in on him again.

Hank panicked. *Good thoughts, try again, good thoughts…*

"Too late for that," Shot in the Leg said. It clicked the safety off Hank's gun.

He tried to think of his wedding to Linda. It shimmered for a moment just at his periphery. He thought about the church, the cake, the champagne glasses, the dance, the way it pissed him off that his best man leered at Linda all night...

And he remembered hitting her years later, over and over until she'd lost the baby. He didn't know she was pregnant. He hadn't been mad about that.

It had been the dress, the silver one that he thought was too low-cut, the one that hugged her hips and drew attention to her legs, and oh God, how beautiful she'd looked. He wasn't the only one who noticed. A lot of other men did. And she seemed to like that, the bitch. She liked other men looking at her. Didn't give a damn if *he* did—sure she could *say* she'd dressed nice for him, but he knew.

The blood got all over the front of her dress. All over the comforter, too. She'd curled up on the bed, fetal and bleeding, and cried, too much in pain, too hurting to move. And he'd left her there because he couldn't stand to see her bleeding and he couldn't stand to hear her cry. Not like that. No satisfaction in her crying like that. She'd called the ambulance herself.

Abuse held the remains of the broken bottle up by his neck, as if trying to eyeball the best angle to stick it in.

He tried to think of something, anything, but each time he tried, they overwhelmed him. He remembered the village in Viet Nam with the little wide-eyed girl and her grandmother, and the American fire that fell across their bodies in an effort to route out the Viet Cong they were hiding. He remembered the punk on the convenience store floor, bleeding, scared, hurt, a kid again, the way his head blossomed red on the floor when Hank shot him. He remembered how his dad used to beat his mom and then leave and he would find her on the floor, curled up and crying, mumbling between tears about having to make dinner for the boys, both of them, even after Robbie had died. He remembered being terrified every night when his father came in his bedroom to say good night, terrified because it wasn't such a stretch to imagine those big hands that liked to hit and punch also liking to push, or to hold a throat underwater until it filled up. And every time he did something bad, he imagined that his dad had given Robbie that same look, that same disappointment and barely simmering disgust, right before he drowned him.

Fathers who cared that their youngest sons accidentally drowned

251

didn't say *accident* as if it was a blessing in disguise, and they didn't share a look with their eldest sons that said *You could be next, if you cross me.*

"Wait," he muttered. "Wait."

Shot in the Leg trained the gun on his head. It would get its turn last. Finish him off, probably, after each of them had gotten in a good lick.

Inside, he chuckled, but he knew it wasn't really funny. None of them had opted to use the toaster.

Death in the Family took a step forward. "Good-bye, Hank."

"Wait," he said again, his gaze darting around the room for an exit, an opening between them through which he might escape. There was none.

He swung at Nam blindly, but Abuse must have warned them. Nam blurred—everywhere but the wrist and the hand that held the rake—just seconds before Hank's broom handle passed through its chest, then grew sharper and more solid again in its wake.

The first blow from its rake cracked against his skull. His head froze and the room in front of him wavered like heat off hot pavement. Then the pain thudded black spots across his eyes.

The chilly draw of glass across his cheeks and forehead, the wet of blood running into blood, felt strangely right.

What was his brother's name?

Death in the Family swung the baseball bat. Home run.

Hank felt another sharp crack. He smelled perfume but he couldn't remember whose it was. His eyes were painted black, and he slumped down onto something soft. Couch.

He heard a crunch and felt something give above his left eye. He felt light. Soft, like the couch. Even the pain in his head felt fuzzy. Bad reception. Couldn't see Kelly and Michael.

He'd been in the army. When? Where? It didn't matter.

It all stopped with thunder against his head.

«««—»»»

A few weeks later, Detective Cauley stood in the den of Hank Swanson's house. Without the yellow tape, the swarming CSIs, the investigating officers, and the miscellaneous craning necks and curious frowns of neighbors and news people, Cauley could think alone, in the center of everything.

His gaze wandered to the couch. The clean-up crew had gotten most of the blood out of the middle cushion, and all of it from the carpet. Cauley had known Hank for years. He'd gone to his retirement party, in fact, down at the station. He knew Hank had problems—lady trouble, mostly—but Cauley couldn't imagine anything that would have driven the man to suicide. Hank just never seemed too troubled by anything.

The medical examiner said that Hank's body had been worked over pretty good—baseball bat, broken bottle, rake—before the shot to the head. But the only fingerprints on any of the weapons were Hank's, and there was gunpowder residue on his fingers. Given several of the angles of the cuts, the ME had concluded that he'd done most if not all the other injuries to himself.

Cauley could almost feel the sum total of Hank Swanson's life swirling heavy around him in the room and throughout the house. The darkest of corners did not go unused there. The dusty shelves, the bare furnishings, the wear and tear of lonely routine—none of it was empty. In that house, Cauley still felt the man who'd lived there, or at least remnants of the man. The house hadn't cooled yet. The spirit—or spirits—of his past hadn't left.

"Shame," he muttered to himself. "He was one of our own."

Behind Detective Cauley, Dark Alley, "Accidental" Shooting, and First Homicide waited, pelting his back with black-eyed daggers of frustration. They felt strong in that house, stronger than they ever had before. They felt alive. And they felt angry.

THE VIKING PLAYS PATTY CAKE

Brian Keene

The air burned their lungs, thick with smoke from the fires—and the stench of the dead.

Chino pushed a branch out of the way and peered through the bushes. "What's wrong with him?"

"Don't know." King shrugged. "He ain't a zombie. Looks more like a Viking."

They studied the giant on the park bench. He was impressive; early forties but in good shape, well over six feet tall, decked out in tattoos and earrings. His hands clutched an M-1 Garand, the barrel still smoking from the round he'd just drilled into a zombie. The creature sprawled on the ground ten feet away—minus its head. The grass and pavement were littered with more bodies. An assortment of weapons lay scattered on the bench; two more rifles, four grenades, a dozen handguns, and boxes of ammunition for each. Next to those was a large backpack, filled with bottled water and food.

The Viking sat like a statue, his eyes roving and watchful. Another zombie closed in on him from the right. The rifle roared and the creature's head exploded.

The Viking never left the bench. He brought down three more before the rest of the creatures fell back. From their vantage point, Chino and King heard one of the monsters ordering others to find guns. Several of them raced off.

The Viking began muttering to himself. "Patty cake, patty cake…"

Chino crouched back down. "The fuck is wrong with him? Why don't he hide?"

"I don't know," King said. "Maybe he's crazy."

"Got an awful lot of firepower," Chino observed. "We could use that shit."

"Word."

The Viking fired another shot. From far away, deep inside the city, more gunfire echoed.

Chino's fingers tightened around his .357. "That the Army guys shooting?"

"Maybe," King said. "They've been trying to take the city back. Held it up to the railroad tracks down on Eight Mile, but then they got overrun by them things."

Chino shook his head. "Why bother. Ain't nobody in charge anymore. Why don't they just bail?"

King peeked again. The zombies still kept their distance from the man with the guns, but more were coming; dead humans, dogs, cats, squirrels. The Viking calmly reloaded, still mumbling under his breath.

"Patty cake, patty cake, baker's man…"

"What's he doing?" Chino whispered.

"Playing patty cake."

Chino grunted. "Whole world's gone crazy."

"There're still people in charge. You know Tito and his crew?"

"The ones holed up inside the public works building?"

King nodded. "I was talking to him three days ago. Went out there and traded six cases of beer for some gasoline. They got a ham radio."

"How they working it? Power been out for a week."

"Generator," King said. "They heard some military general got parts of California under control. And there's a National Guard unit in Pennsylvania that's taken back Gettysburg. Could happen here, too."

Chino frowned. "That would suck. I like the way things is. Do what we want, when we want. We got the guns."

"Not as many as that guy." King nodded at the Viking.

Both men peeked out of the bushes again. The zombies inched closer, circling the park bench. Some now carried rifles as well. The Viking put down the Garand, and picked up a grenade. His eyes were steel.

"*Open fire,*" one of the zombies commanded. "*He is just one human.*"

With one fluid movement, the Viking pulled the pin and tossed the grenade toward the undead. There was a deafening explosion. Dirt and body parts splattered onto the grass. The Viking threw a second grenade, but one of the creatures snatched it up and flung it back. The explosive soared towards the bushes—the bushes concealing Chino and King.

"Shit…" King shoved Chino forward. "Move your ass!"

The grenade failed to detonate, but neither man noticed. They were too busy dashing from the shrubbery—and directly, they realized too late, into the firefight. The M-1 Garand roared, and the zombies returned fire.

"Motherfucker," Chino shouted. "We done it now!"

Bullets plowed through the dirt at their feet and whizzed by their heads. Chino and King opened fire, helping the Viking mow down the remaining zombies. Within seconds, all of the dead were dead again.

The Viking turned his weapon on the men.

"Whoa!' King held up his hands. "We're alive, yo. Don't shoot!"

The Viking didn't respond.

"Chino," King whispered. "Put your gun down."

"Fuck that." Chino spat in the grass. "Tell that puta to put his down first."

King smiled at the Viking. "We don't mean no harm. Hell, we just helped you."

"Why?"

King blinked. "Because you were in trouble, man. Why you sitting out here in the open like that, Mister…?"

"Beauchamp." The Viking's shoulders sagged, and he put the rifle down. "Mark Beauchamp."

Chino lowered his weapon, wondering what King was up to.

"Why you out here on this bench, Mr. Beauchamp?" King's eyes flicked over the stranger's arsenal. He licked his lips. "Wouldn't it be safer trying to find some shelter? Come wit' us, we can hide you."

"No." The Viking shook his head. "I don't think so. I'm waiting."

"Waiting? For what?"

The Viking's eyes turned glassy, and King realized the man was fighting back tears.

"I had a job at the Ford stamping plant, just south of the city. Wasn't what I wanted to do with my life, but it was okay. Fed my family. Had a wife, Paula, and four kids. My son's twenty-one. My daughters are fifteen, fourteen, and five months."

The Viking paused, and despite the tears welling up in his eyes, he smiled.

"I think raising my boy was easier than the girls."

King nodded.

Chino shifted from foot to foot, his finger flexing around the trigger. Was King just going to talk the guy to death?

"I was at work when it happened. I heard it all started in Escanaba, but it spread to Detroit fast. By the time I got home, Paula and the kids were gone. No note. Nothing. The evacuation order didn't go out until a day later, so I don't know what happened."

His face darkened, and then he continued.

"There was blood in our kitchen—a lot of blood. I don't know whose it was. And one of the windows was broken. But that's all."

"Sorry to hear that," King said.

"I spent the first twelve days looking for them. But then I got an idea. We used to come here. I'd sit on this bench with my daughter, Erin, and we'd play patty cake. So I'm waiting, see? They'll come back. Paula wouldn't just leave like that. She knows how worried I'd be. I'm waiting for my family. I miss my kids."

"And just shooting zombies?"

"Yeah. I've become a pretty good shot. Used to have a kick-ass pellet gun."

"What about the birds, man? How you gonna shoot them?"

"Haven't bothered me yet. And my family will be here before the birds show up. You'll see."

King glanced at Chino, then back at the Viking. He tried swallowing the lump in his throat.

"Sure you won't come with us?"

The Viking shook his head.

King slowly approached the bench. Chino tensed. Here it came. King had the guy off guard. Now he'd pop him, they'd grab the shit, and get the hell gone before more zombies came back. But King didn't waste the guy. Instead, he shook his hand.

"Good luck."

"Thanks."

King turned back to Chino. "Come on. Let the man wait in peace."

Chino's eyes nearly popped out of his head. "Say what?"

"You heard me," King growled. "Let him be."

King trudged across the grass, and Chino ran to catch up with him. He grabbed King's arm and spun him around.

"The fuck was that all about? We could have smoked him."

"No," King said, his voice thick with emotion. "We ain't touching him."

"Why not?"

"Because," King sighed, "I miss my kids, too."

An artillery shell whistled over the city. The explosion rumbled through the streets.

Beneath it all, they heard the Viking playing patty cake.

SHADOW CHASER

SIMON WOOD

I spotted the ramshackle farmhouse from the dirt road. The directions were vague and the house wasn't marked, but I knew I had the right place. It was the kind of place I would have chosen.

Turning into the long driveway, I noticed three tall figures shoulder-to-shoulder on the porch. *That* I wasn't expecting. The meeting was meant to be a one-on-one affair with no spectators. Alarm bells rang in my head, but there was no way I could turn tail and run for the hills. I had to see things through, no matter how bad they got—especially after the phone call.

"Cam, you have to meet me," he'd said. "You have to help me stop you. If you don't, people will die."

I'd recognized the voice immediately and knew I had no choice. There'd been too much killing over the years and if I could prevent any further bloodshed, then I would do my best. It was the least I could do, considering the amount of blood on my hands.

Pulling up in front of the farmhouse, I recognized my welcome party on the porch: Klein, my lawyer; Westerman, my doctor; and Trant, my professor. Except these men weren't waiting. They were hanging from the porch rafters, strung up with clothesline, their hands tied behind them. From their contorted and discolored features it was obvious their necks hadn't broken. They'd died from strangulation, a sign of a bad hangman, but I knew the hangman well and he was anything but incompetent. He'd wanted their deaths to be long and agonizing. The corpses swayed, slapping together like a human wind chime producing an off-key melody.

I slipped from my car and went up to the trinity to pay my respects. They were the ones who'd saved me from a guaranteed death sentence and gotten me my subsequent release from the state hospital. We'd corresponded for a year or so after the treatment had ended, but our lives had moved on and we'd lost touch. But I could always find out what was happening with Trant. His name and face were featured regularly in the headlines over the years, thanks to the famous "Trant method." I lingered in front of Professor Trant, my savior. Good old Trant. He'd convinced the world he had the answer to society's nightmares. He really believed he could save the human race from itself. Poor bastard—look where that thinking had gotten him.

"Like Icarus, did you dare to fly too high?" I asked the professor as I patted his leg.

I tried my best to ignore the stench. All three men had messed themselves, and an untidy cocktail of feces and urine pooled at their feet. It was impossible to tell if fear or death had been the cause. At one time, the repugnant scene wouldn't have disturbed me. I suppose it just goes to show what a good job Trant did with me.

I climbed the four steps to the porch and called out through the open doorway. "I'm here, just as you requested." I glanced back at the hanged men and my voice lost its power, trailing off to a whisper. "I thought you said we could prevent death." I wasn't sure whether I said these words or just thought them.

No one replied.

I took another step and stood at the threshold to the farmhouse. The early evening light illuminated little beyond the welcome mat. A tightening in my stomach prevented me from venturing inside. I'd used abandoned places like this to inflict pain and death. I rubbed my fingers together, feeling the blood that had once slid between them. Images of what I'd done engulfed me and I had to take a step back lest they wash me away. I leaned against the window ledge to steady myself.

"Show yourself, Mac," I demanded.

This time I received an answer.

"I'm glad you came," a voice said from the darkness within the house.

Although I'd heard his voice on the phone, it was nothing compared to hearing it from just feet away. It was too much, and my resolve to confront him melted. I didn't want this anymore. It would have been so easy to run, but how does anyone outrun his shadow?

He came to the front door, and for the first time since Trant's separation tank, I saw my other self. The sep-tank was like a deprivation chamber, except it wasn't filled with water, but with an energy field. For days without rest, Trant had ruthlessly psychoanalyzed me in the sep-tank, forcing me to confront the killer inside. In my delirium he had appeared not as a delusion or an apparition but as a physical being. The tank's construction was able to support and solidify my mental projection and I came face-to-face with my other self—the tumor that had been eating me alive. As soon as I was free of Mac, Trant had me dragged out of the tank a cured and sane man. He'd entombed Mac for further research.

"Cam, it's been a long time," he said. "Too long."

He stopped inches from my face and examined me. He'd come from me and we should have been identical twins. We shared the same height and build, even the same thinning hairline. What we didn't share was his leer, which failed to hide its contempt for the world and everyone who inhabited it. Deep lines that mimicked the curve of his smile seemed to have been carved onto his face with a box cutter. His hungry hands flexed continuously, as if ready to ensnare his next prey. The eyes were the biggest difference between us—his were hollow, absent of soul. To stare into them meant staring into a bottomless pit.

"How have you been, brother?" he asked.

Brother. That word raked broken glass down my spine. He wasn't my mother's child. If anyone had breathed life into him, it was me. I was father to this monster. Of course, Dr. Westerman would have disagreed. In his opinion, Mac wasn't in fact born but was a product of my environment. I preferred Klein's courtroom analogy. It's the one that made the most sense to me. He described my other personality as my shadow—someone that was me and at the same time not me. The concept helped me sleep easy at nights. But standing here, in front of Mac, I knew I would never sleep easy again.

Mac took a step back from me and nodded to himself, acknowledging an unasked question. It was difficult to read him, but I could hazard a guess as to what he was thinking. Just as I could see the cruelty manifested on his body, he could see the meekness and empathy that had become part of me. Although polar opposites, I was sure we could agree on one thing. We had nothing but contempt for one other.

"I didn't think you could survive outside the sep-tank," I said.

Mac smirked. "What can I tell you? Trant's technology had a little side effect. The longer I stayed, the more real I became."

"Did Trant know?"

"Let's just say it was a little something he didn't want the press to find out about. It wouldn't have been good for his image."

Trant, what a fool you were, I thought. He'd played with fire and had gotten burned.

"Did you have to kill them?" I asked. I wanted to sound harsh, but lament filled my words. Pathetic, really. I should have been stronger than this, but strength was a trait that belonged to my shadow. Anger and conviction had become impotent emotions since the separation.

"Of course I did." Mac wandered over to his handiwork. He brushed a lazy hand across the back of the dead men's legs, causing the human wind chime to sing its dull song again. He leaned against the porch railing. "What did they ever do for me?"

"Were they meant to do anything for you?"

Mac stiffened, a flush of anger consuming his features. "Yes, they were. They owed me. They gave you liberty and freedom, while they gave me institutional purgatory. What kind of deal was that?"

"You got what you deserved."

"Bullshit. My hand was your hand when we took a life. I didn't do it by myself. You were there every step of the way. We should have been locked up together or not at all."

"So what will square it for you? Killing me too?"

And how I wished he would kill me. Freedom had worn me out. In the eyes of the law I was innocent, but that didn't stop the guilt. Mac was right. My hand had been his hand when we killed, and removing him like a strip of tape from the mouth of one of our victims didn't change a thing. I was still a killer—just a remorseful one. If my shadow wanted to string me up with Trant and the others, that was cool with me. I welcomed death and all the oblivion it offered.

Mac took three swift strides so that he was directly in my face. "No, killing you isn't the answer—rejoining is."

264

My breath caught in my throat. I didn't want any part of his insanity. I thrust him away with my hands, but achieved only partial success. My hands sank into his shadow flesh, absorbing him and dissolving into him at the same time. There was no pain, but the sensation scared me. Through our contact, I saw into my shadow self. I had total access to his mind. Within a handful of rabbit-fast heartbeats, I witnessed the killing of Trant, Westerman, and Klein—and so much more. I experienced his rage, absence of conscience and murderous desires, all burning white hot inside him. His emotions were contagious. What he wanted crept into me, igniting a starved part of my psyche. Like exercising muscles atrophied from years of neglect, I flexed thoughts that I believed were long since amputated. Regardless of how much those desires warmed me, I didn't want any part of them and I yanked myself away from Mac.

My hands came away easily, more easily than I'd expected. My momentum carried me backward and I bounced off the porch railing and down the steps. I jarred my spine and cracked my head on the ground before landing on my back. I scrabbled away, preparing to defend myself against an attack, but it wasn't necessary. In spite of my vulnerability, my shadow was frozen in a moment of rapture.

"My God, did you feel that?" Mac clutched his chest where my hands had passed through him. His eyes blazed. "That was one hell of a mental hand job. I haven't felt that good since we were one." He took a step down the stairs toward me.

"Stay the hell away from me." Still reeling from my fall, I scooted away from him using my hands and legs like a crab.

Mac halted his descent. "Don't tell me you didn't enjoy that."

"Christ, no."

Mac relaxed. He lounged against the stair rail. A smug smile crept across his lips.

"I read you," he said. "I saw your life, if you want to call it that. Pitiful really. It hasn't been much fun since they turned you loose—that tedious little job cleaning streets for the county, the pokey condo and sad nights alone watching TV while you eat those plastic-flavored TV dinners."

I jumped to my feet. "Fuck off."

My shadow raised his hands in mock surrender and grinned. "Temper, temper," he cooed. "Trant wouldn't like that."

Schoolyard tactics, but they were working. I kept my silence, not wanting to be drawn in to Mac's childish games.

"You've fallen a long way," he said. "You used to be magnificent—and you can be again. Just take my hand."

"No."

Mac retracted his offer, letting his arm fall to his side. "Then I'll have to take what I need."

"Take *me*? What for? You don't need me. You did well enough killing them." I pointed at Klein, Westerman, and Trant, their bodies now still.

"It's not the same."

Mac spoke with sincerity. Whether it was intentional or not, he'd shown me a chink in his armor. He was reaching out for help for the first time in his existence. He wasn't the all-powerful killer I believed he was. He was fallible, and it was clear we'd both lost something when they had separated us. I don't know what you'd call it—spirit, soul, or *what*—but we lacked it and we hungered for that void to be filled. Unfortunately, sating that hunger came at too high a price for me.

"And rejoining would change that?" I suggested.

"Of course. Isn't that obvious?"

He descended another step toward me and I backed away.

"That's far enough," I said.

"I can't believe you're resisting."

"Like you said, isn't that obvious?"

"You disappoint me," Mac said, descending another of the porch steps, "but you don't surprise me."

He was gearing up for an attack, but for once he would have to play it safe. He couldn't risk hurting me. If he killed me then he couldn't complete his plan. It gave me another edge, a better chance to stop him. Mac stepped off the porch, but I stood my ground.

"I told you to stay where you are."

My car was close, but there was nothing inside it that would protect me. I hoped a weapon was inside the house. I had to get in there, but I had to be smart about it. Running around to the back door wouldn't do any good. Mac would be all over me. No, the only way in was through the front door.

"You know I'm going to have to stop you," I said.

Mac laughed, but before he could say anything, I charged at my shadow. Leading with my shoulder, I thundered into him. My shoulder slammed into his gut and the air exploded from his chest before we merged again. I knifed through his flesh and we dissolved into each other. We crashed to the ground at the base of the steps, conjoined. I tried to tear myself away as I'd done before, but my strength deserted me.

Memories and feelings bled out, but I didn't die from this wound thanks to a transfusion from Mac. His past nourished my depleted character. Vivid images poured into my consciousness. I was with him in Trant's institution. He tricked a young doctor into the sep-tank during a therapy session and stabbed her to death with her own pen. He then slaughtered two guards with the same pen before relieving them of their weapons. I closed my eyes to blot out the visions, but the avalanche kept coming. The finale to Mac's escape was brilliant in its depravity. He'd broken out all the other shadow personalities, unleashing a hundred other killers imprisoned by the Trant method. Fueled by disgust, I wrenched myself away.

"My God, what have you done!"

I scrambled toward the house, climbing the porch steps on my hands and knees. I didn't find my feet until I was through the doorway. I slammed the door shut behind me and locked it before he could recover. I knew it wouldn't hold him for long, but I just needed some breathing space. I wondered if he had a gun, but didn't think so. That wasn't his style—*our* style. Knives were. I raced into the kitchen ripping out drawers, their contents spilling onto the floor.

"You can't prevent the inevitable," Mac shouted.

"That's what you think," I muttered to myself as I groped among the fallen cutlery for a butcher knife.

Mac slammed a boot heel against the door. Wood splintered. The door wouldn't last much longer under that kind of punishment, but it didn't matter. I was ready to end his plan before it had the chance to blossom.

After two more devastating blows, the door exploded off its hinges. Mac raced into the kitchen. I stopped him in his tracks, though. I jammed the knife against my throat. My move was a little too zealous and I broke the skin. Blood trickled from the wound.

Fury contorted his face into an ugly caricature. Is that how I'd looked to my victims? Was that the last image the innocent had etched onto their retinas before they died? Poor bastards. Well, no more. It wouldn't happen again.

"Do you really think killing yourself will stop me?" Mac's question was full of contempt.

"Yes, or you wouldn't be here."

He didn't say anything, but a faint tremor shook his body. He knew I was right and he was screwed.

"You need my body because you're not complete."

"Neither are you," he spat back.

"But not like you. Me" —I bounced the tip of the knife off my chest— "I'm devoid of a personality trait. That's no hardship. I can get by just fine without you, but you—you're a snakeskin to be sloughed off and left to rot."

It was clear Mac wanted to kill me with an intensity that threatened to split him, but knew he couldn't if he were to survive. I had the upper hand, but I wasn't safe. A cornered animal reacts unpredictably and can't be trusted.

"You won't do it," he barked. "I've seen inside you. You're a mundane little nobody. You need this second chance."

A few hours earlier I would have agreed with him. I hated my life and the shapeless excuse for a person that I'd become. The opportunity to be my old self and to kill again was a temptation I was only inches from accepting, but experiencing the victimization I'd handed out to so many people changed that. I learned something Trant's treatment and Westerman's therapy hadn't taught me. I valued life—*all* life—including my own. If I were pushed, I even valued Mac's.

"I've read you, too. Without my body, you'll die," I said. "You're weak. Your battery is running down. How long have you got left—months or days?"

"What are you going to do, wait until I shrivel up?"

I didn't answer. I wasn't sure what I was going to do.

"Why did you let the others out?"

"Did you like that? I thought it was cool." His mouth broke into a grin. "I couldn't let my comrades in arms rot when there was a chance for everyone. Besides, it helped with my escape. With so many of us on the loose at once, the cops couldn't launch an effective manhunt to catch anyone."

SIMON WOOD

"Trant never should have tried to study the shadow personalities. He should have destroyed them when he had the chance."

"Well, I think he knows that now."

I detected an air of change in Mac. His frustration dissipated. He'd thought of something or I'd missed something. Whatever it was, he believed he had an edge. His gaze fixated above and to the right of my head. Unease settled on my shoulders and my poker face was lost.

"Where are they now?" I asked.

Mac shrugged. "Who knows? Probably trying to find their host selves."

"Is that how you see me—as a host?"

Mac shrugged again. "Seeing as we're being honest and all, and that it's unlikely this little reunion is going to end pretty, yes, you're a host, a sweet ride for me to travel about in."

He made some unnecessary hand gesture to distract me and edged half a step toward me, still looking at the spot over my damn shoulder. I wasn't supposed to notice, but I was shit scared and I noticed everything. I still couldn't see what he was looking at. I didn't want to take my eyes off him to check. Fresh waves of sweat dotted my forehead and trickled from my armpits.

"Well, you just lost your ride."

"Is that right?" He spoke directly to the spot this time and edged another half step. "You keep talking about ending it all, but I don't see you doing anything about it." He edged another half step.

He was a mere stride from being within arm's reach. My butt was backed against the countertop and I had nowhere to run. If he lunged, he would ensnare me. I had the knife in my favor, but I didn't have his murderer's dexterity. I reckoned it made us less than even—in his favor. I didn't think he could prevent me from slashing my own throat, but I wasn't sure I could do it.

The moments we'd merged had shown me another possibility. I had something to live for now. I had a plan and a future, but for it I needed my shadow back. I knew it would break Trant's heart if he was alive, but I needed to be one again. What the hell was he looking at? I turned and saw nothing over my shoulder. It had been a ruse and I'd fallen for it. I knew what would come next. Mac lunged. From the corner of my eye, I caught his smile. He thought he had me, but this is what I wanted him to do.

I whirled to face him. His arms were outstretched, aiming for my throat. I lashed out with the knife. The blade was sharp and his shadow flesh was weak. The knife severed his right hand. Shock felled him, but didn't curb his momentum and he lumbered forward, embedding himself into me. His chin melted into my neck. My chest dissolved into his. I caught a glimpse of our Siamese twin act in the reflection of the pots and pans hanging over the kitchen island. The curved surfaces distorted our merger beyond revulsion.

"What have you done?" he murmured, as we exchanged thoughts and he glimpsed my plan. I fought to push him away and separate us. We couldn't rejoin yet, not while he still had his other hand—a killer's hand—or I would never have control. I had to remove his remaining hand. He knew this. My thoughts were his thoughts as we dissolved into each other and he bear-hugged me to prevent our separation. He sank deeper into my flesh.

"Don't do this," he pleaded.

"I don't have a choice."

I swung a leg behind his and leaned my weight against him. It unbalanced us and we tumbled. I aimed our entwined bodies at the kitchen table. Mac connected with the wooden surface; I didn't. Flesh and shadow flesh were entangled, but the merger made them weak. I thought we'd simply separate, but the impact tore us apart. Flesh ripped, bones snapped, and veins severed.

Now we really did need each other. Sinew kept my destroyed jaw in place. A gaping hole in my chest resembled a matching wound in Mac's. A portion of his missing skull clung to a knot of flesh at my neck. He writhed on the linoleum, blood pumping from his wounds. I crawled over to him with the butcher knife still in my grasp. I grabbed his arm and he tried to fight me off, but it was a feeble effort. I pinned his remaining hand to the ground and placed the blade over his wrist.

"No," he murmured.

I ignored him and leaned my weight on the knife. The blade passed through flesh and bone but I didn't rest up until I felt it bite into the vinyl below. Mac whimpered in defeat.

I tossed the knife away and rolled on top of my shadow. Neither of us fought our reunification. We let nature take its course. I felt him invade me. That rage and total disregard for humanity wormed its way into my way of thinking, refreshing old tendencies. I feared I'd made a mistake and for all I'd done to prevent the beast roaming within, it wouldn't make any difference. But the fear didn't last long. What was bad about him bled into me, and what was good about me bled into him. My humanity tempered his lack of one. Happiness bloomed within me and I would have smiled if unconsciousness hadn't claimed me.

When I awoke, daylight was breaking over the horizon. I moved my body and found it obeyed me. I struggled to my feet. I was blood-soaked and so was the kitchen, but I wasn't injured except for a pair of old-looking scars encircling both wrists.

As I ran my head under the faucet, my body felt like my own. Mac wasn't trapped genielike in the recesses of my soul or a puppet master operating my strings. We were integrated, but not like before. I was someone new, in possession of certain skills that I would now need.

I burned the farmhouse, using gas siphoned from Trant's car. The fire claimed my three wise men and I didn't want to leave until their bodies were ashes, but I drove off when the sirens drew close. I couldn't be apprehended now. I hit the road, but I didn't head home. That life, like the one before it, was over. I picked up the interstate instead to begin a new life—chasing shadows.

"Kieran Malcolm," I said to myself, naming the man who had entered the sep-tank after me. Kieran lived the closest, just across the Nevada border. I hoped his shadow hadn't caught up with him yet, because I wanted to be waiting. His would be the first—the first shadow I would kill.

THE FOLLY

ROBERT DUNBAR

Thick and viscous floodwaters lapped at the small island. Mud particles swirled in the current, as did nearly microscopic organisms upon which thousands of tiny fish gorged before being swallowed in turn by their larger brethren. Egg cases clogged the vegetation. Tadpoles and water moccasins teemed in this primordial soup, and a fetid stench pressed the islet almost as heavily as the swamp waters. In spots where accumulated ooze drizzled back from the leaves of sodden trees, it seemed to rain perpetually.

The monster approved.

Fluid churned darkly as the creature waded onto denser mud, then heaved itself onto a tilting oak. Green with slime, even the trunk felt slick, but claws dug in. One thick branch led to another, then to one still further and the next. Drawing as near as it dared to the giant alligator, the monster settled on a limb to watch.

«««—»»»

The child turned away from the kitchen door. "It will kill us all."

"Hush!" exclaimed Grandmother Fontaine, rattling her cup and saucer. "What's wrong with that girl?"

"Stop upsetting your grandmother, Cass." Daphne reached for the cream. "Apologize at once." At the far end of the table, older siblings smirked, but their mother shot them a look. "And don't you muscle-bound louts utter a word."

"I am sorry to upset you, Grandmother," intoned Cassie. "But it will kill us."

"Cass!" The child's mother massaged her temples. Barely even dressed yet, Daphne could already feel the migraine starting. She tugged at her dressing gown. Though hardly the way she preferred to appear at the breakfast table, she found it *so difficult* to maintain standards on the island anymore, especially after being abandoned by the last of the servants. Unpaid wages indeed. Surely some things in this world were more important than mere money. And now the child showed definite indications of having inherited "colorful behavior" from her father's side of the family. (Not that much *else* remained *to* inherit.) *So difficult.* The pain in Daphne's skull throbbed. Twining a stray lock of unnaturally blond hair behind one ear, she reached for the crystal decanter and poured a generous slug of brandy into her coffee. Perhaps she could dress for lunch.

"It will." Ignoring her mother, which required little effort, the child calmly buttered another piece of toast, spreading the butter with meticulous precision. Obviously, it needed to be exactly even. When at last it met with her approval, she cast an expectant glance toward her Aunt Pandora before taking a bite.

At the far end of the table, Pandora noted the look and nodded. "I saw it again."

"But you're insane, dear," said Grandmother. "Pass the butter, Cassie, if you're *quite* through."

"I saw it," repeated Aunt Dora (as they sometimes called her) undaunted. She was accustomed to this sort of treatment. Many years before, while watching an old Bette Davis film on television, Pandora Fontaine had been struck by the moment when the leading man asked, "Is it Miss or Misses?" only to have the heroine reply, "It's Aunt—every family has one." Pandora had never forgotten it, if only because people so often insisted that she looked like Bette Davis, which she never interpreted as a compliment. Davis' glamour eluded her. She thought the woman just looked nuts. "Yes, Horace," Pandora acknowledged. "I see you. Here, Virgil, pass this to your brother before he pitches a fit. And I did catch a glimpse of it from my bedroom window last night. It came all the way to the edge of the garden and stood there, looking up at the house."

"They put people away for saying stuff like that," said Great

Uncle Jason, nodding in simultaneous disapproval (of her remark) and approval (of his own). "Y'all just remember your grandmother," he added to the group at large.

"I beg your pardon!"

"Not you. The other one."

"I tell you, it was there again," insisted Pandora. "Didn't you hear the dogs barking?"

"Ain't there no more bacon?"

"Where them dogs at anyways?" wondered Uncle Jason.

"Outside somewheres, I suppose," Daphne hazarded. "Where else would they be? Now let's have no more of this unpleasantness at table, shall we?" Daphne hoped to steer the conversation toward a trip into town she planned to make this week. Perhaps *planned* was too strong a word. She'd need someone to handle the boat, and of course some cash would be pleasant. "Coffee, Uncle Jason, dear?" She leaned forward and played with her curls in what she ardently prayed still constituted a fetching manner. While smiling, she allowed her gaze to stray toward poor Pandora—now that's who *truly* needed a trip to the beauty parlor, as Daphne had so often helpfully suggested. But would Dora listen? Stubborn creature. The old maid of the family—small wonder she looked prematurely middle-aged. Her figure had *possibilities*, one had to admit, and her eyes might not be bad, what one could see of them, if only she would learn not to stare so intently through those thick glasses. But as for that hair (which had obviously never been cut in her life) and this unfortunate tendency to wear her dead father's old clothing…

"So when's that photographer coming?" asked Virg suddenly.

"Uncle Jason, dear. I was wondering if…"

"What photographer?"

Daphne frowned at the interruption. Actually, she frowned a great deal when it concerned her boys. Constantly in fact. Especially now that the twins, often fondly referred to by their mother as "those oafs," neared twenty. Could they be small-boned and delicate boys whose diminutive stature belied their (and her) age? No. Of course not. Virgil and Horace just *had* to be overgrown goons.

"They don't never miss breakfast," Horace mused.

"Photographers?"

"No, stupid, the dogs."

"What photographer?" asked Cassie.

"Don't be all the time calling your brother stupid," said Grandmother. These carryings on did not amuse her. Why could they never have a civilized meal?

"How come? He is, ain't he?"

"Next week sometime."

"Am not!"

"What photographer?"

"What's this about next week?" Grandmother felt herself growing heated. More than anything in the world, she detested being ignored and when frustrated resorted to volume. "And why is everybody always picking on poor Horace?" she shouted.

"Thanks, Grammy."

"Don't you call me that! If I've told you once…"

"Another magazine wants to do a piece about the house," explained Pandora patiently, though they'd had this conversation several times already. Repetition remained one of her major functions within the family.

"I trust they're paying you this time," assayed Great Uncle Jason with a disgusted air, as though he already knew the answer to that one. They all looked up. Rarely did anyone, let alone Uncle Jason (who liked to play at being patriarch), ever acknowledge that the house they all lived in had been left to Aunt Pandora.

"Why?" the child inquired. "I mean, why should they pay?" She felt sincerely puzzled. And why take pictures? The house was just the house, after all. She knew of nothing unique or interesting about it. Weren't all houses shaped like alligators? Admittedly, her experience of other people's dwellings had been extremely limited. She had almost never been off the island, and as for the stunned horror on the faces of their (very) occasional visitors, well, she had long ago privately decided that it was the sight of her older brothers that provoked this reaction. They were certainly gruesome enough.

Though quite bright, she remained quite wrong about this. (The house, not the brothers.) Encountering their home for the first time, everyone always just gaped, much like the house itself. Huge claws supported either side of the entrance, molded concrete providing texture and details, as the giant gator reared its head and hunched its back to create the upper story. With the heavy green shutters tightly closed, even the incongruous windows vanished, completing the illusion. Of course, Cassie knew some of the history. They all did. It had been built three generations earlier, lifelong project of an ancestor with more money than sense, and had been known as "the Folly" ever since, especially now with the family fortune decimated and the house itself crumbling. On this point (and no other), the family unanimously agreed: the only thing worse than living inside an alligator had to be living inside a decrepit one. Aunt Dora was forever trying to get the building declared a landmark so they could at least get some funding for repairs, but the response always came back the same—'bizarre' did not equate with 'significant.' Besides, what would be the point of a landmark in the middle of a swamp?

Watching her mother pour more brandy into a teacup, little Cassie just shrugged. No one answered her questions, but no one answered anyone around here. Never. They were always too busy squabbling. And this morning's argument went on for quite some time.

«««—»»»

They'd taken the news of the photographer reasonably well, thought Aunt Dora. Probably best not to mention that it wasn't an architectural magazine this time but a publication dedicated to the paranormal. One never knew how they might react. To anything. Even for an inbred clan deep in the swamp, she thought they might well be considered a peculiar bunch, but then the family always had run to eccentricity. Putting her sunhat on backwards, she stepped out into the garden and took a deep breath with every semblance of calm. Breakfast had been far from relaxing. "Crazy as loons, the lot of them," she muttered to herself. Never mind. To the best of her knowledge, she hadn't inherited anything like the worst of that. (Suddenly noticing that her blouse was buttoned wrong, she paused a moment to correct it.) What she had inherited resembled her father's obsessive relationship with his studies. He had been a classicist (like his father before him), and their library bulged with reference works, several of which he had written himself. She knew these books intimately, having grown up with them. With them? Hell, she'd practically grown up *in* them and possessed barely a single childhood memory that did not involve some imposing tome open on the library desk or the kitchen table or spread out on her bed at night. Never mind that her father, unlike herself, had traveled the world in pursuit of knowledge. The passion felt the same, though she had not herself been educated as a classicist. Or as anything really. (Even in her youth, the family fortune had already dwindled to the point where little could be squandered on the education of a mere female.) Nevertheless, she considered herself an accomplished amateur folklorist, and several academic journals had endorsed this opinion by publishing her monographs. Yes, the passion felt the same. In recent years, however, the primary focus of her enthusiasm had shifted into…well, yes, she admitted it, more *eccentric* areas. These days (and nights, *late* nights), she often found herself immersed in reference material pertaining to the Yeti or Sasquatch, to Mothman or the Jersey Devil. And as for interpretations of these myths…

As in most things, she had her own theories. She *knew* they were all real. Further, she knew them all to be the same, whether appearing in the Pacific Northwest, a Scottish moor or some remote mountain range in Tibet. It was all the same beast.

She also knew they had one on the island. Not that anyone had ever actually seen it, of course, but the creature had always wintered here, lurking in the most overgrown and secluded areas. Her father had been aware of it and had seemed to relish the knowledge, and her grandfather had known it before him. It virtually qualified as a family legend.

But this year everything had changed.

Heavy rains had pelted throughout the winter as hurricanes shredded the coast. Repeated flooding had drastically altered currents and channels throughout the swamp, submerging whole areas, until waters sank to unknown depths. Finally she understood the danger.

Never had she sensed the creature's presence so intensely. (Just last week, Uncle Jason had been complaining about the sudden scarcity of game.) Intriguing, she thought, as she passed beyond the parameter of the enormous curved tail that served as garden wall. If the creature remained trapped here in this unprecedented fashion, no one could predict…

She stopped walking. She stopped breathing. At the edge of a weed-strewn remnant of a flowerbed: a footprint. Broader than a man's and longer, hooking deeply into soft earth. No mistaking it— the clearest she'd found so far. Must get the camera, she thought. Yet she remained, sunlight pounding down upon her as she stared. At last, she began to breathe normally again and became aware of a bird trilling in the thicket. Then another sound filtered into her consciousness, a shrill, furious yapping. How long had that been going on?

A vague sort of path strayed through undergrowth, and she followed it into a stand of elms. One of the trees appeared to be emitting all the noise. (Odd, she noted, not even a dogwood.) Around the other side, she encountered the actual source—a fat little spaniel deep within a hollow trunk. "Hey, Circe, what's going on? How did you get in there? Where are the big dogs?" Most days, sporting an air of disgruntled martyrdom, the spaniel supervised a pair of smelly, noisy and untrained hounds of no particular usefulness. (So similar were their attributes, it often proved difficult to discern which pair of 'twins' was being referred to at any given time.) Imperiously, the dog continued to bark. "Oh, you want me to lift you out? Why ever did you climb in there? Hang on." She crouched and hefted out the squirming, porcine beast. "Heavens," she said, grunting. "You have got to cut back on the biscuits, girl." Placing the dog on the ground, she was rewarded with a burst of flatulence, as the small beast scrambled toward the garden, then halted and glared back. When Pandora didn't follow at once, Circe snorted impatiently. Clearly, the animal had no intention of returning to the house unescorted.

"I'm coming," Pandora said. But she continued to survey the woods. "Yes," she told the dog as a slight breeze stirred the foliage. "I'm worried too."

«««—»»»

"What the devil is the matter with that bitch?"

Grandmother started to object.

"I'm speaking of the dog." Great Uncle Jason sounded annoyed—another breakfast ruined. "She's been hiding behind that damn stove since yesterday."

"Perhaps she's smarter than she looks," muttered Pandora.

"Almost have to be," said Jason as he leaned both elbows on the table. "And where are the twins? And I'm *still* speaking about dogs."

Pandora poured herself a cup of coffee. "Gone, I'm afraid."

"What?" No one had noticed the child enter the room. "Where have they gone to?"

"Don't worry, sugar." Uncle Jason kept his voice low and comforting, while he glowered at Pandora. "We'll go look for them later."

"You won't find them." Dora stirred her coffee.

"Just what do you mean by that?" He pounded his fist down hard enough to make all the plates jump. "I believe I've had about enough of this nonsense." Horace and Virgil giggled expectantly.

"I saw a footprint in the yard yesterday. Wait. Don't say anything. I knew you'd never believe me so I sat by my window all night. Almost missed it. If it hadn't moved, I would never have seen it. It must have been watching me the whole time, which made me feel pretty stupid. Perhaps it's always been watching. I got a pretty good shot though. Infrared. Telephoto lens. And I spent this morning in my darkroom." She slid the print across the table. "You can see it pretty clear."

The explosion she expected never occurred, only a soft "Jeez, look at that" from one of the twins, followed by a low whistle. The silence continued for a long moment. Everyone stared at the photo. For the first time in her life, Dora had their undivided attention.

"This could make our fortune," Uncle Jason announced finally.

"Restore our fortune," corrected Grandmother.

"As you will," he conceded, "but catching the monster would certainly..."

"Don't you understand the importance of this?" Nothing in their faces encouraged her, so Pandora changed her tactics. "Besides, it could be dangerous."

"That's just why we need to set traps."

"That...might be a good idea," she conceded.

"I thought you'd think so, once you calmed down. Then, after we sell it..."

"That's not why we're trapping it. I'm a scientist."

"You're not."

"You ain't."

"In my own way, I am, and..."

"Would you rather we shot it then, dear?" Grandmother inquired. "Had it stuffed maybe?"

"We will do neither," insisted Pandora. "We are not a circus family."

"Of course not," Grandmother explained. "We'll sell it to a circus family."

"Don't be an idiot all your life, Dora," advised Uncle Jason kindly. "Besides, we won't sell it to a circus, necessarily. We'll sell it to the highest bidder."

Even Daphne looked interested now.

"But I want to observe the creature, study its habits," objected Pandora. "This is a priceless opportunity to…"

"To make a lot of cash." Grandmother rose from the table and drew herself up to her full height—an impressive four foot eight. "You are being inexcusably selfish. The family needs this, and I cannot allow you to jeopardize it."

"Don't be too harsh on her, Grammy," suggested Virg.

"Don't dare call me that, you lout." She threw a piece of toast at him. Though most people found it difficult to distinguish between the boys, Grandmother apparently perceived sufficient differences to justify doting upon Horace while remaining as indifferent (if not downrightly hostile) toward Virgil as she was to the rest of her family.

Uncle Jason cleared his throat. "Maybe we can work out some deal so's the buyer gets poor Dora as well—you know, like an expert thrown in. That way she'd get to do her little research or what have you," he went on. "After all, no particular reason she shouldn't be happy too. Maybe she'll finally meet some man." This provoked loud guffaws as Uncle Jason leaned back in his chair and folded his hands over his gut. "Now, here's how we'll catch it…"

«««—»»»

From the kitchen doorway, Pandora watched them stroll down the garden path with shovels and picks. Knowing she could do nothing to stop them, she kept busy in the kitchen, amazed by the number of things she found to occupy her time (if not her thoughts). First the spices required alphabetizing, then the stemware needed to be sorted by size and type.

Throughout the morning, laughter occasionally drifted back to the house, and from time to time Uncle Jason's voice boomed, shouting orders as usual. Finally, she abandoned her labors and just stood at the backdoor.

"This will be bad," a voice said.

Not having heard the child creep up behind her, she jumped a little. "Yes," she agreed finally. "It is going to be bad."

«‹‹—›»»

Dora gazed out her bedroom window. A smear of moonlight blotted the prehistoric shadow of the house across the sodden trees. "You know, don't you?" she whispered. "You see everything."

She could sense a difference in the woods. All her life, she'd imagined an affinity with the elusive creature. Her father and grand-father had allowed themselves the same fantasy, believing that—because they took notes and drew sketches—they had somehow befriended the beast. Madness. Even if over the years they had achieved some sort of rapport with it, what would happen when the creature felt... betrayed?

This would be very bad indeed.

«‹‹—›»»

She came down early to find the boys already up, gulping cups of foul-smelling coffee and attempting to make toast. (Smoke filled the room, and the kitchen appeared to have been ransacked by chimps. Evidently they'd prepared the coffee themselves.) Before she'd made much of an inroad on the mess, the twins headed out, having first equipped themselves with a baseball bat and an old fishing net.

"Where are you going?" she called from the backdoor.

"Checkin' the trap."

"Wait, I'll come with you," she said. Letting the screen door slam behind her, she shuffled quickly along the garden path in her slippers and robe. "Where's Uncle Jason?" The boys already ranged far ahead of her, laughing and hooting, and she yelled after their broad backs. "I said, where's Uncle Jason?"

"Ain't up yet, looks like."

"We're gone surprise him with monster for breakfast."

"Should a made more toast." Evidently, this was hilarious, and both brothers guffawed and fell against each other as they headed into the woods. In the dawn light, birds warbled and insects hummed.

She joined them at the edge of the pit.

"Jeez," remarked Horace, staring down.

Virgil blinked rapidly. "Is that...?"

"Uncle Jason," Horace conceded. "Right?"

"Most likely," agreed Pandora.

They continued to stare. At length, Virgil ventured another utterance. "Where's the rest of him at?"

Pandora shut her eyes.

«‹‹—››»

A long day ensued, full of arguments and hysterics. Their voices rose and then subsided into exhaustion, only to soar again, riding each fresh gust of outrage. Dora wanted to call the authorities, but Grandmother proved very insistent. "Have state troopers and the press and whatever else down here, getting it all for free? I think not." Daphne just kept drinking, while little Cass lingered on the sidelines, pale and somber. To no one's surprise more than his own, Horace took charge. Uncle Jason had just been careless, he decided. In a few days, surely they would catch the beast. (Grandmother backed him up. Of course.) And so it went. Hour after hour.

Day after day. Night after night. "Madness," insisted Pandora.

Daphne vanished first, whether into the woods or the water no one knew… until Pandora discovered their launch missing from the boathouse. Then Cassie noticed bits of the little boat floating nearby. After that, the child became even quieter and more withdrawn.

"We should have known even Daphne wouldn't just abandon her child," said Aunt Dora.

"No?" Grandmother made a face. "Well, you may be right. I couldn't say, I'm sure. But more importantly, now none of us can leave."

"No," agreed Dora. "We're as trapped here as it is."

Cassie disappeared next. She simply didn't come down to dinner, and no one could remember where they'd seen her last.

The day it got Horace, Pandora found Grandmother on her back in the garden, her expression still seething with outrage. Apparently, she'd seen more than her old heart could bear. Possibly just as well. Blood had spattered everywhere.

«‹‹—››»

The next morning, Pandora wrestled with Virg in the kitchen. "Please, don't do this."

"I'm on kill it," he slurred, weaving drunkenly toward the door while loading the rifle. She made one last attempt to block him. He shouldered her out of the way, and she hit the wall hard, slumping to the floor as the screen slammed behind him. Straightening her glasses and rubbing a bruised arm, she did not even try to get up.

A single scream followed the gunshot… then that terrible silence.

At last, she rose. Latching the screen, she bolted the inner door and stumbled slowly into the parlor, pausing only to retrieve an old shotgun and a box of shells from the gun cabinet. "Well, old girl, it's just us now." As she sat heavily in an armchair, she felt the dog press close to her legs. "Last living things on the island." In the hallway, the grandfather clock ticked loudly. "Except for the monster."

There was a knock at the door.

"No!" When the momentary paralysis faded, she rushed to the door and screamed at the wood. "You don't get in that easy!" She clutched the shotgun to her chest, while Circe barked fiercely (from behind the sofa). "I'll blow you to pieces."

"Beg pardon?" came a muted reply.

She fumbled with the latch and flung open the door. "Who are you?"

The woman stammered, "Umm… my name is…"

"You have a boat? Yes, of course. Where is it? The dock of course, yes. Hurry." She grabbed the other woman by the arm. "Come on!"

"Hold on there." Brandishing a metal tripod like a club, the woman tried to pull away. "What's with the rifle?"

"It's a shotgun," she said as though that explained everything. "Drop that. And the case. Just run." She practically dragged the woman out under the jaws of the house, and they jogged down the path toward the dock. The dog scrambled along behind, keeping up remarkably well on little legs but barking all the while. "Circe, shut up!"

And suddenly Circe did.

Pandora whirled to look back. Eyes bulging, the dog had planted all four paws stiffly. "You know, I never noticed it before, girl," she told the dog, "but you pretty much look like Bette Davis too."

"Umm." The other woman just stared at her in alarm. More precisely, she stared at the shotgun.

"It's all right," Pandora assured her. "I'm not crazy."

"No, of course not. Silly idea. Umm... is there anyone else on the island?"

"No one you want to meet."

"Lovely." The woman drew a deep breath. "Look, I think I've about had enough of... Where's my boat?"

"I'm afraid I can guess." Dora paced to the edge of the dock, and the other woman followed. The motorboat rested on the muck at the bottom, close enough for the splintered hole to be clearly visible.

"And the little man who brought me?"

"You won't find him. We'd best get back to the house." Her voice held a sad and jagged quality, reminiscent of shattered glass. "See that? Those green mounds way out there? They're the tops of trees where islands used to be. A week ago, you couldn't even see that much. The water's receding at last. If we can just hold out..." She turned away from the dock. "Stay close now," she said softly. Suddenly, she discharged the shotgun into the foliage, and Circe took off down the path, a chubby blur in a low cloud of dust. "Run." Staggering from the recoil while she fumbled for shells, she lurched forward. "I mean it. Go!"

They pounded back along the path. Lagging a few paces behind, Pandora tottered awkwardly with the weapon. Sweat blurred her vision, and the vine-choked woods seemed to press forward. She fired again, wildly, at nothing in particular. Finally, they reached the maw of the house and paused there, breathing hard and looking back at the woods, while Dora pumped more shells into the chamber.

"You want...?" The other woman wheezed. "I have *got* to stop smoking. You want to tell me what we were running from?"

"Where are you, girl? Girl?"

From behind them came a small sound. Circe's face squeezed through the barely open door and emitted an inquiring yip.

"Yes, we're coming in," she told the dog.

"May I bring my equipment?" asked the woman.

"Oh," Pandora considered the woman's luggage at last. "You're the photographer. I forgot." For the first time, she took in the woman's appearance. Aggressively short, she radiated a wiry energy. Even her khaki trousers seemed selected for vigorous activity, and the reddish hair had been severely cropped.

"If now is inconvenient," she said, "I can always come back some other time."

"Please." Waving her in, Dora slammed the heavy door behind them and bolted it.

"Well, you sure know how to make a girl feel wanted. What did you say your name was?"

"Sorry. Pandora Fontaine."

"You're kidding? Like with the snaky hair?"

"No, that was…never mind. Grab that end of the sofa."

"Wait. You're the one I was coming to see." The photographer fished in her pocket until she found a slip of paper. "P. A. Fontaine."

"Pandora Ariadne. Don't ask. If you'd help," she grumbled, "this would be a lot easier." Together, they began to drag the heavy sofa toward the foyer. "Great outfit by the way," Pandora added, looking away. "But don't you experience some difficulty locating combat boots in children's sizes?"

"Shut up. What? You're a fashion plate?" Grunting, the woman shoved the sofa against the door. "You want to tell me what this is all about now?" Her freckled face fairly simmered with intelligent frustration. "Or can't I ask that either?"

«««—»»»

Circling the library erratically, the dog padded across the ancient oriental carpet, clicked along the wooden floor, then settled under an oak desk.

"Well, it's why you're here really, though I'm afraid it may be more of a story than your magazine ever anticipated."

Nodding for her to continue, the photographer studied her hostess. The longhaired woman seemed exhausted, beyond tears and panic, as though she had reached a plateau of functional numbness. Periodically, she would go very still and appear to listen for something.

"I guess this is what you should see first," Dora said. Opening a file, she slid a photograph across the desk.

"Old boyfriend? I only ask because he appears to be… umm… happy to see you."

"What? Oh." Dora stared at the photo. "I hadn't noticed."

"You're kidding? You *so* need to get out more. You know what it looks like?"

"A snake?"

"The *whole* monster." The photographer rolled her eyes. "More than anything, it looks like a sort of giant muskrat. Don't you think?" She studied it. "Except for the ape arms and stuff. Not a bad shot really. You do this?"

"Don't humor me." Pandora slid the rest of the file across the desk, and the woman began to go through it. "I didn't quite get your name."

"Well, it's been a little hectic." Without looking up, the redhead turned a page and said, "I'm Alix. Just Alix."

«« —»»

"Funny I'm not more scared," Alix said later. "Just kind of cold." The light had begun to dim when she pushed the file away. "So your entire family...?"

"The only one I really mind about is Cass." Pandora held her gaze. "You think I'm insane?"

"I've met up with much stranger things than just monsters." Alix shook her head. "People have been telling me I was psychic since I was a kid. Plus spirit photography *is* my specialty. Now you're looking at me like *I'm* the one that's nuts. Is that nice?"

"Do you ever get any?" asked Pandora.

"Beg pardon?"

"Pictures of ghosts."

"Oh. Sort of hard to tell," said Alix. "Smears of fog in a room is all that ever shows up. But I'm trying to perfect a film process that... why are you smiling?"

"Nothing. I was just thinking what a good match we are. I mean, how much we have in common."

"Don't blush."

Suddenly, Dora got up and paced around the library. "If you're psychic, why didn't you know what you were walking in on here?"

"Impressions come when they come. And anyway I knew you were going to ask that." Alix shrugged again. "So this monster of yours—the one I came all this way to get pictures of—why has no one ever seen it close up before? If it's everywhere, I mean?"

"They live only in the most inaccessible places. And they're nocturnal, mostly. And I can't imagine there are more than a handful of them left, though they must have been around an awfully long time."

Returning to the desk, she reaching into the file and rooted out a map. "Observe the distribution. I tell you, continental drift is the only explanation. These land masses…"

"Could you maybe give me the simple version?"

"They might be an ancestor of man's. Or perhaps the result of parallel evolution. The point is they must account for so many of our legends." She ticked them off on her fingers. "Werewolves, forest spirits, boogey men…"

"Boogey men?"

"I know it sounds peculiar. You have to understand—my family has been obsessed with myths for generations. Consumed by them in fact."

"Literally."

Dora ignored that. "Even if the creatures aren't killers by nature, their survival depends on staying hidden. So if no one who ever met one is around to talk about it afterwards, I don't find that especially comforting."

Alix snapped her cell phone shut. "Still can't get a signal. I don't suppose there's a phone here. Electricity?"

"Generator's busted again."

"Always said I had a yen for the simple life."

"Funny, we bicker like…"

"I know."

And so the two of them spent that first afternoon fastening shutters, bolting doors and reinforcing barricades. Sunlight bled through the cracks, but with each drawn curtain it grew darker inside until Pandora lit the oil lamps. They also loaded every weapon they could lay their hands on, including an old dueling pistol (from Grandmother's night-stand and doubtless possessing a colorful history) and a birding rifle the boys hadn't touched in years.

Finally, they picnicked on sandwiches in the library, while Circe insinuated herself between them and demanded handouts. Dora stood up suddenly. "What if it got inside?"

"That wouldn't be good," agreed Alix.

"No, I mean, what if it *got* inside? The door was open, remember?"

"I think I'd feel something. I'm sure I would." Alix closed her eyes, concentrating. For a moment, blankness suffused her face. "Oh dear." She blinked several times and then just stared at the ceiling. "What's upstairs?"

"Bedrooms mostly," Pandora replied. "My grandmother is laid out in one of them."

"Well, something up there is alive." Alix stared fixedly upwards. "Alive and hungry."

«««—»»»

"How lovely." Holding the lamp, Alix stayed close behind Pandora, as shadows swung along the mottled walls. "Like being digested by the house." Scrabbling claws made a din on the tight, spiral staircase, and twice she nearly tripped over the dog. "Going out the backdoor must be an unforgettable experience."

At the top, Pandora started along the hall.

But Alix turned away. "What's this?" Voice hushed, she indicated a broad, short door that seemed to have been designed for trolls.

"The gator's head," said Dora. "Not much of a room. Storage mostly." Pandora pushed forward to fiddle with a latch. "Bring the light closer." As the door swung, a stench of dust and mildew rolled into the hallway. Precariously maneuvering the shotgun, she stooped to peer into darkness.

"Careful," Alix whispered, ducking to enter. As a cobweb melted across her face, her vision slowly adjusted. Being inside the head felt weird—the opaque portals of the house's eyes discharged only a dim glow on the old luggage and crates and carpets that crammed the tiny space. She raised the lamp as high as the sloping ceiling permitted.

Shadows shifted in the murk. From behind a huge carton, twin orbs blinked at them, and the dog barked once. The shotgun trembled as a shape rushed forward.

"Oh, Circe. You're safe!" On her knees, Cassie buried her face in the dog's fur while the animal groaned affectionately.

"Hi," said Alix. "You're Cassandra? I'm a friend of your Aunt Pandora's. She's sort of having a little trouble getting her voice to work at the moment. Apparently. Sweetie, what's with the filth? Honestly, I can hardly tell you're blond under there. Let's get you cleaned up, shall we?"

«««—»»»

Even through the shutters, silent incandescence patterned the curtains until thunder rocked the house. "Well, the waters *were* receding," whispered Pandora.

Finding the child had changed everything.

"Okay, enough of this being trapped business." Alix paced back and forth, her boots clicking on the library floor. "We need to *do* something. Come out here in the hallway. What's under here? Do these panels come up? Is there a pickaxe? Drag that rug in here."

Half an hour later, Cass got up from her nap on the sofa to investigate the sounds of chopping, shoveling, scraping and grunting. She had already explained, while they'd sponged and fed her, all about how she had decided to hide from the creature. ("Eminently sensible" had been her aunt's considered assessment.) She paused to retrieve some leftovers from the sideboard.

"It will not work," the child mumbled around a mouthful of sandwich.

"Knock it off, sweetie," Alix told her.

"And Uncle Jason doesn't like anybody touching his toolbox."

"He won't mind," insisted Pandora. "And perhaps he had the right idea." She helped Alix turn over a small table. "Digging the trap outside is where he went wrong." She began sharpening table legs with a file.

Thunder rumbled.

««—»»

The scariest part had been propping the backdoor open and scampering back in the dark to hide. Crowded into the closet, they must all hear her heart still pounding, Pandora felt sure.

"Hush now, Circe." Cassie kept one hand clamped over the dog's snout.

Pandora pressed her ear to the door: the house whispered, and the rain whispered back. After a long time, something clattered, possibly from the kitchen.

"Aunt Dora, I'm scared."

In the quiet, a dry scratching grew louder…until a thud shook the floor.

"We got it!" cried Cassie.

Shifting the shotgun's weight, Pandora started to open the door, but Alix caught her sleeve.

290

"Too dangerous. I'll go." In the cramped darkness, Alix edged to maneuver past the child and dog.

"No, I need you safe. I mean, to look after Cass." In the charred shadows, their hands grappled, then gripped. "I'll be okay," said Dora. "You have to let me. It's my monster."

"I can't hold her," Cassie complained about the struggling dog.

"Me neither," Alix said softly. The door closed. They waited. The storm drummed distantly now.

"Aunt Dora will never come back."

"Shut up, kid."

When the closet door opened suddenly, the dog immediately launched away into the darkness. "It's all right, Cass," said Pandora, leaning in the doorway. "Take the dog upstairs, please."

"Is the monster dead?"

They followed the low growls to find Circe, patrolling the edge of the pit while baying like a twenty-pound Hound of the Baskervilles. A rank, wet smell filled the hall.

The trap had worked perfectly, and the creature huddled at the bottom of a space beneath the house. Hunched into itself, it looked surprisingly small. Blood glistened in the fur. The small rug lay in a heap, and one of the sharpened legs of the splintered table appeared to have snapped off. "No, it's not dead." Pandora lowered the shotgun. "But I want you to take Circe and go to your room. Now, young lady."

"But…"

"Go on, sweetie, please," added Alix, and the child complied without further argument.

"You're good with her."

The two women stared down into the pit, and Alix slid an arm around Pandora's shoulders. "Please, don't shake like that," said Alix. "We're all right. For heaven sakes, what am I thinking? Where's my camera? I've got to get shots of this while it's still breathing." She raced for the library.

The cowering beast scuttled even deeper into a corner, and the acrid sting of urine tinged the air. Listening to the labored hiss of its breathing, Pandora fancied she heard a faint, hopeless moan. "I knew this would be bad." After a moment, she paced to the window and pulled back the heavy draperies. Straining to raise the window, she unlatched the shutters. Rainy wind gusted in, cool and fresh, fighting back the stench, and murky evening light flooded the hall, augmented by a flicker of lightning.

She returned to the brink of the pit, and at last the creature raised its head. Even in the gloom, the savage yellow eyes seemed desperate, imploring.

«««—»»»

When Alix lugged in the tripod and several cameras, she found Pandora, sitting in an old straight-back chair. Lit now, the lantern smoked. Dimness seemed to seep from the corners of the room, but the glow formed a quiet pool, barely trickling over the edge of the trap.

The hole now contained another chair, a bentwood coat rack, and several drawers from the china cabinet. Of the creature only pools of various fluids remained.

For a long moment, no one spoke. A wet breeze snapped sodden curtains as Alix moved to the window. Rain struck the house with a clatter, and wind clapped through the trees. There were things Alix wished to say, things she wanted to shriek. *Are you mad? Why would you do this? It could have killed you. Could have killed all of us. Still might.* But words didn't slide easily into this quiet, and finally her pulse hammered with less insistence. Still, other questions churned her thoughts. Would it die out there? And how long before anyone came to the island? Even issues as simple as what they would make for dinner plagued her. Surely the child would be hungry again soon. Beyond the window, each spurt of electricity revealed a world of teeming green, shoulder-high grasses and ancient shrubs, thrashing limbs that blurred into swaying shadows. The downpour made a rapid patter, soothing, hypnotic. "Sap rises," whispered Alix. "Leaves hang low and wet." She was barely conscious of having begun to speak. "Water slaps the bank. The mud. Sinking. Waiting and watching through all the seasons. Always alone. The blood. Does it stop? Is this death? Alone." Thunder rumbled in the floor. "Is it life?"

Pandora's voice could barely be heard above the rain. "Is that the creature's mind you're reading? Or mine?"

"Not yours." Almost at once, storm sounds dimmed to a droning, repetitive hush. "You're not alone."

Neither of them spoke again for a long time.

SPIDER GOES TO MARKET

GERARD HOUARNER

Spider was walking from one village to the next when he came upon a dozen men from each arguing over a debt. Their words were loud, and their voices flew close to the pitch of war. Drawn to their passion, and knowing that men of passion are distracted and easily tricked, Spider hid in the grass to listen.

"You must pay what you owe," shouted the Big Man of one village.

"Such a price has never been asked," answered the Big Man from the other village, waving a fist.

"But not impossible for you to meet."

"We are the judge of what is possible and what is not. And if we were to pay, what will you do with our young men?"

"Sell them for what we want."

"And what would happen to our young men?"

"They will be sent to work some place far away, and never return."

"If that happens, we will never see our young men again."

"Do you ask to see again the grain, or the goat, or the pot you traded away last season?"

Spider had never heard of such a thing. He understood what everyone of the land knew, that wealth was counted in obligations a man was owed. He wondered, how could debt be settled by sacrificing the very thing that made a man wealthy? Give away enough young men, and soon there would be no one for the Big Men to call on for tribute, or service, or sustenance. Bonds forged by satisfying needs and appetites would vanish as debt and debtor were sold off to strangers. The web of dependency and power on which Spider danced would collapse!

It was the kind of scheme Spider himself might have designed, thinking himself clever. The kind of scheme he sometimes came to regret.

As shouts and screams erupted, Spider decided to act. No one on either side of the argument appeared as clever as himself, since both groups had gone from words to blows. Spider crept closer to the battle, hoping to discover who was responsible for changing how and why bargains were made. And to steal something of value from fighters knocked out in the fray.

The battle swung back and forth and suddenly ran over him. Fists and limbs and sticks and clubs flew one way and another. Then there was quiet, and the men from the victorious village took Spider prisoner, tied him up and roped him with a string of other captives from the losing group.

"Off to market you go," the Big Man told him with a smile. Spider decided that was not a bad idea, for he still wanted to meet the trickster responsible for passing off such a scheme on his neighbors. Here was a chance to learn a new trick or two. And there was always the challenge of deceiving someone who thought himself more cunning than Spider.

His captors led Spider far from the villages of his choice. Under the thick canopy of a forest, men marked by foreign tribal scars welcomed them with strange speech. Spider's captors bargained until darkness wove the branches over their heads into the blanket of night.

At last, the new men gave Spider's captors a bundle of sticks with metal heads whose strength and sharpness he had never before seen. Spider and the other men bound with him were given over to the new traders, who roped them with strings of other captives. During the celebration that followed, Spider slipped out of his bonds for a short while, stole the metal-headed sticks and replaced them with sticks with heads of stone.

The next morning, the two groups parted company. The new men led Spider and his fellow captives through hills and valleys until they came upon a different people. Once again, Spider and his company were handed over, this time for bags of pale flour. Once again, Spider was thrown into an even larger gathering of captives. During the night's celebration, Spider shrugged and his bindings fell. He stole the powder and replaced it with dirt.

In the morning, the groups parted company. Spider and his fellow captives were led across rivers and swamps until they came upon a town by the sea. An old man struggled to free himself from the string of captives, shouting they were all being sold to the Lord of the Dead.

"His followers are pale," the elder yelled, "and they will take us across the water where the dead wander. Our bodies will be crushed, and from our flesh they will squeeze the oil they use to cook their food. From our blood they will make the red wine they drink. Our broken bones they will grind to powder that turns to fire in their iron tubes."

The old man wailed, and the despair in his voice brought a moan to the lips of all the captives. Even Spider, for a moment.

A group of men came out of the town, and Spider saw they were indeed pale, and not like any men he had seen before. Their dress, manner and speech marked them as from a world Spider never knew. They handed bundles of shell money to Spider's captors. The strings of captives were given over. Spider was led into town. There was no celebration, which suited Spider. He did not want to steal shells.

Spider and his company were brought to pens and crowded together like herds of animals. One by one they were branded, their ritual scars defaced by the town's sign. When Spider's turn came, he asked the man in charge:

"Why do you chain and brand us? If you want our labor, can we not strike a deal and both gain in the bargain?"

"Does a human ask permission of a horse to ride him?" replied the man in charge. "Does a human beg a cow for milk, or ask forgiveness of a pig for taking its flesh?" He cracked his whip across Spider's back.

Spider flinched. "But we are not beasts."

Again the whip cracked. "You are naked."

Spider shuddered. "The cloth I wear is enough to protect me."

Once more, the whip cracked. "You stink."

Spider's body shook as blood trickled down his back. "Surely not as badly as you, in the sweat-drenched layers that hide your shame." The whip cracked a third time. "You live among beasts, like beasts."

Spider fell to his knees in a pool of his own blood and tears. "We live as we choose, as our customs and spirit tell us to live. But you do not understand, do you, whipmaster? Let me prove we are no different from you." The old excitement coursed through Spider, easing the pain of his punishment slightly, as a plan blossomed in his thoughts. "I'll wager freedom against service. Already, you hear that I can speak your tongue. I will wear your clothes, use your tools, balance your ledgers. I will take the blessing of your god, and worship in your temple, and you will see your god loves me as my own creator in the sky loves me, for I am made no different than you."

"A beast taught tricks and dressed like its master is still a beast. Besides, how can beasts wager with men? Such a thing does not belong in the natural order of life."

The man's assistants rushed forward and burned the town's mark in Spider's flesh. Others placed a collar of iron around Spider's neck, dragged him back to the pens, and chained him to men from tribes which had no name for him.

Lost among strangers, Spider sat stunned by the failure of his trick. What kind of men were these, who did not tumble before his wit and charm and cunning? He was used to being punished when caught stealing or making a fool out of a man, but not before he enjoyed his prize, or the fool was already made. He considered the problem.

That night, Spider slipped out of his shredded skin and into a fresh coat. The wounds he had suffered to his body healed. The cuts to his pride remained open. The sea's waves crashed onto shore, carrying the cries of captives trapped in the darkness of ship holds and in the fields of strange lands. From his place of hiding, Spider took out the sharp metal-headed sticks and gave them to his fellow captives.

"Rise with me," he told them, "and show these servants of the Lord of the Dead that the living are not prey, but lions with strength and courage. Show them how we bury the dead, and keep the spirits of evil from our houses."

From the pens rose a roar that shook stars from the sky. Walls fell.

A tide of sharp-edged rage spilled over brick and wood and flowed towards the town. Voices rose in alarm, and the darkness in front of Spider seethed with lights and motion.

Then the night shattered with a hundred lightning bursts, and thunder cracked, drowning the sound of chains rattling and lions roaring. A hail of angry hornets flew past Spider's ear. Men fell, dragging Spider down with them. Lightning flashed again, like the eyes of demons opening and closing. Thunder boomed over him, and clouds of acrid smoke chased after the sound. Men screamed. Blood flowed into the earth. Plumes of fire lit the ships waiting in the harbor. The keening of spirits filled the air. Then the earth trembled and split and swallowed men whole.

«««—»»»

Men with whips and iron tubes picked among the bodies, killing the crippled, taking the living and wounded back to the pens in chains. Spider went along with the rest, once again shocked that his trick had failed. How could he have known the monster's strength matched its terrible appetite?

The next morning, Spider was taken to the market, the destiny his first captor had promised him. Men inspected him, probing his mouth and prodding his arms and back. When men began haggling over prices, pointing to wounds suffered by one or another prisoner, Spider regretted not stealing shell money when he had the chance. What a fine trick it might have been to join the bidding and win freedom for himself and his fellow prisoners. But as the whipmaster dragged him off to be branded once more, this time with the mark of his new owner, Spider realized his bid and money would not have been accepted. He could hear the mocking reply: a beast cannot buy its freedom, especially when there is work to be done. The vast monster's blindness cast his mood in such darkness that he barely smiled when the whipmaster was himself whipped because Spider's first brand had disappeared.

That night, Spider slipped out of his bruised and branded skin and into a fresh coat. He discovered a wound to his soul was keeping company with the one to his pride. He listened as waves crashed on shore, carrying with them the drowning cries of neighbors lost to the sea. From his place of hiding, Spider took out the flour and tried to give it to his fellow prisoners.

"Join me," he told them, "and show these servants of the Lord of the Dead that they cannot use the living to do the work they themselves are too weak to do. Cover yourselves with the powder so you will seem like the men who keep us. Carry your chains, follow me over the walls. I will guide you, and together we will walk like the chameleon."

Spider stood and, after showering the flour over himself, became as pale as the moon. No one joined him. He stepped out of his chains and went to the pen wall. No one followed him. Those who had survived the previous night's slaughter looked away as he climbed out.

"Are you afraid of freedom?" Spider asked them.

"When we see it, we will tell you," a broken voice answered.

Spider left them behind and walked past guards, who saw only a flash of white. He made his way into the trees. He ran, feet barely touching the ground so no one could track him. He thought himself free.

Laughter and song from the town and ships stopped him. He looked back. Lights, like the many eyes of a monster, flickered with amusement. The wounds to his pride and soul deepened as he imagined the monster taunting him with a trick well-played. Run to your freedom, the monster seemed to say. Leave these worthless souls to me.

But no drums filled the night air with talk between one village and the next. No stories were being told around hearth fires. Instead, the breeze brought Spider the clink of shell money, the cries of battle, the clang of new chains being forged. An insatiable monster was devouring the freedom in the land he had assumed would always be his.

The truth struck him. These new men were afraid of the world and their place in it. They did not know how to appease the demons haunting them, or settle the restless spirits living among them. They were blind to the ways of the world because they feared it, and blindness fed their terror.

Spider understood that they were blind, as well, to wonders not of their making or under their control. Their eyes were pinched shut by the desire to overcome what they perceived to be greater than themselves, for in that greatness they found dread. The sea, the sky, the land, all were enemies to be conquered and used. Prisoners to their clever instruments of power like their killing iron tubes and the sea-spanning vessels in the harbor, the new men took comfort in the vision of a world filled with material wealth theirs for the taking. They dared not risk the moment's gain for the rewards of kinship with other men and higher forces. Such sentiments only frightened them.

And as long as illusions of power separated these new men from the feeling that drove them, he could not use that passion against them in his play. But the game was not over. Was he not Spider, surely filled with wit enough to best a mere monster?

Spider returned to the pens and placed himself back in chains. He stared at the monster he had dared challenge, searching for a way to heal his pride and win back his soul.

The next day, the captives were divided according to brands. Voices rose in anger over Spider's missing brand, but he gained no satisfaction from the momentary confusion. Soon enough, he was marked again, brought to a ship and quartered below decks with the other captives who lay on their backs on narrow shelves piled one atop the other. The sweat and sorrow of many passages rose out of the wood to choke him. The ship moved before the wind's breath, rocked in rhythm to the sea's restless motion.

He thought of men's eyes blinded by tear to his tricks and illusions. That night, he kept his skin with its mark of ownership. His wounds festered. Waves and wind brought the songs of captives from the other side of the sea, where the old man had said only the dead wander. The songs were driven by the pounding beat of ceaseless labor, and were filled with pain and loneliness. And hope.

Spider spoke to no one. He bit his tongue and lips until blood ran from his mouth. He pressed and rubbed his face against wood, letting the rough grain pit and peel back skin.

"What are you doing?" asked a man across the aisle.

"I am coming down with a terrible illness," Spider replied, grinning broadly. He worked a splinter loose and used it to prick bloody holes all over his body.

"The owners will only throw you overboard if they think you'll infect the rest of us," said another man.

"But what if we're all infected already?" Spider asked. He moaned softly and rubbed his stomach. "Can the owners throw us all overboard? Will they dare?" He coughed up phlegm, which he mixed with the blood in his mouth and sprayed liberally across the aisle. "Do we care if they do?" he whispered.

For a while, Spider's low moans and occasional coughs were the only sound in the hold. Then someone else coughed. A leg iron thumped against wood as someone's leg trembled. The smell of blood, and piss, and shit grew thick in the hold.

"I think a plague has come to curse our owners," Spider said.

Laughter rippled through the night.

Guards came down to the hold in the morning with food. They were greeted by a chorus of wails and moans. Captives vomited at their feet, clutched at their leggings, bled on their flesh.

Spider crawled to where the guards stood, frozen in place. "Help me, " he cried out, rattling his chains while he trembled as if seized by fever.

The guards retreated back up the stairs. The shock and wonder in their eyes drained away, leaving a glaze of terror over the emptiness that remained. Spider reached out to them, bloody foam on his lips. "Help us," he pleaded.

The master of the ship pushed the stunned guards aside and inspected the hold from the top of the stairs. He wrinkled his nose at the stench, turned to the guards, and pointed at his cargo.

"Go down there and clean that filth out," the master said.

"They're dying," said one guard.

"It's the plague," said another.

Spider put a hand on the bottom step and drew himself forward, reaching for the light, and for the ship's master. Behind him, the others massed, weeping with imagined suffering.

"Throw the lot overboard," the ship's master commanded. "We'll go back to port. Those thieves won't get away with selling us spoiled merchandise."

"I'm not touching them," replied a guard.

"We'll catch what they have," replied another.

"Then shoot the poor beasts before you throw them overboard."

"I'm not going into that devil's pit," a guard said, letting his weapon fall and backing away from the stairs.

"The ship's a plague carrier," said another guard. "To the boats, before we all die."

Cries and footsteps sounded from the deck. Bodies splashed into water. The ship's master cried out, waved his cutlass and fired an iron tube into the air. But his crew ignored him, and finally he looked down into the hold, at first with despair, and then with resignation.

"At least I'll have the insurance," he said, closing down the hold.

Moments later, the crackle of flames and the smell of smoke filled the dark space. Spider slipped out of his chains, worked out the latch's trick and opened the door. The ship's master was already gone, urging a small band of rowers to pull harder on their oars. Spider went back to free the other captives, and together they put out the flames and saved the sails and masts.

Wails and moans turned to laughter, and a great cheer rose among the men.

"Are you afraid of freedom now?" Spider asked the old man who had answered him in the pens.

The old man smiled and rubbed the place where iron bracelets had chafed his skin. His gaze passed over the sea, and he said, a little sadly, "I am not certain I see it."

"Then we will go find it," Spider said. The wound to his pride closed a little, and some of his soul grew back as he watched the ship's master and crew flee. He laughed at the trick he had played, until the wind and waves brought him the songs of captives from far away.

He heard their cry of pain and knew the monster had them all in its terrible maw. And Spider understood that he still had many tricks to learn and play before he found a land where his spirit and the people to which it belonged could once more run free.

PEST CONTROL

C. Dennis Moore

Sixteen hours he'd been on the move. He had to stop soon. Not to sleep, that was too risky. But his feet screamed with raw pain and he had to rest. His lungs burned like he'd been breathing acid. His mind reeled, still, with the images he'd seen since last night. And to think they'd been there all along, hiding, waiting, biding their time. And when they struck, they'd done it with a vengeance.

He clambered up a hill, using exposed roots and jutting rocks for purchase, reached the top and looked over the area. He couldn't see far, the sun was a mere whisper away from setting.

Across a field at the bottom of the hill he saw a guard shack, a factory or warehouse behind it.

It would have to do.

He took off down the hill. The breeze felt good against his forehead, and he pulled up the tail of his shirt to let it caress his stomach as well.

He breathed in deep, filling his lungs despite the razors that tore at his insides with every inhalation.

The shack was further than it looked and it took nearly another half hour to reach, but when he did he thanked God for bringing him such a gift. It looked deserted, and the factory parking lot was empty. He approached the small building cautiously, listening for the clitter and clatter, for the taps or chirps. There was nothing but the wind blowing about his face and the sound of his own ragged breath.

He crept to one of the windows slowly and silently. He peered through the dirty glass, cupping his hands around his eyes. There was a chair and a long counter with monitors and telephones and a computer, but not much else that he could see.

Around the side of the guard shack, he found the door ajar. He nudged it open and let what little light the moon provided reveal what it would. Which was nothing.

He let out his breath in relief and stepped inside. He didn't touch anything, not until he could more fully discern there was nothing in here with him. He eased the door closed behind him, then sat down in the guard's chair and collapsed forward onto the desktop and tried to hold in his vomit.

After several minutes of dry heaving he looked up, looked around again, and realized he was too visible. He worked himself under the desktop where the monitors stood, then stretched out, letting his muscles rest and his feet get some air. He took off his shoes and socks, peeling them back where his blisters had broken and started bleeding. The circulation flowed and his feet sang praises of relief, but that just made them hurt worse.

He laid his head on his arm and listened to the silence outside. If not for where he was hiding and the state of his body, he could almost fool himself into thinking nothing had happened, that all was calm and peaceful in the world. He *wanted* to pretend. Who would have thought the world could be turned upside down in so little time?

«‹‹—›››

Kevin wasn't much for the crotch rockets; he didn't feel the need for speed. He just liked being out by himself, cruising along and feeling a nice breeze whipping past him. He rode a CVO Softail Convertible and he rode it alone, as he did most things, because the company of others tended to make him claustrophobic after too much exposure. So he'd learned a long time ago to enjoy things he could do by himself.

This wasn't to say he didn't have friends, he had several. He had simply learned to keep them at arm's length because sometimes he just needed solitude.

Tonight was definitely one of those times. His boss had just come back from a week's vacation, which Kevin had been covering, to tell him half the things he'd done—which Kevin had done from the notes his boss gave him—were wrong. Kevin's opinion, however, was that he'd done everything right; his boss, a fat, smelly lump of nothing named Snyder, just didn't tell him about the shortcuts he always took. And now here he was, riding along a road he'd never seen before, knowing only that it was far from home, far from work, and thus far from the bullshit of his otherwise lackluster existence.

And then the bike chugged, coughed, and sputtered until Kevin managed to get control of the wheel and the brake and bring himself to a slow halt. The engine sputtered one final time, then died. He put the kickstand down, swung off the seat, and crouched next to the engine to see what was the trouble.

It was dark. He could barely see the engine at all, let alone determine the problem. He heard something coming from inside it though, some kind of clack-clack, like the rustling of thick tissue paper. Was there a short circuit in the wiring somewhere?

He leaned in closer, trying to see past the dark, but it was all just black shadows and moonlight-glinting chrome. But the thing that really confused him was how the shadows shifted. He put his head next to the engine, his ear close enough to feel the heat coming off it, and the clatter inside grew louder. Then something tickled the rim of Kevin's ear. He swiped at the ear, then looked around, like something might be on him.

Something tickled his ear again, then the other one, and the clack-clack from the engine was replaced by a buzz, and soon Kevin's vision was blurred by a swarm of flies, dive-bombing his face, causing him to squint when they tried to fly into his eyes. He shook his head to get them away from his ears and nose, trying to swat at them with his hands, but they wouldn't be stopped and soon Kevin was backing away from the bike as flies issued from the engine by the hundreds; if there was a space, a fly had taken it, and now they were moving out—right for Kevin's head.

He backed up across the road, tripped and fell, then rolled around in the dirt and grass, trying to treat the flies like fire and put them out. But they just hovered above him until he was done, then went in once he stopped.

He got to his feet, looked around as best he could, picked a direction, and ran.

«《—》»

Doug's seasoning mix was simmering, which gave him time to get the tomatoes and onions chopped while the shells were in the oven. He set the tomato on the cutting board, removed the sticker with the edge of his knife and a flick of his wrist, then the power went out.

There was that brief moment where he could only think *Huh?* and then he set the knife down and went for the flashlight under the sink. Two other voices said, almost at the same time, "Power's out!"

"I kinda figured," Doug mumbled as he headed for the basement door.

The breaker box hung on a column of brick in the middle of the basement, behind the furnace, on the other side of an obstacle course of Christmas decorations, old toys, and busted furniture Doug hadn't bothered to get rid of yet. He traversed the jungle, got to the breaker box, and opened it, shining the light on each switch.

If there was a blown breaker, he didn't see it.

Then he heard the clitter and clatter above him. He pivoted the light overhead and the ceiling of the basement was covered in bugs—waterbugs, it looked like, maybe beetles—dozens of them. Doug backed up, as if this would keep them from raining down on him, nearly toppled over the Christmas tree box, then righted himself and moved away from the center of the room. How did he not hear that as soon as he came down?

Didn't matter. He shined the flashlight around the rest of the basement and saw they weren't just on the ceiling. The bugs came through the floor and the back wall, which was dirt like the floor. A stream of them issued from the ground and hundreds of big black specks of exoskeletal nastiness scurried here and there. Doug darted up the stairs, pulled the door shut and locked it behind him, and went to get the boys.

"Jason!" he called.

His oldest son replied from upstairs, "What?"

"Come down here for a second. Cory?"

The younger of his two boys said, "What?" He was in the living room, sitting in the dark. That was Cory, calm in the face of the unknown, just waiting to see what happened.

"You guys get your shoes and jackets and come help me."

"What's up?" Jason asked, joining them in the living room.

"Come on," and he turned around, headed for the basement. His sons followed. Doug grabbed the broom from next to the refrigerator, handed Jason the mop.

"We're gonna knock them off the ceiling and crush em. Cory, you take the flashlight."

"Knock what?" Jason asked.

"You'll see."

Doug opened the basement door and stepped down, but what he'd seen moments ago was nothing compared to what he faced now. Cory aimed the light into the darkness, but it wasn't just a few dozen beetles and waterbugs, it was hundreds, probably thousands of them.

They backed up and closed the door and everyone moved back into the kitchen.

Doug supposed he'd call an exterminator, because he couldn't imagine who else there would be to call for something like this. He'd never heard of an infestation this bad, not even on A&E. He found the listings, dug the phone from his pocket, and saw there was no signal.

"That's new," he said. "Jason, you got a signal?"

"No, it doesn't look like it."

"Okay." He scratched his head, closed the phone book and paced around the dining room table.

"Did you see how many there were?" Jason asked.

"Yeah."

"We've got bug spray, that'll do it, right?"

"I don't think one can's gonna take care of all of them."

"It'll help."

"Anyway," Cory said, "they're just bugs."

"Just bugs," Doug echoed. He got the can from the top of the fridge, shook it to see how full it was. It felt almost new. He put his hand on the basement door, but hesitated. It didn't feel right. They're bugs, they're inevitable, they're everywhere, but that many? It definitely felt wrong. But, like Cory said, they're just bugs.

He opened the door and sprayed. Bugs fell by the dozens from the ceiling and doorway, the walls, and he stepped out onto the landing to crush them under his feet as he fought his way to the bottom of the stairs. By the time he got there he realized Jason and

Cory were still at the top. He didn't know if he'd expected them to follow or not, but he knew a few more feet doing the job would help.

"Jason, I need the flashlight," he called up the stairs, but when he turned around to look, he saw he'd made no progress at all. It didn't matter how many he'd killed, they had the numbers to replace them and it seemed as if he'd not even made a dent. And now he was downstairs, in the dark, surrounded, with a can that was almost empty. He couldn't see the stairs, nor the door at the top. He didn't know if Jason had heard him.

He was supposed to be eating tacos right now.

Bugs fell from the ceiling, tangled in his hair, fell into his shirt collar, tickling his skin. He tried to shake like a dog and get them off him. That's when the sheer number of them hit him. He didn't understand why they were in his basement, why they were attacking him—and Doug knew this was an attack, simple as that—or why they'd chosen his house. What he did understand was that he had to get back upstairs. Never mind the power. He'd made a mistake coming down here, had greatly underestimated them. He charged toward the direction of the stairs, only to run face-first into the concrete wall. His nose throbbed and gushed blood. Doug brushed the bugs from his face, trying to clear his eyes and see where he was. He tripped over the stupid Christmas decorations again, felt bugs squish under his hands, and got to his feet. He felt their legs on him, then something like tiny points of fire burning into him, like a thousand pinpricks, and he knew they were biting him.

"Fuck!" he yelled, fighting to get them off him, but there were just too many and the pain finally brought him to his knees.

«««—»»»

His boys heard the scream upstairs. It overpowered the clicking of the bugs on the other side of the basement door, which Jason had closed when his dad went downstairs and he, Jason, saw the bugs were still coming. Cory jumped and looked up at his brother in the dim glow from the flashlight. Jason couldn't find anything to say. Words of hope felt like a lie in his mouth.

"Dad?" Cory asked.

Jason moved to the door and leaned in, hoping to hear his father climbing the stairs, trying to open the door. He turned the handle, pushed open the door, but the flood of bugs that fell out answered his question. He leapt back, brushed off the few that had landed on him, and grabbed his brother's arm.

"Come on," he said, and they ran out the front door.

"What about Dad?" Cory asked.

Jason couldn't bring himself to say the words, but silence felt like ignoring it, and that felt like a betrayal.

"I don't think he's coming up," Jason said.

"But you don't know."

"No," Jason said. "He's not coming up."

"He's hurt down there."

To that, he had no answer. Could he go to the police station? Or the hospital? He really didn't know. But once outside and looking around, it appeared his wasn't the only house with a problem.

The neighbors a few houses down were all standing outside, staring back at their house, as if it had grown legs and tried to come after them. He dragged his brother down the street and asked them, "What happened?"

The father—Jason didn't know any of their names—looked over at him as if drugged, and said, "They just came out. There was a crack in the plaster in my daughter's room, and they came out of it. They were in the walls. It was just a crack, but they came through and it got bigger. God, there were so many of them."

"So many what?" Jason asked, knowing the answer.

"They were cockroaches," the man said. "We never had cock-roaches before," he made sure to add. "Jesus, they were everywhere."

Jason and Cory went back down to their house and Jason told his brother, "Get in the car, I'll be back."

He went inside to get the keys off the hook by the door, and found the floor was covered in bugs. They crawled and shuffled over each other in a macabre dance, vying for space. He had the flashlight in his hands, and hearing something from the kitchen, he shone it through the living room, across to the kitchen table, where he saw what remained of his father.

Doug was swarmed in them, every inch covered, and in the glare of the light, Jason could see they'd eaten away chunks of his face, including both of his eyes. He was coming forward, finding his way by feel in the constant, shifting and creeping dark. Jason's heart pounded and he wanted to throw up. Doug fell forward and when he didn't get back up, Jason fought back a scream. He backed away and got the hell out of there, for his brother's sake, if for no other reason.

He got in the car and he and Cory pulled away.

«««—»»»

"Are we going to get an ambulance?" Cory asked.

"Ambulance for what?" Jason asked.

"For dad."

That wasn't something he wanted to talk about just yet. But Cory hadn't seen him in those last few seconds, so he didn't know how bad it really was for their father.

"Um, we're gonna try and find some help, yeah," he finally replied.

Jason wound the car through the streets, not really having a direction in mind, thinking in the back of his head they could go to their uncle's house. They certainly couldn't just drive around all night, and parking the car somewhere and waiting was no solution either.

He'd only driven to his uncle's house once, but he thought he knew how to get there. Uncle Dean lived out past the highway, all he had to do was take the Avenue out past the hospital, then turn.

"We're gonna go see if Dean's home," he told his little brother. Cory didn't argue.

The drive out didn't assuage any of Jason's trepidations; all was in darkness. No house lights, no streetlights, no traffic lights. Houses stood open to the world while people stood out on their lawns, or walked down the street in socks and shorts, whatever they'd thrown on after work that afternoon, families displaced and lost. Whatever was happening, it obviously wasn't just Jason and Cory's neighborhood. It looked like it was all over town. A lot of families were in their cars as well, but he didn't know where they might be driving to. Was there some kind of shelter? He turned on the radio to see if there was any news, but heard only dead air.

He checked his phone, but it still had no service.

No phones and no radio meant no lines of communication. As bad as he'd felt just moments ago, Jason suddenly felt ten times worse.

Then he almost hit a man running down the Avenue. Jason swerved and slammed on the brakes, skidded, but maintained control.

The guy ran over to the window, yelling something, but Jason was shaken and not paying attention. He rolled down the window a crack.

"What?"

"Let me in. Please. Get me out of here."

He looked over his shoulder, like something might be there.

Jason hit the unlock button and the guy dove into the back seat. Jason pulled away and turned off onto Dean's road.

"You okay?" he asked the guy in the back.

"No, not even close. What the holy motherfuck is going on?"

"We don't know," Jason said. "What did you see?"

The man told them about the flies that had clogged up his motorcycle engine, about taking off down the dirt road, approaching the first house he'd seen and knocking on the door.

"Nobody answered, and the lights were out, but I heard something inside. Cupped my face over the front window and could barely see, but I could tell something in there was moving.

"It was bugs, man. A million of 'em. Crawling all over everything. God, the sound they made; there were so many of them all at once, I could hear it outside."

"Where was this house?" Jason asked.

"Just up this road, big white house."

"Was there a boat?"

Jason wasn't familiar with this part of town, only knew his uncle lived out here. He couldn't remember how many, if any, neighbors Dean might have. It might not be Dean's house this guy was talking about, but Jason knew his uncle had a boat.

"Yeah yeah," the guy in the back said. "Boat, parked over on the side."

"Is that Uncle Dean's house?" Cory asked.

"Yeah, I think so."

"What does that mean," the passenger asked.

"Means we're not going there. And if not there, I don't know where else to go."

«‹‹—››»

So they drove, and introductions were finally made. Jason wasn't as familiar with the streets as he wished he had been. He didn't know where he was going, but everywhere he went the sights were the same. No streetlights burned, no houses were lit up. The McDonald's on Main Street was dark, but they drove by slowly, staring into the big plate glass windows at the bugs covering the inside of the restaurant.

"What is going on?" Jason asked. "I mean, really, man: bugs?"

"Cockroaches, crickets, flies. I've seen grasshoppers and beetles. It's not just one kind, it's all of them," Kevin said.

"How?" Jason asked. "Why? They're not just swarming, they're attacking. They got our—" but he cut himself off here, for Cory's sake. He looked at his little brother, but Cory was looking out the window, staring at his school as they drove past it.

"I bet it's safe in there," he said. Jason glanced over to see what he meant, saw the school.

"It's locked up, though," he said. "And anyway, that place is so old, there's probably a million ways they could get in there."

"Then we could go someplace else," Cory countered, "someplace just like it."

"But where?" Kevin asked from the back seat.

"You think we should try the hospital?" Jason said. "Lots of people. And those places have back-up power, don't they? For the machines and stuff?"

"Makes sense," Kevin said. "We could try it."

Jason turned the car around in a Dollar General parking lot, and headed back toward the highway. Cory turned on the radio and started scanning every station, hoping for at least one of them to still be on the air, but they heard only static at every stop along the dial, on both AM and FM bands.

Since none of the traffic lights worked, Jason stopped at every intersection, and every time he did, the chirp of the crickets got louder for a second. And the longer they were out, Jason noticed, the fewer and fewer people they saw. Some cars were left abandoned in the street, the doors open, lights on. Several houses they passed were also open, the doors wide, with nothing but complete black glaring out at them, daring them to step inside. Jason thought of how his father looked in those last few seconds. They weren't just swarming him, they were *eating* him.

Kevin saw the lights of the hospital first and couldn't contain his excitement. It infected the others and soon all three were eager to get there, to sit in the light, to be surrounded by people. The parking lot was as full as could be expected and Jason wondered if others had the same idea of safety out here. That would come as a huge comfort, especially to Cory, whose state of mind he worried about. Whatever was happening, it had to be even harder on a thirteen-year-old.

Kevin pointed out a parking spot, the closest one nowhere near any of the doors.

"I don't see any bugs out here," Cory said.

"Yeah," Jason agreed. "Haven't *seen* any outside, but we've heard plenty of them."

"We'll run," Kevin said.

Jason pulled into the spot. "Cory, you hold my hand," he said. He'd expected an argument on that point, but his little brother merely nodded.

They climbed out of the car, Jason taking Cory's hand, and all three took off for the first door they saw. Halfway there, Jason had a moment to wonder if it had been locked, if someone had tipped them about what was happening, and someone in charge had locked the door against anyone else getting inside. Then, for a second, he knew it was true. They'd never get in. The people inside had everything they needed, they could survive for a while, probably, if this thing—whatever it was—went on long, so why would they ever want to let more people in and diminish their finite supply? They wouldn't, he realized. The doors were locked, and the run back to the car was going to be even longer. And what if they didn't make it, because there could be a million and a half bugs with sharp pincers hiding under every single car in this parking lot, and Jason could easily imagine those bugs working their way out of hiding this second, waiting for them to find the doors locked and have to turn around and come back, only to find their way blocked by a sea of insects.

But the door wasn't locked. Kevin got there first, tore it open and held it for Jason and Cory, then darted inside behind them.

There was light, but not the bustling crowd of people Jason had expected to find. In fact, the halls were empty. The gift shop stood open, but empty. Same for the chapel.

"It's so quiet," Kevin said as they traveled down the hall. "It's so weird."

"No bugs anywhere, though," Jason said.

"Yeah, that's good," Kevin replied.

"We should find the ER," Jason suggested. "If there's lots of people, that's probably where they'd be."

They found a map of the hospital, located the emergency room, then headed toward it.

"Maybe they can send an ambulance back for Dad?" Cory asked.

"Yeah," Jason said. "We'll see."

They turned the last corner to the emergency room, and all three stopped dead. There was no refuge here.

Bodies lay scattered, half-eaten, and still teeming with skittering, clattering bugs of every imaginable kind. They went halfway up the walls, meandering about, crawling over each other. A few hundred were on the ceiling. One fell onto Jason's shoulder, a cockroach, big as any he'd ever seen, nearly the size of a small mouse, and he flinched, swatted it half a dozen times, trying to get it off without actually making contact.

It fell into a pile of beetles and lay there, legs flailing until the beetles shifted around, turning the cockroach over, and it crawled away.

Crickets chirped randomly somewhere under the moving mass of insects.

Cory had already backed away half a dozen steps. Jason couldn't take his eyes off the corpses. Bugs spilled from inside them, as if they'd set up hives or dens or whatever it was bugs typically lived in. A nurse lay slumped over a keyboard at the desk. A chunk was missing from her open left eye. With her chin resting against the keys, her mouth was closed, but Jason saw movement inside her cheeks and for a moment he imagined it was his own mouth those tiny, rapid legs were tickling. He wiped at the phantom sensation with his tongue, then bit the inside of his cheek.

The chirping of the crickets quickly changed from random bleeps, merged, fell into synch, and in the span of a few seconds they all chirped as one loud voice. It didn't take a rocket scientist to know that couldn't be a good thing, especially when the mass of bugs all seemed to stop and take notice of them as a whole.

Kevin didn't bother with words; he grabbed Jason's arm and hauled him away. Cory was already running.

They tried to run back the way they came, but before they reached the chapel, the hallway was teeming with cockroaches and the boys took the first turn they found. They ran, legs pumping and muscles burning, their chests pounding with their heartbeats. They had no idea where they were going, but as far as they were concerned, if there weren't any bugs in front of them, they were headed in the right direction.

They turned into the cafeteria, and Cory headed for the counter, probably to hide behind, Jason thought, but he only lasted a second before they all realized the roaches were eating everything they found back there, every sweet, half-rotted, or exposed bit of food was swarming.

"Where the hell are we going?" Kevin asked.

"I don't know, man. How do we get out of here?"

"Hold up," Kevin said, and they all stopped to catch their breath and decide on a plan. The hallway was bare and silent, except for their ragged gasps. Kevin leaned against the wall, bent forward with his hand on his knees, holding himself up. Cory couldn't run as fast, but he was definitely in better shape. He was breathing heavy, but didn't seem on the verge of collapsing.

"You think that was on purpose?" Kevin asked.

"What?" Jason replied.

"They blocked the way we came in. They pretty much herded us further inside."

"That can't be. They're bugs."

"I know what they are, but you saw them back there. Those crickets. All at once?"

"They're communicating," Cory offered.

Jason looked from his brother to Kevin, who nodded, then said, "I think so, too."

Jason shook his head.

Cory looked at the floor, then said, "Listen."

The other two went silent, cocked their heads. The rustling came through very faint, but just noticeable under the hum of the lights. From further down the hall. They crept forward, the bathroom and supply closet doors giving way to patient rooms. The rustling came from inside. Jason knew what he'd find, but he had to open one of the doors anyway.

The room was painted in bugs, the remains of a patient sprawled across the bed with tiny black and brown bodies nesting in the abdomen, crawling through the hair, over what was left of the face. When the door opened, the bugs came for them, and the three took off again, back the way they'd come, still trying to get out of the maze.

Jason pulled them over to the side and said, "We're going to have to go through them. I know there's a lot, but if they're between us and the doors out of here, we have to. How many of us can they get if we're running, anyway?"

"How many do they need to get?" Kevin asked. "One's too many for me, especially if I'm that one. Are you nuts?"

"No, I'm trying to protect myself and my little brother."

"Did you not see what they did back in the ER? And do you think we're any stronger or faster than any of those people?"

"Stay here, then. Cory and I are gone."

Jason grabbed his brother and said, "Come on." Cory followed, but his reluctance was plastered all over his face.

Kevin followed too, under protest.

It didn't take long to find the bugs, or for the bugs to find them. And that was the moment Jason saw the flaw in his plan. Kevin noticed it, too. The beetles clacked and clattered, barricading the hall, but not coming for them. It almost looked as if the bugs dared them to come further.

"We're nowhere near the door," Kevin said.

"We'll be fine. We're bigger, faster, and we're going to keep moving, and killing as many of them under our feet as we can."

"We don't even know how far it is to the door," Cory said. His terror was evident, and Jason knew if Cory was showing a reaction, he had to be affected in a huge way. Cory was the ice king, the inspector, the one who looked objectively at every situation and simply got through it to see what happened on the other side. But how do you remain objective when the whole town is in blackout and the one place you've found with lights is full of bug-infested corpses— and you're next?

You don't. And Cory was the proof of that.

"You'll be okay, Cory," Jason said. "Just keep up with me."

"You know I can't."

"It's okay," Kevin said. "We'll be here, too."

Jason ran through his memory of where they'd been so far, trying to remember landmarks like artworks on the walls or where the snack machines had been, anything that might clue him in when to turn and which corridors to take.

He grabbed Cory's hand, held it tight, and they took off.

The crunch beneath their feet sickened them and a few times they slid in guts when too many of the disgusting things got under them.

Cory tried to keep up, but mostly it was a matter of Jason slowing down for him.

The further they ran, the thicker the carpet of crickets and cockroaches; the bugs were fortifying their position and not making this the least bit easy on them. Soon the thin sheet of bugs had grown to a shallow pool that came to the tops of their feet, and then they were struggling through a swamp that covered their ankles and had to contain several million bugs. Their progress was nearly halted, but they fought through, taking down as many as they could. The door was in sight when Jason glanced over his shoulder and saw several dozen bugs working their way up Cory's legs, some as far as his abdomen. In his fight to freedom, Cory didn't notice.

Jason stopped to swat them off. What he didn't see until it was too late were the ones crawling up Cory's back. They'd reached his shoulder, crawled up his neck, into his hair, a few smaller ones slid into his ears too quick to be stopped, and took Cory to his knees.

Jason swept bugs from his brother's hair, off his shirt, away from his face. But he only had two hands and they got into Cory's nose. He gagged when they crawled up and down through his nasal passages and into his throat.

Jason shouted, "Help me!" but Kevin only stood there, a blank look plastered on his face.

Cory doubled over, clutched his gut, and that's when the rest of the bugs swallowed him in a rippling, writhing cocoon, and Jason snatched his hands back so quickly he lost his balance and fell backward. He went wrist deep in the cockroaches, slid in their smashed bodies, and scrambled to his feet, sweeping bugs off him and telling Kevin, "Get them off my back."

Kevin grabbed his arm and hauled him toward the door, but Jason fought him, yelling, "We got to get him out, we got to get him!"

Kevin got him outside, away from the building, leaned him against the trunk of a car.

"You can't get him," Kevin said.

For the first time since the attack started, Jason lost it.

He punched the trunk until his fist left dents, ignoring the pain, yelling "Fuck fuck fuck fuck" over and over. He turned and ran back toward the building, with Kevin giving chase.

Jason stopped before the automatic doors could open and watched the diminishing bulk of his brother buried beneath the swarm as they devoured him. He cried as they finally retreated. What was left was his brother sprawled face-first on the floor, covered in a hundred thousand bite marks, bleeding and gasping. When Jason saw Cory move, he tried to go back in, but Kevin stopped him again.

"You saw what they did," he said. "They got inside him, man."

"Fuck you," Jason said, and turned around. He had to close off his heart now and find the car. But this hadn't been the way they came in and the car was two lots over. They approached cautiously, wondering if the bugs had anticipated this and come out to head them off, but they got the doors open, inspected the seats, floor and ceiling as best they could with the dome light until Jason found the flashlight in the backseat.

The car was clean, so they got in and closed and locked the doors.

On the highway again, Kevin asked, "You want me to drive?"

"No, I got it," Jason said.

Several times, Kevin opened his mouth to speak, but nothing came out, so he closed it again. What would he say anyway? Nothing Jason wanted to hear.

He drove aimlessly, watching the people in the streets. The bodies weren't hidden inside their homes anymore. They saw more and more dead outside, on lawns, sidewalks, slumped over steering wheels. The bugs were getting bolder, branching out, expanding their attack.

"Fucking madness," Jason muttered. "We have to get some gas."

"Where?" Kevin asked. "No one has power."

"I don't know. But if we don't try, we'll be walking soon anyway. My old man never was one for filling the tank. Ten bucks here and there always seemed to do just fine for him. Nice going, Dad."

"I'm sure he wasn't anticipating this."

"Like it matters. He's dead. Cory's dead. At least I *think* he is. I'd know for sure if I'd gone back inside for him."

"And you could have wound up right next to him on the floor."

"Well, thanks so much for saving my life, I guess. Keep your eyes open for a gas station."

«««—»»»

Kevin directed him to a truck stop at the edge of town. "They might be on a different grid? Hell, maybe it's just us this is happening to."

"Sure thing," Jason said. They pulled into the darkened lot, though, and knew it was for nothing. "Forget it, then," Jason said. "We're done. Low fuel light's been on since the hospital."

"Maybe one of these others has some gas in it."

"You know how to drive one of those trucks?"

"No, but there's cars, too."

Jason drove around the lot, both of them scanning for prospects. The entire place was barren, with the exception of all the abandoned cars.

"There!" Kevin said, pointing. At the far end of a row of gas pumps they found a pickup with the doors open, nozzle hanging out of the gas tank. Jason pulled up alongside it.

Kevin got out, checked inside the cab. The keys were in it. Then he swept the interior with his eyes, looking for bugs. There were none.

"This one," he said over his shoulder, waving Jason over.

Jason turned off his dad's car, got out and came around to the truck. "Where are all the bodies?" he asked.

Kevin looked around and shrugged.

"I don't know. If they were out here, surely they'd have run away instead?"

"Maybe," Jason muttered. "I gotta get something to eat, man."

Kevin stared at him, dumbfounded. "How can you eat?"

Jason shrugged. "Look, all this shit started while my dad was making dinner. I need some food. I'm gonna check the store.

"Here, take the flashlight, and keep your eyes open. I'll be there in a second, and we can stock up."

But Jason was gone before Kevin got to the end of his sentence.

Kevin put the nozzle back in its cradle, replaced the gas cap, closed the flap, and got into the truck. The engine roared and he had

319

to restrain himself from howling with joy. There'll be time to celebrate once all this is over, he thought. He pulled the truck up alongside the store.

It was dark inside, but he'd expected that. He had almost reached the door before it dawned on him it was *too* dark. Jason was in there, with the flashlight.

Kevin pulled open the door cautiously, watching the floor just across the threshold in case a wave of bugs washed over his feet. "You in here?" he called. Jason didn't answer. Kevin stepped inside. "Where are you?" He didn't hear a thing inside the store. He went down the aisle closest to the front, past the motor oils and atlases, headed for the refrigerators. He heard a noise and turned toward the corner, then realized it was the urinal flushing, and the men's room door opened, accompanied by the glow of the flashlight and Jason. "Shit, dude, you scared the hell out of me."

"Had to piss. I grabbed a bunch of waters, they're on the counter. I'll grab some food."

"I'll take the bottles out to the truck," Kevin said. He gathered them in his arms and shouldered the door open, loaded them into the truck, and came back in to find Jason standing in the middle of the aisle, staring down at the floor. "What's up?"

"They got it all," Jason said.

Everything, every bag of chips, every candy bar, anything the bugs could get to, lay open, some of it scattered on the floor, some torn open on the rack, but there was nothing here that hadn't been touched and partially eaten by the bugs.

"Fucking everything. What the fuck?"

"Fuck it, let's go. We'll find it somewhere else."

"Where else is there?" Jason asked. "They've gotten everywhere. We're not gonna go anywhere they haven't already been. These things have been around how many millions of years? Dude, they're everywhere."

"We'll find someplace, but let's go."

Then they heard it, the familiar clack-clack-clack as legs shuffled over carapaces and a thousand cockroaches, beetles, crickets, and grasshoppers maneuvered into position behind them.

"Let's go, now," Kevin said, turning and seeing them forming outside.

They approached the door and looked at the writhing black and brown roadblock.

"It's not gonna end, is it?" Jason asked. "There's too many of them."

"What are you talking about? You're in shock, man. Knock it off, and come on. It's only a few, we'll stomp half of them on the way to truck. You ready?"

"I'm not in shock," Jason said. "I'm seeing the truth. Look over there," he said, pointing to the truck.

Bugs poured out through the grill.

"Shit," Kevin said, thinking about his motorcycle.

"You go on," Jason said. Kevin looked at him, but Jason's eyes were dead, defeated. His face had a numbing glaze to it and Kevin thought if he could be Jason for just a second, he'd feel the tears beating at his chest, struggling to get out. Not that he could blame him. Kevin didn't have a family, and the few friends he counted as his, he hadn't even wondered about them all night, so he obviously didn't consider them too important, did he? But Jason had literally watched his family being eaten alive.

He didn't question Jason's state of mind or condemn him for slipping away from reality for a moment.

"Come on," he said. "We can't stand around here, let's see if there's a back way."

The back way, however, was closed off, too, as they heard the bugs coming out from wherever they'd been hiding inside the store. The sound they made as they came up the aisle with the decimated chip bags and candy wrappers was like a giant strand of firecrackers amidst the utter quiet of this new world.

As for the flies, they heard the buzz only seconds before the swarm hit them both in the face, blinding, deafening, and disorienting both men. Kevin, facing the door, ran forward, pushed through to the outside, whipping his head back and forth and swatting at the air with his palms. Jason, however, turned toward the aisles to see the approaching wave, and as the flies attacked, he swatted, flinched, and fell back into a display of anti-freeze jugs, tumbled to the floor, and was met by hundreds of pinchers going straight for his fingers and hands.

He yelped and the flies got into his mouth. The bugs scurried up his arms and legs, overwhelming his frantic attempts to shake them off. He stood up, but fell back again, this time into a rack of motor oils and brake fluids. Kevin heard the clatter inside the store, but he'd made it through the pool of bugs and . . . he couldn't bring himself to go through it again to help. He cursed himself, but right now he had his own issues. The flies still swarmed his head. The bugs crawled up his pants. Some slipped under the cuffs and crawled up his legs.

He squashed these with his fists against his legs, but he had to move before they became too many to control.

He hated himself for it, but he turned and ran.

«««—»»»

He woke up an hour or two after sinking into the dark of the guard shack. He hadn't meant to fall asleep. He listened for bugs, but the shack was silent around him.

The sores on his feet and hands were open and stinging. He shuffled his position, trying to find one that didn't hurt. His hands were stiff and felt like welts had been raised on his palms. His scalp itched and he quickly ran his hand through it, afraid it would be crawling with bugs.

He flexed his knees and tried to find the energy to stand. His knees popped, but he didn't get any further.

Kevin tried to think of what his next move would be. He'd run away from the truck stop with no plan, no direction. He'd simply moved, and kept moving. Who knew how much distance he'd covered since then? Or how much there still was to cover before he found some place safe to stop. He certainly couldn't live in a tiny guard shack. He wasn't even sure what this place was supposed to be guarding, the lights had been out and he'd been too preoccupied to pay much attention to the warehouse or factory or whatever it was behind the shack. He'd only known he probably wouldn't be able to get inside there, so he'd focused on the shack instead.

He thought for a second about Jason and wondered if, at the end, he'd thought Kevin as much a coward as Kevin thought himself. He tried to justify his abandonment by reminding himself Jason had told him to go, and really, at that point, Jason wasn't going to be of any use to him anyway. But none of his rationalizing made him feel any better about how quickly he'd cut and run.

God, his feet hurt. I might not be going anywhere for a few more hours, he thought. Maybe not even until tomorrow.

He had to bandage them, if he could. He wondered if there would be a first aid kit here in the shack. He leaned forward and searched under the counter that served as the desktop, using his hands to help him in the dark. He maneuvered around the supports, into the corners and crannies, searching blindly, until his fingers sank deep into a hidden pile of cockroaches, and those tiny legs crept over his knuckles, up to his wrist. They tickled as they scurried up his forearms and Kevin jerked back, flailing his arms, trying to shake them loose, smash them, and it suddenly occurred to him what was so peculiar about the stinging in his soles.

Through the skitter of the bugs up his arms, Kevin realized the burning on his feet wasn't caused by having been on the move all last night, all the following day, and into the next evening—during which the signs of the insects' total reclamation of the world was evident in every empty building, abandoned car, and half-eaten, egg-laden corpse he saw—but by the scurrying bugs that were crawling around, inside and out, of his broken blisters. They were inside him. Not the big ones, not yet. But God, he felt them. He felt them under his skin. He felt them tiptoeing across his muscles and tendons. He felt them inside, gnawing on his bones and trying to get into his organs. The cramps doubled him over and he screamed and the bugs got in that way, too. The only other sound besides Kevin's scream, for miles around, was the clattering of the bugs scurrying over one another, and the chirp of the crickets calling the forces to battle.

I'M SO SORRY FOR YOUR LOSS

RONALD MALFI

Unable to sleep, Buddy Tupelo peeled the bed sheet off his body and dropped one foot to the floor. Careful not to wake Marie, who slept soundly beside him, Buddy climbed out of bed and, with his hands feeling around in the darkness ahead of him, zombie-walked across the bedroom to the door. Once he made it out into the hallway, he eased the bedroom door closed then flipped on the hall light. The single naked bulb in the ceiling caused him to wince.

He made his way to the living room, nearly walking right into the Christmas tree he kept forgetting was there, and over to the small table that sat at the bend where the two sofas formed an L. On the table was their shared laptop, an outdated piece of crap Buddy had purchased a few years ago for around four hundred bucks. Marie had wanted one of those fancy-schmancy MacBooks, but Buddy, who had learned frugality at a young age, hadn't seen the point. Sure, their cheapo laptop often froze up or lost the Wi-Fi connection—and lately, the goddamn curser had a tendency to drift to the upper right corner of the screen for no apparent reason—but for Buddy, who was about as skilled on the computer as a dog is behind the wheel of a school bus, the thing worked just fine. Also, he thought MacBook sounded like something you'd read at a McDonald's.

He groped for the laptop in the dark, working his fingers around to where the power cord was plugged into the back. He unplugged the power cord, tucked the laptop under his arm, then continued on down the hall toward the bathroom. Sure, there was a bathroom off their bedroom, but Marie often complained that he woke her in the middle of the night, particularly when his gastritis was really boiling up his guts. Also, the bathroom at the other end of the house was just far enough away for him to indulge in…less seemly activity…without his wife's knowledge. (And if she suspected he looked at porno-graphic websites at night while hunkered down on the toilet, even after he'd gone through the trouble of clearing the Internet history, she'd never said anything to him about it.)

In the bathroom, he flipped on the light and the ceiling exhaust then set the laptop on the counter beside the sink. Marie's hairbrush was on the edge of the sink, its stiff black bristles bursting through a meshwork of his wife's dirty blond hair. Buddy dropped his boxer shorts and scanned his doughy, middle-aged frame in the large mirror with some mild disdain. He could stand to drop a good twenty-five pounds. Maybe even thirty. Once the holidays were over, he promised himself, he would buckle down and start working out. Hell, maybe he'd treat himself to a gym membership. At the very least, he could watch the soccer moms doing Pilates while he huffed and wheezed along a treadmill's conveyor belt.

Buddy dropped the toilet seat, grabbed the *el cheapo* laptop, and settled himself down. God, the lousy gastritis had been doing a job on him this week. And with all the holiday food they would be eating, it only promised to get worse. A lover of all this salty, fatty, and spicy, was Buddy Tupelo.

He winced and leaned to the left as he released an almost mournful expulsion of flatulence. Then, briefly, he contemplated masturbating, precariously balancing the laptop on one knee while he downloaded porn and worked himself into a sweaty little mess, but in the end—and mostly due to the gastritis, thanks so much—he decided to forgo such recreation and pulled up his Facebook page instead.

It had been Marie who'd showed him how to use Facebook. Buddy had resisted for as long as he could, uninterested in the tech-nical shrewdness he believed he would have to cultivate in order to use the site. Also, what was the point? If he needed to talk to someone, he'd just pick up the phone. Not to mention he had little interest in turning into a clone of Marie—always hunched over the laptop, clacking away at the keys, sometimes tittering or chuckling or sighing or saying *oh oh oh* whenever she'd read someone's happy or funny or sad post. It wasn't until Marie set up his profile and starting connecting with his old school friends on his behalf did he finally acquiesce, and even then it was so his friends wouldn't mistake his wife's silly little comments as his own.

Yet to his surprise he found he had become quickly addicted, and in less than four months, he had managed to accumulate more Facebook friends than Marie—nearly four hundred at the moment. Some were colleagues at the foundry, others were neighbors and relatives, and some were even his old high school buddies, many of whom he hadn't spoken to in nearly a decade. Buddy didn't post on his own page very often—what did a middle-aged, overweight factory employee really have to say that was so pressing?—but he did find voyeuristic pleasure in scanning his friends' pages or reading the messages others had posted on his page.

As he squeaked out another odorous spurt of flatulence, Buddy entered his screen name and password into the appropriate blocks then logged onto the site. The little horizontal bar at the bottom of the screen incrementally turned green as the site began to load. A few seconds later, his personal avatar appeared at the top of the screen. It was a photo of him when he was a bit younger, his hair a little longer, his weight more manageable. Unlike many of his online friends, Buddy shied away at posting current photos of himself, opting instead for pics of his favorite album covers—Steely Dan's *Can't Buy a Thrill* and Bob Dylan's *Blonde on Blonde*, among others—or the occasional can of Natty Boh or Dale's Pale Ale sitting comfortable on a coaster. Maybe after the holidays, once he hit the gym and dropped down to a more presentable weight, he'd take a nice photo of him and Marie. Some of his old high school cronies had been pestering him to do so.

He saw now that he had not only one post on his homepage, but a whole column of them. He read the first one which said, simply, *I'm so sorry for your loss.* He looked at the one below it, which said, *My condolences.* And below *that,* a third post read, *You are in our hearts and prayers.* In its infinite wisdom, Facebook saw it fit to amputate the majority of messages and hide them behind a link that said, *See all 109 messages.* Buddy gaped at that. Then he clicked on it and, sure enough, the page loaded with over a hundred messages, all of which conveyed some genus of condolence for some apparent great loss. Even the comments that had been pecked out in the abbreviated gibberish of computer lingo—*we r there 4 u!*—carried the same general theme.

Buddy's first thought was that he had gotten hacked—that someone somehow had managed to usurp his Facebook page and was playing some sort of prank on him. That was certainly possible, wasn't it? Sure. But what he thought might *not* be possible was for that Internet hijacker to have also appropriated all his *friends'* Facebook accounts as well, for all the posts, Buddy suddenly realized, had come from his cache of Facebook friends. These weren't strangers. These were people who knew him.

His second thought was that this had to be some kind of joke. Christmas was only a week away, so it was a bit soon to be laying on the April fool's jokes...but what other explanation was there?

"A mistake," he muttered to himself, his voice barely audible to his own ears beneath the whir of the exhaust fan. Sure—that was it, wasn't it? A simple mistake? Someone had gotten some piece of information wrong and, before they knew any better, these Facebook drones had simply started commenting on his page. This seemed the most likely explanation, and Buddy was somewhat surprised that it caused him noticeable relief.

He clicked on Bob Sherman's name—old Bobby Sherman, who had posted, ever so meticulously, *u in my tougts bro*—and waited for Bob's page to load. Buddy figured he'd shoot old Bobby a message and ask him just *why* he was in his "tougts." But Bob's page didn't load. Buddy clicked the name again, but again nothing happened. He tried someone else—Margot Lucille-Miller from the foundry, who had expressed her sympathy in a conga-line of X's and O's—but Margot's page didn't load, either.

"Okay, you stupid piece of crap," Buddy grunted at the laptop. "Don't you freeze up on me now."

He scrolled back to the top of the page, intent on hitting Refresh, which was when he noticed something that, at least for a moment, caused his confusion to drift toward fear...

The date of the most recent post was January 11...of next year. The earliest posts were dated January 9, also of next year—approximately three weeks away. Buddy stared at the dates for an inordinate amount of time, as if to stare them into making sense.

A cool sweat broke out along his scalp. A glitch in the system—surely that was what this was. Lord knew it happened to Facebook all the time—the site froze up, or posts simply vanished into the ether for no apparent reason. And if it wasn't Facebook screwing up, it was probably the lousy *el cheapo* laptop.

But, he wondered, *how could this be the laptop's fault?*

Suddenly very frightened, he hit Refresh.

The page went blank and the little horizontal bar at the bottom of the screen turned from white to green again as the new page loaded. Buddy held his breath. He wasn't sure what he had just been looking at, but whatever it was, it didn't sit well with him. He didn't like it, not one bit.

The fresh page loaded. There was his avatar, the old Buddy Tupelo with the longer hair and the slimmer waistline. There was a series of comments on his page, too…only they were different now. The first comment was no longer *I'm so sorry for your loss;* now it was Derrick Porter asking if he was up for bowling on Saturday night. The comment below Derrick's was from Bob Sherman, suggesting they skip bowling and just head over to Shooter's and put down a few Fat Tires. Buddy scrolled down the page, searching for any of the bizarre comments that had just been there a moment ago, but they were gone. All of them—gone. And when he checked the date of Derrick's and Bob's posts, they were from earlier today—December 19.

Buddy stared at the screen for a long time. He hit the Refresh button a few more times, yet each time the screen reset, it was unchanged. Bowling or Shooter's? The list of a hundred-plus sympathetic comments had vanished into cyberspace.

Five minutes later, after he'd finished up in the bathroom and set the laptop back on the table between the two sofas, Buddy got into bed and pulled the sheet up nearly to his chin. Beside him, Marie slept soundlessly. He thought about waking her and telling her what had happened, but in the end, decided not to. If it still bothered him at breakfast, he could bring it up then.

Buddy turned over and closed his eyes, though he knew sleep would not come to him anytime soon.

TIMOTHY MEEK

GORD ROLLO

*Seek ye the Lord, all ye meek of the earth, which have
wrought his judgment; seek righteousness, seek meekness:
it may be ye shall be hid in the day of the Lord's anger.*
Zephaniah 2:3 (King James version)

Buffalo, New York, USA
June 14th, 2039

Tim was scared of a lot of things—admittedly, too many damn
things—but at the moment his biggest fear was that he'd run out of duct
tape before finishing; not that there was much he could do about it. The
stores were all closed now, and more than likely sold out or looted long
ago anyway. He'd either have enough silver tape to finish sealing the
apartment in heavy clear plastic or he wouldn't. Simple as that.

Heaven help me if I run out, though, Tim thought. He was getting
itchy just thinking about it and needed to stop and go wash his hands
again.

Fucking germs...

Tim scrubbed and scrubbed and scrubbed his hands practically
raw but eventually got himself under control and headed back to
work; worried he was taking way too long. There was only the big
dining room window left to cover but he knew he was running out of

time. Back a few hours ago when he'd taken his last break there had still been four hours to prepare, but time was flying and down to a little over two hours until crunch time now. One way or another, the world as he knew it was about to end. The planet wasn't going any-where, of course, but human civilization certainly might be. Two hours and change until the scientists and global leaders initiated *Project Red* and finally found out if they could stop the devastation they'd unleashed.

Tim didn't have much faith in them.

None, actually, which is why he was taking his own precautions.

His friends and neighbors here in the building thought he was insane but he'd fully expected that much. The President of the Earth Council himself had ordered (not asked, or suggested, or pleaded—*ordered*) that every able bodied man, woman, and child be outside at 8:00 p.m. Eastern Standard Time tonight for the scheduled bomb drops in his area. *Screw that!* When the sky turned red tonight Tim planned to be in his apartment, cocooned inside his little fortress of plastic. There was just no way he could handle being outside tonight. Not with all the bugs. He was starting to sweat just thinking about them crawling all over his skin...in his ears...in his mouth. *God no!* They'd be too small to see, but still, he wasn't doing it. He *couldn't* do it. Was he making a big mistake, like everyone told him he was? Who knew?

They'd all find out soon enough.

From his window, Tim could see people already starting to gather in LaSalle Park beside his apartment building. He was on the fourth floor and his dining room window looked directly out over the kid's play park and ball diamond beyond it. Downtown was only a few clicks west from here, and Lake Erie directly to the north but dis-tances and directions didn't really mean much in the grand scheme of things anymore. The coming apocalypse had reduced everything down to the here and now. Even though LaSalle Park was fairly small Tim imagined it would hold several thousand bodies if they packed it to the max, but so far there were only a hundred or so men and women milling around, most huddling together with the people they'd arrived with and keeping a close eye on the sky.

Tim was reaching for his last roll of tape, just about to seal the window up when he spotted a familiar face outside in the park. A woman named Wendy Harding was exiting the building and walking into the growing crowd below. All five-feet-eight, blond-haired, long-legged, perfect-bodied inch of her. Even at a time as dire as this, her beauty stopped Tim cold and he let the heavy plastic wrap drop to his feet, forgotten for a moment. Secretly he'd been in love with Wendy for years, and although Tim had promised himself one day he would walk up and let her know how he felt, he'd never summoned up the courage to actually talk to her. The closest he'd ever come was sneaking one of her real estate business cards off the community cork board down in the lobby and dialing her cell phone number listed at the bottom of it. He'd waited until she'd said hello twice, then hung up before making a fool of himself trying to ask her out on a date. He just always figured someday he'd ask her properly, you know…face-to-face.

Odds were, now he'd never get the chance.

With a sigh of regret, Tim got back to the business at hand and finished sealing off the dining room window. Just to be sure, he took another twenty minutes rechecking every nook and cranny of the seams for possible leaks where the chemicals or man-made viruses or whatever the fuck else might try getting in, but things were about as good as he was going to get them. For better or worse, he was ready.

He needed to go wash his hands again, though.

Fucking viruses…

And then Tim got out his journal.

Project Red Survival Journal
Entry #1
June 14th, 2039

My name is Timothy Meek. I'm 38 years old and I live in apartment 412 of LaSalle Towers, in Buffalo, New York. I'm not very good at describing myself, but I guess I'm about 5' 8" tall and weigh 160 pounds. I'm a pretty average white guy - Caucasian I think they call it - with short brown hair and hazel colored eyes. Suppose none of that really matters all that much but it makes me feel better knowing there will be documentation of me if things go to hell in the coming days, which is definitely possible. There may not be anyone around to read this journal either, but as far as I can see it, it can't hurt.

For the record, I disagree with the Earth Council's desperate decision to implement Project Red, and have subsequently locked and sealed myself within my apartment and will be disregarding the President's order to be outside at 8:00 p.m. tonight. I am not in principle a troublemaker or a lawbreaker, but I have made my decision and must stand by it now. If the truth be told, I hope the government scientists are right but I don't think they will be. If I'm wrong and ever called out to answer for my disobedience, so be it. I'll deal with it then.

I'll try to keep this record simple and to the point as much as possible, even though I'm sure I'll end up rambling. My personal feelings and thoughts aren't all that important so I'll try just relating the facts and the play by play as things go down. No promises though. Okay, in case whoever reads this has no idea what happened, let me go back about six months and tell you what started all this madness.

On January 19th of this year, there was a terrible explosion at one of the United States major centers for disease control in Atlanta, Georgia. Deep within the bowels of the CDC, there was a hidden laboratory where top secret research into biological and chemical weapons had been going on for nearly 100 years. Joe Public like me would never know about any of this but the scientists had really fucked up this time and accidentally released a nasty genetically mutated superbug that swept across the planet killing 250 million people in the first 3 weeks alone. The virus, known only as V-2283 initially (before everyone realized we'd been given a one way ticket to hell and someone clever in the media had dubbed it Dante's Flu) was an airborne disease that started with flu-like symptoms such as cough and fever but soon escalated to weeping sores, internal hemorrhaging, and liver, kidney, and respiratory failure. Basically, within a week of contact, a person's body would shut down on them, Dante's Flu eating them from the inside out.

The viral weapon had been designed to masquerade as a common cold or mild flu so the infected individual would have time to make it back to their troop, army, country, whatever, and then pass it along before the real symptoms hit. By the time their doctors and leaders discovered what was really happening, it would already be way too late.

Somewhat luckily (if 250 million casualties can ever be considered lucky), the bio-weapon didn't quite work as planned or it might *have killed off every man, woman, child, and animal on the planet. When the death rates started to slow down on their own, the Earth Council began to think maybe we'd gotten off as easy as possible under the circumstances, but they were flat out wrong. Those who didn't catch Dante's Flu and die quickly weren't getting away scott free. They weren't immune to the bug as initially hoped; their bodies just reacted differently to the spreading disease. Long story short; the entire world population is dying of cancer.*

So am I, I guess.

It's in our lungs, they say. In our blood too. I don't seem to have any of the visible lumps most people are developing and I've never even once coughed up a mouthful of blood but I'm sure it's only a matter of time. The government says if we do nothing, we'll all be dead within a year. What we need is a miracle, but what the Council has given us is Project Red. Starting tonight, the bug bombs are going to heal us, supposedly. Well, obviously not me. I'll be sitting this one out.

The clock read 7:52 p.m. and Tim couldn't recall the city ever being this quiet before. Hell, this was Buffalo after all. Morning until night, this city was *always* crazy. Not tonight, though. Nothing was moving around out there and no one was talking. All those desperate people gathered outside and it was as silent as a tomb. It was seriously creeping Tim out. Through the dining room window he could see a mass of blobs down in the park but the thick plastic was distorting his view and he couldn't make anything out clearly. Probably for the best. If he could see the people outside, his best guess was they'd all be facing the same direction; heads tilted to watch the horizon, waiting to catch their first glimpse of the planes they hoped were coming to save them.

Tim sat down, back against the outside wall and tried to clear that haunting image out of his head but just couldn't shake it. Then he started to imagine the people a few minutes from now, standing out there covered in the bugs raining from the sky and he nearly lost it. Suddenly light-headed and nauseous Tim closed his eyes, grabbed his knees and held on tightly.

How can they do it? How can they just stand there and let...

Tim dashed to the sink to vomit.

It was only after washing his face and thoroughly scrubbing his hands again that he realized he hadn't sealed the drain in the kitchen sink yet, like he'd planned. He had lots of bottled water and buckets to use for washing himself or going to the bathroom and had already sealed the bathroom tub and sink, but not this one in the kitchen. *Idiot!* The bombs would be dropping any minute and he clearly wasn't ready. Tim knew the sink had a water trap inside the pipe that would more than likely keep the bugs out but didn't want to take any chances so he quickly twisted in the drain plug, filled the sink with water, layered plastic over the top and used the last of the duct tape to seal the edges to the countertop.

He finished just in time to hear the drone of the approaching plane engines and ran to the dining room window even though he couldn't see outside very well. Seconds later, the blurry crowd below started to cheer and there was even a brief chant of USA…USA… that started up but for the life of him Tim had no idea what they were all so happy about. Desperation and blind faith can do strange things, he guessed.

Fucking people…

Through their collective noise Tim heard the first of several detonations. Maybe it was because he was sealed inside a plastic bubble, but the bombs sounded strangely muffled and farther away then they really were; more of a bass deep *THUMP* than the loud explosions he'd been expecting. Then again, these weren't missiles smashing into buildings or tearing up the ground; these warheads had been designed to blow up in mid air, to release their payload above the heads of the gratefully cheering crowds.

Tim considered turning on the television set to watch the drama unfolding simultaneously around the globe but his heart just wasn't into seeing the end of the world in blazing Technicolor right now. *No thanks.* He'd eventually want to check the news feeds to get updates on how things were going, but tonight he was far too depressed to watch the idiotic smiling faces of the reporters on CNN. Instead, Tim turned on the portable air compressor and homemade filtration system and said a little prayer they'd hold out long enough for the air outside to clear. It might be a couple of days; it could take as long as a week. Regardless, he was on his own for a while.

Outside, the sky was turning red.

Project Red Survival Journal
Entry #2
June 15th, 2039

Project Red is supposed to purify our blood; hence, in my opinion, the rather silly name. To do that, the scientists have developed these tiny creations called nanobots: microscopic 'bugs' that are half living organism and half computerized machine. Crazy stuff straight out of science fiction novels if you ask me, but they've been around for a while now and will be released into the air by the billions and infected people will breathe them into their lungs where they can then apparently go to work healing the sick from the inside out. Call me cynical, but I don't buy it that the scientists have just come up with this wonderful cure. That reeks of bullshit to me. There was too much money in NOT curing cancer, if you know what I mean? Governments keep things from the public all the time and there's no way of knowing when they actually discovered a possible cure. Probably years ago. Decades maybe. It just took the whole world standing at death's door before they finally decided to let the rest of us in on the plan.

How inhaling laboratory created bugs can possibly cure cancer is beyond me, but from what I've gathered they will use electrical impulses to stop the damaged cells from reproducing uncontrollably, not allowing the cancer to grow and spread as it normally would unchecked. It's a bit like chemotherapy, but on a microscopic level where the smart bugs can identify and destroy the cancerous cells on a one-on-one basis instead of just wiping out everything in its path like chemo. If Project Red works as planned, the world should go into remission, the cancer stopped in its tracks from spreading or infecting other organs. Further nanobots may need to be deployed on a regular basis to keep people's enhanced immune system running properly but no one really knows what the future might bring. At least the smart bugs will give the world a chance, they say.

I'm not buying any of it.

I think it's a crock of shit. A desperate move made by a handful of controlling desperate men and women. Lies and false hopes given to the people to help keep the masses from panicking too much. Hope is a powerful weapon, and as long as the people have some the author-

ities will be able to keep the peace. Once it's gone, though, and the citizens of the world know they've been played for fools; that's when the shit will really hit the fan. I'm afraid that's where we're headed. Anarchy.

The next two days were surprisingly uneventful. Tim sat around the dining room table listening to the radio and occasionally flopping on the living room couch to watch an hour or two of the unending television coverage. There was no end to the parade of scientists and government officials interviewed by the various news media; all of which droned on and on about the apparent success of Project Red and how everyone would start feeling better soon. To Tim, it seemed like they were jumping the gun a little, clapping each other on the back a bit too hard before there was any proof they'd accomplished anything. In fact, if success was so assured as they claimed, why weren't they showing more live coverage from out in the cities? Where were the interviews with the average citizens of the world who were supposedly out there on the mend? Sure, there were hours of footage from the night the bombs had been dropped, film clips from around the world of the skies changing color and all the happy people dancing in the streets literally covered head to toe in a sticky red substance that, no matter how many times Tim watched the replays, couldn't stop thinking looked eerily like they were covered in bucket loads of blood.

The following morning, Tim heard a report on the radio that definitive proof had been collected to verify the nanobots were doing their job, stopping the spreading cancer in its tracks. Encouraged, Tim had flipped on CNN to see what they had to say about it, but was shocked to find out all they were showing was a minute long film clip of a bearded man in a white lab coat standing inside some sterile looking lab somewhere. He was pointing to a graph on a blackboard and explaining about the growing number of reported cases of remission throughout the world. That was it. No patient interviews. No eyewitness reports. No tear-filled mothers or wives beaming at the cameras while they hugged their victorious husband or child who'd just been given a new lease on life. It didn't make any sense, did it? Throughout the day, there were more miraculous newsflashes but they too lacked any real substance. It was all happening too fast for

Tim's liking. All the reports were just that little bit off, not quite ringing true or providing any real proof of anything other than the confident scientists' claim. And why should Tim believe what they were saying? It was them, along with the governing officials, who'd got everyone into this mess in the first place.

Fucking politicians...

Outside his building, Tim couldn't see or hear a thing. After the crowds had dispersed from LaSalle Park swarming with their microscopic saviors several nights back, everything had been quiet as a mouse. No one seemed to be moving around and Tim couldn't even hear the normal yelling and screaming within the paper thin walls of his apartment building. What were they all doing, he wondered? Why was everybody staying inside and being so quiet? Tim had absolutely no idea. All he could go by was what he'd seen and heard on the television and radio—and they weren't telling him shit.

In the days that followed, things would only get worse. Tim continued his journal entries but outside the world had seemingly ground to a halt and there was never much for him to say. The newscasters and scientists were still spouting their messages of hope and victory but even to Tim's untrained eyes he could see the men and women on his television screen didn't appear anywhere near as healthy as their reports claimed. The red lesions and cancerous growths were far more prominent than before, covering huge areas of the broadcaster's visible bodies. These were examples of the scientists' success stories? Christ, they looked worse than before the bombs had been dropped. Worse than Tim, even, and he hadn't showered in over a week now. He quickly stripped and checked again, but Tim still had none of the red growths growing anywhere on his body.

Project Red Survival Journal
Entry #9
June 23rd, 2039

Something has gone terribly wrong. I don't have any proof yet but my gut is telling me things are spinning out of control and the government is lying to the public to try and keep us calm. Was lying, I should say. CNN stopped broadcasting this morning at around 9:30 a.m. and they were the last of the television markets still on the air. Now there is nothing but static and white noise on every station, and the radio signals went dead a few days ago.

The last programming I saw was a badly pieced-together documentary explaining how the bio-engineered nanobots had been created using microscopic computer chips fused with genetic DNA from some small creature. I can't be positive but I don't think they ever revealed exactly which type of bug they took the DNA from. Not that it matters much, I guess, but at the time I remember wondering if the program had been edited and several minutes of information conveniently removed. It didn't make much sense but I had a feeling I was right. Why bother, though? What did they have to hide?

After the documentary, things got even weirder. They cut to a live feed from CNN headquarters in Atlanta, Georgia but there was no one in front of the camera. I kept waiting for the producer to cut to a different feed or run some other pre-taped program but nothing happened. Ten seconds went by, then half a minute. It was as if the studio was empty, or maybe everyone had gone home and just left the camera running. After nearly five minutes of dead air, an old grey haired man with small beady eyes shuffled into view and sat down on the corner of the wooden desk to take center stage in the news studio. He was rake thin and practically drowning in his baggy clothes. His exposed head and hands were also covered in numerous red cancerous growths but he had a constant smile plastered on his face that no amount of sickness seemed able to wipe off. Who was this guy? He had a CNN tag on his chest and although it was a little blurry, when I moved closer to the T.V. I think his name was Jim something. Jim Argen...something; the last part of the man's name was lost in a fold of his baggy sweater. Whoever he was, surely he wasn't one of CNN's newscasters. Couldn't be. Hell, the old bugger had to be close to eighty years old. Maybe older. He'd walked onstage from behind the angle of the camera though, so for all I knew maybe he was the cameraman; or used to be. I had no way of knowing but I had the feeling that maybe he was the only one left at the studio. Some old diehard who'd worked there his whole life and now, even when the world was falling apart around him, stubbornly refused to go home.

I never did find out. Old Jim just kept sitting there smiling into the camera until the picture cut out and the network went static. After

that I had no contact with the outside world at all. No T.V., no radio,
no noisy neighbors, no nothing.
What the hell is going on?
A couple of days they'd said. Three or four tops. The skies would
clear and people could go about their regular lives while the
nanobots worked their invisible magic from the inside. Lying bas-
tards. They've fucked things up good this time.
Real good.

When Tim woke up the next morning, naked and sweating
beneath an old wool blanket, it took him a moment to figure out there
was something different about his surroundings. Something had
changed and it wasn't until he got shakily to his feet and walked over
to the dining room window that he realized what it was.

Outside, the sky had turned back to blue.

Incredible as it seemed, it was true. Beyond his plastic sheets, the
world seemed to be returning to normal. Maybe the scientist had been
right after all. Their time frames had been off a week or so, but still,
here was finally the potential proof Tim had been waiting for. Trouble
was, he couldn't really see out the window to see if things were back
the way they used to be or not. The thick layer of plastic obscured
everything. He couldn't even tell if anyone was outside in the park.

The urge to tear off the protective sheet was incredible, but Tim
stopped himself in time and sat down to think things through first.
The last thing he wanted to do was unseal his room too early and con-
taminate his sanctuary with bugs. In his mind, he could picture millions of microscopic creatures straight out of a science fiction movie
hovering outside, just waiting for their chance to get inside and attack
him. Even though he was sweating, the thought made him shiver.

Fucking Nanobots...

No way. Opening the window was out of the question. At least
until he had more proof than a blue sky to go on. An idea flashed into
his mind about how he used to coat the windows of his old apartment
with plastic to keep the cold weather out in the winter. Someone had
shown him that if you took a hairdryer and blew warm air onto the
plastic, it magically stretched tightly onto the window frame and
became almost transparent. The plastic on these windows was much

thicker than that old stuff he'd used, but there was a chance it might work the same way. Worth a try, at least.

Hurrying to the bathroom, Tim grabbed his old hairdryer from under the sink and ran an extension cable over to the wall plug on the far side of the room to fire it up. Careful not to put the nozzle too close to the surface in case the hot air melted a hole through the plastic, Tim soon had the window stretched taut on the frame and he could finally see outside again for the first time in ten days.

Outside, Lasalle Park looked pretty much like it always had, except there was still a thin dusting of red powder covering the ground. It looked like someone had snuck into the park and coated all the grass and trees with sticky cotton candy. The sky was incredible though, the most amazing crystal clear cloudless sky Tim could remember and staring at it brought a huge grin to his unshaven face. At least until he realized that there was nothing moving in it. He studied the skies for several minutes but never found a thing. No birds, no bees, no airplanes, no nothing.

Turning his attention back to the ground, Tim was convinced there was nothing going to be visible there, either. On first glance he was right. Where were all the people? Surely if they'd all been cooped up the last week and a half like him, they'd be dying to get out there and move around on such a beautiful day. The kids at least would be out bombing around in the park, right? Apparently not.

Then Tim heard a dog bark below him and it was music to his ears. He leaned forward to press his head close to the glass so he could see straight down closer to the side of his building, eager to see at least some sign of normal life.

That was when he screamed.

Project Red Survival Journal
Entry #10
June 24th, 2039

I woke up in Hell this morning.

That's not me trying to be symbolic or overly dramatic either; I'm being dead serious. Things are worse than I could have ever imagined. Far worse. I don't know exactly what the scientists have done but I think they've destroyed the world and everything in it. *The sky had miraculously turned back to blue today and I'd just begun to hope this nightmare was finally over, but then I heard a dog bark and looked out my dining room window for it. I wish I hadn't, for what I saw outside on the red grass was something I can hardly wrap my mind around, much less describe. It had obviously once been a cute, cuddly pet, but where before its body had been covered in soft shaggy fur it now was sealed within a series of red shell-like plates interlocking like medieval armor. Its head and throat were covered in red sores so thick I wondered how it could still see and breathe. Its withered legs were more like burned sticks and instead of running like any normal dog might, the poor animal could no longer carry its own weight and was pushing itself along the ground on the scaly carapace of its bloated belly.*

The dog-creature's pathetic barks echoed like gunshots in the early morning silence, and unfortunately I wasn't the only one to hear them. It didn't take long to draw a crowd. I don't know if I even want to try describing to you the scene that unfolded below me in the park after that. Seriously, you're better off not knowing but I think I'd be doing a disservice to whoever eventually reads this if I don't at least try and make you understand how bad things have become.

Hundreds of people from my apartment building, the surrounding neighborhoods, or wherever began to gather in Lasalle Park again. I call them people but that's only because I can't think of any other word to label them. There are no adequate words for what they've become. These people, these things who used to be human beings walked, slithered, and crawled out of their homes on long spindly limbs that stuck out from hard red bodies, bloated like gas-filled balloons similar to that of the deformed dog. Most of their heads had large weeping deformities that encased their entire skulls in smooth red domes that from my vantage point above looked like shiny motorcycle helmets.

For a few minutes they simply congregated, communicating in a series of guttural grunts, strange clicks, and high-pitched hisses. I'd never heard anything like it before but they sounded almost alien in nature, like the gibberish dialogue for some bad science fiction movie. When the poor dog-creature started yelping in misery again, the human-things pounced on it and began tearing into its scaly hide with their elongated teeth and razor sharp claws. The masses made short work of the unfortunate animal but once the smell of death was in the air, the creatures who had recently been my friends and neighbors began to turn on each other, their bloodlust ravenously awakened. The fight was relatively short but incredibly violent and gruesome. From above it seemed like there were no allies or teams; it was every creature for itself, biting and tearing at anything within reach until more than half of the original number of creatures lay dead or dying, mutilated on the gore-drenched grassy field.

And then the feeding began.

That part I'm not telling you about. No way. Trust me; some things are better left unsaid.

Tim spent the following few days living in fear, terrified one of those creatures had heard his scream and might come looking for him. When none did, he relaxed a little but still stayed away from the windows during the day and was forced to leave the lights off during the night so no one would know where he was hiding.

On day fifteen, the electricity went out anyway so there were no lights to put on, even if he'd wanted to. His air filtration system was shot too but electricity was the least of Tim's problems. He was nearly out of food and worse, he only had half a jug of water left to drink. When that was gone, Tim had no idea what he would do.

He wondered if things were this bad all over the world. They probably were. Had to be, really, if he thought about it logically. The world government had coordinated Project Red around the globe and if the scientists had screwed things up here in America, odds were they'd royally fucked up everywhere, right? Of course they did.

Fucking Scientists…

Then Tim was struck with another thought, one so sobering it literally sent chills down his back and forced him to sit down for fear his legs might give out. *What if I'm the only one left? The only human?* Crazy as the notion was, the more he considered it the less insane it began to sound. *I mean, how many other people out there are so bug phobic they've sealed themselves in plastic?* Good question. Was there anyone out there on the planet as fucked up as him? He had no way of knowing but he seriously doubted it. Even if there were people who hadn't stood outside for the bombs like they'd been told (and surely there were many), unless they'd taken extreme precautions like he had, the microscopic nanobots would surely have found their way into their homes and ultimately, their bodies by now.

Was he the last man on earth? Was he? It said in the Bible that the meek would inherit the earth, but Tim had never dreamed it would come down to a singular meek, him, Timothy Meek, the good book had been referring to. This thought made Tim burst out laughing, startlingly loud in his silent apartment, and the fact that he didn't care who—or what—might hear him was his first true indication he was losing his mind. He wondered what had taken him so long to finally snap.

Two days later, just as Tim was sitting at the dining room table swallowing his very last gulp of tepid water, he noticed the growth developing on his left forearm. It was red and scaly and hard as rock to the touch. Frantically, Tim jumped to his feet, stripped naked, and checked the rest of his body but there were no other crimson sores to be found.

Not yet.

Tim sat back down at the table and began to cry.

Project Red Survival Journal
Entry #13
July 3, 2039

This will be my final journal entry. I apologize for my last few entries; they were just the scribbling of a bitter, scared man. I'm feeling better today; a little anyway, and I'll try wrapping this up in a way that makes more sense. I can't go on any longer. Living, I mean. My food and water are gone and worst of all I have many more large red welts developing on my skin. My left hand is already hooked and withered and basically useless to me trapped within its rigid shell. My writing hand, my right, isn't much better and I steadfastly refuse to go look in the mirror to see what has become of my face.

I thought I had the room sealed, I really did, but I suppose I've been kidding myself all along. Really, what was I thinking? There's just no way to completely seal a room air tight enough to keep the nanobots out, not when all you have to work with is heavy plastic and a few rolls of duct tape. It was predictable right from the start that I'd be contaminated along with everyone else; I just managed to prolong things, I guess.

For the record, I'm not angry at anyone and I don't blame the President of the World Council. Hell, he was just doing what he thought best. At least he, along with the rest of the council tried to save everyone and for that I am somewhat grateful. Doesn't mean I'm not pissed off, but what can I do but accept things as they are? I have no idea what will become of the world or the new breed of human creatures that we are all becoming. If they have the capacity, maybe it will be one of them who finally ends up reading my account here on these pages. Who know? All I am certain of is I have no desire to become one of them. I can't stomach the thought of that. My body is metamorphosing at an incredible rate, the nanobots continuing to work their secret dark magic inside me as I write these last few lines, but while I'm still in control of my body and mind I've chosen to stop this nightmare before it reaches its inevitable conclusion. I know suicide is a coward's way out, but I'm okay with that. Death is the only choice I have.

I won't...I mean I can't...become one of them.

Tim finished writing and closed up his journal. In his heart he knew it was a sadly inadequate collection of entries and didn't come close to explaining the horror of what had happened outside of his walls but he'd done his best to try and make some future inhabitants of earth understand what had become of the human race. Tim sealed the book inside two zip-lock freezer bags and left the journal sitting in the center of the dining room table.

Standing on spindly red legs, he lurched his way over to the kitchen countertop and dug through a drawer of junk until he found what he was looking for: A real estate business card with a picture on it of a pretty blonde-haired woman smiling up at him. Moving to the phone, Tim carefully punched in the phone number printed on the woman's card and hoped she'd not only be home, but still be capable of picking up the receiver. Someone answered on the fourth ring, or at least knocked the handset off onto the floor. Tim could hear a series of wet clicking noises, and the sound of heavy, labored breathing.

"Wendy?" Tim asked, knowing she couldn't answer him but refusing to die without at least trying to finally speak to the woman he'd fallen in love with from afar. This might not be the Wendy Harding he remembered and had desired all these years but Tim hoped there was enough humanity left in her she might somehow still understand his words. "It's Timothy Meek from upstairs in apartment 412. I've never had the courage to tell you this but I've always thought you were the prettiest woman I've ever met. I know things are all screwed up now, but I was just wondering if there was any way you'd consider coming upstairs to meet me. I don't know why, but I think I'd like that a lot. What do you think?"

There was no response. Just more heavy breathing.

"Apartment 412, okay? Come up and say hi, Wendy. Please..."

Tim hung up the phone and went directly into the living room to start tearing off the semi-transparent sheets that had been all he'd seen of the world for so long. Within minutes he'd removed all his hard work and was just rolling the plastic into a big ball when suddenly there was a loud knock at the apartment door. The pounding, which was more of a *thud-scrape-thud* than a real knock, startled Tim but didn't surprise him. Steeling his nerves, not knowing what he'd find but knowing this was how his life would end, Tim took a deep breath and opened up the door.

Outside the door, a massive five-foot-eight red bug stood looking in at him. This was the first time Tim had seen one of the creatures up close and it was only now he noticed the tiny flickering antennae on top of its head and realized what animal DNA the scientists had used to graft onto the nanobots. Unbelievable, but it all made perfect sense really. Everyone had always said they'd be the last creatures alive if the world was stupid enough to engage in Nuclear War. They'd escaped that particular end of days scenario, but somehow, through no real action of their own, these creatures had still managed to come out on top of the food chain after all.

Plain and simple: They were survivors.

The thing that had once been Wendy Harding shuffled into the room with teeth and claws ready, and as hideously deformed as she was Tim still found himself strangely attracted to her. Maybe it was the growing creature within him, or maybe he'd just finally gone completely crazy. Instead of running away or trying to protect himself Tim simply opened his arms and waited for her deadly embrace.

Fucking cockroaches...

TRAPS

F. Paul Wilson

Skippy Super Chunk peanut butter worked best.

Hank smeared it on the pedals of the four traps he'd bought. Victors. Something about the way the big red *V* in their logo formed itself around the shape of a mouse's head gave him a feeling that they knew what they were about.

Not that he took any pleasure in killing mice. He may not have had the bumper sticker, but he most certainly did brake for animals. He didn't like killing anything. Even ants. Live and let live was fine with him, but he drew the line at the threshold of his house. They could live long and prosper out *there*, he would live in *here*. When they came inside, it was war.

He'd had a few in the basement of their last house and caught them all with Skippy-baited Victors. But he always felt guilty when he found one of the little things dead in the trap, so frail and harmless-looking with its white underbelly and little pink feet and tail. The eyes were always the worst—shiny black and guileless, wide open and looking at him, almost saying, *Why? I don't eat much.*

Hank knew he could be a real sentimental jerk at times.

He consoled himself with the knowledge that the mouse didn't feel any pain in the trap. Better than those warfarin poisons where they crawl off to their nest and slowly bleed to death. With a trap, the instant the nibbling mouse disturbs the baited pedal, *wham!* the bow snaps down and breaks its neck. It's on its way to mouse heaven before it knows what hit it.

Hank was doing this on the sly. Gloria wouldn't be able to sleep a wink if she thought there were mice overhead in the ceiling. And the twins, God, they'd want to catch them and make them pets and give them names. With the trip to Disney World just three days off, all they could talk about was Mickey and Minnie. They'd never forgive him for killing a mouse. Best to set the traps before they came home in the afternoon and dispose of the little carcasses in the morning after everyone was gone. Luckily, this was his slack season and he had some time at home to take care of it.

He wondered how the mice were getting in. He knew they were up there because he'd heard them last night. Something had awakened him at about 2:30 this morning—a noise, a bad dream, he didn't remember what—and as he was lying there spooned against Gloria he heard little claws scraping on the other side of the ceiling. It sounded like two or three of them under the insulation, clawing on the plasterboard, making themselves a winter home. He was ticked. This was a brand new two-story colonial, just built, barely lived in for six months, and already they had uninvited guests. And in the attic no less.

Well, they were in a woodsy area and it was fall, the time of year when woodsy things start looking for winter quarters. He wished them all a safe and warm winter. But not in this house.

Before setting the traps, he fitted a bolt on the attic door. The house had one of those swing-down contraptions in the hall ceiling right outside their bedroom. It had a pull-cord on this side and a folding ladder on the upper side. The twins had been fascinated with it since they moved in. The attic had always been off-limits to them, but you never knew. He had visions of one of them pulling the ladder down, climbing up there, and touching one of the traps. Instant broken finger. So he screwed a little sliding bolt in place to head off that trauma at the pass.

He took the four traps up to the attic and gingerly set the bows. As he stood on the ladder and spaced them out on the particle board flooring around the opening, he noticed an odd odor. The few times he had been up here before the attic had been filled with the clean smell of plywood and kiln-dried fir studs. Now there was a sour tint to the air. Vaguely unpleasant. Mouse b-o? He didn't know. He just knew that something about it didn't set well with him.

He returned to the second floor, bolted the ceiling door closed, and hit the switch that turned off the attic light. Everything was set, and well before Gloria and the girls got home.

«««—»»»

Kate crawled into Hank's lap as he leaned back in the recliner and watched the six o'clock Eyewitness News. She was holding her well-thumbed "Mickey's book." As soon as Kim saw her, she ran in from the kitchen like a shot.

So with his two pale blonde seven-year old darlings snuggled up against him, Hank opened up "Mickey's book" for the nightly ritual of the past two weeks. Not a book actually, just a brochure touting all the park's attractions. But it had become a Holy Book of sorts for the twins and they never tired of paging through it. This had to be their twentieth guided tour in as many days and their blue eyes were just as wide and full of wonder this time as the first.

Only three days to go before they headed for Newark Airport and the 747 that would take them south to Orlando.

Hank had come to see Disney World as a religious experience for seven-year olds. Moslems had Mecca, Catholics had the Vatican, Japanese had Mount Fuji. Kids had Disney World on the East Coast and Disneyland on the West. Katie and Kim would start out on their first pilgrimage Thanksgiving morning.

He hugged them closer, absorbing their excitement. This was what life was all about. And he was determined to show them the best time of their lives. The sky was the limit. Any ride, any attraction, he didn't care how many times they wanted to go on it, he'd take them. Four days of fantasy at Mickey's Place with no real-world intrusions. No *Times*, no *Daily News*, no Eyewitness Special Reports, no background noise about wars or floods or muggings or bombings…or mousetraps.

Nothing about mousetraps.

«««—»»»

The snap of the trap woke Hank with a start. It was faint, muffled by the intervening plasterboard and insulation. He must have been subconsciously attuned for it, because he heard it and Gloria didn't.

He checked the clock—12:42—and tried to go back to sleep. Hopefully, that was the end of that.

He was just dozing back off when a second trap sprang with a muffled snap. Two of them. Sounded like he had a popular attic.

He didn't know when he got to sleep again. It took a while.

«««—»»»

When Hank had the house to himself again the next morning, he unbolted the ceiling door, pulled it down, and unfolded the ladder. Half way up, he hesitated. This wasn't going to be pleasant. He knew when he stuck his head up through that opening he'd be eye-level with the attic floor—and with the dead mice. Those shiny reproachful little black eyes…

He took a deep breath and stepped up a couple of rungs.

Yes, two of the traps had been sprung and two sets of little black eyes were staring at him. Eyes and little else. At first he thought it was a trick of the light, of the angle, but as he hurried the rest of the way up, he saw it was true.

The heads were still in the traps, but the bodies were gone. Little bits of gray fur were scattered here and there, but that was it. Sort of gave him the creeps. Something had eaten the dead mice. Something bigger than a mouse. A discomforting thought.

And that odor was worse. He still couldn't identify it, but it was taking on a stomach-turning quality.

He decided it was time for an inspection tour of the grounds. His home was being invaded. He wanted to know how.

He found the little buggers' route of invasion on the south side of the house. He had two heating-cooling zones inside, with one unit in the basement and one in the attic. The compressor-blowers for both were outside on the south side. The hoses to the upstairs unit ran up the side of the house to the attic through an aluminum leader.

That was how they were getting in.

There wasn't much space in the leader, but a mouse can squeeze through the tiniest opening. The rule of thumb—as all mouse experts knew—was that if it can get its head through, the rest of the body can follow. They were crawling into the leader, climbing up along the hoses inside, and following them into the attic. Simple.

But what had eaten them?

Up above the spot where the hoses ran through the siding, he noticed the triangular gable vent hanging free on its right side. Something had pulled it loose. As he watched, a squirrel poked its head out, looked at him, then scurried up onto the roof. It ran a few feet along the edge, jumped onto an overhanging oak branch, and disappeared into the reddening leaves.

Great! He was collecting a regular menagerie up there!

So much for the joys of a wooded lot. Gloria and he had chosen this semi-rural development because they liked the seclusion of an acre lot and the safety for the twins of living on a cul-de-sac. They both had grown up in New Jersey, and Toms River seemed like as good a place as any to raise kids. The house was expensive but they were a two-income family—she a teacher and he a CPA—so they went for it.

So far, theirs was the only house completed in this section, although two new foundations had just started. It would be nice to have neighbors. Until recently, the only other building in sight had been a deserted stone church of unknown age and long-forgotten denomination a few hundred yards south of here. The belfry of that old building had concerned him for a while—bats, you know. Very high rabies rate. But he spoke to the workmen when they bulldozed it down last week to start another cul-de-sac, and they told him they hadn't seen a single bat. Lots of animal droppings up there, but no bats.

He wondered: Would a squirrel eat a couple of dead mice? He thought they only ate nuts and berries. Maybe this one was a carnivore. Didn't matter. One way or another, something had to be done about that gable vent. He went to get the ladder.

«‹‹—››»

He had everything taken care of by the time Gloria and the girls got home from their respective schools.

He'd tacked the gable vent back into place. He couldn't see how that squirrel had pulled it free, but it wouldn't get it out now. He also plugged up the upper and lower ends of the hose leader with an aerosol foam insulation he picked up at Home Depot. It occurred to him as he watched the mustard-colored gunk harden into a solid Styrofoam plug that he was cutting off the mouse exit as well as the mouse entryway. Hopefully they were all out for the day. When they came back they'd be locked out and would have to go somewhere else. And even more hopefully, the squirrel hadn't left a friend in the attic behind the resecured gable vent.

«««—»»»

Hank hardly slept at all that night. He kept listening for the snap of a trap, hoping he wouldn't hear it, yet waiting for it. Hours passed. The last time he remembered seeing on the clock radio LED was 3:34. He must have fallen asleep after that.

Dawn was just starting to bleach out the night when the snap came. He came wide awake with the sound. The clock said 5:10. But the noise didn't end with that single snap. Whatever was up there began to thrash. He could hear the wooden base of the trap slapping against the attic flooring. Something bigger than a mouse, maybe a squirrel, was caught but still alive. He heard another snap and a squeal of pain. God, it was alive and hurt! His stomach turned.

Gloria rolled over and sat up, a silhouette in the growing light. She was still nine-tenths asleep.

Suddenly the attic went still.

He patted her arm and told her to lie down and go back to sleep. She did. He couldn't.

«««—»»»

He approached the attic door with dread. He did *not* want to go up there. What if it was still alive? What if it was weak and paralyzed but still breathing? He'd have to kill it. He didn't know if he could do that. But he'd have to. It would be the only humane thing to do. How? Drown it? Smother it in a plastic bag? He began to sweat.

This was crazy. He was wimping out over a rodent in his attic. Enough already! He flipped the attic light switch, slipped the bolt, and pulled on the cord. The door angled down on its hinges.

But it didn't come down alone. Something came with it, flying right at his face.

He yelled like a fool in a funhouse and batted it away. Then he saw what it was: one of the mousetraps. At first glance it looked empty, but when he went to pick it up, he saw what was in it and almost tossed his cookies.

A furry little forearm, no longer than the last two bones on his pinkie finger, was caught under the bow. It looked like it once might have been attached to a squirrel, but now it ended in a ragged bloody stump where it had been chewed off just below the shoulder.

Where the hell was the rest of it?

Visions of the squirrel chewing off its own arm swam around him until he remembered that auto-amputation only occurred with arresting traps, the kind that were chained down. Animals had been known to chew off a limb to escape those. The squirrel could have dragged the mousetrap with it.

But it hadn't.

Hank stood at the halfway point on those steps a long while. He finally decided he had wasted enough time. He clenched his teeth, told himself it was dead, and poked his head up. He started and almost fell off the stairs when he turned his head and found the squirrel's tail only two inches from his nose. It was caught in the bow of another trap—the second snap he had heard this morning. But there was no body attached.

This was getting a bit gory. He couldn't buy a squirrel chewing off its arm and then its tail. If anything, it would drag the tail trap after it until it got stuck someplace.

Nope. Something had eaten it. Something that didn't smell too good, because the attic was really beginning to stink.

He ducked down the ladder, grabbed the flashlight he always kept in the night table, then hurried back up to the attic. Light from the single bulb over the opening in the attic floor didn't reach very far. And even with daylight filtering in through the gable vents, there were lots of dark spots. He wanted the flashlight so he could get a good look along the inside of the eaves and into all the corners.

He searched carefully, and as he moved through the attic he had a vague sense of another presence, a faint awareness of something else here, a tantalizing hint of furtive movement just out of his range of vision.

He shook it off. The closeness up here, the poor lighting, the missing animal carcasses—it had all set his imagination in motion.

He gave the attic a thorough going over and found nothing but a few droppings. Big droppings. Bigger than something a mouse or squirrel would leave. Maybe possum-sized. Or raccoon-sized.

Was that the answer? A possum or a coon? He didn't know much about them, but he'd seen them around in the woods, and he knew every time he put turkey or chicken scraps in the garbage, something would get the lid off the trash can and tear the Hefty bag apart until every last piece of meat was gone. Raccoons were notorious for that. If they'd eat leftover chicken, why not dead mice and squirrels?

Made sense to him. But how was it getting in? A check of the gable vent he'd resecured yesterday gave him the answer. It had been pulled free again. Well, he'd fix that right now.

He went down to his workshop and got a hammer and some heavy nails. He felt pretty good as he pounded them into the edges of the vent, securing it from the inside. He knew what he was up against now and knew something that big would be easy to keep out. No raccoon or possum was going to pull this vent free again. And just to be sure, he went over to the north side and reinforced the gable vent there.

That was it. His house was his own again.

<<<—>>>

Wednesday night was chaotic. Excitement ran at a fever pitch with the twins packing their own little suitcases full of stuffed animals and placing them by the front door so they'd be all set to go first thing in the morning.

Hank helped Gloria with the final packing of the big suitcases and they both fell into bed around midnight. He had little trouble getting off to sleep. There probably weren't any mice left, there weren't any squirrels, and he was sure no raccoon or possum was getting in tonight. So why stay awake listening?

The snap of a trap woke him around 3:30. No thrashing, no slapping, just the snap. Another mouse. A second trap went off ten minutes later. Then a third. Damn! He waited. The fourth and final trap sprang at 4:00 a.m.

Hank lay tense and rigid in bed and wondered what to do. Everybody would be up at first light, just an hour or so from now, getting ready for the drive to Newark Airport. He couldn't leave those mouse carcasses up there all the time they were away—they'd rot and the whole house would be stinking by the time they got back.

He slipped out of bed as carefully as he could, hoping the movement wouldn't awaken Gloria. She didn't budge. He grabbed the flashlight and closed the bedroom door behind him on his way out.

He didn't waste any time. He had to get up there and get rid of the dead mice before the girls woke up. These damn animals were really getting on his nerves. He slid the bolt, pulled down the door, and hurried up.

Hank stood on the ladder and gaped at the traps. All four had been sprung but lay empty on the flooring around him, the peanut butter untouched. No mice heads, no bits of fur. What could have tripped them without getting caught? It was almost like a game.

He looked around warily. He was standing in a narrow cone of light. The rest of the attic was dark. Very dark. The sense of something else up here with him was very strong now. So was the odor. It was worse than ever.

Imagination again.

He waved the flashlight around quickly but saw no scurrying or lurking shapes along the eaves or in the corners. He made a second sweep, more slowly this time, more careful. He crouched and moved all along the edges, bumping his head now and again on a rafter, his flashlight held ahead of him like a gun.

Finally, when he was satisfied nothing of any size was lurking about, he checked the gable vent.

It had been yanked loose again. Some of the nails had pulled free, and those that hadn't had ripped through the vent's plastic edge.

He was uneasy now. No raccoon was strong enough to do this. He didn't know many *men* who could do it without a crowbar. This was getting out of hand. He suddenly wanted to get downstairs and bolt the attic door behind him. He'd call a professional exterminator as soon as they got back from Orlando.

He spun about, sure that something had moved behind him, but all was still, all was dark but for the pool of light under the bulb. Yet...

Quickly now, he headed back toward the light, toward the ladder, toward the empty traps. As he sidled along, he checked in the corners and along the eaves one last time, and wondered how and why the traps had been sprung. He saw nothing. Whatever it was, if it had come in, it wasn't here anymore. Maybe the attic light had scared it off. If that was the case, he'd leave the light on all night. All *week*.

His big mistake was looking for it along the floor.

It got him as he came around the heating unit. He saw a flash of movement as it swung down from the rafters—big as a rottweiler, brown scruffy fur, a face that was all mouth with huge countless teeth, four clawed arms extended toward him as it held onto the beams above with still two more limbs—and that was all. It engulfed his head and lifted him off the floor in one sweeping motion. For a few spasming seconds his fingers tore futilely at its matted fur and his legs kicked and writhed silently in the air. As life and consciousness fled that foul smothering unbearable agony, he sensed the bottomless pit of its hunger and thought helplessly of the open attic door, of the ladder going down, and of Gloria and the twins sleeping below.

SEARCHING

MONICA J. O'ROURKE

He's spent years searching for me. Traveling through deserts rife with expansive waves of heat, through rivers of sand that stretch into the sky further than the eye can see. His thirst is great yet he never stops, never gives up. Longing for shade doesn't slow him. He swims vast oceans, endures fierce waves and brutal winds, his face whipped by icy, salty water, his eyes stinging.

I thought I saw him the other day. I have his eyes: chocolate brown, with flecks of green. We have the same chin, the same mouth. I would easily recognize him. I know I would. It will be like looking at my own reflection. Playing checkers will be his favorite game. He'll like chamomile. One spoon of sugar and no milk, just like how I drink mine, like I'm grown up. He'll want to play dolls, but I don't care for dolls. They're silly. I like my stuffed bears and cats. They look like the real thing, and sometimes I imagine they really are real, and I talk to them and read Mercer Mayer books to them until they fall asleep. I'm too big for such books now, but I still read them out loud, because they enjoy it. Books left over from when I was a little girl, not big like I am now.

Years and years he's spent driving across the country searching for me. I can't remember how he lost track in the first place. Maybe I once knew and forgot. He drives and drives for hours and days at a time, calling out my name, stopping people in the street to show them my picture. He has my photo because he imagined what I would look like and he created it, because he can do anything he wants. He's like a magician, only better, because he's real.

I lie on my bed with my feet up on the wall and my head hanging off the edge. It makes the blood rush to my brain and makes my ears ring. Looking at my room upside down makes me giggle. My stuffed animals hang from shelves from the bottoms of their feet. My board games are suspended in midair, defying gravity. The tiny hotels and houses and Monopoly money never fall to the floor.

Mom yells at me. "Get your dirty socks off the wall." She picks up my underwear and throws it in the hamper. "Young lady, you can be such a slob." I'm not a slob. I'm just lazy. When I'm sure she isn't looking I stick my tongue out at her.

"I have to write a paper for science," I tell her as she flits around my room like a warm breeze. "Make a poster too."

"Of what?"

"Our solar system."

"That's nice," she says on her way out the door, but I don't think she really thinks it's nice. I don't think she cares much about it at all.

He's still looking. I can tell. He's looked in every toy store because he thinks that's where all kids hang out. But I like books. And suddenly he thinks of that, because he likes books. He suddenly realizes we're so much alike his search for me grows even stronger. In fact, he *vehemently* searches for me. (Vehemently: eagerly, passionately. This is today's word in my word-a-day calendar.)

Mom calls me for dinner and I bring my science book with me.

"Look," I say, opening to page fifty-three. "This is our solar system." I hold up the book so she can see.

"Put that away during dinner." She scoops macaroni and cheese onto my plate.

I place the book on my lap. "Where's Dad?"

"He's coming." She calls his name again and I hear him getting up from the sofa, the fake leather making a noise like fingers rubbing a balloon. It also sounds like farting sometimes, and that cracks me up. In the summertime when it's hot and no one remembers to turn on the air, my legs stick to the sofa cushions and I have to peel them off.

Dad sits and starts eating. We're having meatloaf, which I don't like.

When *he* finds me, we're going to have duck every night for dinner. I've never had duck before, and I don't even know if I'll like it, but it sounds very elegant and it's the kind of food I'm sure he eats. Duck, and shrimp cocktail. And oysters. Those are grown-up foods and we'll eat them every night.

"I have to do a report, Dad."

He looks at Mom. "Gas prices are going up. Again."

"So?" She sits down and starts eating her dinner.

"What? *So*? So it's insane."

"We don't even have a car." She eats her green beans before anything else. Mom always eats her vegetables first.

"Dad?"

He shoves food into his mouth and talks anyway. "That doesn't bother you?"

Mom shakes her head. "We've got our own problems. No need to worry about the cost of gas on top of everything else."

"Daa-aad, *look*. Lookit this. Da-ad!"

He glances over his shoulder, and even though he's looking at me, he's talking to Mom. "Cost of gas goes up, then taxes go up, it never ends."

Mom laughs and says, "Oh yeah?" and eats another forkful of green beans.

"Dad?" I say quietly, holding up my textbook, staring at the photographs of the galaxy.

After dinner Dad sits on the sofa and Mom washes dishes, so I sit on the sofa too. I don't want to have to dry but she'll probably yell for me to do it anyway.

I hold up my science book and open it to page fifty-three. "Lookit," I say, laying it across his lap, running my fingers over the glossy picture. "Daddy? See? I have to do a report."

He's staring ahead, at the television. The news is on. I hate the news.

"Dad?" I wait for an answer. "Dad?" I stare up at him. "Dad? Daddy?"

"Can't you see I'm busy?" he yells, knocking the book off his lap. It tumbles to the floor. He makes a sighing noise and goes back to staring at the television.

I pick up the book and bring it to my bedroom.

Later in my room, I start my assignment. "The Solar System, by Karen Brown. Our solar system has eight planets. We used to have nine but now it's only eight. One planet that's not a planet no more is Pluto, and they named that one after a dog. The other eight planets are—" I copy the names of the planets. I copy some other stuff too. I draw a picture that looks like the one in the book.

Sometimes I pretend he stops watching the news and comes in to see me and throws his arms around me and tells me how much he loves me. But that doesn't happen.

Sometimes I wonder if *he's* any closer. It's taking him so long to find me. My real father. The one who looks like me, talks like me, loves books the way I do. The father who would never ignore me to watch TV.

There must be a way for me to send him a signal, to let him know when he's close. One time I asked Mom who my real father is and she looked at me funny and asked me what I was talking about. So maybe she doesn't know. Maybe she thinks the man who lives with us is my real father. Maybe they switched places one night, and this stranger took my father's place. Because he can't be. He can't be my real father.

He just can't.

My real father is searching for me. He walks or runs when he can't find a car or a plane. Sometimes he even hitchhikes, because he'll never give up. He knows he'll find me if he just keeps looking. I know my science projects will be fantastic when he helps, because he's really good at stuff like that. He's a scientist, and a doctor (brain surgeon), and even a lawyer. An actor too, I'll bet. He searches, and I'm looking too. Like the other day, I saw a man who looked like me. That had been so close. I know it's going to happen. I just have to be patient. And when my real dad finds me, it'll be great.

Everything will be perfect then.

FIRE

ELIZABETH MASSIE

Mac heard the familiar rumble outside his apartment and turned from the stove, shoved the heels of his hands against the wheels, and coasted to the window. Pushing back the thin, sun-bleached curtains, he stared down at the street three floors below where the silver Mercedes had come to a stop, the front right wheel on the curb, the engine still running and some indecipherable song pounding a bone-rattling bass through its glistening sides, making the car appear to be breathing.

A few moments later the engine was cut. The music died. Another moment and two people climbed from the front—one, the driver, was a huge, muscular man in an expensive dark suit, black tie, felt fedora tipped forward, and polished, boat-sized shoes. He walked around the front of the car with a decided swagger, kicking his feet out as if knocking back invisible dogs, until he reached the passenger who was standing on the sidewalk, arms crossed, chin tipped up in feigned confidence, light brown hair brushing her shoulders. Even at this distance, Mac could see the new wounds on her face, a prominent bruise to the right eye, a gash on her chin. The man put his arm around her shoulder and turned her toward the apartment building. The large gold ring on his finger matched the size of the bruise on her face.

As they vanished beneath the apartment's front awning, Mac turned back toward the kitchen. The water was hissing, almost ready for the pasta. If nothing else, Mac was a whiz with foods. A former chef who had lost his job following his accident, he continued to read about cooking online and study cookbooks lent him by his crusty yet generous landlady Alva Ricardo. He ordered a wide variety of foodstuffs over the phone from the local Korean store, Greek store, Japanese store, Pakistani and Indian store. What was delivered in cardboard boxes once a week offered a unique combination of aromatic, globally-integrated culinary possibilities. When Alva was free for an evening, Mac invited her to dinner. Sometimes Alva brought her daughter, Elena and her six-year-old granddaughter, Bunny. They would sit about the battered yellow 1960's-era kitchen table upon the wobbly kitchen chairs, but with the paper towels folded just so, and the candles lit and flickering, with the fragrances of the food practically pushing the lids from the pans and baking dishes, the evening became one of temporary elegance and grace. Even Elena, an overweight and naturally gruff young woman, seemed to absorb a bit of polish, and sat up straighter and spoke in a more civil tone when dining at Mac's. One evening, she'd even risen to the occasion and complimented Mac and his cooking.

"You pretty damn good with this stuff, you know," Elena had said as she scooped up another serving spoon full of kha'geena and shook it off onto her plate. "You really should get a job in a restaurant. Or cook here and sell carry-out. No, probably not. Got to have a license, don't you? But I like your food, much better than what my Mama used to cook when I lived at home. That was some nasty shit. I mean stuff. Sorry."

"You're livin' at home again, don't you forget," said Alva, her lips pressed and thin.

"Just temporary 'til I find another place," said Elena. "But anyway," she turned back to Mac, "you got a good thing goin' here. It's a shame you don't cook for hardly nobody but yourself. And you ain't a half-bad lookin' man, beside you not having no legs and all."

Bunny, who'd been sitting silently, chewing on the sesame seeded roll her grandmother had buttered for her, looked around the table at Mac's lap and the emptiness beneath it. When they'd first met, Bunny had been clearly disturbed and confused by his physical appearance, but with time she had come around to accept that the man in the chair was a real person, that he didn't bite or drool, and that he was nice to kids.

Alva and her family weren't the only ones Mac cooked for, though. He also fixed meals every so often for his next-door apartment neighbor, Lisa Sterling, though he had no idea if she'd ever eaten what he'd left by her door. She never returned the dishes. Lisa was young, pretty, and shy, a waitress by trade and a drug dealer's girlfriend by happenstance.

The two had met through the wall five months earlier, when Mac had moved into the building. He'd wanted a first floor, but Alva only had the one on the third floor available. She'd given him a cut rate on the apartment, promising that as soon as a first floor opened up, it was his. Mac had little choice but to take the offer. His sole means of income—his computer—had been stolen from his previous flat, as had his television, stereo system, cell phone, and cash. Mac had fought the intruders as best he could but the boys, fourteen years of age at the oldest, had pistol whipped him out of his chair and left him dazed and bleeding on the braided rug. The landlord had been pissed and had kicked Mac out as a proven liability.

"They see you and know they got their easy mark," he'd said, one hand on the door, the other scratching his chest beneath his t-shirt. "Fuckin' easy pickin'. You're out of here, this time tomorrow."

Mac didn't have the money to fight the eviction, so he gathered up what was left, moved into a shelter for a couple weeks and then landed the vacancy in Alva's building. He bought a used laptop with what remained on his credit card, but by the time he had his "Mac's Cheap Yet Exotic Cooking" site up and running again (featuring the popular "Recipe a Day" and "Ask Mac" column), it had been nearly a month, and he'd lost a number of subscribers. Only a few remained.

The second evening after moving to Alva's building, Mac had heard someone crying through the wall. He'd listened, then knocked tentatively. He knocked again and spoke into the plaster, "Are you okay?"

A soft voice had replied, "Yeah, I'm okay," though he could tell that wasn't true by the raggedness of the sobs. He began to watch through the window and the peek hole in his front door to see who was so sad and scared, and thus came to know his neighbor, Lisa. Once he'd wheeled out of his apartment to her door but she refused to answer. He could tell she was watching him through her own peek hole, could hear her voice pressed up against the door. "I can't take the chance of Darien knowing I was talking to any man but him."

And so Mac's life consisted of re-establishing himself on the Internet, cooking, reading, and waiting for Lisa to be alone so he could talk to her through the wall.

Lisa and Darien could be heard on the stairs now, moving up to the third floor. The man sauntered even when there was no one to see but his girlfriend, his voice affecting a deep tone that was more growl than language. They made it to the landing. Mac wheeled to his door, pushed himself up until his eye was at the peek hole, and gazed at the couple in the tainted light of the overhead bulb.

Darien was all scars and sneers, unpredictable, as likely to kiss and snuggle Lisa as to punch her for saying something wrong, for moving wrong or standing wrong. This afternoon, Darien was in a particularly sunny mood. He spun Lisa around, rubbed her breasts through her pink knit top, then shoved his hand down the front of her tightly fitting jeans, wiggling his hand and his hips simultaneously, leaning in to draw his tongue across the bruise beneath her eye.

"Babe," he snarled with a savage grin, "you just wait for me, you hear? I'll come back sometime tonight. You be waitin' for your daddy, you be ready."

"I will, Darien."

"Call me Daddy, Babe. I like it you call me that."

"Daddy."

"You keep yourself hot and wet for me."

"I will. Daddy."

"You damn right you will." Darien laughed and shoved his hand even deeper. Lisa threw back her head and squeezed her eyes shut. Then the dealer withdrew his hand and strolled down the steps. Lisa clung to the railing, her head dropped toward the floor, then moved out of Mac's sight to her own door. Mac could hear her key in the lock, the door creaking open then slapping shut. He waited a good sixty seconds before going over to their adjoining wall and rapping lightly.

After a few moments, Lisa rapped back. Then, her muffled voice said, "Hey, there."

"You okay?"

"Sure, Mac. How about you?"

"Okay."

"Good."

"You have plans for supper?"

"What?" It sounded as though she were shedding her clothes, breathing irregularly as she peeled off the tight jeans and the pink top.

"Supper? I could bring something over."

"I'm not very hungry, Mac."

"I've got freshly made pasta. Tomatoes, peppers, onions, a little garlic. It's almost ready. I think it's some of the best I've ever made."

Another pause. "No, thanks."

"You have to eat something."

"I'm really tired. But thanks."

"You can reheat it later."

"Well."

"All right?"

"Okay. All right."

"I'll bring it over, put it by your door in just a little bit, then."

"Okay."

Mac finished the pasta dish—lovingly sautéing the vegetables with olive oil and rosemary, then letting them cook over a low heat. When the sauce was perfect, he ladled it over the pasta in a casserole dish, securing the lid, then wheeling it out into the hall on a thick, folded towel. He knocked on Lisa's door, his heart beginning to race.

Maybe this time she would open the door. Maybe this time, for the first time, he would be able to see her face to face.

It took a good minute before he heard her at the door. He held the towel-padded dish up toward the peek hole.

"Looks good, Mac. Thanks. Just leave it there."

"If you open the door I can just hand it to you. I'll be real quick, I promise."

"No."

"Lisa..."

"Darien could be back any time now."

"His car is gone."

"He's fast, Mac. You can't know how fast."

"He can't be that fast."

"He can be anything he wants."

The dish was growing heavy but still he held it out. "Come on, Lisa. You know what I think of him. You know what I think you can do, what you *should* do. Yet there you are, still letting him control your life. You're way too good for that."

"Mac." She sounded exasperated, defeated. And in that single utterance Mac heard, yet again, her inability to shed the man who so abused her. Then she said, "Please just leave the food or take it back with you." He heard her withdraw from the door and back into the bowels of her apartment.

Mac put the dish on the floor. He ran his thumbs along the padding on the arms of his chair and stared at the door—the water stains, the mildew, the frayed veneer at the bottom that resembled dried fronds of an old hula skirt. Then he went back to his apartment.

In the kitchen, he dumped the remaining pasta and sauce down the disposal, and took his time grinding it into nothing.

«««—»»»

Darien returned to Lisa's apartment three hours later, bringing along two of his friends. The friends were stoned but Darien sounded sober. Mac had heard Darien boast to Lisa that the best dealers don't mess with the shit they sell. They just let the morons lose their minds and their money.

Mac lay in his bed against the adjoining wall, his hands pressed to his chest, his heart thundering, afraid of what would Darien might do to Lisa, wishing he could kill the man, and wanting Lisa more than anything he'd ever wanted in his life. He listened to the feral laughter next door, the grunts, the meek, indecipherable responses from Lisa to whatever the men were saying or doing.

If he had arms of steel, Mac would slam them through the wall and catch up the criminals by surprise. He would snap them up, wring their necks, and then drop them one at a time out the window to let them splatter blood and brains on the quartz-sparkling sidewalk. Warning signs for anyone else who might want to mistreat Lisa. People would step over the carcasses, afraid to move them, afraid that whoever put them there wanted them there, and who would challenge such a powerful man?

"Then she would want me, too," he whispered to the ceiling and to a spider that hung from a fragile line. He closed his eyes, trying to think louder than the men next door. He saw in his mind Lisa coming to his apartment with the empty casserole dish. She was dressed in her tight jeans, thin t-shirt, no bra. She sat beside Mac on the bed, telling him he was right, that she was better than to let herself be treated so poorly. Telling him that she hated Darien and that she had only stayed with him because he had terrorized her into staying, that she wanted to run away with Mac and never look back.

She fell onto the bed on her side. Mac tenderly stroked her hair and kissed her tears away. Lisa moaned, rolled onto her back, and placed his hand upon one of her soft breasts. Mac felt the delicious stirring in his blood, the sudden electrical current that would not be denied, flowing outward from his soul like sun's rays, coursing to his mind, his heart, his groin. Lisa lifted her body to kiss Mac's lips. He reached between her legs to find the jeans gone and her dark and secret place trembling and damp.

Somewhere beyond there was a heavy sound, a thud, a groan...

Mac found his own shorts gone, his underwear as well, and he was swollen and ready. As Lisa opened her legs she whispered, "I love you, Mac. I love you so much you can never know." He drove himself into her, into her, into her, into her. His muscles cramped deliciously with each movement. Lisa clung to his back with her fingers.

Somewhere beyond there was a muffled cry...

Lisa cried out in ecstasy. Mac's explosion was exquisite, divine, and he threw his head back, thanking God with a loud and primal roar that made the hairs on his arms and chest stand at attention.

Somewhere beyond there was a swearing, and the words, "Fuck, you hear that?"

Mac opened his eyes. His throat was dry as gravel. He was wet below the waist. He stomach spasmed.

It was Darien next door. "You hear that?" The dealer laughed and pounded on the wall with what sounded like his foot. It made Mac's headboard rattle. "Cripple over there's jackin' off! Holy shit!" There were other male voices now, joining in the laughter. Beneath it all, Lisa's soft weeping.

Mac let his breathing slow. He swallowed against dryness, and then wiped his forehead. The laughter through the adjoining wall dropped off and the voices shifted, moving on to conversations about something that sounded more serious, something that was hard to hear. Mac wondered what they had done to Lisa to make her cry. Was she hurt or just sad?

Surely she had heard Darien making fun of Mac, banging on the wall.

He must pay.

Mac switched on his clock radio to his favorite oldies station and turned the music up.

Hot town, summer in the city...

He once again saw himself with steel arms, bashing in Darien's brains and sweeping Lisa up and away.

He fell asleep to jovial radio co-hosts giving a weather report and talking about an upcoming festival of some sort, something to do with water, with cleaning up the river, or fishing or boating, he couldn't quite tell because the world was falling away.

«« — »»

He awoke to a headache so heavy, so fire-hot, that all he could do was to crush his skull between his hands to alleviate the pressure. His pillow was soaked with sweat and dream-tears, though he could not recall the dreams with any clarity. The radio droned on, playing some nondescript classical tune defined by violins and oboes. The clock face read 6:07 a.m.

Is Darien still there with you, Lisa? Or is he gone?

Mac eased off the bed onto his chair, sponge bathed in the bathroom, and put a kettle on for morning tea. While waiting for the water to hiss, he went to the adjoining wall, pressed his ear to the scabby paint, and listened. There was no snoring, suggesting that Darien and his minions had left. He looked out his living room window; the Mercedes was gone.

Turning on the computer, Mac pulled up his e-mail, discarded the spam, and then went back for his tea, black, straight, no milk and no sugar. He worked on his site for several hours until he heard gentle noises next door. He rolled to the wall, rapped.

A return rap, and "Good morning, Mac." She sounded exhausted but not terrified. She was obviously alone.

"Hi. How was the pasta?"

"The—?" She hadn't even tasted it. She likely put the whole thing at the bottom of a trash bag. Mac felt a flush of heat—frustration, disappointment—at the back of his neck. "It was...very good."

"It was?"

A hesitant, "Yes."

"You didn't really try it yet, did you?"

"No, Mac, I'm sorry. I didn't mean to lie. I didn't want to hurt your feelings."

"It'll reheat in your microwave if you still have it. Or…you could bring it over here and I can reheat it if you want."

"Don't be silly."

Mac rubbed at the fire on his neck, pushing it down, away. He took a long breath, held it, let it out. He changed the subject. "You on your way to work?"

"In just a while. I have to put on my makeup."

Lisa served pizzas at a "child-friendly" restaurant five blocks over, where families held frantic birthday parties and children crawled through pools filled with plastic balls and played Skee-Ball and Whack-A-Mole. Lisa worked part-time, three days a week, ten-thirty in the morning until nine in the evenings. She wore the uniform of the establishment—beige polyester slacks and short-sleeved white blouse with a little plastic nametag reading "Lisa." She usually put her hair up into a ponytail, making her look younger than her twenty-four years. The makeup was often used to hide the evidence of Darien's mistreatments, applied heavily from what Mac could see through his peek hole and window.

Mac scrambled for something else to say, something to keep her talking. "I was looking at some of the National Parks online last night. Gorgeous places. I'd love to see the Grand Canyon, the Smoky Mountains, some of the rest. Wouldn't you?"

"I dunno."

"Just imagine, traveling across the country." He tried to make his voice sound even, not overbearing. "Think of all the stuff there is to see. I'd especially like to visit all those different restaurants spread across the states, the big city eateries with the high reputations, the little diners off forgotten roads. I bet I could find a new job some place unique and exciting, start over. I've never had the chance to do that, to go anywhere much. How about you?"

"No," said Lisa. "It sounds like fun."

Mac took a deep breath. "When was the last time you had fun?"

It sounded as if she spit air. "Never."

"You need to leave Darien." It came out faster than he thought it would, though he wasn't sorry he'd said it.

Silence. Then, "I can't, Mac. He'll kill me."

"He's killing you now."

She sighed.

"How did it get like this? How did you let him take over your life so much?"

"I don't want to talk about it."

"Why? This is me, remember."

"Fuck. Okay. I was out of a job. Darien was great. He set me up in my place, paid the rent, still pays for most of it. You think I can afford even this mouse-infested shit box for what I make at the restaurant?"

"I don't know what you make."

"Well, I can't. And even if I could, he's been around a long time, more than a year, Mac, longer than I've known you. He's told me over and over he'll kill me before he lets me go."

"You need to get away. It's not his decision to make."

Silence.

"Call the police. Get him arrested."

"He'll kill me. They'll hold him, let him out, and he'll find me and kill me."

"Get a restraining order."

"Ha! You think that'll stop him? He brags he's never been held by the cops before, he's too smart."

Mac clenched his teeth together. It felt as though matches had been struck behind his eyes, pinpoints of red hot. "He's not smart, he's evil."

Her voice dropped, becoming almost inaudible. "The only thing that will get him away from me is if he was put in prison or killed. That ain't never going to happen."

"Never say never, Lisa."

A very long silence. Mac thought for a moment that she had moved away but then he heard her shifting.

Mac put his hand on the wall, willing her to feel his love through the plaster.

"Lisa, let me help you."

The reply was loud and abrupt. "You? You're kidding, right? How can you help?"

Mac was taken aback. He withdrew his hand. She saw him as only the cripple next door, the young man who had nothing to offer but pasta, pie, and a friendly word through the wall.

Her voice softened as if she had read his mind. "Mac, it ain't about you and the way you are. It's Darien and the way he is. Nobody can help. Not you, not the police, not God, not even Superman."

Mac had a sudden, silly, brilliant idea. His heart rose with the revelation, the clear vision of what they could do. "Hey, let's just leave together. Right now. I don't have money to buy a car but I can afford two bus tickets. Head out to where we've never been before. Leave all this mess, this pain, this fear in the dust."

"I can't."

"Wait. Think. Don't say you can't. You can."

"Darien knows people everywhere, he pays for information. He'd find us. He'd find the bus we take. He'll kill us both and nobody will ever find us."

"Lisa, please..." *Can't you tell I love you?*

"No, Mac. I have to get to work. You have a good day, okay?"

And she was gone.

The day was long, the afternoon sun hanging for an inordinate amount of time atop the building across the street, sending stifling heat into Mac's apartment. The curtain was no good at holding the heat at bay, neither was the torn plastic shade. There was no air conditioning, of course, another reason the place was so cheap. Mac worked on his site, paced, flipped through a cookbook, read the first three chapters of a novel Alva had given him a month ago, then put it aside, bored. He drank iced coffee and patted the fire away with wet washcloths.

He thought about Darien, he thought about Lisa. He imagined himself and Lisa on a bus west, her head in his lap, his chin atop her brown hair. He imagined the two of them having inexpensive roadside picnics at rustic tables where squirrels watched from treetops, the scents of honeysuckle and a near-by sun-warmed stream drifted in the air, and the world glowed like the fires of heaven.

Lisa got home a little after nine. Mac prepared to tap on the wall to say hello but heard Darien's car pull up in front of the building, and seconds later Darien come up the stairs. Through the peek hole, Mac could see the man had a crystal vase filled with roses for Lisa, as scarlet as the blood he drew from her at his whim.

Lisa had said, *The only thing that will get him away from me is if he was put in prison or killed. And that's never going to happen.*

Mac heard Darien open the door, call cheerfully for Lisa, and then everything went silent. It was silent for a long time and then music began to play, the same heavy stuff Darien listened to in his car. Mac sat on his bed, not wanting to listen beneath the music, afraid not to listen.

The beating came around midnight. Darien's blows, Lisa's cries. It lasted a good twenty minutes. There was a shattering on the sidewalk outside. Mac knew it was the vase of flowers, tossed out by Darien to prove some point. Then Darien left, cursing, stomping, down the stairs to his car.

The only thing...prison or killed.

And that's never going to happen.

Mac didn't have the strength to kill Darien. And if he did, he wouldn't survive prison. He'd be shanked to death, tormented, or tortured by Darien's buddies on the inside. The only thing left was to get the man arrested and imprisoned for a long time.

The rest of the night Mac stayed awake, knocking futilely on the wall to get Lisa's attention, listening to her sob. Mac had never heard such despair in his life, nor had he ever felt it as strongly or completely himself.

«‹—›»

Two days later, Darien drove to the apartment building with Lisa in tow. He'd picked her up from work and had a need he wanted her to fill. He brought her up the stairs, past Mac's peek hole, and into her apartment. Darien's mood was hard to pinpoint, he seemed distracted though not particulary angry. He didn't stay long with Lisa, but when he came out he encountered a legless young man in a wheelchair blocking the staircase.

"What the...?" said Darien, pushing back his hat and scratching his forehead. The man's eyes were rimmed with red, dangerous, narrowed. "Whoo hoo! Who let the cripple out?"

Mac leaned forward in his chair, his arms folded and resting in his lap. His body burned with determination and dread, though he fought to keep his words cool, calm. "You're not getting past me, Darien."

"You's a stupid fucker, man," laughed Darien. "Get out my way before I make you get out."

That's what I want, Darien. Make me get out, hit me, knock me cold. Then I'll have you arrested. I'm not afraid to call the cops on your pathetic ass. And Lisa and I will be out of here before you're on the streets again.

"I'm not moving."

"Hell you ain't." Darien stuck out his foot and shoved it against the chair, trying to kick it sideways and into the wall beside the stairs. The chair bucked up against its brakes and scooted back a foot. Mac grabbed the wheels and pulled the chair back into its original position.

"You brain damaged, that's what you is. I said get out of my way. I don't ask nice twice."

"You're not even good enough to be called an asshole, Darien," said Mac. "You're a shriveled up little shit-smelling nothing. You're an asshole's asshole. Beating up women, how brave is that?" His breathing came in shallow, irregular pulses. His heart banged at his chest, warning him to stop what he was doing.

How much will it hurt when Darien actually strikes?

Darien laughed loud and long then, hands on hips, head thrown back, his hat wobbling. He couldn't believe what he was encountering. Mac could hear Mrs. Carter across the hall, thumping against her front door, peering out. That was good. A witness.

Then Darien's laughter cut off, dead in his throat. He leaned over and slapped Mac soundly on his face. It stung mightily. "Move that chair."

Mac just stared at the man, locking his jaw to keep it from trembling.

Darien lifted his boat-sized foot and drove it into Mac's chest. Mac felt something crack in a bright explosion of pain. A rib. Breath rushed out; he gasped, nothing came in. He gasped again, again. Nothing. And then, a pain-filled rush of salt-tasting air.

Okay, he's done it now, back up, let him by!

"You fucker," snarled Darien. "You got what you asked for. Now move!"

Lisa, he's going to jail, I can promise you!

Mac tried to pull his wheels to let the man get by, but the agony in his chest wouldn't give him the strength.

"I said move!"

Mac forced himself to lean forward over the pain.

"Move!"

He grabbed the wheels, pulled, grit his teeth yet cried out involuntarily. The chair inched back. But it wasn't enough, it wasn't fast enough.

"Fuckin' *move!*" It was a flash then, a movement of body so rapid that it only registered in residual ghost-image after it was done. Darien's hands locked together and he swung them up, around, and down, driving them against Mac's shoulder with such force that Mac and his chair toppled over and down the steps. Mac's hands shot out, grasping for something to stop the fall, but it was happening so fast, another rib breaking as he struck a step and flipped again, falling, falling. A shoulder cracking. His wrist. The chair bouncing over his head, reaching the second floor landing before Mac did.

Mac knew he was going to die the moment before he did. He saw how he was to land, and knew with certainty that he would never travel with Lisa to the west, never find those exclusive, exotic, and curiously old-fashioned restaurants, never get another job as a chef, never fix himself and Lisa lunch at an old picnic table off a two-lane highway where vintage metal trashcans were tethered to concrete blocks and cars hummed by, not caring who you were or where you came from. In this moment he was indescribably sad, until he saw that Alva was on the second floor, staring up at him in horror and up past him at Darien with rage.

She had seen the assault. She had watched the drug dealer slam Mac down the stairs to his death. She and Mrs. Carter could tell the police all they would need to know. Lisa wouldn't have to do anything, just let her angry, righteous neighbor and landlady take charge. They wouldn't be afraid to testify. Murder would put Darien behind bars for many years. If not for life, then at least long enough for Lisa to start over, to come up from the shadows in which she'd been living, to move, to grow, to find the beauty that was there that she had never truly seen before.

Or will she just go on to another like Darien? Will she even know how to save herself? Who will help her?

"Lisa!"

Mac's head struck the floor at an angle, the weight of his body following, driving him hard against the unpolished wood, snapping his neck in a burst of golden and silver flames.

The fire went out.

DANCE OF THE BLUE LADY

GENE O'NEILL

Timothy Shaw winced when his mother said, "Goodbye, Timmy, I'll see you at lunch." Timmy was really a little boy's nickname, but Tim was thirty years old now. Today, he didn't complain though as he slipped out the front door. His mom had been sick lately, and Uncle Liam was here to drive her over to see the doctor in Jackson.

Tim paused outside the door and listened for a moment as they talked. Earlier they'd been whispering loudly back and forth, as Tim had dressed for work in his room. Uncle Liam was always pretty bossy. He liked to give everyone advice, including Tim's mother. That's what he seemed to be doing this morning.

"Kathleen, the boy is a man now. It's past time to discuss his future—"

"Can't it wait?"

"No, we need to make some decisions, just in case things don't go well in the next few days at Sutter Memorial Hospital, and well…" His uncle's voice tapered off.

There was a long pause, then his mom said in a barely audible voice, "We'll talk tonight, after dinner, Liam. After I have a chance this afternoon to explain the situation to him."

"That's fine."

Tim wasn't too good with numbers or reading, but he usually picked up well on what people meant when they talked, especially how they felt. Even though he wasn't sure what they were talking about, he knew his mom was definitely upset.

It was nippy outside. He blew on his hands, pulled up his collar, hurried over to Main Street, along the two blocks of wood-planked sidewalk of Marshall Creek in the Sierra Nevada foothills, past the boarded-up storefronts called downtown, seeing no one out on the street. As he came to the end of Main Street, before it climbed away from the town and headed over the hill toward Jackson, he crossed the road to the town park. A neat, green area of grass, bushes, and oaks, much smaller than the city park over at Jackson. With no play equipment, no statues, no birdbaths, no fountains, no picnic tables or grills. Only two buildings in sight. The old gazebo back on the mound of grass that rose up then sloped down and dropped out of view before reaching Marshall Creek. And far to the right under a large spreading oak, the restrooms.

Tim headed toward the cinderblock building.

Waiting for him near the public toilets was Chatterbox, and the gray squirrel was indeed chattering away this chilly morning: *Click, click, click, click.*

Tim approached the men's side of the building, slipped his hand out of his jacket pocket and kneeled near the squirrel. In his palm were five *Cheerios.* "Hi there, boy," he said, as the little animal set up on its back legs, carefully plucking each individual piece of cereal out of Tim's hand, and then popping them into its mouth. "Hungry this morning, eh?"

Quiet now, with puffed up cheeks, Chatterbox turned and scampered up the nearby large oak. Tim watched the squirrel disappear up the tree, and then smiled to himself. Chatterbox was his only friend left in Marshall Creek.

After checking around the cinderblock building for non-existent trash, he peeked into the open door of the men's restroom. Everything looked fine, just as he'd left it yesterday. The women's side was in the same condition. No one had used either restroom. In fact, the toilets were rarely used now that almost everyone had moved away from Marshall Creek. Still, Tim had his job to do.

He checked the wastebasket, then the paper towel and toilet paper dispensers. Nothing needed servicing today. Now for the cleaning.

He went to the supply closet at the far end of the women's restroom and took out his equipment.

With his green duster, he brushed imaginary spider webs and dust from the spotless cinderblock walls; next, he swept the polished concrete floor with the big mop-broom after spraying it lightly with a coat of pine-scented oil; then, he thoroughly scrubbed both sinks and the two toilet bowls with *Comet*, wiping the fixtures down with a thin coat of *409*; and finally he sprayed and cleaned the big mirror with *Windex*. Mr. Spinoza, the Mayor, had shown Tim the routine years ago. Back when he was first hired. His mom said the money to hire him came from an old bank account his grandfather had left to keep up the park. But the money had run out last year around Easter time, and the town could afford nothing more. Tim had continued working five days a week in the small park, taking money for his supplies and gas for the power mower from his savings. Actually, he only needed to come for half a day now that no one regularly used the facilities. It wasn't necessary to do anything in the afternoons—except Fridays when he mowed the lawn and trimmed bushes.

He repeated his cleaning routine next door on the men's side. By the time Tim finished polishing the mirror in the men's restroom it was almost 11:00. He took all his supplies and equipment back to the cleaning supply closet on the women's side, carefully storing them away.

Then, Tim walked around behind the men's restroom to the storage shed, the padlocked door marked, *Staff Only*. He took out his key and unlocked the old shed, his pulse speeding up slightly. He opened the squeaky door, ducked his head in, clapped his hands, and smiled broadly. Inside the storage shed, next to his neatly arranged small tools, shovels, rakes, hoes, and big power mower, was a piece of casted sculpture, a statue roughly shaped into a feminine figurine, five feet high, her face lacking distinct features. She wore a coat of greenish-blue rust. On her base were two words faintly stamped into the metal: *Prima Ballerina*. Tim couldn't read the inscription, but he'd carefully written down the letters and asked his mom what they meant. He'd seen the ballet on TV a number of times and loved the dancers in their funny costumes. So he understood the elegance suggested by the unknown artist.

He'd found the statue with three other sculptures, a birdbath, a number of metal picnic tables and benches, and a bunch of other stuff, all packed tightly into an old Quonset hut down by the creek. He'd gone exploring down there after his mother told him that his grandfather had odd ideas about a park. She said that before Tim was born, when his grandfather agreed to set up a trust fund for maintenance of the existing park, the old man required it be cleared of all the donated clutter from the gold rush days. Tim's mother said her father insisted a park should be kept as *pristine* as possible—a word Tim liked the sound of, but didn't fully understand. He knew it meant something like: just green grass, bushes, and trees. The old man had reluctantly agreed to keeping the gazebo donated by the owners of the Fort Ann Mine Company for concerts, and allowing the construction of the restrooms as a modern necessity. But the rest of the stuff had been given away or stored down out of sight in the Quonset hut. When Tim first uncovered the figurine, its natural beauty had taken his breath away. He called her simply, the Blue Lady.

Eventually Tim had drug the Blue Lady up here to the restroom storage shed, nearer to where he worked. Each day after he finished his janitorial chores, he opened the shed and rewarded himself with a long look at the beautiful sculpture. Sometimes, like today, Tim lifted the Lady out of the shed, closed his eyes, and after a second or so, he'd imagine classical music playing down at the gazebo—violins and all the other instrumental sounds. Then, for a few minutes the Lady would dance for him. *Graceful* and *elegant*—two words his mother often used describing the ballet on TV. Oh, how wonderful. He never touched the Lady when she was dancing. No, he didn't dare. Neither did Tim clean off the rusty stuff. It was like a special blue-green costume she wore. No, the Blue Lady was marvelous just the way she was. And her special dancing and the classical music were Tim's secret.

After the dance today, Tim carefully put the Lady back in her hiding place. He locked the shed, circled once around the park to ensure that everything was in good shape, and waved goodbye to Chatterbox in the oak tree, before heading back home.

It was still early so he walked slowly along Main Street, glancing at the signs above the boarded up window fronts, finally pausing at SHAW'S HARDWARE/DRY GOODS—the second part of the sign almost completely faded out now. He wasn't sure what DRY GOODS meant anyhow. His grandfather had started the store back when the mines and mills were still running at full strength, maybe fifty or even a hundred years ago, he wasn't sure. Then, his mom took over when Grandpa died. Tim had been just a young boy then, a real Timmy. She said the town had 3,000 people back then after the Mother Lode was discovered. But people had moved away as the mines closed and the lumber mills shut down. She said the unlucky town was off the beaten track and didn't get the tourists, like Jackson and Sutter Creek over on well-traveled Highway 49. Tim didn't understand the numbers or much of what she called economics, but he'd watched his mother shrivel up and grow old unsuccessfully trying to make ends meet at the hardware store. Until last year after the 4th of July parade in Jackson, when she finally closed it. Then just before Christmas she found something wrong in her chest, a bump or something. Tim shook his head. Thinking about stuff like that made him feel funny, kind of sad, nervous, and helpless all at the same time. He sighed and continued along the boardwalk.

As he passed by the boarded-up windows of the GROCERY STORE/U.S. POST OFFICE, he heard a voice behind him, "Hey, Timmy." It was Mr. Spinoza, who lived behind the grocery store he once ran. Mr. Spinoza had been the Postmaster and Mayor, too, back when the town had been full of people.

Tim nodded and smiled.

"How's your mother doing, Timmy?" Mr. Spinoza asked, the use of the nickname making Tim clench his teeth. The ex-Mayor was like the rest of the old people left in town: they all called him Timmy. "Haven't seen her out and about for a while."

"Fine, Mr. Spinoza," Tim said politely. He knew his mother wasn't fine, and he didn't feel like mentioning the doctor visit today. He also hoped if he were quiet that Mr. Spinoza would mention something about his daughter, Ava. When the store closed, maybe two years ago, Ava went away to Sacramento to college. Before that she used to occasionally come over to the park and bring Tim a tuna fish sandwich and a cream soda or root beer at lunchtime. "Least I can do for all your hard work, Timothy," she'd said. Ava was only seventeen then, but she seemed older to Tim. Sometimes he'd pretend that she was his girlfriend. But he knew that was silly. He was too old for her, and, besides, she already had a boyfriend—a football player from Sutter Creek. She was sure pretty though, and had been a really good friend. He missed her. He'd never actually had a *real* girlfriend to take over to the movies in Jackson or anything like that.

Mr. Spinoza didn't say much about Ava, just that she was doing okay at Sacramento State, maybe going to be a nurse pretty soon. He said to give Tim's mom his best, then the ex-Mayor disappeared around the side of his grocery store. Tim watched the stooped old man go, the smells of something cooking reminding him it was lunch time.

«««—»»»

At lunch that afternoon, Tim's mom had fixed his favorite, meatloaf and mashed potatoes with gravy. But he hadn't really enjoyed it all that much, because he felt something was wrong. For one thing, his uncle was not eating with them, out walking, checking out the Fort Ann up on the hill. And his mom's eyebrows were drawn together in that funny kind of way. She wasn't eating, just sort of moving her food around on her plate. At last she set her fork down.

"Timmy, we need to have a little talk."

He knew this wasn't going to be like that sex thing, because she didn't have that silly-nervous smile on her face, her voice strained and high pitched. No, she was really serious…and almost looked scared.

Tim nodded, "Okay, Mom." He set his fork down beside his plate and paid close attention.

"Ah, well, you know, I went over to see Dr. Mikkelsen in Jackson today," she said, not looking him straight in his eyes.

"I know."

"And you remember that Dr. Mikkelsen had sent me to the hospital in Sacramento for a bunch of tests and to see a specialist last week?"

"Sure, I remember, Mom."

He'd gone with her last Monday, missed work at the park. Aunt Martha had come and picked them up real early, then driven them to Sacramento. After dropping off his mom, Aunt Martha had taken him to the zoo near William Land Park. And they'd had a hot dog, coke, and pink popcorn. Like a long time ago, when he'd been younger. But his mom had stayed at that Sutter Memorial Hospital all day. She'd looked really tired and worried when they picked her up late Monday afternoon. No one said much on the ride back to Marshall Creek.

Which was funny because Aunt Martha was like Chatterbox. Tim also noticed that his mother was doing that thing with her eyebrows.

"Well, son, those tests came back, and I had to go over to Dr. Mikkelsen's this morning to talk about the results. What needs to be done for me to get well. You understand?"

He nodded and waited, because he could tell there was more.

His mother took a deep breath and managed to look him square in the eyes now. "The news isn't real good, Timmy. I have to go back to Sacramento, have an operation, and be in the hospital for a little while. You are going to have to stay over there with Aunt Martha and Uncle Liam, until I can come home. That's why your uncle took off work, came over this morning, and brought his Lexus SUV to haul us and some stuff back to Sacramento."

Tim liked Aunt Martha okay, but Uncle Liam made him real nervous. Always interrupting everybody, never listening. Whenever they'd visited them in Sacramento, Uncle Liam never let his two girls, Fiona and Kara, be alone with Tim. Funny. He wouldn't have been rough with them. He knew they were just little girls. In fact, he wasn't really interested when they tried to drag him outside to play in their tree house in their backyard. He didn't have to worry, because Uncle Liam was right there, sending the girls to their room or some place else. His uncle acted like he was...sort of scared of Tim. Like Chatterbox when Tim first tried to feed the squirrel from his hand. But Uncle Liam was as big as a bear. So he didn't understand, or even much like, his mother's younger brother.

«««—»»»

After dinner that night, Tim went in to his room. Uncle Liam had helped him pack a suitcase full that afternoon. Seemed like an awful lot of stuff for a few days.

He turned the TV on to *Friends*, while he looked over his CDs. He didn't always understand all the jokes, but the familiar voices of Rachel, Chandler, Joey, and the others always made him feel good. Sometimes he wished he could go visit them in New York City. But it was too far, perhaps even farther than San Francisco. On his wall was a poster of Barry Bonds, who played for the San Francisco Giants. Ava had given it to him. He'd never seen the Giants play, but he listened to their games sometimes on the radio. Looking over his collection, Tim had to pick out ten CDs—that was all he could take. At least that was all Uncle Liam said he could take. Hmm. The Eagles...the Righteous Brothers, his mom's favorite...Janis Joplin...Joe Cocker...and Arlo Guthrie, his best favorite.

In the kitchen, Tim could hear his mother and Uncle Liam arguing over the sound of the TV.

"*No*, I won't agree to that," his mother was saying in a loud, forceful tone. She rarely used her loud voice to him or anyone, but when she raised it to this level, Tim always listened carefully.

He edged closer to the door.

"Kathleen, be reasonable," Uncle Liam said, his voice calm, lower than usual. "He's a boy in a man's body and...well, you know. Sonoma State has a terrific program, like I've been saying since you found out about him way back when he was a baby—"

"Timmy is very high functioning, especially his social and verbal skills, he doesn't need to be institutionalized. I've discussed it thoroughly with Dr. Mikkelsen. The people at Sonoma State are all lower functioning."

"That's not true," Uncle Liam said, his volume increasing. "Besides, there are many his age. How many young people left in Marshall Creek? Any at all? And who does he have here to look out for him? Tell me that."

"Me."

"Maybe. But what about if this operation and the treatments don't work out? Who knows? Maybe you've put this off too long. What then, Kathleen? Martha and I can't provide a permanent home for him. Not with the girls growing up and—"

"Oh, for God's sake, Liam." His mother sounded really disappointed and hurt. But her voice wasn't so loud now.

Tim listened on for a while, finally realizing that Uncle Liam wanted to send him away. Away to someplace called Sonoma State Hospital. And he was starting to convince Tim's mother. He could tell she was weakening.

"Okay, okay, but let's see how the treatment goes."

"Well, I think it is past time now, Kathleen. Time to face up to reality. The boy needs to be with his own *kind*. Sonoma State Hospital is a great spot for him."

My own kind? Tim thought. And go away to a, a…hospital? He didn't feel sick. Leave his mother? Marshall Creek? His job? The Blue Lady? The flood of questions made his head hurt, his chest tight, his throat dry, and his eyes teary. He didn't want to go away anywhere. Tim sucked in a long breath, turning up the sound on the TV.

《《《—》》》

Late that night, after his mother and uncle were asleep, Tim dressed and slipped out of the house.

A full moon lit up Marshall Creek, almost as if it were daytime. The stars were out and twinkling. A beautiful night. But cold. He'd forgotten to slip on his coat, and rubbed his arms through his sweatshirt, shivering in the early spring air.

Tim crossed Main Street, then walked across the park to the restrooms. He stopped for a moment and looked up into the darkness of the oak. Despite not seeing Chatterbox, he whispered, "Goodbye, old friend." Then he took out a plastic bag from his pants pocket, and shook out a small pile of Cheerios onto the ground. Maybe Mr. Spinoza would come over and feed his friend.

With a sad heart, Tim slipped around behind the building. He unlocked the storage shed and gazed inside. "Hello, Blue Lady," he said, dragging the sculpture out and around the building. She was heavy. He sucked in a deep breath, and with an effort, he hauled the statue across half the park to the gazebo. Then, he rested a moment at the steps, catching his breath before pulling the Lady up onto the stage. Placing her in the center of the platform, he stepped back and nodded to himself. Grandpa had been wrong about her. She belonged out where people could see her. With moist eyes, he whispered, "Goodbye, Blue Lady, I will miss you very much. But I have to go away with Mom and Uncle Liam, maybe go live at a hospital far away in a place called Glen Ellen—"

Timothy, don't feel bad, a soft voice said in his head.

Shocked, frozen in place, Tim just stared at the Blue Lady. She'd never spoken before. Her features seemed finer now, too, and she was smiling, staring directly at him.

Come here, Timothy, to me. She held out her hands, beckoning with her fingers.

Clumsily, he shuffled forward.

Good, now take my hands. Tim reached out and clasped the Lady's hands. They were not cold and metallic like usual. No indeed. The Blue Lady's hands were warm and alive. He could feel an electric tingling moving up his arms, into his chest, and spreading through his body.

Feel the magic?

Yes, I do, he thought, puzzled by the sensation.

Good. Close your eyes. Listen. Can you hear the music, now? Guitars were beginning to play, but not the usual classical music.

Yes, I can hear it. And he recognized the song! "City of New Orleans." His best favorite.

That's right, she said, a smile in her voice. *Let's dance, Timothy.*

But I don't know how, he thought, blinking, trying to pull away. *I never went to any of the high school dances over at Jackson. I just don't know how.*

The Blue Lady laughed, gripping his hands tightly. *Oh, but you do now, Timothy. Yes you do.* At that moment she pulled him closer, Tim slipping into her arms. She was soft, but strong, too. And her head leaned against his shoulder. She smelled nice. *Keep your eyes closed for now. Listen to the music. It will talk to your feet. Listen and feel.*

He listened...He felt. Then, they began to dance, slowly at first, Tim a little stiff and tentative. But after a few minutes he began to catch on, the appeal of the music seeming to grip and lead him.

Relax, give yourself up.

He could indeed do it.

Around and around, they danced on the stage, as one. Gracefully. And the music played on—"Hotel California," and "You've Lost That Lovin Feelin," and "Me And Bobby McGee," and "Desperado,"—playing all of his favorites. It was too wonderful.

She whispered in his ear, *You can open your eyes now, Timothy.*

He blinked, staring into a perfectly lovely face, her sparkling eyes matching the color of her emerald gown. The moon overhead was shining down on them like a spotlight, as they laughed and twirled about like TV dancers on the stage, Tim and the Blue Lady, the magic invading them in the cool evening air under the twinkling stars. The magic, the magic, the magic...

«««—»»»

Despite the customary 72-hour waiting period, the Amador County Sheriff ignored the missing person statute after Liam Shaw's concerned late night phone call; and early the next morning, he sent over three of his deputies to Marshall Creek. All day the lawmen led search parties of volunteers through the dilapidated buildings, abandoned mining junk, and open shafts surrounding the dying town, searching for the missing young man.

But Mr. Spinoza was too crippled up to scramble around with any of the search parties. Instead, he checked out the park at 9:00 a.m., hoping to find Timmy there. He was positive the conscientious boy would show up for work, that he'd find him cleaning the restrooms or mowing the lawn. But Timmy wasn't anywhere around the park.

In fact, the grounds were empty.

Completely empty, except for a gray squirrel chattering over at the gazebo.

Mr. Spinoza shuffled closer to the bandstand. *Hmmm—needs paint*, he thought, stopping at the foot of the stairs up to the platform, looking over the structure, then noticing the new addition in the middle of the stage.

Looked like Timmy had recently drug up one of the old rough sculptures to the gazebo from the Quonset hut down near the creek. Mr. Spinoza shook his head, thinking, *Old Man Shaw had been right locking this stuff up years ago—most of it nothing but lumpy blobs of poorly casted metal.* He shook his head, snorting dismissively, and saying to himself: *Modern art, who needs it?* But he peered more closely at the piece, not really remembering this one, which didn't look too bad actually. Nope, not really so abstract as the others...Looked like a pair of dancers, twirling around with smiles on their faces.

DINOSAUR DAY

GARY A. BRAUNBECK

Well, you got some idea of what happened then or else you wouldn't be here talking to me now, would you? Don't look at me like that. Every couple of years one of you new reporters over at the *Ally* stumbles on that old story and then comes around asking your questions, so if you don't mind I'll tell it in my own way, thanks very much.

Besides, this has got nothing to do with me. Not really. This is about a couple of folks I used to know and the nice little kid they had who they didn't much like and so did everything they could to horse-whip the nice right out of him. I understand all about the so-called "tough-love" approach to raising a child, but I think these folks carried it a little too far. Seems to me more and more folks these days want their kid to pop out of the womb fully-raised and don't much have the patience or care to take the time to teach them things, instill values and such. They let the movies and video games and cable channels do all of that for them, or else the belt and fist, then wonder why in hell it is every so often a kid or two walks into their school and opens up with a Howitzer or rocket-launcher or something. I'm getting off the subject, sorry. My mind wanders a bit these days. Got that tape recorder running? Good.

Jackson Banks is the name. Appreciate it if you spelled it right this time. I've lived in Cedar Hill all my life, including the last six years here at the Healthcare Center. Got a nice private apartment-

389

style unit all to myself, round-the-clock care, and—I'm proud to say—money in the bank, thanks to the retirement package I had waiting when I punched the clock for the last time at Miller Tool & Die almost a decade ago. That's where I knew Don Hogan. Him and me worked the line there. On the job Don seemed a decent-enough fellow, hard-working, friendly, never what you'd call antisocial. We'd go out for some beers and burgers with the other fellows after the shift and bitch about the foreman's brown nose or some such—you know, the usual guys-after-work kind of talk. We'd make jokes about the wives (except me, my Maggie had passed on the year before and the fellahs were always careful not to make jokes about wives buying the farm), piss and moan about the economy (when you work the line in a place like Cedar Hill, the economy's always in the crapper), and then get on to things like sports.

That's when something about Don would change. Other guys, they'd be talking about the game that had been on TV over the weekend or what OSU's chances were of winning the national championship, and Don, he'd talk about this some, but then the other fellahs'd get on about their kids; so-and-so's boy was going out for football at Cedar Hill Catholic this year, or such-and-such's daughter was making a name for herself on the Blessed Sacrament volleyball team, that sort of thing. That's when Don'd clam up. Oh, he'd listen and nod his head and ask questions, but you could never get him to talk about what sports his own son was into. There was a reason for that, but I need to tell you about something else first, so bear with me.

This was back in 1970. We still had boys over in Vietnam and the Kent State shootings were so fresh the wound hadn't even begun to scab over yet. Our involvement in Vietnam had been good for *Ohio's* economy but not so hot for Cedar Hill's. We didn't have any major manufacturing plants that could fill military contracts fast enough to suit Washington, so most of that went to places like Columbus and Dayton. Even back then the industrial heart of the city was starting to murmur (it wouldn't ever completely stop, but it's been on life-support since the mid-80's) and the city needed some kind of new industry to come in and boost the local economy. So Cedar Hill got into the gravel business.

See, there was this rock quarry a couple miles out past the old county home that had gone under during the Great Depression. For decades it'd just been sitting there, this big-ass hole in the ground, no use whatsoever, except during the rainy season when it'd fill with water and high-school kids'd go out there to skinny-dip and smoke dope. Well, the city leased this land to a gravel company, and they came in with their Allis Chalmers and their feeder hoppers, radial stackers, jaw crushers, and a couple hundred jobs to fill, and set about the business of digging the living shit out of that quarry. Now, they had this one piece of equipment called a PIP (short for Portable Impactor Plant) that was basically a sixteen-wheeled horizontal hydraulic pile-driver. They fired this bad boy up every Sunday afternoon and the operator'd drive it up to one of the quarry's lower walls and start hammering away. One hit from the impactor would go about twenty feet into the wall, and inside of a couple hours, there'd be tons of rocks and boulders for the workers to go at on Monday. Thing is, it made a noise the likes of which shook the ground and rattled windows over a good quarter of the town. Imagine an hour or two of continuous sonic booms. It wasn't so bad for folks who lived far away from the area, but if you lived anywhere near the north side of Cedar Hill, it felt like bombs going off in your backyard.

I know this last part because Don Hogan and his family lived on the north side, and every Monday he'd come in to work with another list of things that had happened during the previous Sunday. Mostly it was minor stuff like windows rattling or his wife's glassware being shook off a shelf, but it was Don's kid usually provided him with the biggest complaints.

"I swear to Christ," he'd say, "that damn kid's afraid of his own shadow. Yesterday, when they started in over at the quarry, he comes running into the house all crying and shaking because he thinks there are giant monsters coming. I keep telling Cathy not to let him stay up on Friday nights and watch Chiller Theater, but does she listen to me? *Hell* no. Then we gotta put up with him having nightmares and shit and thinking that giant monsters are out there walking around Cedar Hill every Sunday afternoon. I don't know what we're gonna do with the likes of him, I really don't."

The likes of him. That's just what he said, and in those four little words I knew right away that Don and Cathy Hogan didn't much like their own son. I felt for the kid, I did, but how a man manages his own house is his own business and it ain't nobody else's place to tell him how to do things otherwise.

I got to meet his kid a couple of weeks later. There was a company picnic out at Mound Builder's Park that Sunday, and rare as it was for the company to shell out any extra money for its employees' benefit, everyone came and brought their families with them. (You offer an afternoon of free food and beer and soda pop, you'd better watch out.) Anyway, Don's kid was named Kyle. He was seven. A small, thin, fair-haired and -skinned nervous kid who wore glasses and spent most of the afternoon with his nose buried in a stack of comic books while the other kids played games and sports. He struck me as having a lot on the ball, had those kind of eyes where there was always something going on behind them. None of the other kids paid him much mind, which seemed like something he was used to, so he'd brought the comic books along.

I wandered over to where he was sitting and introduced myself. I have to tell you, he was one courteous and well-mannered little guy. He stood up and shook my hand all adult-like and said it was a pleasure to meet me. "It's a real pleasure to meet you, sir." Said it just like that.

"I work at the plant with your dad," I said. "He talks about you a lot." Which was within spitting distance of a lie, but I didn't think it my place to tell this kid that his dad hardly ever talked about him, except to make fun of him.

Kyle seemed to sense right off I was white-washing something, because he got this look in his eyes like he *wanted* to believe me—it would've been the greatest thing in the world if his dad *did* talk proud of him, you could just tell the kid wanted that more than anything—but then he looked over to where the other kids were deep into a serious ball game, saw the way his dad was cheering the kids on and not looking over in his direction, not even once, and his whole body kind of deflated.

"What'cha reading there?" I asked, pointing to the stack of comics.

"Just comics."

"Anything good?"

He shrugged. "*Ghost Rider*, mostly. I think he's a neat hero."

"Ever read *Green Lantern*?"

"No, sir."

"How about *Prince Namor, the Sub-Mariner?*"

"You know about *Sub-Mariner*?" Ought to've seen the way he looked at me right then. There's a grown-up who reads comics? What's the world coming to?

So I sat down next to him and we talked about Prince Namor and Spider-Man and Hawk-Man and monster movies and the like (I had a nephew who was really into those things so, being a good uncle, I stayed current on important matters such as these), and somewhere in there I happened to look down and see that one of Kyle's shoes had a thicker sole than the other one, and that's when I realized, genius that I am, that he had a club foot. Turns out he also had asthma, because he had to use his inhaler once when he got real excited talking about *The Green Hornet* and lost his breath.

"So what'cha want to be when you grow up, Kyle?" I asked after he'd settled down and got his breath back.

"I wanna...I wanna write stories. About spaceships and monsters and ghosts and things, like that Rod Serling does."

"You watch them *Twilight Zone* re-runs, do you?"

"Uh-huh. And that one movie? *Night Gallery*? A man on television said that they're gonna make a weekly series out of that this year. That'll be so *cool*. So I'm gonna be a writer."

"That'll make your folks proud," I said because it seemed like the kind of thing you ought to say to a kid. Then Kyle looked over at his folks, at the way they were cheering the other kids on, and he started to cry.

I felt about an inch tall right then. Here I'd come over to give the kid some company, cheer him up and make sure he wasn't feeling too lonely, and I wind up reducing him to tears. Me and Maggie, we never had any kids, but I'd like to think if we'd had, we would've been real supportive of whatever dreams they found appealed to them. I'd've been damned proud to have me a kid who wanted to be a writer. Ain't nothing better to me than to spend the weekend curled up with a good book, nosir. I read Raymond Chandler and Ray Bradbury and writers like that who tell stories like they're reciting poetry. Never much good with words myself, I admired that, and I thought it was just terrific that Kyle wanted to write and I told him so but it didn't stop him from crying and trying to turn away so I wouldn't see it.

"Don't your folks think that's a good idea?" I asked him, realizing that I was about to cross a line that men don't talk about among themselves, the line where you go from being just an outsider to someone who knows their private business. It's one thing when you're invited to cross the line; it's another thing altogether when you take it upon yourself to do the crossing, but no way in hell was I just gonna get up and walk away from this kid with his inhaler and his club foot and nervous ways. My guess was everybody'd been walking away from him at times like this for most of his life and probably sleeping the sleep of the just after. No snowflake in an avalanche ever feels responsible.

I looked around to see if anybody was watching us, then reached out and put my hand on Kyle's shoulder. "Hey, c'mon now, it's all right."

"No it isn't," he said. "Mom and Dad, they think I'm useless—that's what Dad's always saying. 'You're useless.' I wish I could be a ball-player but I can't run too good, and I can't always catch my breath."

"Those things aren't your fault, though, Kyle. You can't help that you were born with problems like those."

He shrugged his shoulders. "I'm a sissy."

"Why, just because you don't like the things other kids do?"

"Uh-huh." Said so seriously that I knew deep in his heart he believed it. It was easy to understand why: if you were a male in Cedar Hill and wanted to be accepted by the other fellahs, you had to be a White, Athletic, Semi-Articulate, Beer-Drinking Poon-Tang Wrangler who drove a pickup with at least one hunting rifle displayed in the back window, or the son of a man like that. If you were like Kyle, though, if you were a poor, blue-collar, crooked-toothed, skinny, four-eyed, club-footed asthmatic who was more interested in comic books and *Night Gallery* and spaceships than in sports and fighting and hunting, well, then, you were a sissy, a queer, an easy target for ridicule because you couldn't fight back. Don't get me wrong, there's a lot of decent folks in this community, but there's also more than enough assholes to go around—and Don Hogan was definitely an asshole. So was his wife, but I didn't find that out for sure until later, and by then…

Okay, so here I am in the park that afternoon and Kyle's crying because his dad don't think much of him or what he wants to be when he grows up. "He says it's stupid," Kyle said. "He says that only smart people can write books an' make any money an' I'm not smart, I'm a sissy who can't do anything an' he says…he says that he's ashamed of me."

I didn't know what to say to him about that. I had half a mind to march over and knock ol' Don's teeth right down his throat, but that'd probably come back on Kyle real hard so I just stayed put.

"Do *you* think it's stupid?" I asked.

"I think I'd be a good writer. I already wrote a bunch of stories."

"Ever show 'em to your folks?"

"They don't want to see them. Mom says she can't read without her glasses but she never *looks* for them so she can read my stories. Once I found 'em for her so she could read a story I wrote about the people who live in the caves on the moon, an' she...she smacked me hard in the face. She said I was being smart with her, but *I wasn't*. I *swear* I wasn't."

"Maybe she was having a bad day. I'm sure she didn't mean it." I was trying to give Cathy the benefit of a doubt. The only thing harder than being a blue-collar worker in this town is being the wife of one. It was that way back in 1970 and it hasn't changed much today, you ask me. Most of the gals in this town, they're brought to not to expect much out of life and so they don't. You get yourself a high-school education (Cedar Hill has the lowest graduation require ments in the state), find yourself a job, and if you're lucky you marry a man with a steady job and do what you have to to make a good home for you and yours—and if that means having to back down and suffer his occasional cruelties, that's just part and parcel of marriage. So I gave Cathy Hogan the benefit of a doubt.

"They'll come around, Kyle," I said, hoping he believed it because I for one had my doubts. "I bet they'll come around and be really proud of you."

"Dad scares me."

Didn't quite know how to take that. "Scares you how?"

"He likes scaring me. Sometimes he comes into my room at night after I'm asleep and holds a pillow over my face until I wake up. He makes me fight him off 'cause he says I need to learn to fight on account of I'm such a weakling. And sometimes he'll sneak up behind me and shout and make me jump. He laughs at me then. Says I gotta...what is it? 'Grow a spine.' That's what he says."

The ball game was really heating up now, folks were on their feet and shouting, whistling, making all kinds of noise, and then they started up over at the quarry with PIP. Everybody winced and looked over in the direction of the quarry, shaking their heads and complaining about the noise. Fact of the matter is, the noise and vibrations weren't so bad in the park, not so that the day was going to be ruined. Seemed to me that if anything was going to do that, it was the dark rain-clouds in the sky. I decided right then it was time for Kyle and me to go over and get ourselves a couple of hamburgers, so I turned back to him and said, "Hey, why don't we mosey—"

The rest of it died in my throat.

Kyle was rigid as a board and pale as a corpse. I've never seen a kid that scared before. He was holding his breath and his eyes were so wide I thought they might pop right out of his skull.

"Kyle, hey buddy, what's wrong?" I laid a hand on his arm and felt how he was shaking, the kind of shakes you usually think of when someone talks about getting the DTs; this boy was shaking right down to the insides of his bones.

And he still wasn't breathing.

"Hey, buddy," I said, trying to work his inhaler from his pocket, "are you all right? Do you need—"

"*They're coming!*" he screamed so loud that half the folks watching the game turned around to look at us.

"Kyle, hey, what—"

"*They're coming, they're coming, THEY'RE COMING!*" And now he was up on his feet and looking around him like a bank robber who'd just run out to hear the police sirens screaming down on his ass and I knew he was gonna bolt so I tried to grab hold of his arm again but he was so far into panic I didn't have a chance and then he was off like a shot screaming they were coming they were coming everybody had to hide everybody had to get away before they got here because they'd kill us all and by then I was on my feet and going after him but there's a lot of difference between the speed of a terrified seven-year-old even if he does have a club foot and a fifty-year-old factory worker with a tricky back but now the game was stalled and some of the players got into the act and just as I gained some ground one of the teenagers had easily tackled Kyle and knocked his glasses off and Kyle was thrashing around and screaming at the top of his lungs and crying so hard that snot flew out in ribbons and covered his face which was getting redder and redder by the second and all the time he kept shrieking on about how they were coming they were coming didn't anybody hear them and look up there can't you see their shadows starting to block out the sun oh god please everybody has to hide before they kill us all—

—and then he stopped screaming because he couldn't get air into his lungs; even from where I was I could hear the way he was wheezing, how his throat was making all these wet crackling sounds, so I pushed my way past the crowd of gawkers who'd gathered round and had to shove the teenager who'd tackled Kyle off the boy because the idiot was parked with his knees on Kyle's chest, then I had Kyle sitting up and was holding his inhaler for him but he was still thrashing around in panic and by now Don and Cathy had come over, both of them looking for all the world like the most humiliated couple God had ever created, looking more embarrassed for themselves than concerned over their boy, and I managed to get the inhaler in Kyle's mouth and gave him a couple of pumps but he didn't get it all, he jerked his head away and tried to scream as he saw the shadow that was falling over the park from the rain clouds, I knew that's what was scaring him because he pointed to the shadow and croaked out something like "...sore hay..." and then his eyes rolled up into his head and his legs shuddered and he wet himself and passed out.

An ambulance had to be called to come get him, and they hooked him up to some oxygen and loaded him into the back and took off for Memorial. By now it was starting to rain and what folks weren't running for one of the covered shelters or their cars were gathered around Don and Cathy offering their sympathies and trying to think of things to say to make them feel better about being so embarrassed by their boy.

All I could do was stand there and shake my head, listening to the constant *whump-whump-whump!* from PIP at the quarry and looking at Kyle's inhaler that I still held in my hand.

«««—»»»

By the time I got over to the emergency room the rain was coming down pretty hard. It was lightning and thundering to beat the band, too. I got inside and found Don and Cathy in the waiting room, both of them smoking one cigarette after another (you could still smoke in hospitals back then). I wondered if they both smoked like that around the house, knowing how it would affect Kyle's asthma, but I didn't say anything about it. Didn't seem like the right time for a lecture.

"How is he?" I asked.

Cathy just gave me a look that would have frozen fire and went back to her smoking. Don looked at her none-too pleasantly, then shook his head and said, "They got him back there but we haven't been told anything yet."

I handed him the inhaler. He looked at it like it was a piece of dog shit, then snatched it out of my hand and whirled on Cathy. "How many goddamn times have I *told* that kid to keep this on him? Christ! Sometimes I think he doesn't have the sense God gave an ice-cube!"

"He had it on him," I said. "He just dropped it when he took off like that." I didn't care about this lie, not one little bit.

"Doesn't make any difference," Don said, not looking away from Cathy. "You gonna say something or just sit there like a knothole on a log?"

"I'm sorry that he embarrassed us in front of all your buddies," she said.

"You got that right. Kid's been nothing but a pain in the ass since he came into this world. If you hadn't listened to that quack doctor of yours, putting you on Thalidomide—"

"—which I stopped taking after the first month. I heard the stories. Besides, it made me feel sick all the time."

"You shouldn't've took it in the first place! If you hadn't, maybe we'd've had a normal kid with good feet and healthy lungs and—"

"—so now it's *my* fault Kyle's sickly? Oh, you're really a fucking prize sometimes, Donald, you know that?"

"I'll thank you not to—"

They both realized I was still standing there and got real quiet. I was trying to think of a graceful way to leave when the doctor came out and told us that Kyle was going to be all right but they were going to keep him overnight to just to make sure. "It was a fairly serious episode," he said. "It could have been fatal. Has he been taking his medications?"

"When we can afford them," said Cathy. "But we always make sure he's got his inhaler." She let out a long stream of smoke, and I knew the doctor was thinking the same thing I had when I saw them puffing away.

"Would you like to see him?"

"Not particularly," said Don. "I have to go to work in the morning to make the money to pay for this goddamned hospital visit." He looked at Cathy, who wouldn't look at him, then turned to me and said, "You two were getting all buddy-buddy there. Why don't you go back and see him, Jackson?"

"Think I will, thank you."

They had him off in a room by himself, all hooked up to an oxygen tank with a mask over his nose and mouth. He looked fifty years old, all pale and sweaty with dark half-crescents under his eyes. He smiled when he saw it was me and waved.

"Hello, yourself, little man." I reached into my coat pocket and brought out the comic books he'd left back at the park. "I grabbed these up for you. Didn't think you'd want them getting ruined in the rain."

He nodded his head and reached up for them, but the IV tube and needle wouldn't let him reach very far so I laid them on the bed next to him. "That new issue of *Ghost Rider* got pretty wet, so I stopped off and bought you a new copy, plus they had this Special Issue just come out, so I got that for you, too."

He looked at the comics, then at me, and smiled under his mask. He looked like he was gonna cry again and I didn't know that I could handle that, so I pulled up a chair next to his bed and said, in as light a tone of voice as I could manage, "So…they treating you good here so far?"

He nodded.

"I half expected you to be conked out after what happened. Gave us all quite the scare, is what you did."

He pointed to something in the corner. There was a small black-and-white television on a wheeled stand, tuned to the local PBS channel. Even though the sound was turned down pretty low, I recognized the theme they play at the start of the *National Geographic* shows.

"You want me to turn it up a little bit?"

Nod.

I did, then adjusted the rabbit ears for a better picture, rolled it closer to the bed, and sat back down next to him. "You know, I watch this sometimes, too" I told him, which was true. "This *is* what you wanna watch, right?"

Nod, nod.

"Okay, then."

It was a special about this thing called the "Bog Man" they'd found in the Netherlands. The narrator said the man had been buried in this peat bog for over two thousand years. They had film of it. His brow was furrowed and there was this serene expression on his face. He wore a leather cap that reminded me of my own work hat and lay on his side. His feet and hands were shriveled (I wondered how seeing those shriveled feet made Kyle feel about his own problems but didn't say anything) but aside from that, he looked no different from any number of guys that worked the line. Put a metal lunch bucket in his grip and it might've been me two thousand years from now.

The narrator kept going on about how well-preserved the Bog Man was, and likened it to a similar discovery made in Siberia a few years back when they'd found a fully-preserved Mammoth.

Sometime in there Kyle reached out and took hold of my hand and gave it a little squeeze. I squeezed back.

He fell asleep after about fifteen minutes, so I got up, made sure the comics weren't going to fall off the bed, and then did something that surprised even me; I bent down, brushed some of the hair from his forehead, and gave him a little kiss there. It seemed right somehow. I started to walk away as quiet as I could and then bumped into a clipboard hanging at the foot of his bed. I caught it just in time. As I was putting it back I glanced at what the doctor had written, then read some of the typed material.

On top of everything else, Kyle was diabetic. I felt my heart jump a little. My Maggie had been diabetic, it was what killed her eventually. Thinking this made me sad and I missed her all the more for the thinking, then I saw something about "…macular degeneration," and "…visual hallucinations commensurate with Charles Bonnet Syndrome." I knew that it was pronounced *Shaz Bone-eh* because my Maggie'd had the same problem. You see things that aren't there. She used to tell me toward the end that she always saw this well-dressed Negro butler following me around the house, then she'd joke about how we could use some extra help, seeing as how she'd be blind soon enough. She was totally blind the last ten days of her life.

And Kyle Hogan was slowly losing his sight just like her.

There's some anger that takes on a life outside your power to do anything about it, and sometimes this anger comes wrapped up in sadness like a mummy in bandages. I was that kind of angry. Didn't seem fair, this great kid who held my hand and smiled at me having so many problems and not even ten years old yet. Hell, I've know people *my* age who couldn't handle half of what this kid was dealing with on a daily basis. Don and Cathy had themselves one great boy here, and needed to be reminded of it. So I put the chart back and marched out to the waiting room, all set to cross yet another line.

Don was by himself. "Cathy and me had some words and she took off," he said. "I was hoping I could trouble you for a lift."

"No problem." I figured it'd give me a chance to say a few things to him.

We'd been driving along a couple of minutes when Don said, "I suppose Kyle gave you quite an earful today. Kid'll talk your head off you give him half a chance."

"Right before he passed out in the park, he tried to say something to me. Sounded like 'sore hay' but that don't make any sense."

"'Dinosaur Day,' is what it was. Sunday is Dinosaur Day."

"That something else you use to scare him with?" I asked, making sure I put a hard emphasis on the *else* so Don'd know that I knew things.

He eyeballed me for a second, then grinned. "Yeah, it is. He hears old PIP start up and feels the ground start shaking and he thinks it's monsters, so, yeah, I go with it. I tell him that it's the sound of big old dinosaurs waking up and going for a walk. I tell him that on Dinosaur Day he needs to behave himself or else I'm gonna lock him outside so the dinosaurs can step on him or eat him. Goddamn sissy thinks that pile-driver is a dinosaur's footsteps. No kid of mine's gonna have an imagination like that. Won't do him a damn bit of good later on in life."

"But he's a great kid, Don. He's smart, and he's sensitive—"

"Don't give me that 'sensitive' shit, okay? 'Sensitive' and ten cents'll get you a cup of coffee over at the L&K Restaurant. Big deal. He's a sickly kid who ain't never gonna get any better and on account of the way he is, Cathy doesn't want to have another one…so I don't get to have a boy that I can cheer on while he plays football, or teach him how to duck-hunt, or how to drive—no. I got the likes of him to deal with. You think I don't know how the other guys at work are gonna look at me come tomorrow? 'Too bad about Don, having him-

self a boy like that. Makes you wonder about his being a real man.'
And don't tell me they ain't gonna think that. A man's son is the
measure of his father, and I don't want anyone thinking that Kyle is
any measure of me."

"That may be the lousiest thing I've ever heard anyone say."

"I'll thank you to mind your own business, Jackson."

"For god's sake, man, don't you see what you're doing to that
kid? Scarin' him like that all the time and—"

"—and if he's gonna stand any chance in this world, then
someone *has* to scare him! Don't you get it? I got to put the fear
inside of him so he'll know what life is like. I figure there's only so
much that a kid *can* be scared before it becomes a permanent part of
him, and then he won't be scared of nothing anymore, and *that's* the
only way he's gonna survive in this life. He's got to have the fear
within him."

"You'd best watch out, Don. Things like that have a way of
coming back on you."

"What the hell would you know about it? You and Maggie never
even *had* any kids."

Goddamn good thing we were on his street already or else
he'd've had himself one long walk home.

«««—»»»

Don and I avoided each other at work for most of the next week,
but we weren't what you'd call obvious about it. We sat at different
tables during break, and when the other guys went out after work, I'd
beg off if Don was going along, or he'd make some excuse about getting home to tend to Kyle if I was gonna be there. I don't think the
other guys suspected anything other than Don being embarrassed
about his boy.

An offer of voluntary overtime came up for that Sunday, and I
was the first to get my name on the list. Don signed up for it, as well.
I was getting ready to head home that Friday when he stopped me
near the doors and said, "I hope everything's okay with you and me."

I shrugged. "How's Kyle feeling?"

"He should be able to go back to school next week. Listen,
uh…Cathy's gonna be using the car Sunday to take Kyle over to see

his grandma. Could I get you to swing by and pick me up on your way in?"

"Don't see why not. I've got some comic books that I think Kyle might enjoy."

"*You* read comic books?"

"Bet'cher ass I do. Some of the best stories being told anywhere. Kyle got me interested in *Ghost Rider.* You ought to give it a read sometime. Might teach you a thing or two."

He stared at me for a minute to see if I was joking. When he saw that I wasn't he broke out laughing anyway, pretending that I *was* joking. I went along with him thinking that.

"See you Sunday," I said, punching the clock and heading out to my car.

That Saturday night I sat down to watch another special on PBS about how childrens' personalities are shaped during the first ten years of their lives. A lot of it was a bit over my head, but then they got to this one psychologist who started talking about something called "...consensual reality." Way I understood it is that a child is taught from its first day on earth to see the same world their parents see. That seemed simple enough to me, but then the psychologist showed this film of a nine-year-old girl who'd been raised by her mother who was a schizophrenic. The girl had even worse delusions than her mother did, because she'd been taught to see the world her mother saw and once she got old enough to let her imagination kick in, she "amplified the disorder" because she thought she was dealing with the world her mother gave her, "...one of sleeplessness and incoherence and dementia and paranoia." She was ruined. It broke my heart.

I started to drift off. It's strange the connections your mind will make when you're falling asleep. I thought about the Bog Man and how he looked like the guys I worked with. Then his face became Don Hogan's and he got up out of the bog and said his name was Chaz Bone-eh. He started screaming at Kyle. Kyle was crying because he was scared and was trying to tell Chaz he could see monsters. Chaz said that was good because monsters were real and they were coming for Kyle. Then he lay back down in the bog and his face became mine, so I curled up with my lunch bucket next to the Wooly Mammoth and went to sleep, waiting for someone to find me in a couple thousand years.

«««—»»»

They were screaming at the Hogan house when I knocked on the door.

"...have my goddamn lunch ready on time is all I ask!"

"So because you got to work today that means I can't sleep in an extra half-hour?"

"Bitch! I got a long day ahead of me and—"

I knocked louder and they got real quiet. Cathy answered the door in her bathrobe. She glared at me and then blew smoke in my face. "Your ride's here." She walked away, leaving the door open but not inviting me inside. Don peered out of the kitchen doorway and shouted, "Be with you in a minute, Jackson."

"I got them comics for Kyle," I said. "Mind if I come in and give them to him?"

"Oh, for chrissakes!" said Cathy. "That's just what he needs, more comic books!"

"I'll thank you not to speak to my friend like that," shouted Don.

"Screw him—and screw you, too! And screw that little useless piece of shit of a son you've got!"

That's when I decided Cathy Hogan was as big an asshole as her husband.

"You go on up," said Don to me. "His room's right at the end of the hall."

I knocked on Kyle's door and he opened it just a crack, then smiled when he saw it was me. "Hello, Mr. Banks."

"Hey, Kyle. Got some more comics here for you. *Creepy* and *Eerie* and an issue of *Famous Monsters.*"

"Thank you very much." He seemed a bit nervous to me. No wonder, if the screaming I'd heard from his parents was the norm around here.

"You feeling better?" I asked, ruffling his hair.

"A little."

Downstairs Cathy was shouting, "Pimento loaf's all we got for sandwiches! I haven't been to the groceries yet."

"I *hate* that shit!" Don shouted back about twice as loud.

"Then fuckin' go hungry today, I don't care!" This followed by cupboard doors being slammed and a glass being broke.

Kyle looked at me and shrugged. "They yell a lot, I guess."

I nodded. "So you'll be visiting with your Grandma today?"

He brightened. "Yeah! My gramma's really cool."

"Treat you nice, does she?"

"Yes, sir."

It was good to know that there was someone in this world who was good to this kid.

I started to say something else, but then PIP kicked in over at the quarry and every window in the house shook. I checked my watch and saw that it was only nine-thirty in the morning; they usually didn't get started until noon on Sundays.

"Now, don't you go gettin' all excited, Kyle," I said. "That's just—"

I got real quiet when I looked back up.

When I was over in Korea during the war, my unit came across a little boy whose entire village had been wiped out the night before. He'd been the only survivor, and our interpreter told us that the kid had seen the whole slaughter. I never forgot the look on that kid's face. There was this gruesome *calm* to his features that somehow got worse when you looked into his eyes; he was staring at something only he could see, something so far away and so terrible there would never be words to describe it, so he'd just decided to embrace it.

The look on Kyle's face made the one on that kid's seem like a grin over a birthday cake.

"What is it, buddy?" I said.

"You need to leave, Mr. Banks."

The *whump-whump-whump* from PIP was getting a lot louder and a lot stronger.

"Are you okay?"

"I'm fine, sir," he said, taking hold of my hand and leading me out of the room. "But you really need to go outside."

"You sure you're okay?" I asked him as he led me out onto the front porch. I figured there was something he wanted to tell me and didn't want his folks to hear. 'Course, he could've done that upstairs, but that look on his face and the hollow sound in his voice told me this was serious, so I went along.

"I'm fine, Mr. Banks. See? I'm not scared anymore."

The next bunch of whumps from PIP were so violent I thought for a second the sidewalk was going to crack open. I could hear Cathy screaming at Don about how it was his fault they couldn't afford to move someplace where this goddamned noise wouldn't shake loose her fillings every week, and Don shouted something back at her that I couldn't make out but I heard the slap clear enough, and by then I couldn't hear or feel anything else but the noise and vibrations from PIP.

Kyle yanked me off the porch and all but dragged me to my car. "You have to get in now," he shouted. "Please, Mr. Banks."

"What the hell is wrong, Kyle?"

He stared at me, then blinked. "Can't you see it?" He pointed over the roof of the house.

"See what?"

Whump-Whump-WHUMP!

"Please get in your car, Mr. Banks." He opened my door and started pushing me. He was a lot stronger than he looked. Before I could say anything more, he slammed closed the door and turned back to house, looking at something over the roof, and then the noise became these explosions that rocked the ground so bad I actually hit the top of my head against the inside roof of the car and by the time I got my vision cleared there was another series of explosions that shattered every window of the house and then another one that shook the trees and then another one that caused one of the streetlights to come loose and fall across the middle of the sidewalk in a shower of sparks and broken glass and by this time I was so scared I couldn't move so I sat there gripping the wheel and wishing to hell I'd never said yes to coming over here today but wishing and ten cents'll get you a cup of coffee and then Kyle spread his arms wide and lifted them over his head and started laughing and the explosions kept coming closer and harder and louder and faster and I didn't think that PIP could work that fast and then another part of my brain said *I don't think it's PIP* and I closed my eyes as the vibrations rattled by bones and my dentures and everything there was inside me right down to the stalks of my eyes and all the time I could hear Kyle laughing laughing laughing—

—and then it all stopped.

No noise.

No vibrations.

No sound or movement at all.

I didn't want to open my eyes, I was still that scared.

GARY A. BRAUNBECK

"Mommy, Daddy," called out Kyle. "Come look. It's *so cool!*"

I heard the front door open and then I heard Cathy and Don start yelling for Kyle to get his ass back up on the goddamned porch they were going to give him what-for real good and then Cathy gasped and Don shouted *"Jesus H.-fucking-Christ!"* and then they both screamed but that was drowned under the sound that came next.

It was a roar from something so big and so angry that it swallowed nightmares whole for breakfast.

I pressed my head against the steering wheel and whispered Maggie's name over and over.

Then the roar came again, twice as loud as before, and then Kyle laughed again and the whole world became noise and thunder and one massive explosion and then there was a sound like a jet engine sucking in all the air from the earth and then there was a silence the likes of which I hope never finds me again.

I don't have to tell you what I saw when I finally opened my eyes, do I? You've seen the pictures of the house, the way the whole front of it was smashed to rubble. There wasn't enough left of Don and Cathy Hogan to scrape up with a shovel. The official explanation was that PIP had accidentally hit on a batch of dynamite embedded in one of the quarry walls and caused an explosion that sent rocks and boulders flying, and that one of them landed on the Hogan's house and killed them. Which would've explained the indentations in the ground, all six-feet-wide and three-feet-deep of each one, except that there was no boulder. They say it must have hit with such impact that it broke apart, because there was plenty of rubble. The fact that the gravel company denied any such accident and that PIP was unharmed didn't come into it. Every house on that street lost its windows that Sunday. A couple of family pets were killed by furniture toppling over on top of them. One woman had a heart attack from the noise. The gravel company got the pants sued off them and pulled up stakes and Cedar Hill was no longer in the gravel business by fall.

I asked you once already to not look at me like that. I know how it sounds, believe me. It's been over thirty years ago that it happened and not a day goes by that I don't go over it again, and every blessed time I do I keep coming back to the same conclusion. I told Don that putting that kind of fear inside a boy would come back on him somehow. I *told* him.

Kyle's doing fine. Went to live with his grandmother who made sure he got the right kind of care. He still wears glasses, but he ain't lost his sight yet. He writes me every month and calls me every other weekend. He's real excited about how well his new book's doing—you know that boy's had three Number Two bestsellers in the last few years? Seems folks can't get enough of his spaceships and monsters. He sends me copies of every new book and story he publishes, and he always inscribes them the same way: *To My Buddy Jackson, Who Knows What the Bog Man Knows: It's Always Dinosaur Day.*

He signs him name *Chaz Bone-eh.*

Kid's got a lot on the ball, he does.

ABOUT THE AUTHORS

David Bain is the author of thrillers such as *Gray Lake* and the Will Castleton series (*Death Sight, The Castleton Files, Purgatory Blues, Return to Angel Hill*) which mix crime and the supernatural, as well as several story collections—his boxed set *Until You Can Scream No More* contains more than 700 pages and more than 50 stories. Subscribers to his newsletter—http://smarturl.it/FriendsOfBain—get a free, exclusive Will Castleton story just for signing up, plus a brand new free story every 90 days—you can vote on which story Dave writes next at http://smarturl.it/VoteForBain.

Gary A. Braunbeck is the acclaimed author of the Cedar Hill Cycle of stories and novels that includes *In Silent Graves, Destinations Unknown,* and the forthcoming *A Cracked and Broken Path*. His award-winning non-fiction book, *To Each Their Darkness*, is now being used in some university Creative Writing classes. His short story "Rami Temporalis" was made into the award-winning short film *One of Those Faces*. His work has won 6 Bram Stoker Awards, an International Horror Guild Award, 3 Shocklines "Shocker" Awards, a Black Quill Award, and a World Fantasy Award nomination. He hails from Newark, Ohio (the city that serves as inspiration for his fictional Cedar Hill) and currently lives in Columbus, Ohio where no one has heard of him. As a result, he takes much medication. If you see him at a convention, approach with caution.

Born and raised in Dungarvan, Ireland, **Kealan Patrick Burke** is the Bram Stoker Award-winning author of five novels (*Master of the Moors*, *Currency of Souls*, *Kin*, *The Living*, and *Nemesis: The Death of Timmy Quinn*), over a hundred short stories, four collections (*Ravenous Ghosts*, *The Number 121 to Pennsylvania & Others*, *Theater Macabre*, and *The Novellas*), and editor of four acclaimed anthologies (*Taverns of the Dead*, *Quietly Now: A Tribute to Charles L. Grant*, *Brimstone Turnpike*, and *Tales from the Gorezone*). He also played the male lead in *Slime City Massacre*, director Gregory Lamberson's sequel to his cult B-movie classic *Slime City*, alongside scream queens Debbie Rochon and Brooke Lewis. When not writing, Kealan designs covers for print and digital books through his company Elderlemon Design. To date he has designed covers for books by Richard Laymon, Brian Keene, Scott Nicholson, Bentley Little, William Schoell, and Hugh Howey, to name a few. His short story "Peekers" is currently in development as a feature film from Lionsgate Entertainment.

At present, **Sandy DeLuca** is a full-time writer and painter. She's written and published numerous novels, two poetry collections and several novellas, including the critically acclaimed *Messages From the Dead* and *Descent*. She was a finalist for the Bram Stoker award for poetry in 2001. She lives with three faithful felines in an old Cape Cod House in Rhode Island.

Robert Dunbar is the author of several novels, including *The Pines* and *The Shore*, and the collection of short stories, *Martyrs & Monsters*. His latest project—*Vortex*—is a nonfiction book about the intersection of folklore and horror fiction, which explores some of his major obsessions. To learn more about his work, visit www.uninvitedbooks.com.

The son of teachers, **Greg F. Gifune** was educated in Boston and has lived in various places, including New York City and Peru. Often described as "one of the best writers of his generation" (*Roswell Literary Review* & author Brian Keene) and "among the finest dark suspense writers of our time" (author Ed Gorman) Greg is an acclaimed, internationally published author who has penned several novels and novellas as well as two short story collections. His work has been published all over the world, has been translated into several languages, and has recently garnered interest from Hollywood. His work is consistently praised by critics and readers internationally (including starred reviews in *Publishers Weekly, Library Journal, Kirkus, Midwest Book Review* and others), and his novel *The Bleeding Season* is considered by many to be a modern classic in the horror genre. Also an accomplished editor, for seven years Greg served as Editor-in-Chief of the popular fiction magazines *The Edge* and *Burning Sky*, where he helped launch the careers of many name writers working in various genres today. Greg was also Associate Editor at Delirium Books for three years, and for more than a decade has worked as a freelance novel editor for numerous up-and-coming as well as established professionals. He currently holds the position of Senior Editor at Darkfuse Publications. Greg resides in Massachusetts with his wife Carol, their dogs Dozer and Bella, and a bevy of cats. For more information on his work, visit his official web-site: www.gregfgifune.com or visit him on Facebook.

Christopher Golden is the *New York Times* bestselling, Bram Stoker Award-winning author of such novels as Snowblind, O*f Saints and Shadows, The Myth Hunters, The Boys Are Back in Town* and Strangewood. He has co-written three illustrated novels with Mike Mignola, the first of which, *Baltimore, or, The Steadfast Tin Soldier and the Vampire*, was the launching pad for the Eisner Award-nominated comic book series, *Baltimore*. Golden has also written books for teens and young adults, including the *Body of Evidence* series, *Poison Ink,* and *Soulless*. As an editor, he has worked on the short story anthologies *The New Dead, The Monster's Corner,* and *Dark Duets*, among others. Golden was born and raised in Massachusetts , where he still lives with his family. His original novels have been published in more than fourteen languages in countries around the world. Please visit him at www.christophergolden.com.

Janet Joyce Holden was born in the North of England and lives in Southern California. She is the author of *Carousel* and its upcoming sequel, and writes short stories about otherworldly creatures and things that creep about in the dark. Her blog can be found at http://louis-eldest.livejournal.com

Gerard Houarner works by day at a psychiatric institution and writes at night, mostly about the dark. Recent appearances include stories in the anthologies *Into The Darkness, Eulogies II, Dueling Minds, Torn Realities, Dueling Minds*. Crossroad Press has published ebook editions of *The Beast That Was Max, The Bard of Sorcery* (also available on Audible), and *A Blood of Killers*, with more reprints and new material coming.

Jonathan Janz grew up between a dark forest and a graveyard, and in a way, that explains everything. Brian Keene named his debut novel *The Sorrows* "the best horror novel of 2012." *The Library Journal* deemed his follow-up, *House of Skin*, "reminiscent of Shirley Jackson's *The Haunting of Hill House* and Peter Straub's *Ghost Story*." Samhain Horror published his novel of vampirism and human sacrifice, *The Darkest Lullaby,* in April and his serialized horror novel *Savage Species* this summer. Of *Savage Species*, *Publishers Weekly* said, "Fans of old-school splatterpunk horror—Janz cites Richard Laymon as an influence, and it shows—will find much to relish." His vampire western *Dust Devils* will be released in February, and his sequel to *The Sorrows* (*Castle of Sorrows*) will be published in July 2014. He has also written three novellas (*The Clearing of Travis Coble, Old Order*, and *Witching Hour Theatre*) and several short stories. His primary interests are his wonderful wife and his three amazing children, and though he realizes that every author's wife and children are wonderful and amazing, in this case the cliché happens to be true. You can learn more about Jonathan at www.jonathanjanz.com. You can also find him on Facebook, via @jonathanjanz on Twitter, or on his Goodreads and Amazon author pages.

Brian Keene is the author of over thirty books, including *Darkness on the Edge of Town, Take the Long Way Home, Urban Gothic, Castaways, Dark Hollow, Dead Sea,* and *The Rising*. He also writes comic books such as *The Last Zombie*. His work has been translated into German, Spanish, Polish, Italian, French, and Taiwanese. Several of his novels and stories have been developed for film, including *Ghoul, The Ties That Bind,* and *Fast Zombies Suck*. In addition to writing, Keene also oversees Maelstrom, his own small press publishing imprint specializing in collectible limited editions, via Thunderstorm Books. Keene's work has been praised in such diverse places as *The New York Times,* The History Channel, The Howard Stern Show, CNN.com, *Publisher's Weekly,* Media Bistro, *Fangoria Magazine,* and *Rue Morgue Magazine.* Keene lives in Pennsylvania. You can communicate with him online at www.briankeene.com or on Twitter at @BrianKeene.

Jack Ketchum's short story The Box won a 1994 Bram Stoker Award from the HWA, his story Gone won again in 2000 — and in 2003 he won Stokers for both best collection for *Peaceable Kingdom* and best long fiction for *Closing Time.* He has written over twenty novels and novellas, the latest being *The Woman* and *I'm Not Sam,* both written with director Lucky McKee. Five of his books have been filmed to date—*The Girl Next Door, The Lost, Red, Offspring* and *The Woman,* the last of which won him and McKee the Best Screenplay Award at the Sitges Film Festival in Germany. His stories are collected in The Exit at Toledo Blade Boulevard, Broken on the Wheel of Sex, Sleep Disorder (with Edward Lee), Peaceable Kingdom and Closing Time and Other Stories. His novella The Crossings was cited by Stephen King in his speech at the 2003 National Book Awards. In 2011 he was elected Grand Master by the World Horror Convention. He has four cats.

Champion Mojo Storyteller **Joe R. Lansdale** is the author of over thirty novels and numerous short stories. His work has appeared in national anthologies, magazines, and collections, as well as numerous foreign publications. He has written for comics, television, film, newspapers, and Internet sites. His work has been collected in eighteen short-story collections, and he has edited or co-edited over a dozen anthologies. He has received the Edgar Award, eight Bram Stoker Awards, the Horror Writers Association Lifetime Achievement Award, the British Fantasy Award, the Grinzani Cavour Prize for Literature, the Herodotus Historical Fiction Award, the Inkpot Award for Contributions to Science Fiction and Fantasy, and many others. His novella *Bubba Hotep* was adapted to film by Don Coscarelli, starring Bruce Campbell and Ossie Davis. His story "Incident On and Off a Mountain Road" was adapted to film for Showtime's "Masters of Horror." He is currently co-producing several films, among them *The Bottoms,* based on his Edgar Award-winning novel, with Bill

Paxton and Brad Wyman, and *The Drive-In*, with Greg Nicotero. He is Writer In Residence at Stephen F. Austin State University, and is the founder of the martial arts system Shen Chuan: Martial Science and its affiliate, Shen Chuan Family System. He is a member of both the United States and International Martial Arts Halls of Fame. He lives in Nacogdoches, Texas with his wife, dog, and two cats.

Jonathan Maberry is a *N.Y. Times* bestselling author, four-time Bram Stoker Award winner, and freelancer for Marvel Comics, IDW and Dark Horse comics. His novels include *Extinction Machine, Fire & Ash, Patient Zero* and many others. His award-winning teen novel, *Rot & Ruin*, is now in development for film. He is the editor of *V-Wars*, an award-winning vampire anthology series that is also in development as a comic from IDW; and *Out of Tune*, a forthcoming dark fantasy anthology. Since 1978 he's sold more than 1200 magazine feature articles, 3000 columns, plays, greeting cards, song lyrics, and poetry. He teaches Experimental Writing for Teens, is the founder of the Writers Coffeehouse, and co-founder of The Liars Club. Jonathan is a frequent keynote speaker and guest of honor at genre conventions and writers conferences, often speaking on the craft and business of writing, the publishing industry, social media and other topics. He's a member of the Mystery Writers of America, International Thriller Writers, Horror Writers Association, and the International Association of Media Tie-in Writers. Jonathan lives in Del Mar, California with his wife, Sara Jo and fierce little dog named Rosie. Visit him at www.jonathanmaberry.com

Ronald Malfi is the award-winning author of horror novels, mysteries, and thrillers. In 2009, his crime drama, *Shamrock Alley,* won a Silver IPPY Award and was optioned for film. In 2011, his ghost story/mystery novel, *Floating Staircase,* was nominated by the Horror Writers Association for best novel; the book also won the 2012 IPPY National Gold Medal of Honor. Most recognized for his haunting, literary style and memorable characters, Malfi's dark fiction has gained acceptance among readers of all genres. He currently lives along the Chesapeake Bay, with his wife and daughter, where he is at work on his next book. He can be reached online through his website, ronmalfi.com, or on Facebook and Twitter.

Elizabeth Massie is a Bram Stoker Award- and Scribe Award-winning author of horror novels, short horror fiction, media tie-ins, mainstream fiction, historical novels, and nonfiction. Most recent works include short stories in the anthologies *Vampires Don't Sparkle, Mammoth Book of Ghost Stories by Women, and Shadow Masters,* her zombie novel *Desper Hollow* (Apex Books) and historical horror novel, *Hell Gate* (DarkFuse), and a new middle grade horror series, Ameri-Scares, which has launched with the first two novels - *Virginia: Valley of Secrets,* and *New York: Rips and Wrinkles* (Crossroad Press). Massie the creator of the Skeeryvilletown slew of cartoon zombies, monsters, and other bizarre misfits. In her "spare" time she manages Hand to Hand Vision, a Facebook-based fundraising project she founded to help others during these tough economic times. Massie lives in the Shenandoah Valley of Virginia and shares life and abode with the talented illustrator/artist Cortney Skinner. She can be reached through her website: www.elizabethmassie.com or through Facebook.

C. Dennis Moore is the author of over 60 published short stories and novellas in the speculative fiction genre. Most recent appearances were in the *Vile Things* anthology, *Fiction365.com, Dark Highlands 2, What Fears Become, Dead Bait 3* and *Dark Highways.* His novels are *Revelations* (available in hardcover, trade paperback and ebook formats from Necro Publications), *The Third Floor,* and *The Ghosts of Mertland County.*

James A. Moore is the author of over twenty novels, including the critically acclaimed *Fireworks, Under the Overtree, Blood Red, Deeper,* the *Serenity Falls* trilogy (featuring his recurring anti-hero, Jonathan Crowley), and his recent novels *Blind Shadows* and *Seven Forges.* He has twice been nominated for the Bram Stoker Award and spent three years as an officer in the Horror Writers Association, first as Secretary and later as Vice President. He cut his teeth in the industry writing for Marvel Comics and authoring many role-playing supplements for White Wolf Games, including *Berlin by Night* and *Land of 1,000,000 Dreams,* and the novels *Vampire: House of Secrets* and *Werewolf: Hellstorm.* He currently lives in the suburbs of Atlanta, Georgia. To find out more, visit him at genrefied.blogspot.com or at twitter.com/jamesamoore.

Gene O'Neill lives in the Napa Valley with his wife, Kay. Gene has two degrees, neither having anything to do with writing (or much of anything else). Since 1979, Gene has seen over 120 of his stories published, most notably: two in *The Twilight Zone Magazine*, six in the *Magazine of Fantasy & Science Fiction*, two in *Pulpsmith*, four in *Science Fiction Age*, three in *Cemetery Dance*, and many in specialized publications like *Dragon* and *Starshore*, with numerous anthology placements, including *Borderlands 5* and *Dead End:City Limits*. Stories have been reprinted in France, Spain, and Russia. His short story collection *Taste of Tenderloin* won the Bram Stoker Award in 2010 year for collection, and also garnered a 2009 starred review in *Publishers Weekly*. His most recent story collections are Dance of the Blue Lady & Other Stories, and *In Dark Corners*. His novels include *The Burden of Indigo, Collected Tales of the Baja Express, Shadow of the Dark Angel, Deathflash, Lost Tribe,* and *Not Fade Away*.

Monica J. O'Rourke has published more than one hundred short stories in magazines such as *Postscripts, Nasty Piece of Work, Fangoria, Flesh & Blood, Nemonymous,* and *Brutarian* and anthologies such as *Horror for Good* (for charity), *The Mammoth Book of the Kama Sutra,* and *The Best of Horrorfind*. She is the author of *Poisoning Eros I and II,* written with Wrath James White, *Suffer the Flesh,* and the new collection, *In the End, Only Darkness*. Her latest novel, *What Happens in the Darkness,* is available from Sinister Grin Press. She works as a freelance editor, proofreader, and book coach. Find her on www.facebook.com/MonicaJORourke.

Gord Rollo was born in St. Andrews, Scotland, but now lives in Ontario, Canada. His short stories and novella-length work have appeared in many professional publications throughout the genre and his novels include: *The Jigsaw Man, Crimson, Strange Magic, Valley Of The Scarecrow, Only The Thunder Knows,* and *The Translators*. His work has been translated into several languages and several of his titles are currently being adapted for audiobooks and film. Besides novels, Gord edited the acclaimed evolutionary horror anthology, *Unnatural Selection: A Collection of Darwinian Nightmares* and co-edited *Dreaming of Angels*, a horror/fantasy anthology created to increase awareness of Down's Syndrome. He can be reached through his website at www.gordrollo.com or via his publisher at www.ene-myone.com.

Mary SanGiovanni is the author of a number of books, including the *Hollower* Trilogy, *Thrall*, *Chaos*, and the novellas *For Emmy* and *Possessing Amy*. Her short fiction has appeared in periodicals, anthologies, and chapbooks for over a decade. She has a Masters degree in Writing Popular Fiction from Seton Hill University, Pittsburgh. She is currently a member of The Authors Guild, The International Thriller Writers, and Penn Writers, and was previously an Active member in the Horror Writers Association. She lives in New Jersey with her son and her cat.

Lucy A. Snyder is the Bram Stoker Award-winning author of the novels *Spellbent, Shotgun Sorceress, Switchblade Goddess*, and the collections *Sparks and Shadows, Chimeric Machines*, and *Installing Linux on a Dead Badger*. Her writing has appeared in *Strange Horizons, Weird Tales, Hellbound Hearts, Doctor Who Short Trips: Destination Prague, Chiaroscuro, GUD*, and *Lady Churchill's Rosebud Wristlet*. You can learn more about her at www.lucys-nyder.com.

Jeff Strand is the Bram Stoker Award-nominated author of such novels as *Pressure, Dweller,* and *Wolf Hunt*. If he was ever killed and then brought back to life, he likes to think that he wouldn't get all vengeful and stuff, but he honestly can't say how he'd react until it happens. Visit his Gleefully Macabre website at www.jeffstrand.com.

T.T. Zuma is the author of various genre stories in numerous anthologies and is one of the editors of the *Eulogies II* anthology. He also reviews horror novels for Horror World and *Cemetery Dance Magazine*. He lives in New Hampshire with his wife Paula.

Shirley Jackson Award-nominated author **Tim Waggoner**'s novels include *Like Death* and *The Harmony Society,* and his latest short story collection is *Bone Whispers*. In total, he's published over thirty novels and one hundred stories, and his articles on writing have appeared in *Writer's Digest* and *Writers' Journal,* among other publi-

417

cations. He teaches creative writing at Sinclair Community College and in Seton Hill University's Master of Fine Arts in Writing Popular Fiction program. Visit him on the web at www.timwaggoner.com.

F. Paul Wilson is the award-winning, *N.Y. Times* bestselling author of forty-plus books and many short stories spanning medical thrillers, sf, horror, adventure, and virtually everything in between. More than 9 million copies of his books are in print in the US and his work has been translated into 24 languages. He also has written for the stage, screen, and interactive media. His latest thriller, *Dark City*, stars the notorious urban mercenary, Repairman Jack, and is the second of The Early Years Trilogy, following *Cold City*. He currently resides at the Jersey Shore and can be found on the Web at www.repairmanjack.com.

Simon Wood is a California transplant from England. He's a former competitive race car driver, a licensed pilot and an occasional P.I. He shares his world with his American wife, Julie. Their lives are dominated by a longhaired dachshund, four cats, four chickens & ten thousand bees. He's the Anthony Award winning author of *Working Stiffs, Accidents Waiting to Happen, Paying the Piper, Terminated, Asking For Trouble* and *We All Fall Down*. His latest thrillers are *Hot Seat* and *No Show*. He also writes horror under the pen name of Simon Janus. Curious people can learn more at www.simonwood.net.